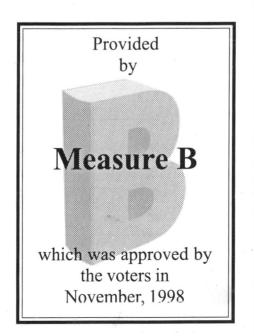

Provided
by

Measure B

which was approved by
the voters in
November, 1998

Slow Way Home

Slow Way Home

A NOVEL

Michael Morris

HarperSanFrancisco
A Division of HarperCollins*Publishers*

HarperCollins books may be purchased for educational, business, or sales promotional use. For information please write: Special Markets Department, HarperCollins Publishers, Inc., 10 East 53rd Street, New York, NY 10022.

HarperCollins Web site: http://www.harpercollins.com
HarperCollins®, ☙®, and HarperSanFrancisco™ are
trademarks of HarperCollins Publishers, Inc.

FIRST EDITION
Designed by Joseph Rutt

Library of Congress Cataloging-in-Publication Data
Morris, Michael, 1966–
Slow way home / by Michael Morris.
p. cm.
ISBN 0–06–056898–4 (alk. paper)
I. Title
PS3613.0775S57 2003
813'.6—dc21 2003050814

03 04 05 06 07 RRD(H) 10 9 8 7 6 5 4 3 2 1

For Linda Maultsby, whose passion for language,
laughter, and life itself continues to inspire the spirit.

$\mathcal{O}ne$

———◦•◦———

$\mathcal{N}$ana always said the Lord works in mysterious ways. Every time she would say that, I would think of Darrell Foskey. If it hadn't been for Darrell, I don't know where I might've ended up. Probably tossed around in a system of Foster homes just like the clothes did in the dryer the night we first met Darrell. He came into our lives thanks to a jammed quarter at the Laundromat. As the night manager, Darrell saved the quarter and won my mama's heart all at the same time.

I was eight that summer day in 1971 when he moved to the apartment with us. The window air conditioner made a rattling sound as it fought the heat that Darrell let through the door. He put down a water-stained box filled with records long enough to snatch the G.I. Joe figure from my hands. The smell of his soured tongue rolled over me the same way he rolled G.I. Joe's head between his fingers.

"Boy, what you doing playing with dolls?" Red lines outlined brown pupils and when he smiled I saw the chipped tooth that he claimed was a sign of toughness. "Hey, just kidding, big guy." When Darrell flung the action figure, I jumped to avoid being hit by G.I. Joe. Little did I know then how I'd keep on jumping to avoid Darrell.

Mama was as shocked as I was seven weeks later when Darrell quit his job at the Laundromat and announced he was taking us out for supper. "Daddy, that's what I love about you. You just go with the gut," Mama said. She nibbled his ear and talked in that baby way I hated. "That man said he'll be at JC's party tonight with a new stash. Let's go on down there, Daddy."

They didn't see me roll my eyes big as Dallas right in front of them. He sure wasn't *her* daddy, and I'd throw up before *I* was fixing to call him any such thing. Before I could ease out of the beanbag and make it to my room, I heard Mama giggle.

"Boy, go on in there and get ready," Darrell yelled. "You gonna get yourself a steak dinner tonight."

Darrell was still going on about Canada and all the good jobs he could get working the pipelines. The pretty waitress reappeared and put another drink before him. Although I couldn't bring myself to look her directly in the eye, I liked the way she smiled and winked at me. Darrell licked the juice remaining on the steak knife and washed it down with a loud smack.

More than usual I was nervous around Darrell tonight. Not so much because of his erratic behavior—I was getting used to the outbursts. But the restaurant was too much. Casting my eyes across the room, I watched a group of women Nana's age laugh while one of them opened brightly wrapped gifts. I couldn't help wondering how they would take Darrell if he got on one of his "spells," as Mama called them.

The more glasses of gold liquid Darrell consumed, the more he bragged about all the gold he could find in Canada. "There's an ol' boy who used to work with me already up there. They tell me he's making fifteen dollars an hour on that pipeline." Darrell licked the excess from the A-1 bottle top and slammed it on the table. I flinched and looked over at the ladies, who were so caught up admiring a gift of crocheted dinner mats that they didn't notice.

The pretty waitress appeared again and poured tea into my glass. "Boy, you best leave off the tea and go to studying your plate," Darrell said with a point of his knife. The waitress glanced at Darrell and then smiled back at me.

"Go on, Brandon, and eat your steak now," Mama said. She lit a cigarette and gazed across the restaurant. "Don't start no problems."

Picking at the slab of meat surrounded by pink juice, I rested my case. Mama knew I wanted chicken. But Darrell was determined and ordered steak for all of us. "I'm not very hungry."

"I'm not very hungry," Darrell whined and squinched up his ruddy face. "What's the matter, this place ain't good enough for you? Not good enough for the little king?"

I stiffened my back and dug my nails into the vinyl seat. Trying to gauge how to respond, I looked at Mama, but she was staring at her reflection in the tinted window and flicking the ends of her newly blonde hair. "Just eat the steak, Brandon."

"We ain't leaving until you eat ever bit of that steak, you hear me." Elbows planted on the plastic red-and-white tablecloth, Darrell enforced his message with another point of the knife.

"It's got icky stuff coming out of it." I followed the tip of the knife up to the brown eyes. It was that look. The same vengeful stare that Mama excused as the dark side in each of the two men she officially met at the Justice of the Peace plus the four she had let in without signed papers. The same dark side that made Darrell throw plates, punch holes in our apartment wall, and kick in my bedroom door.

Mama blew cigarette smoke at the plastic gold lamp dangling above the table. "Brandon, just don't, okay."

Darrell threw his napkin on the plate and steak juice stained the once white material. "Most kids'd be happy to eat at a nice restaurant, but no, not you. Not the king. You little no good piece of . . ."

"Oh, Daddy, don't. Don't get all riled up. Not tonight. He's just being a kid." Mama leaned into Darrell and whined, "Come on, shug. The man's gonna be at JC's and everything. And they're having that band."

All I could do was stare at the steak bone remaining on Darrell's plate. I never flinched when he yelled, "I'm so pissed off right now I don't wanna go nowhere."

Mama's eyes felt as hot as cigarette ash on my skin. I looked up to find her bright red lips pursed and blue eyes bugged as if to tell me in some sign language that she was at her breaking point. "I need a refill over here," she finally yelled.

Soon Mama's body leaned on Darrell, and her hand was inside his shirt. When she put into nibbling his ear, my neck became hot. What I wouldn't give to be able to walk out and leave. To run away and hide until this part was over. Sometimes I almost hated her when she was with one of the boyfriends. Not so much out of jealousy, but because when she drank alone I could handle her. With another man to compete with, I always lost. Some battles were never meant for a boy, I overheard my teacher say the time I showed up at school with a cut above my eye.

So I learned long ago to remove myself when I had to. I convinced myself that I was the only boy in North Carolina or maybe even the whole entire United States who could shrink in his brain and become tiny like G.I. Joe. Searching for an object to stare into and focus the way I had taught myself, my eyes fell upon the group of older women. The one with apple earrings gave me a pitiful sideways smile, and I jerked my head away.

After Darrell was pampered and slurped on proper, he agreed to go on down to JC's party and meet the man with their supply. But not before he vowed to never take me out to eat again. Fine with me, I thought and folded my arms as the waitress supplied the Styrofoam take-out box.

Just as Darrell moved to stand, it happened. The low-hanging lamp shaped like a mushroom struck the side of his forehead, and the carton tumbled to the floor. The slab of undercooked meat rolled onto the green carpet decorated with cracker crumbs and a piece of wilted lettuce. Darrell's face twisted even tighter. Blue veins around his eyes bulged, and he hissed in a way that made me think any minute he would turn into a snake. Holding the side of his head, he let out a loud moan that caused the ladies at the table next to us gasp and clutch their blouses. With the lamp dancing above us and the moan never ending, all I could do was picture Darrell in some sort of cartoon, like Roadrunner and Wily Coyote. In this case the pestering

Wily Coyote just had the heavy weight slammed against his head. And before I could help myself, laughter broke free.

"Sophie, I'm telling you right now that boy's got attitude," Darrell said between clips of electric guitars on the radio. The entire ride from the restaurant I sat on guard in the backseat, arms folded, back stiffened.

"I ought've knocked a knot on his head to show him how it felt. Then we'd see who'd be laughing." Darrell kept one hand on the steering wheel and used the other to reach around the backseat and swat wildly in the air. I pulled my legs in close and watched his oil-stained fingers stretch within inches of my knees.

"You're gonna have a damn wreck," Mama screamed. And then she returned to that baby voice. "Daddy, I just need less stress in my life."

"I tell you where you gonna find less stress. Either away from that snot-nosed brat or in a morgue. You got no more control over him than a whore dropping acid."

"Shut up! Just shut your damn mouth," she screamed.

For a second the sound of guitars on the radio overtook the car. I think Darrell was as stunned as I was at the outburst, but instead of cheering, like I was about to do, he slammed the side of her head against the car window until she begged forgiveness.

As soon as the door of our apartment opened, I headed straight for my bedroom. Predicting trouble had become a sixth sense. I knew even though Darrell said he forgave Mama and would pay for the pills that calmed her nerves, he had not forgiven me. Laughing at him had hurt his manly pride, he had said in the car. I guess like it hurt him when he got part of his tooth knocked out. Pushing a chair under the door-knob of my bedroom door, I pictured myself standing on a stool, holding a bat over my head, and knocking the rest of that tooth out of his square jaw.

Sitting in the chair to add weight for extra protection, I heard their words clipped and broken like some sort of secret code. "Sorry." "Money." "I need it." Within minutes, Mama's little-girl voice disappeared behind a slamming door. The car engine started, and the apartment grew still. Beyond the bedroom window crickets chirped and my heart regained some sort of stable rhythm. With peace came the return of hunger and the image of a fat peanut butter and jelly sandwich.

Returning the chair to its proper place, I eased the door open and tried to remember the schedule for Saturday-night TV. But my plans for dinner alone were cut short when I saw the steel-toed work boots propped up on the coffee table. Our coffee table. The one I found hidden in the corner at the flea market.

Darrell laughed a deep stomach howl. "You look like you just crapped in your pants, boy." He shoved the table with his foot, and I jumped as it slid pass me. My reaction only made him laugh harder, and I scolded myself but good.

When he rose, I stepped backwards, feeling the cool night air that was trapped inside the cinder-block wall. He kept those tiny brown eyes locked on me, even as he turned the radio dial and music blasted out. "Sophie's done gone, sissy boy. And just 'fore she left she give me strict instructions." Darrell lit a cigarette and blew a ring of smoke. "She told me to straighten you out for her. See, here's the deal. You got yourself a respect problem when it comes to your elders."

My heart began to pick up speed again, and I braced myself by sticking my fingernails inside the wedged out places in the wall. Just like a magician, he moved forward and pulled the white take-out box from behind his back. He held it up in midair and stomped the work boot. I dug my nails in deeper, feeling the flecks of gravel in the quick of my nail. The front door was only a few steps behind Darrell, and the chain lock dangled free. Sliding along the wall, I thought of punching him in the privates and leaping over the coffee table to safety. But the magician must have read my mind. At the air-conditioning unit, Darrell slammed the work boot against the wall. The long leg penned me in like the hogs on my grandparents' farm.

"You ungrateful bastard. I paid for this steak and you're eating ever bit of it."

My lip flinched, and I fought to control it with the edge of my tooth. "Can we . . . can we just cook it a little bit and then . . ."

"Now, right there's what I'm talking about. You didn't see your mama and me whining about our steak. Boy, why do you go and do things just to piss me off?"

I wanted to ask for forgiveness like Mama had done. I wanted to say the words that would make him remove his leg and let me go free. But when I opened my mouth, it was dry and the tongue heavy.

Darrell shook his head and took a long drag off the cigarette. He studied the filter and twirled it between his fingers like a minibaton. The red tip shined and the ash grew long, sagging towards the floor. And then with that look in his eye, he stepped forward. I wanted to yell, but my mouth would not let me. The image from an old western Mama and me watched a few nights back ran through my mind. All I could picture were the eyes of the cow from that movie. The eyes of the creature being branded into submission.

The day Darrell decided to officially move to Canada, I packed the small suitcase Nana and Poppy had given me for Christmas and waited in the living room. By this time I had been trained to follow Darrell's golden rule: not to speak unless spoken to. He said that's how I showed respect.

Mama fussed around trying to latch beat-up suitcases and finally settled for wrapping them in black electric tape. I was surprised that all of our earthy possessions could fit into a total of three bags and couldn't help but think that some things were being forgotten.

Darrell acted downright happy and even playfully thumped me on the back of the ear as he walked back and forth carrying battered luggage. Mama was dressed up in new hot pants, and her hair was stacked high. She laughed when I told her she looked like a movie star.

Inside the car Darrell described the apartment he wanted to find. "Out on a lake somewhere. I'm talking about a big-ass apartment with high ceilings and marble floors."

The way he waved his hand was hypnotic, and all I could picture was some sort of apartment like the one Mr. French kept for Buffy and Jody on *A Family Affair*. "And a great big patio too. We can eat supper out there and everything," I said.

Silence lingered for a couple of miles.

Darrell finally hit the steering wheel with his fist. "You ain't told him?"

Mama looked straight ahead and adjusted her sunglasses.

I leaned towards Mama's seat. "Tell me what?"

"Boy, your mama's too chicken-shit to tell you, so the heavy falls on me. Always the heavy 'round here." Darrell sighed in such a way that if it had come from anybody else, I'd guess they were being sympathetic. "Now's not a good time for us to be watching after you. I might even be traveling with the pipeline and all. And you got school."

My hand slowly slid down the plastic seat cover, brushing Mama's shoulder, before I sank back into my proper place.

"Hell, we're even having to sell the car. I'm dropping it off to the man right now. Money is tight and you'd just be . . ."

"I can cut back on my eating. Peanut butter and jelly don't cost much. And I love that."

Mama patted her curls and coughed. "Brandon, don't start, okay. It's just for a little while. Just for a month or two, I promise. Besides, it'll be good for you to spend time with Nana and Poppy. You know, getting to know them better and everything."

Nobody said a word after that, not even Darrell. I never saw my mama's eyes that day. She sat looking straight ahead with loops of curls stacked on her head.

At the bus station, I slid to the end of a wooden bench advertising a furniture store and watched them from a distance. Mama kept pulling at the pants that matched the color of her hair while Darrell kept counting the wad of cash he had made from selling the car.

As black fumes floated around the bus, passengers lined up to board. Mama made one final attempt. "Now, Brandon, you know if Mama could, she would." She handed me a Greyhound bus schedule. "Right up here is Poppy and Nana's phone number. You're better off with them right now. Trust me on this one. Me and Darrell gotta get settled first and then we'll come back for you. I promise it's just for a little while. Hey, look at it as our new destiny. I'm going up there to get things ready for you."

I fought from blinking so I could tear right through her daisy-shaped sunglasses with my eyes. I won't cry. I won't cry. The words rang in my head to remind me I was tougher than anything she could dish out. My jaw clinched, and all of a sudden I found myself wanting to rip every fake blonde curl right off the top of her head.

"Brandon, don't give me that look. Just don't, okay. This is hard enough on me as it is."

Darrell yelled from the door of the bus, and with one final brush against my arm she drifted away. At the top of the bus step she kissed her index finger and pointed it right at me. Her feet looked as tiny as doll feet standing on the wide step. With a final climb nothing was left of her at all.

Before I called the number on the schedule, I watched the bus move slowly forward and then with a roar lurch towards the intersection. Unable to stop it, my eyes burned with emptiness, so I turned to study the red-and-white swirls on the nearest Coke machine. Staring into the bright colors, I felt myself becoming smaller and smaller until at last nobody could make out the pity that weighed on my shoulders.

People of various colors and classes moved about the station as if it was just an ordinary day. Only a few looked down with a smile that they might offer a new puppy in a pet-store window. The garbled call for Columbus, Georgia, blared from the loudspeaker. Families with sons dressed like G.I. Joe clumped around the bus. Mothers with crisp white handkerchiefs dabbed their eyes. All the while, I watched and massaged the callused place on the inside of my arm, a nervous habit I had acquired right after the run-in with Darrell and his cigarette. A free tattoo, he called it. A branding meant to make a man out of me.

After nine more buses had pulled away, my grandparents' white Ford appeared at the curb. Nana's forehead was wrinkled with worry. The way she held on to the string of her plastic bonnet and searched the crowd, I figured she was wondering if she would recognize me. When she turned in my direction, her brow softened and a smile formed as if she was simply picking me up after an afternoon spent at the library. As she made her way through the crowd of servicemen, the hem of her houseshift flapped around her knees.

Her touch was soft to my shoulder, and she pointed towards Poppy. He was sitting in the car with a cap pulled down close to his pointed nose like a getaway driver about to flee a robbery.

"You'll feel better when we get something in your stomach. Now on the way home I want you to study about what you'd like for supper. A hamburger maybe or how about I fry up a breast of chicken?"

Her words hazed my mind the same way the bus exhaust blanketed the air. As we walked towards the car, her arm drew me closer to the folds of her stomach. Poppy cocked his hand forward as if we were about to set off on a vacation. No words were spoken as they took me away to their farm outside of Raleigh. The hum of the engine and cries from a steel guitar on the radio filled the car. An urge tempted me to turn around and look back at the bus station one last time. But I kept my fingernails dug into the vinyl backseat and managed to win that one.

By the time we had reached their farm, mist from the air conditioner covered the car window. Nestled between a thicket of pines and a field blanketed with tobacco, the white farmhouse teased me like an oasis. Ancient ferns swung from chains on the front porch as easy as jewelry on a rich woman.

When I was in the big claw tub that evening, their words drifted from the kitchen and rose above the sound of hot grease popping in a skillet.

"The worst kind of trash wouldn't do something so sorry," Nana said.

"I'd skin her alive if she was standing here right now," Poppy added.

I leaned against the cold surface of the tub and tried to picture Poppy skinning Mama with the switchblade he used to clean catfish. But I gave up trying to picture it, deciding there was not enough flesh on Mama's bony frame to allow such punishment.

For the first few months at Nana and Poppy's farmhouse, whenever I went to the bathroom or got ready for bed, I would glance at the black phone propped on top of a Sears and Roebuck catalog on the hallway table. It was a carefree glance, like one someone might give a penny on a busy sidewalk. I didn't want to stare too long and make Nana and Poppy think I wanted hear from her. But the concern was short-lived. By the time Thanksgiving rolled around, I realized there would be no good-night calls offered from the land that seemed as far away as the North Pole. By Christmas, I had even stopped praying that God would make Mama come back at all. It was then that I let the house's perfume of pine needles, mothballs, and cooking grease seep into my system. I pictured the scent running up my nose and through my blood, ironing out all the nervous places as perfectly as Nana pressed the collar of my church shirt.

"A fresh start" were the words the school guidance counselor used when talking about life on my grandparents' farm. Even then I knew the experience deserved more than a dime-store cliché. It was more than a new start. Life on the farm would be nothing less than a resurrection in which the past and the future are called up and transformed into perfection.

$\mathcal{T}wo$

"Hurry up, slow poke," I heard my cousin call out. She skipped barefoot through weeds and over small branches. Her paint-chipped toenails brushed across the top of the soil barely touching the earth before her legs would fly up again. If I didn't know her better, I would've thought she was timid, but by now I knew she hated more than anything else to get her feet dirty. "Nice Nasty," her brother, Mac, called her.

A branch from a pine sapling slapped the side of my head. I snatched it away and pulled at the leaves of a maple tree, fighting to break free. Dusk had chased away a layer of muggy air. An eerie blue outlined the trees and wild vines that separated my grandparents' farm from the double-wide trailer Mac and Mary Madonna lived in. Their land was a wedding gift from my grandparents to their daddy, Uncle Cecil.

Breaking free from the limbs, I spotted Mac by the pile of dirt Uncle Cecil delivered on weekends for extra money. Money that Nana said paid for all the big bills Aunt Loraine ran up at the stores. Mac was holding a Mason jar high above his head as if offering a torch to light our way.

I tried to gauge the moment their greenish lights would blink, and soon Mary Madonna reached out for the lightning bug I had laid claim to. "That's mine," I shouted more because I thought she would expect me to than for any other reason.

"Tough titty said the kitty and the milk's not free." She kicked up her tan leg and pulled up the edge of her dress before running off. Even her run had sassiness to it. Named for Aunt Loraine's Catholic side of the family, Mary Madonna was a princess in two people's minds: hers and her mama's. My cross to bear, Nana would tell me whenever I complained about my oldest cousin.

"No lightning bug's gonna just fly in your jar. You gotta go for it. Go on, catch it," Mary Madonna said, dancing circles around us.

Watching her hold the hem of her red-and-white dress and run in circles with flashes of blue-green from the lightning bugs all around, I felt steady and strong. There was an ordinariness to it all that satisfied me as much as the food from Sunday dinner.

After the stars filled the sky and the last lightning bug had been captured, Mac stretched out on the floor pallet Nana had made for us out of hand-sewn quilts in the living room. Like always, Poppy warned of the dangers of color TV. "You boys gonna go blind sitting too close to that thing." The jars filled with our catch were right next to us, and during commercial breaks we'd recount to verify how many bugs were still flashing.

Mary Madonna reclined against Nana's chair and instructed Nana how to properly comb the knots out of her long blonde hair. It was a package deal. I could be sure that whenever I asked Mac to spend the night, Aunt Loraine would see to it that Mary Madonna would have her pink Barbie suitcase in hand, leading the way across the trail of flattened weeds that separated our grandparents' home from theirs.

"This girl has the prettiest head of hair. You sure must get that from your mama's side of the family. Lord knows you don't get it from me. I always had the wiriest hair."

Casting a watchful eye on Mac, I casually rubbed the top of my hair, satisfied that there were a few waves.

"This mess of mine never would do a thing but nap up just like a colored woman's hair," Nana said as she pulled the comb out of Mary Madonna's mane.

"Ouch, Nana."

"Sorry, sugar." Nana smoothed the injured spot with her broad, weathered hand.

Mary Madonna tilted her chin and stared at the TV screen. I wanted to reach over and yank it but good.

"You got pretty hair, Nana," I said.

She looked up at me as if I had cussed. "Well now."

"See there, Pearl." Poppy nudged Nana from his easy chair. "You're a regular silver fox." We all laughed at Poppy, even Mary Madonna. The laughter made me feel light-headed. I thought of the colored pills Mama used to take whenever her nerves would run high and wondered if they made her feel the same way.

"Oh, me," Nana said. Her coarse gray hair was twisted in a braid and pinned into place on the back of the head. The first time I had one of the bad dreams, Nana came into my room with it all loose and hanging wild down her back. The stark whiteness of her hair, bathed in the blue moonlight that seeped in through the blinds, reminded me of a ghost. Before I came to my senses, I told her I didn't like long hair. She laughed and wrapped her arms around me. The roll of skin on the side of her back was cushiony. "Sugar, it's just part of my religion, nothing to be scared of. It's my covering. The Bible says so." Her callused hand squeezed mine, and she lay with me until the past rolled away and sleep returned.

After the television was turned off, Poppy moved towards the porch-light switch, and Nana assigned beds. Mac would sleep with me, and Mary Madonna would take the sofa.

While Nana searched for sheets in the hall closet, Mary Madonna twirled her damp hair and sighed. "I'd sleep on that old hard floor if I was you." Cupping a hand to her mouth, she closed her eyes and smiled. "He pees all over hisself. Just like a little bitty baby."

"He does not, you farthead," Mac said, and then quickly looked at me for confirmation.

I shook my head and glanced at the blank TV screen, trying to lie without coming right out and doing it.

Curling the edge of her lip, she let loose. "Don't tell me. Mama said he wakes up like a crazy person. Screaming and spraying pee all over the place. Poor little thing."

That baby-sounding voice. Mama's voice. Before I could help it, I snatched the brush from the coffee table and whacked it against her golden arm. She screamed, and Nana pulled us away from each other.

"What in the world is going on in here?"

Mary Madonna tried to fake-cry. "Ain't you gonna spank him?" she moaned.

"I tell you who I'm going to switch, the whole mess of you if you don't get yourselves to bed. Now scat." Nana waved her hand for effect, and Mac and Mary Madonna scattered. But I stood still as could be. Fury was one emotion I had mastered, and a play act was something I could detect by the slightest change in voice pitch.

Hours later I rolled over to find the pillow missing and a wrinkled sheet beside me. Tiptoeing into the living room, I found Mac stretched on the old quilt, his hair spiked and legs twisted like a slinky. And at the edge of the hall I paused to look real hard at the black rotary phone. In a moment of weakness I glared and waited, staring until the white panel and black numbers blurred my vision like an early morning mist.

The first time the school secretary called my name over the fat brown speaker box in Miss Douglas's class, my heart began racing. Dewayne Pickings had reported that the principal used an electric paddle on him with no fewer than forty-five spikes in place for added torture. And seeing the brown cardboard that now replaced the lunchroom window, the same window Dewayne broke with a rock just because he wanted to see it shatter, I figured he was an expert on discipline. The hissing sounds from those around me didn't help slow my heart rate, and I gave them a sneer as I stuffed the denim bookbag Nana had made me.

But at the front office there was no electric paddle, not even the principal for that matter, only the school secretary, who sold pencils

and pads of paper each morning, and Poppy. After he explained that I
had an important appointment, I watched Poppy write unsteady letters that spelled his name across a white pad. My chest swelled when I
read the name in Poppy's scratchy penmanship. After I was born,
Mama didn't give me the last name of my real daddy. She gave me the
same name as hers, Willard. It was the best decision Mama made con-
cerning men. The name Willard became an asset the day Poppy and
Nana picked me up from the bus station. Fewer questions from nosy
people like the school secretary. I was one of them, and the same
name proved it. For all people knew, I was their own son. I heard
Nana talking about some lady at her church who'd had a child during
the change. People probably thought I was like that. A child that
changed their lives.

We exited Stalwart Elementary that day to find a green boat attached to Poppy's truck. "Bought it this morning when they auc-
tioned off old man Randell's belongings." Poppy ran his hand down
the boat's side. "Figured you'd help me try her out."

A tradition was soon born, and during Friday homeroom I'd try
to guess if this would be the afternoon Poppy would show up to
whisk me away. Nana only gave in to our ritual after I begged a little
more than usual. "You just make sure you don't get behind with your
lessons," she said, inspecting the string of fish we proudly displayed.

Some days we'd sit in that aluminum boat on Ricer's Pond, and
Poppy would talk about a new hog he had bought or the olden days
when he ran the filling station and fixed fancy cars that passed through
town. Mostly we'd just be quiet and listen to the locusts buzzing deep in
the tall grass and watch the water crack and shatter with the landing of
our lines. Only one time do I recall Mama floating into the conversation.

Poppy pulled the green cap with the John Deere logo low on his
head. "How're you managing?"

"Fine." I didn't look up as I reached inside the faded cottage
cheese container and found a worm wiggling to the bottom.

Poppy's voice cleared, and I heard the steady drum of his boot
tapping against the boat floor. "You know, it's a real shame your

mama's turned away from us. Used to be a good girl and then . . . But, now, none of that has a thing in the world to do with you."

Residue from the earthworm made my hand stick to the pole, and I gripped it even tighter. I cast the line extra hard hoping the pop would drown him out. The sound echoed, and a white bird flew away from a patch of lily pads.

Poppy reeled in his line and stared straight ahead. "Never figured out why she started using dope."

I jerked the line and gasped all at the same time. For added effect, I jerked the line and pretended to strain.

"The way I see it, she just let a bad habit run away with her."

"I got something," I moaned.

The boat rocked as Poppy slid to offer assistance. Grabbing the light rod, he cut his eyes towards me.

Staring into the murky water, I shrugged. "Must've broke free."

There was no need to talk about Mama. I was getting my fill of that from the guidance counselor, Mrs. Hanson. Every Monday while the others lined up for the lunchroom, I was pulled aside, and together Mrs. Hanson and me would have lunch in the conference room by the principal's office. If the door was open when we walked pass, I'd search the wall high and low for the electric paddle. The only thing that came close to being something that could cause bodily harm was a golf club tucked in the corner next to the flag.

Mrs. Hanson was wrinkled but had hair as pink as cotton candy. I liked how two curls on each side of her head twisted and hung free like clumps of grapes. But I did not like how Mrs. Hanson would ask me how I felt about Mama and then turn her head and make an attempt to smile. Her smile always ended up lopsided and looked like any minute she would bust out crying.

"How's Nana and Poppy doing?" she asked between sips from her chocolate-milk carton.

"Fine." I studied the pictures that lined her wall. A girl, little babies, and one old man who most likely was her husband. "Who's that?" I asked pointing to the girl centered at the top.

"Umm. That's Rachel, my oldest granddaughter." The way she clasped her hand with the napkin still caught between her fingers told me that Rachel was the detour.

"How old is she?"

"Fourteen. Lives in Chattanooga. And can dance like you never did see. Wins all sorts of talent shows. Told me the other night that she's going to be a majorette." She wrinkled up her nose and giggled.

"She sure is pretty." And while I learned how Rachel was a walking miracle on account of her being born too early, the big hand on the clock that hung over the file cabinet continued to move forward.

On Saturday afternoons the squeals and yells from Mac and Mary Madonna were the only invitation I needed. I'd run down the path Uncle Cecil had mowed between my grandparents' home and their trailer, pulling my T-shirt over my head in mid-flight.

Three sprinklers fanned water in all directions. We would run up and down Uncle Cecil's mound of dirt, pretending to dodge the falling water. At the top I'd stand so tall I could see Nana's front porch, all the while envisioning I was a king of some ancient terrain. A shove from Mary Madonna would quickly end my reign. "Quit hogging up all the water," she'd scream.

Once the mountain had turned to quicksand, Aunt Loraine would stand on the back steps of the trailer and hose us down. No matter how careful I was not to get too much mud on me, she always said the same line when it came my turn to get hosed. "And you, young man. I'll just have to use the spray nozzle on you. You're downright covered in filth." As the pellets of water stung my legs, I never let on that she was doing anything out of the ordinary. I'd jump around like it was fun and act like she was playing some kinda game. And it was a game in which she always had the last say.

Aunt Loraine was a tall woman who puffed out her hair until it looked like one of G.I. Joe's helmets. Her pug nose turned up just enough to remind me of one of the hogs Poppy kept pinned behind the house.

Her face was painted and pasty, just like Samantha's mama's on *Bewitched*. Although I never shared this comparison with Mac or Mary Madonna, I kept it in the back of my mind. With a woman like Aunt Loraine you never knew when you might need an extra supply of ammunition.

Although Aunt Loraine believed in makeup, she did not believe in public transportation. "Public transportation is for coloreds and white trash. The last time I checked, my children were neither," she said when Mac asked about riding the school bus. Since I got off the bus at the farm alone, Nana felt strongly that someone had to be at the end of the driveway to greet me. "Too much meanness going on now days," she'd say. So every afternoon, humid or freezing, I disembarked to find her waiting inside the car with a cold Pepsi.

She held up the bottle. "Did you do good in school today? I got a slice of pound cake waiting on the table for you." And every day she waited while I checked the mailbox. It was another part of the ritual in living with them. Supper at six, bedtime no later than nine-thirty; everything was set by time and carved out of history. But nothing in the schedule prepared me for an uninvited guest.

Just as I got to the black mailbox, I saw it sitting beyond the trees lurking like a cheetah stalking prey. Between the clump of maples across the road sat the old car with a different-colored door. The driver's head was partially hidden by the branches. Closing the mailbox and walking towards the air-conditioning of Nana's car, I heard the roar as the beat-up car engine turned over. A puff of blue smoke drifted beyond the treetops. Stillness wrapped around me just as it had the day I saw the rattlesnake slither in front of the mailbox.

The driver's face was shielded with sunglasses. She was missing the bright yellow curls, but it was her all the same. The one who brought me into the world and the one who casually put me on layaway at the bus station. Although her eyes were hidden from my view, I could feel them pulling me to cross the road and ride away with her. To live in Canada in a fancy high-rise apartment.

The sun reflected off of chipped rocks at the edge of the road. Their slivers of metal were like magnets pulling me towards the old car.

"Come on, now," Nana called. "Poppy wants us to help him pick peas when you're through eating."

Inside the house I ate pound cake and watched Nana fold the towels piled high in Poppy's recliner. All the while, the woman on the TV cried about the husband who left her.

"Is that cake good to you?" Nana asked while staring at the screen. Even though she couldn't see me, I forced a smile and nodded. I ached to tell her my mama was back in town. To mount up and protect my safe haven. To run out the door and down the driveway and hug my mama. To slap her across the face the same way the woman from Nana's TV story had slapped her wayward husband.

But I did nothing but sit there in the air-conditioned home and feel the nervous past coil around my chest, a feeling that I thought had been long cut away.

$\mathcal{T}hree$

$\mathcal{C}$rowds began filing into the converted livestock arena early. By eight o'clock women with children bouncing around them rolled in like waves surging in between the rows of parked trucks whose tailgates were weighted down with bushels of vegetables and fresh flowers.

If I hadn't seen Mama in that car, I would have enjoyed the day at the market a whole lot better. It had been three days since I saw her, and every afternoon I had stood behind the wide pine next to the mailbox hoping to catch her. Part of me wondered if I had seen her at all. Maybe it was a vision like the kind Brother Bailey preached about during Wednesday night church. A walking dream. A walking nightmare. But the turmoil over how I would respond to a potential reunion did not vanish with a simple rub of the eyes.

While Poppy propped his foot on the tailgate of Mr. Winter's truck and cussed the price of hogs, Nana busied herself with arranging bushels of peas and squash. Without looking up, she would offer an occasional "Well, I declare" to the latest news offered from Mr. Winter's wife, Naomi. Miss Naomi was always talking about a customer or a fellow farmer. The Cuban farmer, Mr. Calato, was a regular topic of her concern.

Most days, after the customers had trickled down to the late sleepers, I would run up and down the arena bleachers with Poco,

Mr. Calato's grandson. But after seeing my mama drive by, I stretched out on the wooden bleacher and pleaded a stomachache. The smell of fresh strawberries baking in the sun rose from Mr. Calato's truck, teasing me into thinking that everything was all right.

After running up several rows of bleachers Poco finally gave up and plopped down on the step below me. With his shirttail untucked, Poco's brown stomach rose up in search of air. I felt sorry for him. According to Nana, his mother had died in a car wreck and his father took off without him. At least I still had my mama, and even though I had never met him, there was a daddy somewhere in the world who would take me in if he thought I ever needed him. After Miss Naomi told Nana that Poco's father was connected with the Cuban Mafia, Nana ordered me to stay away from Mr. Calato's truck.

When customers swirled around Nana, and Poppy was forced to break up his weather talk and help, I would sneak over to the lime green truck with a headlight missing. Peering into the cab, I searched for the evils I was warned to stay away from. With the exception of a bottle wrapped in a brown bag and a string of wooden beads dangling from the rearview mirror, the contents were no different from those in Poppy's truck.

"Poco, do you ever hear from your daddy?"

Poco's stomach continued to expand as he shrugged his shoulders. "Your mom call?"

I stared up at the giant wooden beams and the big lights that dangled above us from the ends of skinny cables. "She's busy working. But I got a feeling she might be calling soon."

"One time he came here." Poco was sitting up, picking at a splinter in the bleacher. "Daddito got in a fight with him so then he left."

"But when he left, did he want you to go?"

"He's busy. Busier than your mom even. My dad . . ." Poco suddenly stood. "My dad travels all the time. Back to Cuba and stuff."

"You know, the time he came here, did he want you to go with him?"

Poco's eyes widened as he spoke louder and he stretched his arms wide. "My dad sends me all kinds of money. Real Cuban money. I'll show you. He sends Daddito money too. My dad is rich. Richer than your mom even."

"But did he want to take you?"

Poco looked out towards the arena where Mr. Calato held up a carton of strawberries for a customer's inspection.

"I just need to know is all. Would you've left if your daddy wanted you?"

Before I could rise, Poco kicked me in the flank with his cowboy boot. Pain settled where the breath had escaped. Watching him run down the bleacher steps two at a time, I did not see a boy two years younger with brown skin and coal-colored hair. I saw myself. And just for a second I saw the pity that hung like a cloud over both of our lives.

Everybody at school thought the trip to the Capitol in Raleigh was a vacation. For me it was also a vacation from thinking about Mama. I even got Nana into the act and talked her into signing up as a chaperone.

The morning we were to leave, Poppy came into the kitchen. He washed the slop from his hands while Nana finished packing our lunch.

"Brandon, I still can't talk you into going to the hog sale with me?"

I pushed the breakfast plate away and shook my head. "We're going to the Capitol today, Poppy."

"Umm . . . that's right." Poppy took off his cap and scratched the bald spot where a mole had taken over. "And I sure didn't hear nobody ask me to go. I'm put out about it too."

My back stiffened against the chair, and I shot a look at Nana. She just smiled and shook her head. In a minute, Poppy started laughing and came over and tousled my hair. "Son, I'm just ribbing you a little. No, y'all go on and see the politicians. I'd rather be around a bunch of hogs myself."

Nana rode in the front of the bus with Miss Douglas. Watching the back of their heads as we drove towards Raleigh, I compared Nana's gray bun to Miss Douglas's short brown hair. It was another reminder that Nana was my grandmother. At times I would forget and think of my own Mama as a younger sister, away at college or some boarding school like rich people on TV. Seeing that Mama was only seventeen years older than me, I guess part of it made sense.

We walked in a straight line beneath an umbrella of tree limbs that guarded the Capitol grounds. Nana was in the back of the group and, not wanting to appear like a baby, I made my way up to the front. Inside, everyone gazed up at the high ceilings. Everyone except me. I liked watching their mouths hang open as they looked up towards the ceiling like some prize might fall at any second.

"Good morning, boys and girls." The high-pitched voice broke through the gazes. The woman before us clasped her hands and tilted her head to the side the same way the guidance counselor did whenever she asked about Mama. Her hair was canary yellow and was framed around her forehead in a spray of spit curls. If the woman's smile would've been any wider, it would have split her lips wide open.

"Boys and girls," Miss Douglas said. "This is Senator Strickland. Remember, she represents our district. Senator Strickland is going to show us around and tell us more about the way government helps us."

"My, what a handsome group you all are," Senator Strickland said while leaning over us as if searching for a lost quarter. "Is everyone having a good time so far?" She nodded with closed eyes. "I've been in office for just little over a year. I took over my late husband's seat. Preston Strickland was a good man, bless his heart. A wonderful senator. Oh, you couldn't ask for finer."

As Senator Strickland led us around the Capitol, she touched each of our heads as if we were being marked. I fought hard not to think of Darrell and his cigarette. Nana kept to the back of the group and would smile whenever I looked back to make sure she had not taken a wrong turn along the winding journey.

"Now, this," Senator Strickland said as she clutched her shiny blouse, "this is where it all takes place." She led us inside the empty Senate chamber, and all the heads flew up to the ceiling again. I even looked up at the gold eagles and colored fixtures on the ceiling. "And this is the desk where I sit and vote on all the bills that come our way. Would anyone care to sit?"

Dewayne Pickings bolted pass Miss Douglas and plopped down so hard that the wood sounded like it had gas. "Careful, Dewayne," Miss Douglas yelled. She flinched when her words bounced off the high ceiling, and Dewayne laughed louder.

One by one we took our turn in the desk. I ran my hand over the finish and could smell the lemon left over from the oil that made it slick.

"Don't rub off all the polish," Nana whispered. She stood next to the desk with her arms folded. When Senator Strickland leaned over me, I saw Nana pull at the bottom of her shirt.

"Do you enjoy school?" the Senator asked.

"Yes, ma'am." I sat up straight, and the scent of her lilac perfume made me feel light-headed. Just when I was thinking she was probably Mama's age, she ran her hand over the desk surface.

"This is real North Carolina cherrywood. Feel how smooth it is."

Her hands were lined with protruding veins and the same brown-colored dots that let me know she was closer to Nana's age. Out of the corner of my eye I saw her look at Nana and smile.

"Is he yours?" she asked.

"Yes, ma'am," Nana said. "He's been excited about this trip all week."

"Well, I think it's absolutely wonderful that you're taking part. Some mothers don't even get involved in PTA anymore."

"Oh, I'm not . . ."

"She's my grandmama and my mama," I announced before Nana had to reveal that she was second fiddle.

Senator Strickland batted her eyes seemingly trying to make sense of it all. "Well, now, even better." She leaned so close I could see the black lines drawn around the sagging eyelids. "My late husband used to say that grandparents were a blessing of the highest order. And I knew what he was talking about because my grandparents raised me. Why, I guess that makes us blood brothers, you and me."

The coolness of her big rings chilled my cheek. "It's somebody else's turn," I said and jumped from the seat.

The rest of the day, the Senator looked at me every time she paused to explain the reason for some room or the history behind a particular statue. She pondered me in a way that caused me to think that any minute she might reach out and prick my finger with one of her fat rings. An initiation into her blood-brother order right under the statue of Sir Walter Raleigh.

That night after we educated Poppy on North Carolina politics, Nana tucked me in with the usual prayer. Free from the bun, her long hair draped like a white rope across her shoulder. Like always, she went through the standard list. But tonight she added the woman senator to the mix of people we prayed for.

"Nana, why did that woman keep on staring at me?"

When she cupped my chin, I could feel the hard calluses on her hand, the marks of honest living she called them. "You're just special that way. Oh, anybody that's around you feels it. You got lots of people who love you, you know that?"

I looked deep into her green eyes and sank right into her words.

"I want you to do something for me," she said. "Go to sleep tonight listing out all the people who love you. There's just a pile of folks. But you best start that list off with me, you hear."

And with a kiss, she slipped away beyond the door. Somewhere in the darkness a whippoorwill cried its lonesome call. It was then, for the first time since moving to the farm, that I let myself cry too.

My birthday was a week before Uncle Cecil's, and it was Poppy's idea to celebrate them together with a fish fry. Aunt Loraine declared it a triple celebration. Mary Madonna had won the Miss Sunbright beauty contest the weekend before, and Aunt Loraine demanded that she be allowed to help Uncle Cecil and me blow out the birthday candles. Standing in front of the special carrot cake Nana had made for me, Mary Madonna kept elbowing me to move closer towards Uncle Cecil so that her sash would show up in the picture that Aunt Loraine was taking. When the camera flash went off, it bounced off of Mary Madonna's crown in a way that made me think of lightning.

The beauty pageant had taken place in the school cafeteria. All sorts of girls and little babies paraded on the stage where the high-school chorus had sung Christmas songs the year before. The only reason I went was because Mac had told me Aunt Loraine would stop by the Dairy Queen and buy us anything we wanted. The only re-quirement was that we scream real loud and whistle whenever Mary Madonna walked across the stage. Watching Mary Madonna prance around that stage with the sparkly crown on her head, I yelled extra loud and glanced up at Aunt Loraine for approval. She sat on the edge of the folding chair with her hair bigger than normal, laughing and crying all at the same time.

After lunch Uncle Cecil and Poppy mined the old Chevrolet that Poppy kept on cinder blocks for spare parts, while Mac and me bounced down the driveway in his new go-cart. When he got to the end of the drive next to the mailbox, my heart began to race. Just as I began to picture Mama following us back up the drive and joining in the family get-together, Mac spun the cart back towards the house and a cloud of dust swirled over us.

Mary Madonna stood on Nana's front porch wearing her banner that spelled out Miss Sunbright in yellow glitter. The tiara was back in place, and she waved her arms real big.

"What do you want?" Mac screamed over the roar of the motor.

With her head thrown back and walking just as prissy as the day she was crowned, she screamed, "Mama said for you to pull me in Poppy's cart. Like in a parade."

Mac nudged me in the rib and then asked her, "How much you willing to pay?"

"I got fifty cents back at the house," she said.

"A dollar."

"Mama!" she screamed.

"All right, fifty cents."

After we hooked up the wooden cart that Poppy used to pick up limbs to the go-cart, Mary Madonna knelt in the scattered bark and pine straw that lined its bed. She waved as we circled the hog pen, the tree swing, and the old Chevrolet.

"Be careful," Uncle Cecil yelled under the hood of the rusty car. Poppy glanced up and shook his head.

"I'm gonna be in the Christmas parade this year," Mary Madonna said as she waved at the trees. "Just like Mama was when she was queen."

"Mama wasn't no queen," Mac said.

"She was too. She was Dogwood Festival queen back in high school."

Mac nudged me. "Prove it. I've never seen no picture of Mama in a crown."

"That's 'cause all the pictures are at Grandma Spencer's house. I saw them. All covered up with wax paper so they won't spoil." Mary Madonna clutched her arm like she might have a bouquet of roses to worry with.

Searching my brain for any pictures of my own mama with a crown on her head, I finally remembered the picture of her holding a baton in Nana's yellow scrapbook. "My mama was a majorette."

Before the last syllable finished coming out of my mouth, Mary Madonna yelled, "Your mama was no such thing."

"Nana's got a picture of her."

Mary Madonna had her hands on the side of her hips. "Well, she must've been dressed up for Halloween, 'cause your mama's never been nothing but trouble."

"Shut up, Mary Madonna," Mac shouted.

"Well, it's the truth. Nobody would pick something like her to be a majorette. All she used to do in school was act trashy. Smoking cigarettes and chasing boys."

"Shut your lying mouth."

"That's how come you don't even know who your daddy is. She didn't know which one to pick."

Wanting to knock that shiny crown right off her head, I turned but realized she was too high above me. Mary Madonna's nose flared as she looked down at me. She smiled and adjusted her sash. "If I don't tell you, who will?"

I wanted the engine to drown her words in the roar. "Shut up!"

"Mama's right, you been babied too much. Birthday or no birthday, you need to hear this."

Mac turned towards Mary Madonna. "Stop it, Mary Madonna. I mean it."

Her words were almost as loud as the roar of the engine. "It's just the truth. Everybody knows it except him."

When Mac turned around to stare Mary Madonna into submission, I spotted his blue sneaker on the accelerator. Before he could push me away, my foot reached over and slammed Mac's shoe. The gas pedal sunk towards the metal floorboard. Our heads jerked and the go-cart lurched forward. At the same time, the make-believe float disconnected from its hook.

"Ma-ma-a-a!" Mary Madonna screamed. The cart flew pass us with a mind of its own, pass the tool shed, pass the back porch, and right into the side of the hog pen.

Mary Madonna screamed and ducked her head as the cart slammed into a fence board. Hogs scattered, and Mary Madonna flew through the fence gap, landing crown first in murky hog doo-doo.

Aunt Loraine screamed and jumped from Nana's back porch. Nana followed, and her look of terror made me realize that I would get a whipping.

After Mary Madonna was hosed down and checked for bruises, the real excitement began. "What happened here?" Aunt Loraine demanded. "I mean it. I'm not budging until we find out."

"Now, honey, it was just an accident. Those kids ought not to've been pulling that cart to start with," Uncle Cecil said.

"It wasn't no accident neither," Mary Madonna screamed and buried her wet face in Aunt Loraine's miniskirt. "He did it." Her finger seemed longer than an elephant's nose as it sought me out for punishment.

Moving backwards, I felt my throat close up. "I . . . didn't . . ."

Aunt Loraine threw her arms in the air. "Why, I should've known."

"Now, hold on," Nana said. "Brandon, did you do this?"

"I . . . uh . . . she was . . ." Watching Aunt Loraine's nose grow red and her eyes twitch, I wanted to run down the driveway and keep on going. The vision of an orphanage with crying babies hanging out of the window flashed through my mind.

"Brandon didn't do nothing," Mac said. "It was me. I hit the gas too hard is all. It was like Daddy said. An accident."

Mary Madonna threw her head back and cried even harder. "Nuh-huh. He's telling a story."

Uncle Cecil molded the brim of his cap. Looking into his eyes, I always thought of Mama. They were shaped in that slanted way like hers, and I figured it was the only way they were alike. "We can stand here to midnight bickering over this. Now look, she's not hurt. It was just an accident, Loraine."

"Cecil's right," Nana said. "They had no business pulling that trailer to start with."

The screeching from a tree limb as it rubbed against the tin roof was the only sound I heard. Aunt Loraine stared at me until finally she was forced to blink. Soon the big fake smile that I figured she'd learned from her days as the queen returned. "Accidents will happen, won't they, Brandon? Even on birthdays."

After Mary Madonna landed in the hog pen things changed. Aunt Loraine halfway agreed it was an accident, but I knew she blamed me. Her eyes would search me up and down while I stood on the wrought-iron trailer steps. I could read the blame as she pursed her lips together and sighed whenever I sought Mac. "He's busy doing homework," she'd say and close the vinyl door.

Though I hungered to run along the creek bank with Mac or swing with him on the tire swing, I knew it was for the best. I had caused him trouble, trouble he didn't even deserve.

Drinking the usual after-school Pepsi, I sat at the kitchen table and spelled all the words Nana called out from the book with a bee on the cover. I hated the baby way the bee was drawn with a big smile on his face and two wide eyes. Staring out at the old Chevrolet propped up on blocks, I mapped out the lonesome journey I would take on a wild safari, all the while sounding out words like "handsome" and "home-coming."

Sitting inside the rusty car, I ran my hand over the navy seats envisioning that my touch made the torn leather covers completely whole and brand-new again. Keeping one hand on the thin metal steering wheel, I watched the African roads before me and turned every so often to see Nana pruning the big fern that rested on the porch rail. Her humming rang out and suddenly what she meant to be "Shall We Gather at the River" became the chant of some undiscovered ancient tribe. Just when I swerved to miss an elephant, I heard the roar. Not a roar like Poppy's tractor, but louder. A roar louder than even a lion.

Nana covered her brow and squinted to make out the noise. Turning to look over my shoulder, I heard the roar make its way around the bend in the driveway. And right pass the crepe myrtle, the beat-up car with the blue door appeared. Frozen, all I could do was hit my leg to make sure what I was hearing and seeing was not a dream. But no matter how hard I tried, the roar and final sputter of the muffler would not go away. Never before had I wanted so bad to jump up and find a wet sheet and Nana's halo of long, wavy white hair standing guard at my bedroom door.

Watching Nana, I wanted to yell. To warn her that the visitor was not a new insurance man making his route. It was the collector, coming to get what was hers. But I did nothing but sit while cool sweat trickled down the back of my neck.

Her hair was black again and, seeing her stand at the car's blue door, I noticed she was skinnier than before. She wore the same big white sunglasses and waited so long before speaking that I hoped against hope that she was just a hippie passing by seeking a handout.

"Hey," my mama said. She eased forward the same way I had eased backward the time I saw the rattlesnake drift across the driveway.

Nana turned her back and continued pruning the fern just like the roar was some sort of thunderstorm that had passed over. Nana casually turned her head and looked right at me. Seeing that wrinkled brow was like reading some kind of secret code, and I slid down the seat until my eyes were even with the rusted piece of metal that was once a door lock.

My mama's voice cracked when she first began. "Now, I know what you're thinking. And yeah, I did wrong. I know it, Mama, but I changed this time. I really have."

Nana continued to cut the fern. "Only thing I see changed is your hair."

Mama sort of laughed and ran her hand through the short hair. "Yeah, I went back to black. Blonde just always was . . ."

"Trashy," Nana said and stripped away another leaf.

Mama raised her hands towards the sky and sighed. "Yeah, well. How's Brandon?"

My hand reached for the door handle, and I fought ripping that door right off its hinge and cussing her out. I'd pretend like I was somebody mean and hateful like Aunt Loraine and yell things like, "Go on, trash," until she cried real hard and begged forgiveness. Then remembering that she had promised to come back and get me when things got better, I let go of the handle. Maybe she was keeping her word. I pictured a big house up in Canada. A two-story house like all the popular kids at school had.

"You don't need to worry about him," Nana said.

"Well, he's my son, okay. I mean I can't help . . ."

Nana turned to face my mama and shook the pruning scissors. "The Lord gave you a good kid, but you sure didn't do right by him."

"Damn it, Mama. I didn't come here to fight, okay."

"Sophie, that's the problem. You never cared enough to fight for the boy when you had the chance." Mama put her hands on her hips and stood on the porch step.

"What the hell does that suppose to mean?"

"Listen to me. Your Daddy and me spent many a night with Brandon. Nights working out all the demons your way of living planted in him. Mending all the scars you and your sorry men left on him."

"Scars? I never laid a hand on my boy."

"You didn't have to. You let everybody else beat on him!" Nana raised the scissors up in the air. "When I think of all the mess that boy's been through. No, no you're not about to see him. That's it now."

Mama stepped backwards, and only then did Nana put the scissors down on the porch railing.

"Well, aren't you Miss Fine Christian Lady with her long glorious hair. I guess you're telling me I'm not good enough for second chances, huh?"

"You know better. Every time we bailed you out of one mess, you'd go fall right back into another. My only regret is that the woman down at social services didn't pay me any attention when I told her to come take Brandon out the first time."

"Listen, that's what I'm trying to tell you. That's all changed. Really, this ain't the same Sophie you're talking to." My mama's wrist fell limp like she was telling town gossip. "See, I went through one of those rehabs up in Canada. Learned I could either be pitiful or powerful." Mama smiled real big like I pictured them teaching her at that place up in Canada.

"And you with no money." Nana shook her head. "Lord, you expect me to believe this foolishness?"

"The government paid for it. Everybody gets it up there. And, besides, I met a man . . ."

"Well, sir, how did I know that was coming."

"Mama, this is different. He's a widower. Got plenty of money. Walter, that's his name. He wants us to get married and everything. He's even gonna open up a beauty shop for me to run."

"Sophie, you beat all. After not hearing a word from you in over a year, you just roll in here wanting him back like nothing out of the ordinary. I declare, if you weren't so pitiful, you'd be a regular Lucille Ball." Nana hadn't yet closed the screen door before Mama fired the last shot.

"Mama, don't you force me to do anything. He's still my boy, okay. Any court will tell you so."

Nana flew out the door and down the steps faster than I had ever seen her move. Before I could blink, Nana landed her hand against the side of Mama's face. I flinched at the pop that was louder than the firecrackers Mac and I had lit last Fourth of July.

Mama stumbled, still touching the injured cheek. "Bitch!"

The beat-up car's engine turned over and over, and just when I feared the fighting was not going to end, Mama drove off in a spray of sand, covering Nana's prized fern.

Watching Nana clutch her apron and half skip to the back of the house yelling, "A.B., A.B., where are you at?" I laid down in the car seat and thought for a second that, if I was real still, maybe I could hide forever.

A blue jay landed on the dogwood branch that dipped down to the old Chevrolet. In a flutter of wings the bird turned his head down towards me. His tiny eyes seemed to be looking right into the fearful parts. But his peaceful stare failed to trick me. I had seen the signs of trouble before.

If anybody had joined us for supper that night, they never would've believed that my mama's visit had rattled any nerves. Poppy told a joke every now and then, and I would fake-laugh to let them know I could play the game. Anything to keep conversation away from the car with the blue door.

It was only after I had dressed for bed that I discovered how bad it really was. Their words floated from the kitchen table and every so often became tangled with the clanging sound of a spoon hitting Nana's cup of cocoa, the same cocoa she claimed settled worried nerves.

"You reckon she'll follow through with this?" Poppy asked.

"I don't know what to think. She mentioned some man. Claimed he had plenty of money."

"They all had money, didn't they?" Poppy snorted, and for a second I thought he might be laughing. "Don't worry none. If she means business, then we'll just find us a lawyer."

"A lawyer costs big money. Big money." Nana almost moaned the words. "I expect we could mortgage the land if we had to."

Crickets outside my bedroom window roared at the silence that followed. The land that Nana's daddy sharecropped and saved years to buy. I pictured the rough and faded number on the porch floor, 1918. The wavy numbers, carved with his own pocketknife, were a permanent memorial. I could almost reach out and touch his long wiry beard every time Nana told me the story of the day her daddy became his own man. "No matter what the world may take away from you, they'll never be able to strip you of where you come from," she'd always say at the end.

Hours later when stillness fell upon the house, I was relieved to awake and find the sheet still dry. Easing the door open, I saw a light glowing in the kitchen. The big black Bible was laid open like a place mat on the table. With her back to me, Nana sat cupping a white card. The words were too faint to read, but the gold seal stood out all bright and shiny. The same gold seal that the Senator, Mrs. Strickland, had pointed out to us when she passed around her business cards. The state seal that was there to remind us that, as long as we lived in North Carolina, we could count on liberty and justice.

$\mathcal{F}our$

———••◆••———

*M*iss Belinda jumped up from her pew and began hitting the tambourine. Chatter from the instrument ignited her husband even more. "Jesus said ask all in my name and it shall be given to you. All! You want a mountain to move? Then tell it to move! You want healing? Then tell your mountain of disease to move on out! You want to have your bills paid up? Then explode your mountain of debt with faith!" As the tambourine chimes died down, so did his tone. "But you can't doubt. No, sir. Doubt will do nothing but put a roadblock on the blessing."

As Brother Bailey wiped the sweat off his brow, I slid along the pew and rested my head in Nana's soft lap. I knew the routine. The excitement had faded, and it was safe to recline. I had learned not to lie down on the pew until he finished his yelling. The words he hissed whenever he got into one of his fits would always end up coming out in a fine mist of spat. So I had learned to wait to take my position, just like Brother Bailey said we had to wait on our blessings.

Poppy liked to say that Nana had been going to Rock Creek Holiness Church ever since Moses was a baby. Wednesday night, Sunday, Sunday night: we were engraved in the count that hung on the little brown attendance board every week. All the ladies in the church wore their hair the same way Nana did, long and pulled up in buns. Whenever I had to get up to use the bathroom, on the way up the aisle I liked to turn around and study the tight, round buns behind me. White, red, black, blonde, and even light blue, they looked like speckles from a rainbow spread out across the congregation.

After the service we stood in the small church foyer until the last member had exited out of the glass doors. The scent of muscle ointment and Juicy Fruit gum still hung in the air. Nana eyed the sanctuary, where Brother Bailey and Miss Belinda wrapped microphone cords until they coiled in submission.

"I need to talk with Brother Bailey a minute. You go on and play outside."

The red car divided the space between Brother Bailey's brick home and the pines that lined God's home. In the moonlight black stripes twirled up at the sides of the car like a bolt of lightning. It was Murphy's car, Brother Bailey's son. He was fresh back from Vietnam and, as I heard Nana once say to a friend on the phone, "never will amount to nothing." The light in the car came on for a second, and I could make out two heads. Easing towards the car, I ran from pine to pine, using each one for cover. A flash of excitement filled me, and I wished Mac was here. He would make me brave enough to do something really funny, like jump on the back of the car and yell like a crazy man. I pictured Mac and me then taking off running and landing shoulder first in a pad of pine straw, laughing until breathing itself was painful.

Without Mac, I settled on mapping out a game of private detective, fixing to capture a white-trash criminal, with the trees as my cover. When I jumped from behind a broad tree, fingers held like a gun, I found I was too late. Someone had already been captured.

Through the back window. Murphy was kissing Trudy Beatty on the neck. Her head was all thrown back and the flow of long red hair cascaded to the edge of her white bra. I stood frozen, watching him pull and twist at the top. Uneasiness swept over me and, though part of me wanted to look closer, all I could do was run. I skidded on the slick pine straw and almost tripped over a fallen limb before reaching the church. When I got to the glass doors, I held the cold handle until my breath regained a regular rhythm.

Slipping into the back pew, I tried to focus on the image of Brother Bailey and Miss Belinda with their arms draped over Nana in a way that reminded me of a football huddle. No matter how weird it looked, the sight didn't bother me as much as seeing Trudy in her underwear and Murphy slurping on her neck. To distract myself, I fished a discarded bulletin from the tiled floor and began making a paper plane. All the while, Brother Bailey's voice circled over me waiting for a place to land.

"Now, sister, the Lord knows all the grief that girl has caused you. He won't put more on you than you can bear. But you have to show Him you're serious." Brother Bailey lifted his fist high into the air, and Nana nodded.

"The Almighty took six days to make the world, so I want you to pray six times a day that Sophie won't come against you. That she won't take that boy."

"Glory," Miss Belinda shouted.

Her words fired up Brother Bailey like a gas stove. "Faith can move mountains, but only if you got enough of it. Call it by name now. Say she won't take my boy."

As Brother Bailey and Sister Belinda stood over her, Nana mumbled and then grew louder. "She won't take my boy."

Brother Bailey had his hand on Nana's shoulder. "I don't know, sister, I always figured your girl had herself a Jezebel spirit. But hear me out, her evil ways shall not prosper against you."

I pressed my sneaker harder against the back of the pew in front of me. Creasing the edges of the paper plane, I licked the point with expert precession. It was sturdy, with a sharp point at the end. Ready for takeoff. As Brother Bailey grabbed the side of his belt and pulled the baggy pants high around his waist, I leaned back with all my might and threw my creation. It glided high above the rows of benches and sailed even with the attendance board. I pictured myself in the pilot seat steering it towards an exotic land yet to be discovered. But before I could call out Mayday, it happened.

Just as Brother Bailey opened his mouth, the plane crashed into the side of his neck. He slapped as if an overgrown mosquito was after him.

"Brandon, what in the world? You could've put out Brother Bailey's eye with that thing," Nana said.

But his eye remained strong as ever. Eyes that were too close together and too small for any normal person pierced right through me. The way he squinted, I knew he thought that my meanness came natural. I was a part of the Jezebel spirit. I'm not like her, I wanted to yell. But the real proof was resting at his feet. Cream-colored paper filled with prayer requests and joyful hymns.

The day the deputy with brown cowboy boots appeared at the door, I sat Indian-style in front of the TV. Even with the papers in hand and the stricken look that made Nana's mouth open, she still tried to pass it off. "Just some business stuff. Don't you worry," Nana said and then slipped the thick white envelope underneath the black telephone. That night at supper we talked about a sick sow, the farmer down the road getting his leg cut on bob-wire, and the decreased price in cattle. Never any mention of the chance that the car with the blue door might appear again and that my mama would swipe me away forever.

Nana continued to follow Brother Bailey's orders to the letter. She even took time to pray at the Farmers Market. She would slip into the truck halfway through the day and close her eyes real tight like she was in a deep trance. Scattered conversations bounced around the high concrete walls until the words themselves sounded to me like they were coming from a gigantic blender.

"What's wrong with her?" Poco whispered. He irritated me the way he liked to kneel down next to the side of the truck and watch Nana's mouth move and twist in silence.

"Leave her alone."

Poco wiped the sand off of his jeans. "Is she sick?"

"No, dummy. She's praying is all. She's just religious, okay."

"How come she don't have her beads?"

"What beads?" I asked, afraid Brother Bailey had messed up part of the instructions.

"The rosary. Daddito has one." Poco pointed towards Mr. Calato's truck and the beads hanging from the rearview mirror. "I bet he'd let her borrow them. Is she praying about your mom coming back?"

"No." I jumped from the truck tailgate. "How come you know about that?"

"I heard Daddito and Miss Naomi talking about it. She said your grandma is worried. Worried to death even."

I stomped my foot so hard the jar from the concrete raced up my leg. "She's not that worried. My mama is here just for a little while. Just for a visit."

Poco sighed like he was older than his own grandfather. "Yeah. Just like my dad."

Before we packed up, I saw Nana and Poppy in front of Mr. Calato's truck. They stood right in front of the discolored beads that dangled from the rearview mirror while Mr. Calato propped his boot on the edge of the bumper. Poppy leaned forward, his forehead almost touching the sweat-stained brim of Mr. Calato's cowboy hat.

"You figure some of your kin, down say in Miami, might be able to help us?" Poppy's words were slow, but his eyebrows stretched with anticipation.

Mr. Calato didn't say a thing. Nana coughed a couple of times as if to signal Poppy to try again.

"It's just that we hear . . ."

"Brandon your boy. Just like Poco . . . my boy. If this storm don't blow over, help will be close."

Nana squinted and held up an open hand as if to grab Mr. Calato's words before the early morning breeze had scattered them away.

Five

———— •◆• ————

M iss Douglas had told us important people were coming to school that day. All the high-ups, she called them. Her chalkboards were as black as a starless night, and all the erasers were lined perfectly along the metal sides. The big map of the United States was pulled down, and Miss Douglas gripped the wooden pointer until her knuckles looked milky.

"Boys and girls, who can tell me the capital of Texas?" Miss Douglas asked with the end of the pointer hovering over Louisiana. She craned her chicken-looking neck towards the opened door. A shuffle of footsteps and soft whispers echoed down the sidewalk.

Dewayne Pickings raised his arm, and the musky scent caused me to jerk my head towards the windows. "Ooh, ooh," he moaned. "I know."

The voices grew louder, and I heard Mr. Jenkins, the principal, tell the group that Miss Douglas was one of the best. When the shuffles stopped outside the opened door, the soft blonde hair stood out from the group of men with wide ties. Her smile scanned the room, and for a second I thought maybe she recognized me.

The lady senator. She was standing right in my classroom with a dress so yellow it almost matched her hair. What if she remembered me? She'd remember what Nana had told her about my mama and what trash she was to show up and take me away. She'd tell Miss Douglas,

and then whenever she came to my name on the roll call each morning, Miss Douglas would mimic the guidance counselor's slanted smile
of pity.

"Uh, yes, Dewayne." Miss Douglas pulled at her skirt and the
pointer fell deeper into Louisiana.

"Baton Rouge."

Miss Douglas's wide eyes looked even bigger behind the glasses.
"Now, Dewayne. We studied this state just last week. Try again. This
time let's put on our thinking cap."

Dewayne propped his hands on the roll of skin that hung from his
chin and pretended to tie a ribbon underneath a cap that only existed
in his mind. "Baton Rouge, Miss Douglas."

She cleared her throat and glanced at the special guests. "No, it's
Austin. Austin, Texas. Now let's move on to . . ."

Dewayne's arm shot back up and his scent must have hit Miss
Douglas too, because she snatched her head towards him real fast.
"You're pointing to Louisiana, not Texas. What'd you expect?"
Dewayne asked.

The group of high-ups snickered, and Miss Douglas adjusted her
glasses before faking a chuckle herself. "Well, Mr. Dewayne Pickings,
you're right as usual. I can always count on my little scholar to keep
me on my toes." Miss Douglas tilted forward and giggled along with
the guests.

And then as the group turned to leave, the lady senator looked at
us once more. The powdered face was lined even with my desk.
When her eyes landed on me, she clutched a necklace of pearls. There
was no half-turned smile of pity. Just a slight nod and wink before she
turned and followed the others.

After the visitors left, Miss Douglas claimed one of her sick
headaches and passed out clumps of worksheets. The way she looked
at Dewayne while she counted the sets of papers reminded me of the
way Brother Bailey had looked at me the night I nearly poked his eye
out with the paper plane.

Halfway through one batch of worksheets, my name rang out over the intercom. The brown box with gold wiring made me flinch as the words flooded out. "Miss Douglas, we need Brandon Willard up at the front office." My stomach tightened as Miss Douglas stopped rubbing her temples long enough to nod.

As I reached down for my book bag, Dewayne leaned down across from me. With his face turned sideways, the fat in his cheeks gathered under his eyes, making his face look like it was a filled cream puff. "Sizzle, sizzle, says the electric paddle."

"Dewayne Pickings! Get to work this minute," Miss Douglas screamed.

As I walked down the sidewalk, Dewayne's words raced in my mind but did little to make my heart beat any faster. Little did he know that a cigarette burn and a punch to the back beat an electric paddle any day.

Rounding the corner towards the office, I saw the school secretary, Miss Parnell, right next to the poster that the art class had made of the American flag.

"I know it can't take this long to get him out here." The raspy voice scarred from too many cigarettes caused my legs to freeze.

Through Miss Parnell's thinning teased hair, the white sunglasses from my past swayed back and forth like a cork caught in a windstorm. I tried to hide between the rows of lockers. I needed time to think how to handle Mama without Miss Parnell getting all nervous the way she did whenever the line to purchase pencils got too long at the front-office window. I pictured Miss Parnell calling the guidance counselor for backup. They would offer slanted smiles as they examined my mama and me standing side by side.

"Baby?"

Miss Parnell's pouty lips and Mama's wide smile were on me tighter than security cameras. "Hey," I said more for Miss Parnell's benefit than Mama's.

The retarded boy who helped sell pencils opened the office door next to Miss Parnell. She never lost her glare on Mama as she moved to let the boy enter. "Now look here, missy. Like I told you, your name's not listed as guardian."

Mama pushed her sunglasses back and flung out her hip. The painted flower on the jeans flapped as if a breeze had just swept pass. "Miss Parnell, you know me, okay. You know I'm the boy's mama. I want you to go on and fill out whatever it is that . . ."

The steady tapping from the feet of important visitors drowned out Mama's official comment. Flocked together like geese with the lady senator as a bright yellow canary, the group rounded the corner behind Mama.

"Now, Senator Strickland, did I mention that we received some of the highest rankings on English in the state?" Mr. Jenkins was still smiling when a man with a black camera showed up to take their picture. If they had been standing any closer, Mama and Miss Parnell would have been in it too.

Mama pulled her tight T-shirt down. She stared at the principal the same way she might examine a potential boyfriend. "He doesn't have time to talk with you. So get that notion right out of your head," I heard Miss Parnell warn.

Before the group broke their posed smiles, another set of footsteps rattled the hall. A brown pocketbook was strapped to Nana's wrist and swung back and forth as she marched forward.

Just as the camera flashed, Mama threw her hands up in the air. "Oh, shit."

"You best watch your mouth," Nana said in hushed tones. "When are you going to learn?"

"Umm, umm, umm." Miss Parnell's hair rotated back and forth as she shook her head.

Mr. Jenkins was speaking extra loud and watching the commotion all at the same time. The only person still looking at me was the lady senator. Senator Strickland's eyes were motionless and seemed lower than they had in the classroom. It was a stare that made me think someone she might have known was standing behind me.

"By the time I'm done, y'all are gonna have your asses in court." Mama jerked away when Mr. Jenkins tried to grab her arm.

"Young lady, either leave or I'll call the police and have you escorted out." Mr. Jenkins propped his hands on his white belt. I wondered if he thought of getting the electric paddle and beating her but good.

Mama dramatically kissed her index finger and waved it at me. All the eyes that had been studying the wild creature slowly drifted towards me. Watching her flower-painted jeans flap like wings, I wished she would've taken flight. Along with their pitiful stares came the weight of being her son. Right then part of me wanted to take flight with her and soar high above the school to a place where nobody knew about a past that always hovered nearby.

If my mama didn't do one thing else by showing up at school, she did manage to put Poppy and Nana into motion. In a weakened condition Poppy even agreed to meet with the colored lawyer that Senator Strickland had told Nana about.

The brightly colored balloons that were painted on the dingy block building seemed out of place. Like fresh ribbon tied around some forgotten gift that had been found in the attic. A big white sign welcomed us: "Child Advocacy Network 'CAN' Make a Child's Destiny." While Poppy scratched the stubble on his chin and Nana straightened her skirt, I studied each of the block-shaped letters. They seemed as foreign as the Egyptian words that were stenciled on the sides of temples in my social studies book.

"A.B." Nana stood at the front door with the pocketbook balanced on her wrist like a scale.

Poppy got out of the car in a hunched-over way befitting an old man. "Never guessed I'd end up using a colored lawyer," he mumbled.

Nana never turned around as she led the way up the sidewalk. "They said she's the best for this sort of thing. So hush your mouth and open up your ears."

Inside, photos of various children ranging from infants to ones older than me greeted us on the bulletin board. Guarding the photos at the front desk was a young woman with braids of strawberry-colored hair.

Slumped in the small vinyl chair, Poppy pulled the brim of the John Deere cap even lower over his forehead. When our lawyer appeared from behind an office door, I heard Poppy mumble again.

She had a wide piece of gold material wrapped around her head. A matching dress dared to touch the points of her body. As she glided towards us there was no smile. For all I knew she might have been toothless. But the way she tilted her head ever so slight told me she was equipped to take on anything that got in her way. The sharpness in her cheekbones made me think of the drawing of Cleopatra.

"Hello." Her earrings swung wildly as she reached out for Nana's hand. "I'm Nairobi Touchton."

Nana smiled and introduced herself and Poppy. His hands were planted deep into pants pockets, and his gaze never seemed to settle on one particular person.

Nairobi leaned down and the top of her dress opened to reveal the edge of brown breast. The way my eyes danced around the room I'm sure she thought nervous eyes ran in the family.

Nanny and Poppy met with Nairobi behind a conference-room door covered with gold-colored plastic grooves. It all seemed to take on the feeling of a CIA type of mission that would be best suited for G.I. Joe. Their shapes were distorted through the imitation glass, but there was no denying where Poppy sat at the table. His slump gave him away.

Drifting closer to the bulletin board, I studied the photographs. Babies lined the top row, and a few had little gold balls on their ears; variously colored adults clutched them with surprised smiles. Orphans, I figured. When my glance fell to the bottom of the poster, so did my spirit.

The boy with the name Alfonso stenciled underneath his picture caused the hair on my neck to stand at attention. It was the emptiness in his eyes. A boy deserted not at a hospital, but most likely in a neighborhood or a shopping center. Deserted like the cat Mama said we could no longer afford, so she shooed him out of the car on a street filled with two-story homes and swimming pools. Taffy, the cat, had long been forgotten, but suddenly his green eyes were as wild as the boy's on the poster and just as frightened. Without a calling card to announce its arrival, the hatred that had been buried beneath a need to take care of Mama rose to the surface. While the lady at the desk was busy writing down instructions from a caller, I snatched the photo off the poster with one clean swipe. Alfonso rested inside the pocket of my Toughskin jeans as comfortable as he would have in any two-story home with a swimming pool.

No matter how many times Nana prayed, my mama never did leave town. The farmhouse soon became a place filled with muffled words and worried stares that would magically turn into tense smiles whenever eye contact was made.

The light from the kitchen bled across the hall floor. I gently stepped on the board that always creaked regardless of where I placed my foot. Nana coughed, and I paused to determine her location.

As I turned the handle to the hall closet, the click from the light switch might as well have been a firecracker. Nana jumped the same time I did, and the hall light shone on me like a police searchlight.

"What in the world are you doing up?" Then she looked down at the urine-soaked pajama leg.

I opened the closet door and reached for the sheets. Her hand was warm against my arm. The pat was as gentle as her voice. "We'll fix it."

Not another word was shared as we stripped the soiled sheets and balled them in the middle of the floor. The popping sound of crisp clean sheets reminded me that all was still in order in the farmhouse. Nana's long gray ponytail swung side to side as she bent down to secure the sheet. She smiled and nodded towards the dresser. Pajamas decorated with cowboy hats were neatly folded in the corner of the drawer. I clutched them to my chest and hoped the clean smell from fall air had been captured from the clothesline. A smell so clean that it would protect me from the darkness that had seeped into my mind and caused it to take flight with nightmare.

When I returned from changing in the bathroom, Nana was smoothing out the wrinkles and had the sheet folded down tight like I'd imagine a fine hotel would do. She fluffed the pillow and lifted the edge of the sheet. After I was secured in bed, she kissed my damp hair. I wanted her to stay and lay beside me, to tell me everything would be fine come morning. I wanted to hear the words from our usual script. But tonight she just smiled from my bedroom door. Against the backdrop of the hall light, she looked like an angel standing at the doorway.

When the door hinge squeaked as she pulled the handle, my heart raced again. Before she had completely disappeared into the hallway, I did it. I called out as loud as I would have if I hadn't been used to nightmares. "I want to talk to that judge."

"Now don't you worry about . . ."

"I mean it. I want to talk to him. Remember Nairobi told me I could if I wanted to."

Nana slid into the bed. Her stomach was soft and warm against the small of my back. "Shh, now," she whispered. The thick arm draped against me and in her clutch I knew there was nothing that the judge from my nightmare, the one with the long white beard and fangs, could do to take me away.

But the judge I faced in real life had no facial hair at all. His white hair was streaked with tints of leftover nicotine. The hair was just long enough that it twirled up at the base of his neck. His gold-wire glasses and easy smile made me wonder if he had ever played Santa Claus down at the mall in Raleigh. My grip on the leather chair loosened.

Rows of wide books lined the shelf behind his desk. The walls in his office were tall and paintings of the beach hung next to me. Mama had always said she wanted to live at the beach. She had always claimed the setting sun helped settle her nerves. Thinking that any minute she might bust into the judge's office and provide a rerun of the act at school, I gripped the chair again. But there was no screaming inside the room, just the steady tick of a brass clock and the ruffle of papers as the judge flipped through my case. Just when I started to lean forward and see if my name was stamped on the side of the file, Nairobi rubbed my shoulders. She winked and nodded enough so that her big silver earrings danced. Her chair was so close to mine that at first I thought they were connected like a pair of Siamese twins I had seen in the encyclopedia.

A skinny man with long sideburns glanced at me over black glasses. He halfway smiled and continued scribbling on a pad. Mama's lawyer. Nairobi had prepped me on who I would find inside the judge's chambers. She had told me to be myself and that everything would work out fine.

"Brandon, I want us to get to know each other a little better. You know, chew the fat as they say," the judge said. "Now this is Mr. Jeffords. He's working with your mother just like Nairobi is working with your grandparents."

Mr. Jeffords smiled bigger this time, and the woman sitting in front of the little typewriter started pecking away.

The judge rubbed his hands and looked up at the ceiling. "So tell me, how's school going?"

"Fine." My comment echoed against the high ceiling, and the woman clicked at the little typewriter.

"I see you make excellent grades." The judge flipped the file open and glanced at the pages. "They tell me you're a smart one."

The clicking of the typing filled my ear. Bouncing off the ceiling, it sounded like clicks from a gun. "Good grades are very important. But what about downtime, are you able to have fun as well?"

"Yes, sir. I play with Mac and Mary Madonna a lot. Poppy put up a tire swing for me. Sometimes we play inside the old car Poppy uses for parts when the tractor gets messed up." I moved to the edge of the chair, hoping to see the notes the judge was making. The vision of my permanent record sprawled open on the guidance counselor's desk came to mind.

"Mac and Mary Madonna are Brandon's cousins. They live next door," Nairobi said.

"I see. Well, tell me about your friends. Do you have friends visit you at your grandparents'?"

I wanted to explain that we lived away from the city, but decided against that for fear that the judge would think that we were back-woods. "Sometimes. My friend Poco comes by."

The judge rubbed his chin the way I used to picture Santa doing whenever he made out his naughty-and-nice list. "Poco? Does he go to your school?"

"No, sir. I see him down by the Farmers Market. He lives with his granddaddy. They farm too so . . ."

"What sort of things do you like to do with your grandparents? You know, special things on the weekend or after school?"

The ticking from the clock sounded louder. "Uhh . . . I go fishing with Poppy. He picks me up from school sometime." More notes were scribbled in my file. "But only once in a while. Nana picks me up after school. We go by the Dairy Queen and have milkshakes. So . . ."

"I understand your mother came by the school recently." The judge quickly looked up, and I gripped the edge of the chair until the grooved wood began to feel like it was apart of me. "How did you feel about seeing her?"

"I don't know. She just showed up is all."

"What did you do when you lived with your mother? I mean after school and on the weekends?"

The scent of Mama's freshly washed hair swept over me, and I turned to see if she had walked into the room. The woman at the little typewriter smiled and glanced back down at the machine.

"We'd go places. To the flea market and stuff."

"Do you miss not having her around?"

The words caused me to flinch. Now I could not only smell Mama, but I could see her too. See her running her fingers through my hair the way she used to do. She smelled fresh and clean. She was renewed. I slipped down in the chair and stared at the letters on the big gray books lining the bookshelf until they blurred into Techni-color red. The judge faded, and suddenly the row of books behind him became a movie screen to my mind. I watched the clip of Mama and me acting the fool one Saturday at the flea market. Just the two of us. She put on an old blue hat with a flower on it and pursed her lips until I bent over laughing. Her teeth were pure white and the hat sky blue. Colors so real and bright that I wanted to reach out and touch her. "Every month we'd go to the flea market. I found a table for us one time. Mama talked the man into giving her that old hat to go with it. It had a yellow flower on the side." The movie played on in silence. Mama was laughing and laughing until she could barely walk and had to lean against me. I could feel the bony spot on her hip as I tried to support her. My eyes burned, and a cloud of tears cut the image.

Nairobi offered a tissue and touched my back. I stiffened at the touch and wiped away the past. I never looked up as the judge continued getting to know me better.

"Do you ever think about living with your mother again?"

The clock ticked, and Mama's lawyer cleared his throat. As if that were my cue, I shrugged my shoulders.

The judge's tone began to drip with sympathy. Without looking up at him, I knew he was giving me that pitiful sideways smile. I could read his tone as easy as he read all those thick books lining his wall. Each word he uttered became softer until finally the Santa Claus disguise had peeled away. "What do you picture when you think of living with your mother?"

"A two-story house." I looked up and held the judge's stare. "A place where Nana and Poppy can live with us too."

Six

Seeing Nana and Poppy dressed in their good clothes sitting on the porch at three o'clock in the afternoon, I knew something was wrong. It was the first day that Nana had failed to meet me at the driveway. The sight of them motionless in the green metal chairs caused me to panic. The roar of the school bus and its fading laughter moved down the highway, and for a second I thought of chasing behind it. All I could think about was Paula Simpson telling everybody at school how she found her granddaddy cold as ice, slumped over in a porch swing, dead from a heart attack. My steps moved faster until the tips of my toes were the only part that brushed against the gravel patches in the driveway. Sweat wove a path down the back of my hair until it tickled. By the time I reached the tire swing, I was running wide open.

Nana was the first to move. She got up and brushed her church dress as if invisible lint had collected on it. "Well, now. I didn't realize it was time for you to be home already. Let me go fix your Pepsi."

Poppy continued to gaze at the field spotted orange with pumpkins. "School good today?"

"Yes, sir."

I kicked a rock against the porch step hoping the constant thud would irritate him enough to turn towards me. He just sat there massaging the pointy part of his chin the way he did whenever he learned the price of hogs had dropped.

The screen door screeched, and Nana came out carrying the Pepsi bottle in one hand and a glass full of ice in the other. She carefully poured the drink and, when she noticed me studying her, tried to smile.

Fuzz from the soft drink engulfed me, and suddenly it sounded as loud as fireworks. My heart slowed and began to accept what my mind had already figured out. The silence, the glances towards the field, the pained expressions whispered the details to me. Nana and Poppy might have been alive, but I was gone.

As Poppy rocked in the swivel chair, a steady creak was in concert with his motion.

Nana brushed the dress again. "Well, we heard from that judge today."

I followed Poppy's gaze out towards the pumpkins that we would cut and take to market next week. The perfectly lined rows finally blurred into a flame of burnt orange.

"He thinks it's best if you stay with your mama for the time being. Naturally we'll keep seeing you along and along. They're going to take it slow. Some visits with your mama to start with and . . . well, let's just see."

Leaning against the porch rail, my eyes burned with tears, but they would never know it. I sipped the Pepsi and wiped away the fuzz from my lip like I didn't have a care in the world. But as strong as I wanted to be, my eyes would not allow me to look at them. I heard the boards pop and knew somebody had gotten up.

Nana's hand brushed across my head. The smell of her Sunday perfume rolled over me. She took a breath as if she wanted to say more, but stopped. I wanted her to pull me up by my hair like a kitten and hold me in her lap. To whisper reassurances that things would be all right.

Poppy cleared his voice. "Son, we're sorry. Just plain sorry."

When his voice cracked, I jumped from the porch and ran towards the tire swing. I swung away from their stares. Tears escaped, and I knocked them away with a swipe of the wrist. Then I jumped down and ran to the old Chevrolet. Watching from the porch, they stared as if I was some wild child who had escaped from a traveling circus. I jerked the steering wheel extra hard and tried to laugh like I was really having a good time. Imitating squealing tires, I screamed and pulled at the gearshift. The way I bounced up and down proved I was a carefree. It was only after they had entered the house that I let myself breathe again. Sliding down into the torn car seat, I looked into the rusted spots on the ceiling light and tasted the salt of tears.

The woman from the child-services agency sat in Nana and Poppy's living room with her knees locked together and a clipboard resting on her lap. The red lips were pursed so tight I thought that maybe she had eaten a sandwich filled with Crazy Glue.

"Now let's see . . . Brandon . . . ," the woman flipped through the pages on her clipboard. "Yes, Brandon. Now for the first few visits you will meet your mother in a public location. Grandmother, you can help select a place if you'd like," the woman glanced over her glasses. The string of crystal beads that was attached to her glasses jingled with the slightest movement of the head.

"When will this all take place?" Nana asked.

With one hand the woman checked off a box and held up the other. "Grandmother, one thing at a time. We're just on item two right now."

Before she left, the government woman decided that Dairy Queen would be the best place to meet. I wondered why the woman never checked to see if my mama could meet at Dairy Queen and how she knew what time would work best for Mama. Watching the woman drive away in her square blue car with the government tag, I decided that maybe she was one of those people with ESP. The kind I saw on TV who could tell pregnant women whether they would have a boy or a girl. I wondered if she could see into my future just as easy.

"Hey, baby," Mama said when she handed me the package

wrapped in paper covered with multicolored balloons. She lightly hugged me the way I had hugged Poppy's cousins at the Willard family reunion last year. The scent of fresh soap lingered on her skin, and her hair was as neatly teased as if Aunt Loraine had coached her on how to fix up.

Her eyes swam around as we sat at the usual red plastic table and drank milkshakes. No matter how fast my mama's eyes fluttered, they never landed on Nana. The blue dots darted back and forth from me, to the government lady, and to the white board that advertised a two-for-one special on chili dogs.

Mama spoke real fast and talked mostly about the beauty shop her new boyfriend, Walter, had promised. The government lady nodded and smiled as if to assure me life would be better than ever.

I smiled back and played that she was the proper mother that we both wanted her to be, a mother full of honor and forgiveness. Hoping against hope that what Brother Bailey had said last Sunday was really true. That you never run out of forgiveness. But later I wondered if Brother Bailey had really ever known my mama.

It was Halloween on our third visit and I was dressed in overalls, with one of Poppy's red handkerchiefs dangling from the pocket. My hair was slicked back, and black dots covered my cheeks.

The government lady pursed her lips and glanced again at her watch. "Oh, good night, I hope she didn't have an accident." Nana just sighed and brushed away salt from the table.

For this visit Mama was thirty minutes late. And the last time she was twenty minutes late. By that visit her hair was back to the flat look that I remembered.

The roar of the car with the blue door made us all turn towards the parking lot. A piercing screech from the opened door warned that Mama would be joining us at any moment.

"Sorry I'm late. I had to run Walter up to the store for a refill of his medicine. In case of an emergency like that, I knew you'd understand and everything." Mama nodded at the government lady, but the woman continued to look at her watch.

When Mama wrapped her arms around my shoulders, the sugared-mint scent of Jack Daniels and Listerine drifted pass. She sat on her fingertips and tried to smile real big. "Hey, handsome," she said with a wink. Black makeup clumped together in little balls that hung around the edge of her eyes. "You still doing good in school and every-thing?"

Stop it, I wanted to yell. Stop trying to act like you're some Carol Brady, some perfect mother, because you're not. "Yes, ma'am. I got a B on my math test."

Nana lightly patted the table. "Math is the only lesson he has trouble with. New math, they call it. It just might as well be Greek to me. I was always the world's worst . . ."

"What are you doing dressed like Howdy Doody or something?" Mama laughed and threw her head back. A black hole filled the side of her mouth where a healthy tooth once lived.

I looked up at the government lady for guidance, but she only made a notation on the clipboard.

"It's Halloween," Nana yelled. Red welts appeared on her neck, and she tried to stand but was pinned in by the edge of the table. "Halloween . . . you ever heard of it? He's just being a boy."

For the first time in weeks, the blue eyes fell directly on Nana. "Well, excuse the hell outta me for not carving a pumpkin. But why should I even bother because I know you already took care of it for me."

Nana regained control by patting her hair bun. "Well, I'm sure you'd manage to mess that up just like you do everything else."

Mama stumbled as she tried to stand, and the chewed-up finger-nail was now pointed straight at Nana. "Old lady, I've sat here listen-ing to your bullshit until I'm just about to throw up."

The government lady clutched the clipboard and leaned away from the table. "Miss Willard, contain yourself. You're going to force me to notify the judge."

The words calmed Mama faster than any pill I had ever seen her take. "I'm sorry. I just got all . . ."

Her words faded as a car with music booming from an open window passed on the highway. The government lady made another notation and sighed.

"Miss Willard . . ."

"It's just all the stress with Walter and everything . . . You know, just one slipup and you'd think the whole world was ending or something." Mama looked at the government lady and smiled. "The only reason I forgot is because I spent all morning filling out papers for that beauty school. You wouldn't believe all the stuff they want to know."

Listening to the government lady reprimand Mama like she was her third-grade teacher, I looked at Nana. With her fist propped against her chin, she gazed towards the highway. The government lady's words seemed to float pass her the same way they did me. They began to sound like garbled words from the radio ads that blared at us from the windows of passing cars. Watching the cars and trucks, I wondered what the passengers thought of us. A casual glance and anybody with good sense would have thought we were having a family reunion. An old-fashioned family get-together filled with ice cream and good memories.

Later that evening the cocktail of whiskey and mouthwash wouldn't leave me alone. Mama's lingering scent kept my insides crunched up like the broken peanut hulls that littered the floor of the Farmers Market.

When I passed on joining Mary Madonna and Mac for trick-or-treating, Poppy and Nana knew I was sick for sure.

Pieces of the dining-room light stretched underneath the bedroom door as if they were bony claws pulling me out of bed. For a moment Poppy's words tricked me into thinking they might be coming from a detective show playing on the TV.

"I knew we should've done something before now. We've just been wasting time with all this notion of hope."

"She sat right there in front of that government lady high as a kite. And that lady just putting on like it was nothing out of the ordinary," Nana said.

"That woman don't care anything about him, any more than Sophie does."

Poppy's words cut deeper than the knife he was using to feed himself. He was wrong. My mama did love me. She loved the only way she knew how. Her love was like the insurance plan that the man came to collect money for each month. It was there if I should ever need it. The only thing was I hadn't needed it.

The more Nana said, the louder her voice became. "And to think we don't have no say in all this. We just pass him back to her like bringing back a loaf of day-old bread to the grocery store. No, this ain't right, I tell you."

Poppy coughed and the sound of tea pouring into a glass of ice drifted from the table. "Well, you know I wanted to do it back when she first got a lawyer."

"I know, A.B. But you don't have to rub it in my face."

"Look, I just don't have no more answers. We've talked it, talked it, and talked it. Brandon's still going with her."

"Why can't they see?" Nana's yell was as loud as it had been at the church revival. "They plain don't care. It makes me so mad I just want to . . . I just got to . . ."

A whippoorwill called out from the night. The familiar sound let me breathe again. But the bird's peaceful call was lost on Nana. Her scream filled every corner of the house.

"Pearl, get a hold of yourself," Poppy shouted.

The sound of a chair hitting the floor made me run into the hallway. An old fear was ready to meet me again. Forgotten sounds of screaming and dishes being broken.

Sliding along the hallway wall, I turned just far enough to see the end of the kitchen table. Clutching a butcher knife, Nana used the other hand to yank her hair free. Wiry gray strands poured out of the bun and down her back.

"All my life I followed the rules. Paid what I owed, went to church, tithed. And what did it get me? The one time I need the Lord, He steps out on me. The one time!"

Poppy's wide eyes were fixated on the knife. "Okay, just settle down. It's all right."

"No, it's not all right! I did the right thing, but God flat don't care. Pray six times a day, no, seven, no, eight. Read the Bible. Had faith. And for what? Just to have the part of me I can't stand to lose snatched back into all that mess. I tell you, I just flat can't stand it! I'd rather be dead first."

"Quit it," Poppy yelled and lunged for the knife.

Staring at the black phone, I felt my heart pound and the back of my head vibrate against the hall wall. The sound of another chair being knocked over echoed in the hall. As hard as I tried, I could not reach the phone. My legs were cemented to the floor. All of a sudden the phone became two and then they faded into blackness. My mind was spinning around in a dust bowl just like the one Mama had left behind the day she drove away. As I slid down the wall, a splinter in the baseboard dug into my back.

Holding my breath, I inched my head so that one eye was exposed to the dining room. Expecting blood and bodies, I found instead strands of Nana's hair clumped together in a nest on the floor. Jagged edges of hair were all that remained on her head.

Poppy slowly moved towards the fireplace mantel like he was a string puppet being guided by a master. His shoulders lifted and sank with each heavy breath. Finally he lifted up the mantel and pulled out two thick envelopes.

"If we do it, you know there won't be no coming back," Poppy said.

Nana never looked up as she continued to sweep the hair into an organized pile. "A.B., all my life I've done what people told me to do because they said it was the right thing. Now it's time I do the right thing for this boy's sake."

It was raining the day I met Poco's real daddy at a truck stop. Round scars tried to disguise the face, but the wave in his hair gave him away. His tall frame filled the corner booth while he rubbed wide hands over coffee like he was sitting before a fire. His hair was ash dark, and he had a cowlick in the front just like Poco.

Drops of rain clung to Nana's plastic bonnet. Each time the restaurant door opened and the beat of the rain drifted inside, Nana would jerk her head and the wet plastic would make a crinkling sound.

We had driven all the way to Brunswick, Georgia, to get the camper and begin our vacation. But the way we left before daybreak, carrying out every stitch of clothing that we owned, caused my gut to keep gnawing in a way that food could not satisfy. A steel guitar cried from a jukebox, and a waitress with hair the shape of a honeycomb approached with a tray filled with pancakes.

Scanning the booths with miniature jukeboxes tucked at the end of the tables, I wondered if Poco would have recognized him. The deep-set eyes only strengthened my charge that this was the man who left Poco for a life in Miami. A life Miss Naomi and others at the Farmers Market described with words like "exotic" and "under-world."

"I appreciate you meeting us halfway like this," Poppy said.

"Had some business in Jacksonville anyway." Every time Poco's daddy turned his neck, the silver chain and rectangle-shaped charm he wore would twist into his chest hair.

"Is everything all set up?" Poppy whispered.

Poco's daddy cut his eyes towards me. "This him?"

Nana wrapped her arm over my shoulder. "Now we're just buy-ing a camper. Brandon is so excited about going on vacation in our new camper." The word "camper" came out of Nana's mouth slow and exaggerated, as if Poco's daddy had a hearing problem.

His dark eyes held Nana's stare. A crooked smile soon formed, and with his chin he motioned towards the door.

Outside in the parking lot black smoke rose from semi trucks to match the color of the sky. Thunderclouds floated away leaving be-hind a fine mist in the air. We stood around the white camper staring at our new possession. I was charged with so much excitement I thought that any minute my feet would start spinning up the asphalt. But Poppy and Nana remained frozen, as if they knew touching the metal siding would require them to travel to a land of foreign tongues.

When Poppy finally began the customary kicking of the tires, I had already pulled away from Nana's grasp. Inside the camper-trailer the smell of freshly laid insulation burned my nose. A bunk bed hung from the ceiling, and a small door hid a sleeper sofa at the other end. A bathroom was tucked neatly in the corner, and a small kitchen separated it from the living room. Poco's daddy reached for the folder on top of the kitchen counter and handed it to Poppy.

"Look, Nana, a TV," I said and pulled a small black-and-white down from a corner compartment.

"Don't mess with nothing. We'll go through everything when we get down the road." Nana tightened the straps on her rain bonnet.

Reaching inside his windbreaker, Poppy offered the envelope that had been hidden in the fireplace mantel. Poppy then busied himself with pulling the truck around and aligning the back bumper with the axle of our new camper.

Pulling the chain from his neck, Poco's daddy squatted down in front of me. His coal-colored eyes pierced mine until my neck grew hot.

"You and Poco are buddies, yeah?"

All I could do was nod and reach for the silver chain.

"Hang on to this for him."

The charm attached to the necklace showed an old man dressed in a robe, carrying someone on his back. The metal was still warm from his skin. I turned it over and rubbed the ridges of the carving.

"It's St. Christopher," he said. "He'll take care of you and Poco." Poco's daddy then got into the truck with red fringe hanging from the back window and drifted away faster than the storm clouds that rolled overhead.

Seven

———◆———

When I woke up, the green sign with orange letters was fast approaching us. The bright sun and the stickiness from heavy sleep made the words blur until all I could make out was a drawing of a smiling sun.

"Here we are, Brandon. Florida. Feel that sun beating down on us?" Poppy began pulling at his sleeves until they were up to his elbows.

"Pay attention to your driving," Nana said. She pulled a container from under the seat.

The confining rows of pine trees on each side of the road made me feel that we were already in jail.

"How about a doughnut? Poppy stopped by Krispy Kreme and got the chocolate kind you like."

"What about Nairobi?"

Soft country music from the radio filled the truck. Poppy glanced at Nana and then turned his gaze back towards the road.

"Well, sugar, what about her?"

"Is she gonna get in trouble?"

Nana folded the flap on the doughnut box. "What makes you ask a thing like that?"

"That lady from the government won't like me being gone. I don't want Nairobi to get in trouble."

When Nana turned to look at me, her eyes looked as if someone had traced the insides with a red pen. "Don't you study about Nairobi. She's just fine."

"Aw, look out now. Don't you start worrying about any of this," Poppy said. "We always said we wanted to go to Florida and now is as good a time as any."

"Well how about that lady senator? What's she gonna do when she finds out?"

Nana leaned forward and pointed to an open-air market painted orange. "Oh look, Brandon. Fresh boiled peanuts. Who in the world heard of boiled peanuts this time of the year?"

Instinctively, Poppy turned into the parking lot covered with sand and lime rock. Pictures of red peanuts and oranges were painted on the outside walls. The store was nothing more than a hut surrounded by two gas pumps. A fat man with tobacco juice tattooed on the crevice of his chin greeted us.

"The finest people in the world pull up to this store," the man shouted from a stool next to the cash register. His pasty-colored arm rested on the register while his fingers fished inside a pack of Red Man.

"How you doing?" Poppy said.

While the two discussed a sale on tobacco, Nana busied herself with the bags of oranges. A pole lined with various colored cowboy belts caught my eye, and soon I pictured myself wearing one with my name stamped on the outside. I wondered if I would be able to keep my name. Everybody on TV who was wanted by the police always had to change their name, and I knew that tight-lipped lady with the government would be after us in no time. She'd probably ride in the back of the police car herself so she could deliver me directly to Mama. She'd drop me off at Mama's new beauty shop, where I'd have to sweep the floor every day as punishment for running off with Nana and Poppy.

"Where y'all heading?" the fat man asked.

"Abbeville, Florida." Poppy propped his boot up on the edge of the wooden counter. "We got us a place down . . ."

"How about the boiled peanuts? They fresh?" Nana tossed a bag of oranges on the counter and glared at Poppy.

"No, ma'am. Frozen. But I bet you five dollars you can't tell no difference. I season them with plenty of salt."

"I'll take a bag."

While Poppy continued to talk as if he had known the man all of his life, I ran my fingers across the indented letters on the belt. Jack. Maybe I could talk Poppy into buying it and use Jack as my new name. Just when I pulled the belt off of the pole, I spotted the blue light.

The light on the highway-patrol car stuck up over a rack of packaged crackers. A broad-shouldered man with sunglasses and a big hat got out. I clutched the belt and looked at Nana and Poppy. She flicked through the stack of cash that lined her billfold, and Poppy propped his arm on the counter like he had decided to stay for a while.

With each step of the patrolman's shiny black shoes my heart sank lower. I pictured that government lady sitting in the backseat with her clipboard tucked in her lap. The belt began to twitch in my hand as if it was some sort of snake coming to life.

"Afternoon, Ervin," the patrolman said.

Poppy jerked his arm from the counter faster than the time he touched the electric fence back home.

"Matt, I was just about to give up on you," the fat man said and then turned towards Poppy. "He comes in every day at noon time. Just as regular as sunrise. Comes in here for a bag of peanuts, nothing more."

Poppy tried to chuckle but it ended up resembling a choking sound. "Well, we can't wait to try them ourselves. Y'all about ready to hit the road?"

The patrolman pulled off his sunglasses and winked at me. A chalky taste built up in my throat, and I fought the urge to throw up all over the green indoor-outdoor carpet.

"Go ahead and bag 'em up," the patrolman said.

By the time he reached the counter, Nana and Poppy had moved towards the truck. But I was still standing there with the smell of fresh leather tempting me to vomit.

Nana slightly turned. "Hurry up now."

I tossed the belt towards the pole and didn't bother to pick it up when I heard the buckle meet the floor. As I ran out of the store, my shirt clung to beads of sweat. When I heard his deep voice, the metallic taste returned.

"Ma'am," the patrolman said. "Hold on, ma'am."

Nana and Poppy stopped at the same time. The flowers printed on her blouse stretched wide as Nana's chest rose higher.

When the patrolman reached her, his sunglasses were back on. The sun sparkled off of the dark lenses the same way it did off the rocks in the parking lot. He reached out and touched Nana's arm. "The peanuts aren't good enough to fill Ervin's pockets more than you have to. You forgot your change."

"I heard that. I'm charging you double today," the fat man called out.

The patrolman laughed and turned to go back inside. "Safe travels now."

The edge of the sky was just turning into strips of pink when we reached our new home. As we drove over the tall bridge at the edge of town, the brown marsh and skinny pines seemed like something out of *National Geographic.*

Leaning over the steering wheel, Poppy breathed deep. "I can smell the salt air clean inside this truck."

Resting off a highway, Abbeville was a fishing village on the Florida Panhandle. A place where pirates might've once hidden in the marshy islands visible from the city streets. I guess that's what Poco's daddy had in mind when he selected it as our new place to live. A place protected and forgotten.

Downtown was made up of two streets that ran right next to a river that connected with the Gulf of Mexico. A pharmacy and a grocery store were nestled across the street from the water. A dime store and other local businesses completed the community.

"I want y'all to look." Poppy pointed to the telephone booth that sat under a chinaberry tree. A small sign next to it read "U.S.A.'s

Smallest Police Station." Right then I breathed deeper than I had since leaving the boiled-peanut stand. Poco's daddy suddenly seemed like the smartest man on earth. Where else could we have gotten a better start than in a town with a police station so small it would fit into a phone booth?

"It says to keep on going two miles up Highway 98," Nana said. The papers that Poco's daddy had provided were scattered across her lap.

Outside of town, modest block homes and trailers dotted the roadside. On the other side of the highway, pine trees and lush vines stood guard over the gulf water. A wooden shack with a spray-painted sign that spelled out "Lazy Lounge" in wavy letters was the last place we passed before the steep curve.

The Rest Easy Campground sat on the right-hand side of the road just like the paper said. Across the highway, a clear view of the gulf welcomed us. A big gray bird crashed into the water and then reappeared with a fish dangling from its long beak. Sections of the water flickered as the final rays of sun were played out.

While Poppy checked in at the double-wide trailer that served as an office, Nana massaged her arm as if a mosquito had gotten her.

"It sure is pretty here," I said.

Even though her hair was short and jagged, her smile was still filled with the reassurance that I had come to depend on. "I got an idea this place is just right."

By the time Poppy parked the trailer and we unpacked, it was already dusk. I eased the door open and surveyed the surrounding campers. The crisp night air teased me into hoping we were still in North Carolina, and I leaned out to see if I could hear the ocean waves. Turning to close the door, I saw the words "Sunshine State" on Poppy's truck tag.

"When did you change the license plate?" I asked.

"Go on and close the door before you let bugs inside," Nana said.

"We've had to make some changes. Things won't be the same as they used to be. Nobody knows your situation like we do. You take that judge, for example. Has he spent a whole entire year with you like we have? And I never did hear . . ."

"We took you away, Brandon, because we thought it was the only thing to do." Soapsuds were still on Nana's hands when she touched my shoulder. She sat on the doll-sized sofa and pulled me close to her. My elbow pressed into the softness of her stomach, and her breath was warm against my neck.

"Sugar, some people might disagree with what we've done. They won't see it the same way we do. So we had to get new tags and come up with new names for us to use down here."

Part of me wanted to pull away from her. But the soft, familiar mushy part of her skin and the reassuring vanilla smell of her clothes kept me close.

Nana picked up the envelope Poco's daddy had given them. "That's why we bought this stuff from Mr. Calato's son. He saw to it that we'd have the right papers and so forth. You know . . . to start over."

Visions of me standing in the principal's office trying to start school with a new name raced through my head. What if I forgot my name and accidentally wrote my old name on a test or a worksheet? "What's my new name gonna be?"

Nana clasped my hand. Hard callused places were now softened by the dishwashing soap. "Well, I didn't want this mess to disrupt you any more than it had to, so you're still Brandon. Only the last name will change."

"How do you like the sound of Davidson? Old Brandon Davidson," Poppy said. "Sort of sounds like a movie star name to me."

"Well, he's pretty enough to be in movies," Nana said. "As for me and Poppy, we're going to be more down to earth. I'm Pauline Davidson from now on and Poppy is . . ."

As he stood, the air-vent handle scraped the bald spot of his crown. "I'm Albert Davidson. Pleased to meet you, sir." I laughed when he shook my hand and massaged his scalp all at the same time.

"Good gracious alive, let me get back to these dishes before the water turns cold." Nana continued to shake her head and wash the dishes until the grime of underworld fingerprints were erased away.

Poco's daddy had even lined up a job for Poppy down at the marina. After years of working on broken-down tractors and old cars, he picked right up on fixing boat engines. He even seemed to like working with the men who didn't ask questions when Poppy introduced himself as Albert Davidson from down the state.

"Down the state" was the answer we gave everyone when asked where we were from. Most people looked at us like any part of Florida that didn't stretch out over the Gulf of Mexico was a foreign country and were not interested in hearing any more about our make-believe address. Everyone except Miss Travick.

My new teacher was fresh out of college and drove over from Tallahassee to teach us. Her hair was golden like the lady senator's back in North Carolina. She wore short skirts, butterfly hair clips, and long beaded necklaces. When I first saw her standing outside the classroom, the smell of butterscotch perfume made me dizzy-headed.

"Where are you from, Brandon Davidson?"

By this time I had the line down perfect. "From down the state. We moved here so my granddaddy could work at the new marina."

Nana's feet shuffled on the concrete sidewalk behind me. "I dropped the records off at the principal's office. It's all in there."

"Oh my gosh, where down the state? I'm from Fort Myers."

My eyes searched behind Miss Travick. Rows of new classmates stared back at me. The pencil I had just purchased from the school office began to feel slick in my sweaty hand. Words and names we had rehearsed swirled in my mind, but the town printed on the school record was nowhere in the script.

"We're from Anglers. Nothing more than a little knock in the road. Down past Melbourne." Nana spoke the words so confident even I was beginning to believe her.

Miss Travick regained with another wide smile. "Oh, well, you never know. We don't get many new people."

The first day at lunch nobody would let me sit at their table. Every time I approached an open seat, someone would move over and stretch their arm across the table so I couldn't put my tray down. The laughter made me hunger for something that food could not provide.

Trying not to capture the attention of the teachers, I smiled like I had wanted to sit by myself all along. Pouring iced tea from a pitcher at the teacher's table, Miss Travick caught my eye and smiled back. I saw her get up and whisper to a boy three tables away. His wide brown eyes searched the room until he saw me. Nodding, he got up and brought his tray to my table.

"Hey," he said. "You're new, right?"

"So?" I said.

He gulped from a carton of milk. "My name's Beau Riley. I sit two rows over from you in class."

"So?"

He shrugged and picked up a french fry. "Don't pay no attention to none of those jerks. They're just testing you is all. Where you from?"

"Mars."

"I hear it sure is cold up there." He cracked a smile and kept on going. "You like to fish?"

"Yeah."

"You ever eat mullet before?"

Turning to see if there was another table to move to, I stopped when I saw the others looking at us. "I don't think so."

"Some dummies think it's a trash fish. Now, I don't know how they think up there in Mars, but it's good eating. My mama and daddy are carrying us mullet fishing this Saturday. You interested?"

Two girls with matching T-shirts printed with smiley faces walked over to our table. "Hey, I'm Ashley and her name's Lisa," the blonde one said.

"He's . . . hey, what's your name again?" Beau asked.

"Brandon. Brandon Davidson, from down the state."

· · ·

Beau Riley was the only person in my life who made me be his friend. Soon it didn't matter if Miss Travick had told him to talk to me or not. Beau was the president of our class and held up his head with a confidence that reminded me of a grown man. By the second day kids who wouldn't let me sit at their tables were lining the lunchroom seats next to Beau and me.

He even worked his magic on Nana and Poppy. When Nana first refused to let me go fishing with strangers, Beau had his mama stop by so we could see that she was decent. She had curly red hair and a beauty mark on the side of her chin just like Miss Kitty on *Gunsmoke*.

"Where y'all from?" Bonita asked. She let the standard answer fly pass and soon started telling Poppy that she heard a big government contract was going to bring in a lot more work to the marina where he was working.

"Well, that sure is good news," Poppy said and brushed away a gnat.

"Yeah, well I heard it the other day down at Nap's Corner. It's a restaurant just the other side of the bridge. I work there four days a week. And what about you, Pauline? You working?"

Nana pulled her shirt down lower. "No, but I've been studying about trying to pick something up. You know, just while Brandon's in school."

Bonita waved her hands like an excited baby. "Ooh, ooh . . . you ought to come down and talk with Nap. But Nap's not his real name. They say it's really Enoch or some other Bible name. Anyway, we got a spot open on the lunch crew. He fired that other girl. I warned her that Nap wouldn't put up with being late. Anyway, the tips are real good and the best thing is you can be home when school lets out." She ran her hands through Beau's hair until he edged away. "I sure believe in being home when my kids walk through the door."

When Bonita and her husband, Johnny, returned with Beau the following Saturday, a boy not more than six was sitting on top of a big spare tire in the back of the truck. Later Beau introduced the boy as his brother, Josh. The dark-skinned boy with auburn hair smiled to reveal a missing front tooth.

Johnny brushed off his hand and removed a faded baseball cap. He nodded patiently and answered Nana's questions about the safety of his boat. Feeling blood burn my face, I was relieved when Poppy patted her shoulder. "I want y'all to bring us back a mess now."

Out on the sea, the heavy sun broke the November chill. The boat rocked with the currents, and a band of seagulls seeking handouts followed close behind. We settled near a marshy island. Besides the seagulls, the only visible life on the island was an eagle's nest tucked on top of a dead tree.

Salt from the air tickled my tongue, and when no one was looking, I stuck it out to see if any would gather.

"Brandon, honey, do you need to put on your windbreaker? It's getting chilly," Bonita said.

I shook my head, and watched as Johnny arranged a folded net on the plywood that covered the back of the boat. The net squished together to form the shape of an accordion that Johnny played like a skilled musician. Then, without saying a word, they all took their places as Johnny drove the boat around in a wide circle.

"Hey, man. You better get over here and help. We ain't catching your supper for you." Johnny's broad smile and a point at the steering wheel was all I needed. Gripping the sun-baked metal, I could see Johnny out of the corner of my eye. He lit a cigarette and pretended like he wasn't watching.

The front of the boat dipped to meet the white-crested waves. I dug my toes deeper into the soles of my shoes and rocked only a little bit. Johnny laughed and yelled to the others. "Look at ol' Brandon. He's working it now." Only twice did he reach down and adjust my direction. His touch was that of leather, and his thick fingers were nicked in a way that made me think of tree bark.

We circled wide, and then Johnny took back control, directing the boat into the middle of the net we had dropped off. Beau and Bonita yanked the motor up with one swift pull. Once inside the net's circle, they lowered it again and Bonita gave him a thumbs-up sign. As if reading my mind, Beau nudged me with his elbow. "He's fixing to turn the motor back on to scare the fish into the net."

Later when we pulled the net, I leaned into it just like Johnny showed me and yanked with more determination than I knew I had. We were all together fighting to bring in our catch. Wearing long yellow gloves like the ones Nana used to wax the floor, Bonita and Beau grabbed a hold of the twitching fish that clung to the net like ornaments on a Christmas tree. "Yeah, man," Johnny yelled as the ice chest filled up with silver-colored fish.

Watching Johnny laugh and tousle the younger boy's hair, I felt the old ache. The same one I used to feel whenever I saw Uncle Cecil driving up the driveway with Mary Madonna and Mac in the back-seat. The same way I felt whenever I looked too long at the picture that now sat on the small dresser in the camper. A family portrait taken at Sears with Mac's stiff hand propped on Uncle Cecil's shoulder and Mary Madonna's arm touching Aunt Loraine's skirt.

Moving away to the other side of the boat, I looked towards the island. I could hear them laughing and teasing each other about who would eat the most fish that evening. The eagle had returned to its nest and turned to see where the noise was coming from. Its head twitched from side to side until the gold beak was directly on me. We held our stare, daring each other to break away. When Johnny cranked up the engine again, the bird snatched a twig from the nest and flew away.

The length of Nana's hair wasn't the only thing that changed. To my surprise she took Bonita up on her suggestion and let Bonita put a permanent in her hair. Nana even took a job at Nap's Corner working the lunch shift with Bonita. Since we only had Poppy's truck for transportation, Bonita would pick her up and bring her home the days she worked. Sometimes they would pick Beau and me up after school and we'd all go to the state park down by the beach. Beau, Josh, and me would sit at the concrete tables and eat the hush puppies and fried fish that were left over from lunch rush. We'd walk along the sand and try to capture tiny crabs in Styrofoam cups while Nana and Bonita sat on the car hood talking. Whenever the wind would shift, pieces of their conversation would roll down to the beach like driftwood that floated in with the changing tide.

Mostly Nana shielded her eyes from the sun and offered a smile or a look of worried concern depending on the information Bonita provided. I figured Nana liked being with Bonita because she never had to do any of the talking. There were no lies that had to be told with Bonita.

No one in Beau's family questioned why I lived with my grandparents. The made-up answer sat on the edge of my tongue ready to be discharged on a second's notice. I had made it all the way to Thanksgiving without the topic ever being discussed; I had been relieved and maybe even too comfortable.

"How much longer till school lets out for Thanksgiving?" Josh asked. The inlet water came up to his knees, and Beau had told his brother to stand still once already.

The long pole that arched above Beau's head looked like a rake except for the net that hung at the end. With one fast jerk, he swatted the water. Through the murky water, we could see the crab race away. "Dog, Josh. I told you to be quiet."

"I didn't even move. You just missed is all."

We trudged towards the tall brown grass and mass of pine trees. The thick mud sucked us down deeper, and I wondered if we had discovered quicksand. When I turned to see if Josh was still with us, the tall bridge that led into town was far behind us.

A pelican drifted inches above the water and then swooped down for lunch. Sunbeams sparkled off of the broken water until the area began to seem like one big kaleidoscope. Splashing sounds echoed from deep within the nearby island, and I pictured the land as one big kingdom. The tall pines became noble kings and bushy stalks of saw grass turned into queens dressed in ball gowns. Bright green palmetto stalks fanned out across the edge of the beach to guard their fortress.

That inlet where sea and fresh water connected made my nerves feel healed right down to the wiry ends that our science book illustrated. A place where the past could be buried deeper than the bottomless mud floor we walked across.

When we had made it to the prickly brown grass, Josh sat down on a patch of sand and poked his finger at the crabs. The sound of their claws rubbing against the tin pail reminded me of fingernails on a chalkboard. "Beau, I need to know. When is school letting out?"

"Next Wednesday. Brandon, you got one to your left."

Hunching over the murky water, I was as still as a trained bird dog. The pinchers on the crab below were wider than his body. He paused when I lifted the pole, and his eyes never flinched as the net came down. "He's mine now," I yelled. Flailing in the net with his underside facing us, the crab displayed a pearl white belly that glistened in the sun.

"Can we have crab claws for Thanksgiving?" Josh asked.

"We'll see if we can't get you some," Beau poked my arm with the side of his pole.

"Yeah, Josh, you should ask your mama to fix you some crab," I added.

"What y'all doing for Thanksgiving?" Beau never turned to look at me as we treaded back through the mud.

"Just stay here I guess."

"Brandon, are you a orphan like Superman was?"

"Shut up, Josh." Beau shook his head at his brother.

"Well, that's what mama said he was."

Trying to ignore their words, I stared at the mud that churned with our steps. If only the sound of sloshing water could have been louder.

"Don't pay no attention to him. He's just a first grader. He don't know nothing."

"I do too. I asked mama how come he don't live with his own mama and daddy and that's what she said."

Jerking the bucket from my hand, Beau held it over Josh's head. "If you don't shut your mouth, I'll throw ever one of these crabs on your head and they'll pinch it shut."

Josh's eyes were big only for a second. He squinted at Beau and twisted his mouth. A spray of spat shot out of his mouth and landed on Beau's T-shirt. Before Beau could grab him, Josh was running and splashing water all the way to the bridge.

Beau waited until Josh had made it to the base of the bridge before he said anything. "Johnny ain't my real daddy."

I stopped, but he kept moving forward, never looking back. When I caught up with him, he was looking down as if reading words from the water's surface.

"My daddy left when I was just a baby. I don't remember him too good. Except for this one time. He sat me up in a kitchen cabinet to see if I would fit in there. I remember him laughing real loud. I can't see him, but I can still hear him."

"What about Johnny?"

"He married my mama when I was just two years old. Josh don't know nothing about it but I just wanted . . . Hey, don't say nothing. Okay?"

Beau didn't know that he was dealing with the master of secrets and part of me wanted to toss the script, but by then it had all become a habit. "I won't. I didn't know my daddy neither."

Beau glanced over at me and nodded. "How about your mama?"

Telling Beau about her travels to Canada working the pipeline and about a trip she made to Hawaii, I felt closer to her than ever.

As we moved towards the bridge, it seemed taller than a sky-scraper. Barnacles clung to the wide pilings that held it in the air.

"How'd she . . . you know, pass?"

"She got killed over in Africa. Doing work in that Peace Corps thing Miss Travick told us about."

"What, a lion get a hold of her?"

"No, worse. A big fat rhino. People don't know how mean those things are. Ripped her right down the middle like a slaughtered hog." The image of a newspaper with Mama's picture as a local hero came to mind. She would be dressed in a safari coat and her hair would be all fixed like it was the time she met us at Dairy Queen.

Beau grimaced. "Dog. When'd it happen?" His words echoed underneath the bridge.

I could see Josh clearly now. He was sitting on the concrete boat ramp, acting like he wasn't listening. "I can't talk about it."

That night Poppy and me watched the tiny black-and-white television with tinfoil wrapped around the antenna. Nana's words competed with those of Hoyt Franklin, the reporter who drove around the country in a motor home until he had found the oldest living veteran or a farmer who had trained a hog to jump through hoops. Watching his show, *Navigating the Nation,* had become a new ritual.

Nana tapped Poppy on the shoulder. "Did you hear what I said about Bonita? She wants us to come over to her place for Thanksgiving."

Poppy's eyes rolled up towards Nana. "A bunch of people gonna be there? We sure don't want a bunch of people asking . . ."

"Nobody's going to be there except Johnny's mama and from what they say she's a little touched. She runs that junk stand just past the curve."

The sounds from the television filled the camper as Poppy rubbed his chin. "Well, if you think she won't get all in our business."

Nana grabbed the recipe box that was stacked on top of the cluttered shelf. A stack of mail fell on the floor near the edge of her shoe, but she never looked down. She began flipping through the cards with an energy that I hadn't seen since she cut her hair with the butcher knife. "I'm going to fix pecan pie and turnip greens. Bonita will know where I can get a fresh mess. Thanksgiving is just not Thanksgiving without my turnips. I can hear Cecil telling me now how he loves my . . ."

Clutching the recipe container as if it were a safe-deposit box, Nana opened the camper door and stood outside. Poppy never looked away as the TV reporter interviewed a woman in Iowa. The sound of crickets competed with the woman's televised voice. All the while, the camera scanned an imaginary world the woman had created for herself out of a collection of dollhouses made from dollar bills.

Beau lived near town in a white block home. When we got there, paper turkeys with top hats, the kind that Miss Travick put up on the bulletin board at school, were taped on every window of the house. Bonita had the front door open before we could get out of the truck.

"Y'all come on in. Now the turkey is a little tougher than I like, but Johnny got to talking to his mama and left it in the smoker too long." Bonita rolled her eyes and imitated a flapping mouth with her hand.

Johnny's mother, Mama Rose, was dressed in a pantsuit the color of Pepto-Bismol and had a matching vinyl purse with an outline of the state of Florida printed on the side. But Nana missed the mark when she told Poppy that Mama Rose would keep quiet.

As the turkey was passed, Mama Rose told us all about her business. A mercantile, she called it. An eternal yard sale, where plywood tables filled with secondhand goods were converted into fancy store displays thanks to colored construction paper and Mama Rose's neat penmanship.

"You heard about that fire over in Panama City? The one that took out that store on the strip?" Mama Rose looked around the table and inhaled real loud. "Well anyway, I got a pile of fancy paperweights filled with beach sand for ten cents each. Ten cents, mind you. I can sale them for at least fifty cents, maybe even seventy-five. Yankees pay big money for anything with genuine beach sand. Now y'all aren't Yankees, are you?"

"Come on, Mama."

Poppy chuckled and nudged Johnny. "No, ma'am. I assure you we aren't."

Mama Rose patted the flamingo pin on her jacket. "Well, you never know these days. Especially with you being from down the state. Yankees come down here and just take over. I can spot 'em in no time flat." She pointed a fork at Poppy and bugged her eyes until the fake eyelashes spread out like wings.

After lunch Mama Rose offered to let Beau, me, and Josh have first dibs on her latest merchandise if we agreed to help her unload it out of the trailer she used as a storeroom. Nana only let me after Johnny said he would drive us down there and pick us up when we were through. When I ran back inside for my jacket, I received Nana's final warning.

"And don't you take food from her," Nana whispered at the front door. "No telling what kind of nasty shape her kitchen's in."

Little did Nana know, but to me Mama Rose's front yard, with long moss that hung like banners from the trees, was a natural wonder. Rows of plastic flamingos were propped around the plywood tables as if they had been frozen there during migration. As we unloaded the boxes that still smelled like smoke, she directed us where to place them.

"No, Beau. Use your head. Don't you know that table can't hold that heavy box. Put it down at the other one. And don't break a thing." Beau never seemed to notice the clipped tones in which Mama Rose spoke to him. He would just change the subject or laugh like it was all a joke. I wondered if she was the only person in town who didn't know he held elected office.

Placing the paperweights on the plywood table covered in a red paper, I examined one of the glass balls filled with water. The sand would scatter whenever I secretly shook it. Mama Rose had given us strict instructions not to shake the weights. Watching the word "Florida" appear as the sand was released from the bottom, I remembered a similar paperweight sitting on the bookshelf in Uncle Cecil and Aunt Loraine's home. Looking into the glass like a crystal ball, I tried to picture what they were doing. They would probably have finished Thanksgiving dinner. Uncle Cecil would be unfastening the top of his pants by now and watching football on TV while Mac and Mary Madonna sat in the old car pretending to search the highways for me. Aunt Loraine had probably stopped criticizing us for leaving by now. Maybe she would even feel sorry for my mama and invite her over for leftover turkey sandwiches. Rubbing the edge of the paperweight base, I felt a hard place where the fire had melted the imitation wood. I rubbed the groove like a lucky penny until Mama Rose snatched it out of my hands.

"You're as bad as Beau. I'm not paying you to daydream. Get to unpacking."

Josh laughed, and Mama Rose winked at him.

"He's probably thinking about his mama getting ate up."

Mama Rose planted both hands on her hips. "What?"

"Josh, you better watch your mouth," Beau warned.

Mama Rose never turned away as she held up her hand towards Beau. "Wait a minute. What is this about your mama?"

I felt her eyes on me tighter than radar; my ears began to ring with the rising blood. "She had this . . . umm . . ."

"She was in the Peace Corps and got tore up by one of them rhinos," Beau yelled.

Mama Rose leaned down closer. A scar lined the side of her wrinkled chin. "You been telling stories to these boys?"

Never turning away, I forced myself to look into her eyes. "No, ma'am. She was down in Africa working with the Peace Corps just like Beau said. A big rhino got a hold of her and ripped her wide open."

Mama Rose waited for me to look the other way, but I only bit my lip like I was fixing to cry over the grief.

"Peace Corps? That bunch Kennedy drug all over the world? Well, they're nothing but a bunch of communists." The thick eyelashes swatted her skin. Before she could ask any more questions, a station wagon with an Ohio license plate pulled up.

As Josh showed the guests some of his favorite things on the stand, Beau moved closer. In a stage whisper he said, "Don't mess with Mama Rose. She's a natural born nut, and a mean one at that."

. ·▮·

Watching Mama Rose smile and wave her hand across the table full of smoldered merchandise, I thought of the warning Poppy had given me about fishing in weedy places. A water moccasin will give off a musty scent right before it strikes. With Mama Rose the only scent she gave off was day-old perfume.

Eight

By the time Santa Claus appeared in the middle of the river on an airboat, we had settled into a normal routine. He landed out of the blue one Friday afternoon and looked as out of place as a flying saucer. As we were passing through downtown, Nana pointed at a snowman sitting on a small boat clutching a fishing pole. "Look, how cute." No matter how much she tried to pretend, I could see her finger twitching as she pointed to the plastic figure. Nana's nerves always got keyed up whenever it was time to call Uncle Cecil.

When we pulled up next to the gas station, Nana slipped out of the truck and used a washcloth to wipe down the receiver of the pay phone. The other washcloth held the necessary change for making a five-minute call to the construction company where Uncle Cecil worked. Every Friday afternoon at four-thirty we stopped at the gas station to make the long-distance connection back to our past. The old man who ran the gas station had gotten used to us by now. Whenever we pulled up, he raised his arm to wave, just high enough so that a roll of pasty skin showed underneath his shirt.

The conversation was always one-sided, with Nana listening to updates that Uncle Cecil might offer. Standing around the pay phone, Nana and Poppy would rotate with the shifting wind that delivered the smell of aged urine from the nearby bathroom.

"How you and the kids getting along?" Nana asked. She wrinkled her brow and nodded. Before the operator could come on and warn her that two minutes remained, the phone was passed to Poppy.

"Hey, son. The mortgage note come in on the farm yet?" Poppy used the toe of his boot to push a piece of gravel deeper into the dirt. "Well, just keep yourself a record, and I'll wire you the money."

"I want to talk to Uncle Cecil."

Nana shook her head. "Poppy's talking business right now."

No matter how many times they called Uncle Cecil, the phone calls never lasted longer than five minutes. Conversation was kept polite and censored like greetings being passed along to an acquaintance in the grocery store. Time was too valuable to pass along descriptions of the good life down in Florida.

Christmas day, I woke up as soon as Poppy opened the camper door. "You better get on up. It looks like somebody left something for you out here."

A spray of morning sun fell on me like a spotlight. I rubbed the stickiness out of my eyes and was grateful that Poppy did not try to claim Santa Claus had stopped by.

Nana was clasping her hands and bouncing to an invisible beat of excitement. Next to her was a brand-new bicycle. A green one with wide handlebars. Just like the kind Beau had gotten for his birthday. Jumping out of the door dressed in my underwear, I grabbed the silver handlebars. Their laughter was loud, and Poppy threw his head back. Touching the cool metal, I knew it was real.

Riding up and down the driveway of the campground, I pictured my old bike back in North Carolina. I was sure Mac was mining it for spare parts by now. It was only right. The bike was his to begin with and came to me only after Aunt Loraine bought him a new one. As I dipped down into another washed-out place in the road, it hit me. They probably thought we'd never come back. Our things would be picked over and tossed around until some family on welfare would benefit from our departure. I pictured Mama walking through the house claiming my things and storing them up for my return.

In the truck to Beau's house, the new perfume Poppy bought for Nana competed with the smell of sweet potato pie. Pulling up to the house, Poppy was still talking about how happy he was that Mama Rose would be spending Christmas day with her other son. "Even if she is Johnny's mama, the poor old thing runs her mouth too much."

I fought to lock hold of the happiness I had felt whenever I saw the sparkling clean bike. But try as I might, the thought of my own mama stayed near. Walking inside the door draped in gold tinsel, I decided that if Johnny could put up with his mama not being with him for Christmas, I could too.

Looking at the colored bowls covering Bonita's kitchen table, Nana served my plate. "You want some ham?" she asked, and then without waiting for an answer she moved to the platter of turkey. "Oh, yeah, you don't like it when it's cold."

I wondered if my mama knew that. Would she be eating ham with her new rich boyfriend in a fancy restaurant? Or maybe she was too busy driving around town in the new car he had given her. One with a convertible top so that she would have to wear a scarf on her head like a movie star.

"Now I know you want some of this corn," Nana said. She never looked at me as she dipped the spoon into the bowl.

Johnny's hand was heavy on my head. "This is good eating. You better try it all." He moved around to the end of the table and motioned for Beau to try a piece of sausage.

Watching the Rileys pass bowls of food like they'd known us their whole entire lives, I wished that my mama would stumble on people like Johnny and Bonita. During the blessing, I silently added a request that a similar woman with a matching beauty mark like Bonita Riley's would walk into her new beauty shop.

The day after Christmas, Beau, Josh, and me had covered downtown and the side of the river twice. Nana had warned me not to ride my bike on the highway, but I did it anyway. Besides, it was the only way to reach Mama Rose's stand. She had promised Josh that she would give him a bike flag for Christmas. Beau and me would get one too if we promised to help her move boxes down from the attic.

Mama Rose used a small key to unlock the door that led up to her attic. "You never know what kinda valuable treasures you might have sitting around in a bunch of dust."

By the looks of it Mama Rose could've opened up a whole new chain. Every square inch of the floor was covered with boxes that looked liked they had been painted with dust. One tiny window let us know that it was still daylight outside. Specks of dust that hadn't yet decided where to settle danced in a ray of sun. The stale smell of unwanted gifts passed along one too many times filled our lungs.

"Now while I'm setting up the twenty-percent-off table, you boys go ahead and straighten up. Then I want you to bring these boxes down to the counter." Mama Rose pointed to a stack of boxes with dried-up electrical tape dangling from the sides.

While she watched, we began dragging the boxes to the edge of the stairs. The thick air made our breathing sound like that of the girl at school who missed PE on account of her asthma. I dared not speak until I had heard Mama Rose's footsteps and the closing door down below. "She sure does have a lot of junk."

"Maybe junk to you, but it'll be a treasure to one of them Yankees." Josh repeated the line he had heard Mama Rose say until he had it memorized.

"Nobody's gonna buy any of this junk," Beau said, the front of his hair now darker from sweat.

"They will so." Josh was wearing a gold necklace with an odd-shaped medallion. "Hey, what about this? It's genuine gold."

Beau brushed sweat from his eyes and moved closer. "That ain't gold."

"Is so." Josh pulled away when Beau tried to reach for the necklace.

"What's that thing hanging off the end?" I asked.

A cross like the one Nana wore was in the center. There were four symbols, one in each corner. Small misshapen symbols like I had never seen before.

"Where'd you find this thing?" Beau asked.

Josh pointed to the box with its side caving in. "Personal" was written across the top in uneven letters.

"Dog," Beau said. He pulled a thin white dress from the box. The sleeves were wide and an image of the medallion was stitched right over the heart.

Snatching it away, Beau flung the material in the air as if setting up a tent. "Must be some big fat woman's dress."

Looking inside the box, I saw the edges of crumbled, yellow certificates. The kind like I had gotten when I had graduated from kindergarten.

Beau brushed against my shoulder and dug his hand deep inside. "There's more stuff down here," Beau said.

The white hat was folded in half. Beau pulled the top, and it stuck up like a dunce cap. A long flap fell forward. Two circles were cut out for eyes, like a homemade mask someone might wear for Halloween.

"This thing's creepy," Josh said.

Beau cast his eyes towards me. A half smile formed across his lips. He held the hat by its pointy tip. "I heard about this. It's one of them ghost hats. Mama Rose probably bought it from some dead man's family. Some dead man kept it stuffed in his closet and wore it to spook people. But then Mama Rose showed up and bought all the man's clothes. This probably got picked up in the deal."

When Beau cast his eyes towards me again, I picked up my cue. "Yeah. Some man who got his head cut off."

Wide-eyed, Josh turned to look in the direction of the door.

"The man's ghost wore this hat 'cause he didn't have a head. You couldn't pay me to put that hat on. Beau, I don't think I'd even be touching it," I said.

Beau's smile widened, and I could tell he was pleased with my performance. Josh picked at the leg of his pants and shuffled his feet. Just when he turned to walk towards the stairs, Beau threw the hat on the floor. "Ooh, I see blood right there on the side. Hey, look, Brandon. Ain't that blood?"

Using a pool stick with a piece of spider's web hanging off of the end, Beau picked the hat back up. The white hat dangled from the pool cue.

I craned my neck, but kept a distance. "That's blood, all right. Pure blood from a dead man."

Stepping backwards, Josh was pinned in by the boxes. The light from the window made his face look even paler.

Beau stretched the pool stick out towards him. He held the stick like a fishing pole and the bait moved closer to Josh. "I'll give you two dollars if you put that hat on."

The sound of Josh's sneakers brushing up against the box made me flinch and look over my shoulder.

Beau laughed and moved it closer. "Scaredy cat. It ain't gonna bite you. Just a little blood from a dead man is all."

As I watched Josh pinned in against the boxes, part of me wanted to tell Beau to stop, but the part that won out tingled at the idea of the fear Josh was feeling.

Josh's eyes bulged and when the tip of the hat brushed up against his neck, he went into a screaming fit, twitching and breathing harder than ever. His arms swung wildly and boxes began falling to the floor. Before we could grab him, the nose of a stuffed bobcat behind the boxes touched his arm. The high, piercing scream that he let out was sharp enough to crack the tiny attic window.

"We're just kidding. We're just kidding," Beau kept repeating, but Josh was too far gone. All he could do was scream and swing his fists. His right fist landed on Beau's chin and caused him to land against the box marked "Personal." When the box landed on the floor, yellowed stained certificates and old newspaper clippings spilled out.

"I hate your guts," Josh screamed. He picked up the pool stick and lifted it high above his head. The anger in his eyes raged as hot as a grown man's. Before he could swing at Beau, I moved behind him and locked my arms around his elbows. "Let go of me, you ol' orphan!" He twisted and turned, trying to bite me.

"What in sand's hill is going on up here?" Mama Rose stood on the top of the stairs with her mouth hanging open and her wig twisted to the side.

Before Beau could put the scattered contents back into the box, Josh was pointing at the hat. "They was trying to put that dead man's hat on me."

"What?" Mama Rose followed Josh's point to the white hat that had landed on top of the stuffed bobcat.

Red streaks appeared on her neck, and she blinked so fast I thought the heavy false eyelashes would leave bruises. She clutched the hat the way a veteran's wife might clutch the flag that had been draped over her husband's casket. "Beau Riley! You keep away from my things."

"I'm sorry. I'll put it up," he said. "We shouldn't be playing with your stuff. I'm sorry."

But Mama Rose was immune to Beau's wide smile. "Have you no respect for honor, Beau Riley? Oh no, why should I think something as no-count as you would have any sort of respect like decent people." She pulled Josh to her side, but he remained stiff, staring at the white hat that hung over her arm.

Beau and I busied ourselves with picking up the contents. Even with our backs to her, I could feel the stare piercing through my shirt. If she thought Beau, the president of our class, was a no-count, I could only imagine what she thought of me.

"Is that really a ghost hat?" Josh asked.

"No such a thing, precious. You don't pay any mind to these boys. This belonged to my second husband." She picked up the white dress that was crumpled in a pile and straightened it out. "He was a great man. Made it up the ranks all the way to Wizard."

Reaching to pick up the torn certificate, Beau met my eyes. I could tell from the way he twisted his lip that he thought Mama Rose was about to go off in a fit of crazy talk.

"Wizard? Like in King Arthur?"

"No, not that foolishness. I'm talking about the Klan. He was the big wheel. He ran things around this town."

Mama Rose sat on the top of a rusted trunk. "You boys don't know about the Klan?" Her eyes raced back and forth and settled on me. "Of course, you don't. Coming from that Yankee place you're from. Anyway, it's a group of men in the community who keep the peace." She opened a cigar box and began shuffling though a stack of black-and-white photographs.

"Are they like the police?" Josh asked.

"Oh no. They handle things that the police are too timid to take on." She held up a picture of a group of men all dressed in white. The flaps of their hats were up so that you could make out their faces. Round, sunken, or scarred, the faces were the same in their lack of expression. Sitting on the tailgate of a truck were five boys mine and Beau's age.

"There's Canton himself. Boys, he was a real looker." Mama Rose pointed to the man dressed in a shiny robe. Judging by his fat face, I wondered how even someone touched like Mama Rose could find that man handsome.

"What are they doing all dressed alike?" I asked before thinking.

She looked up from the pictures and squinted at me. "Well, can't you see? They were having a meeting. They always dressed for meetings. It was when they planned what needed to be done to make it so that decent people would feel safe to walk down the street."

"What sort of stuff would they do?"

"Beau Riley. You should know such. Johnny ought to be teaching you. But that mama of yours probably has him brainwashed by now." Mama Rose sighed and mumbled something under her breath. "They would straighten out people who got outta line. Like wife beaters and such."

"They kill 'em?" Josh asked.

"Nothing more than a good old-fashioned whipping most times. Now I want you boys to look." Mama Rose pointed to the boy sitting on the end of the tailgate. Even with a crew cut, he looked like Josh.

"Hey, that's Johnny," Beau said.

Mama Rose clutched her blouse like she might cry. "And here's Alvin right next to him. My two angels."

Josh moved closer and grabbed the photo. "Is Daddy still in this thing?"

"It's the Klan. *The Klan.*" Mama Rose shook her head and began folding the white hat with military precision. "And no, he is not. When he married that mama of yours, he dropped out. But now Alvin is still regular, thank the Lord."

Before Mama Rose closed the cigar box, I stared at the photo one last time. Johnny's young eyes looked back at me. They were the type of eyes that looked too soft to be on a man's face. His hand was propped on the side of the truck. Hands that were once pure and free from of scars.

It was always a natural wonder to me how Johnny could come from Mama Rose's belly and not be touched in the head like her. But I soon learned that what Johnny missed his brother Alvin had inherited in full glory.

There was no denying that the man with the orange-colored beard was Mama Rose's son. He lived on the edge of Hagan's Hell, a swamp-infested area outside of town. Other than Alvin, no other human being lived in the area. And he didn't take well to company, human or otherwise. It was a known fact that he would shoot any living thing that laid foot, claw, or belly on his property. That's why I did a double take when Beau suggested we ride our bikes out to see him.

"You scared of Alvin or something?" Beau shielded his eyes from the morning sun.

"Look. He's fixing to pee in his pants, he's so scared," Josh added.

Two seagulls landed on the side of a shrimp boat docked at the marina. Anything to divert their attention would have been welcome at this point.

Josh began to sing and flap his wings like a chicken. "Bran-don's scay-erd. Bran-don's scay-erd."

"Shut up, Josh," I yelled. "I just don't know how far it is out there. It might get dark before we can get back."

"It ain't far," Beau said. "We got all day. Besides, if Josh can make it, I think you can."

Josh grinned and revealed another missing tooth. He jumped on his bike and followed Beau. The red flags on their bikes flapped in the wind and, looking back one last time at the marina, I eventually followed.

By the time we reached the sand driveway marked "Private" by a spray-painted sign, I was hoping Alvin would allow me to have one drink of water before he shot me dead. Our tailbones ached so bad by the time we reached the area covered in cypress tress and shrub brush that we rode into Alvin's place standing up on our bike pedals. All the better, so he might recognize Josh and Beau and not shoot them.

"Alvin. It's just me and Josh," Beau yelled as he rode pass a second sign that said "No Trespassing."

"And what about me?" I added.

"And Brandon too," Josh yelled. His voice made its way through the wetland filled with stumps and hanging moss and bounced back at us.

Every other pine tree was marked with a hubcap. Closer to the house we passed the skin of a rattlesnake nailed to a tree.

His house sat on stilts and looked like the house version of Joseph's coat from the Bible. Part of the house was made of bricks, and other portions were formed by various pieces of colored wood. His door was made from slick cypress wood and looked like it might have belonged to a fancy house in a rich neighborhood. A rack of deer antlers hung above the door.

Alvin stood below sawing a piece of plywood. A small transistor radio with a bent antenna was propped on the sawhorse. He scratched his beard and watched as we rode up in a cloud of white dust.

"Hey, Uncle Alvin," Josh said.

He looked at the red flags and scanned down to our faces. "Your daddy know you boys come all the way out here?"

"We just been riding and decided to come on out and see you since we missed you Christmas," Beau said.

"And Mama Rose said you made us a coon hat. One like Davy Crockett's," Josh said.

Alvin laughed, and with his missing front tooth the resemblance to Josh was stronger than ever. "That boy don't miss a thing. I expect if you come on in the house, you might find a hat or two."

Climbing up the stairs, Beau introduced me. Alvin never looked at me, but pointed at a hole in the wooden step. "Watch that'n or it'll tear your foot off."

Inside the house, framed pictures of Alvin dressed in white robes decorated the walls. One showed him shaking hands with a man dressed in a bright red robe. Red as the devil costume I wanted to buy for Halloween but Nana wouldn't let me. Certificates like the ones kept in Mama Rose's personal box lined one side of the cypress wall.

When Alvin stuck his fingers in the groove where a door handle should have been, the closet door came off of its hinge. The muscles in his forearm flinched when he cussed real loud. A tall wooden cross filled one corner of the closet. Its wood was pristine and smooth enough for any church steeple. A gold medallion was nailed to the center of the cross. Rows of sawed-off shotguns filled the other corner, and the smell of old grease suddenly made me want to throw up.

"Why you got a cross in your closet?" Josh asked.

Alvin snatched two caps from the top shelf and tossed them at Josh and Beau. "You don't belong to snoop."

"I wasn't. The door fell off," Josh said.

Beau used the tail of the raccoon hat to hit Josh on the arm. "Alvin, can we get a drink of water?"

It wasn't until we had started to leave that I began to fill uneasy again. Alvin pointed the saw towards me. "You bring that boy here and I let him in this time. Y'all 're family. But, boy, I'm tellin' you right now, if you flap your tongue about my business, I'll cut it out."

Beau nervously laughed and waved as we left. But Alvin never laughed. He just stared until I looked away towards the swamp that protected him.

Never hearing Beau and Josh ride off, I turned to find myself alone and facing the point of Alvin's saw. I pressed the pedals as hard as I could until my foot slipped. The bike tilted to the side and I struggled not to hit my chin on the handlebars. I pictured myself falling and being nailed to one of the vacant pine trees.

Gaining speed, I turned, hoping my imagination was getting the best of me. Even in the distance he still looked like a giant holding that saw. And no matter how fast I pedaled, I could not outrace the feeling that Alvin was not touched like Mama Rose. He was just hammered with meanness like Mama's old boyfriend Darrell.

That New Year's Eve I didn't think of Mama or Uncle Cecil's family the first time. For me it was not a celebration of what the year had offered, but an assurance that it would come to a close. The realization of what Nana had said finally began to settle around me. Things really would get better.

Nana and Poppy had agreed to stay with Beau and Josh while Bonita and Johnny went out celebrating. It was the first time we were all together under the same roof like a real family.

"Now, Pauline, you make yourself right at home," Bonita said. "Y'all fix some Jiffy Pop and have a big time." Bonita looked like she was ready for a big time herself. She wore a red dress with sparkles all over it. Nana looked at her as if she was a stranger. I don't think it was so much the flashy dress as it was the specks of gold glitter in Bonita's hair.

Even Johnny was dressed up, with his hair slicked down like a kid waiting for a formal portrait. Bonita even insisted that we all take pictures.

"All right, y'all bunch together," Poppy said.

"Now wait a minute. Pauline and Brandon need to get in the picture too," Bonita said.

"Gracious, no. Me dressed like this? No, y'all take one of just your family," Nana said.

Bonita turned her head in such a way that caused the glitter in her hair to turn into a mini fireworks display. "Crazy, you are family."

"Get on over here," Johnny added.

As I stood in front of Johnny, he put his hand on my shoulder, and Poppy counted to three. It felt good being all squeezed together, feeling the air that Johnny exhaled on my neck and smelling the sweetness of Bonita's perfume. As the flash went off, I hoped that Nana would add the picture to the cluster of photos on the small nightstand in the camper. Right next to the picture of Uncle Cecil's family.

After they had left, Nana made pallets out of blankets for us. We stretched out close to the TV, and I waited for Poppy to warn us about the dangers of going blind from such reckless behavior.

Josh was the first out. His arm dangled as Poppy carried him into the bedroom. Fighting the heaviness of sleep, I was determined to win the bet I had made with Beau. The first one to give in to sleep had to buy the other the item of his choice from Mama Rose's next shipment. But after the evening news my head slipped out of my propped-up hand, and Nana declared the battle over.

"You two keep this up and we'll be up to sunrise. You'll end up getting sick from lack of rest." She shepherded us into Beau's room, where I fell asleep before he could finish telling another one of his ghost stories.

A blue light cut through the thin curtain and hit the side of Beau's bedroom wall. I jumped up and stared at Beau, still sleeping with his mouth open. Fear gripped my ribs until air itself became thick and heavy. It wasn't supposed to happen this way. We were starting the year out fresh. A new life in a new town. The image of Nana and Poppy handcuffed and sitting in the backseat of a patrol car made me run.

The front door was wide open. Crackle from the patrol-car radio rolled into the house. The blue light swirled around the room until the safe haven began to look like the haunted house at a carnival. Nana and Poppy stood at the door. Dressed in a robe, Nana shook her head while Poppy massaged his chin. The officer frowned and flipped through a small notepad. If he was going to take them, he would have to take me too. The popping sound from the radio was louder this time, and the woman's voice on the other end was shrill and rattled off some type of foreign language. "Signal four down at Dead Man's Curve. Signal seven being transported by Morley's Funeral Home."

Poppy turned and saw me running towards them. "Get on back to bed," he said.

The officer never looked up from his pad. "They're taking her on to Tallahassee Memorial."

"What happened?" I asked

"Are you next of kin?" the officer asked.

"No, just good friends." The blue light continued to slap Poppy's face as he stared at Johnny's boat in the corner of the yard.

The officer took a pen from his shirt pocket. "Who's the closest kin?"

"His mama lives just past the curve," Nana whispered. "Runs that junk stand."

I tapped Nana on the arm, but she just watched as the officer wrote down the information.

"What's the matter?" The cool night air was brisk, and dew began to tickle the inside of my toes. I looked down and realized I only had on my underwear.

"Well in that case, maybe y'all should be the ones to tell the boys." The officer looked down at me in that same pitiful way that the guidance counselor used to.

Running from the news that would doom the house with gold tinsel taped around the windows, I saw Beau standing there with his arms spread across the doorway. The brown eyes that once danced to please were now as hollow as two broken pecan shells. The blue light hit him over and over until it covered him thicker than the early morning dew.

Nine

T hat first day of 1973, Beau convinced Nana that a bike ride
would clear his mind. We hadn't slept at all the night before, and even though I kept waiting for him to break down
like Josh had, he remained empty of emotion. His nervous eyes cast
around the house, never landing on one place for very long.

"Are you really sure you want to go out there?" I yelled from my
bike. We were at the pharmacy about to turn on the side street that
would make the events from the night before cement in our minds.

Beau never looked back as he pedaled faster. As the bicycle flag
flapped in the breeze, the sound of vinyl cutting into the wind echoed
from a corner building.

Thick silver locks secured the garage doors at Rayford's Body
Shop. A closed sign with faded black letters hung from the office window on string that looked like knotted shoelaces. Two pit bulls with
studded collars started barking before we put our kickstands down. A
chain-link fence was all that separated us from their long teeth and the
stacks of automobiles they protected.

The crumpled silver car that Johnny had waxed every Saturday
was balled up next to the gate, waiting to join the torn vehicles on the
other side of the fence. Beau walked over to the part that used to be
the driver's side. The steering wheel was dented inward like a melted

penny. The driver's door was missing, and in its place jagged pieces of metal pointed outward.

Beau's steps were slow as he circled the front of the bashed-in hood. The engine stuck out and curled like a crooked tooth. A circle of cracked glass spread out across the windshield. My stomach tightened, and I tried to fight the image of Bonita's head slamming into it.

Beau moved pass the passenger door that had been sawed in half, pass the missing tire, and ended up at the back bumper. The part that still looked like the same old car that his mama had driven all those times before. He stood at the trunk and rubbed his hand along the surface. Stood there like it was any other day. Like they might have been at the store and he was ready to put a bag of groceries inside the trunk.

The dogs snarled and barked louder when I turned towards them. Foam from their anger clung to the chain-link fence. And no matter how mad my stare made them, their barks never did drown out Beau's crying.

Hidden behind the broken car that had taken the life of the only father he had known, Beau cried and yelled until I heard him struggle to breath. The sound of torment caused me to tuck my head in sympathy. Embarrassment made me move farther away. But before I got pass the chain-link fence, it stopped. As if nothing had happened, Beau got on his bike, brushed his nose with his forearm, and rode away. It was the last time I ever saw him cry.

Any crying that Beau lacked Mama Rose made up for. She walked into the funeral home leaning on Alvin's arm and dressed in a black trenchcoat. A long black wig made her look more like a witch than a grieving mother. Mama Rose howled when they approached the pink-colored light that shone down upon Johnny's coffin. I couldn't fault her for carrying on so. Tucked inside the fancy lining, Johnny resembled the store mannequin that Mama Rose used to advertise the "I Love Florida" T-shirts. His hair was so perfect from all the hair spray that it looked like a wig from Mama Rose's personal collection.

The veil that hung down over the coffin tried to convince us that he was the same old Johnny who just got in from fishing. Poppy patted Alvin on the back. "Don't he look good? I mean to tell you, I hope they make me look that good when it comes my time." But when Mama Rose lifted the edge of the coffin veil and saw Johnny's sunken forehead, Poppy's words were nothing more than wasted air. She threw her head back until the top of the wig revealed natural gray and hollered louder.

Bonita sat on a folding chair draped in black velvet. Nana stood guard behind her holding a cup of water and a cardboard fan with a print of a sun-tanned Jesus on one side and an advertisement for First Citizens Bank on the other. Josh and Beau stared at the gray carpet as people passed by and patted their heads.

Harvey, the cook from Nap's Corner, grasped the tip of Bonita's fingers in his wide black hands. Bonita still had a cast on her arm and a patch to cover the damaged eye. The good eye was covered red from crying. As Harvey whispered into her ear, Bonita nodded and bit her lip. The woman who was introduced as Harvey's wife was much louder. When she leaned down, her wide black hat touched the edge of Bonita's hair.

"Baby doll, you remember me? Sister Delores. I came in last week to pick up that smoked turkey. Well now, if you need us, you call. You hear what I'm saying? Me and Harvey will come sit with you, we'll pray with you, we'll even cry with you if need be."

Bonita used her good hand to unfurl a tissue and dabbed the exposed eye. If Bonita was touched by the appearance of the black couple, Alvin sure wasn't. He squinted at Harvey and Sister Delores the whole time they were in the room. A scowl that seemed more eerie than the makeup that covered Johnny.

After the funeral I told Nana what had happened at the junkyard and how Beau carried on. "Well, you just let him be. If he wants to talk about it, he will. Otherwise just keep quiet about Johnny. People handle grief in all sorts of different ways," she said.

Back at school, Beau ignored all the stares and dodged any questions about Christmas break. In class he even asked a couple of questions about the lesson on Seminole Indians.

After class, I was stuffing my book bag when I saw Miss Travick lean down and wrap her arm around Beau. "Are you feeling better? You know I'm here if you ever want to talk." Ivory beads from her long necklace swirled within inches of Beau's neck. He nodded and smiled wider than ever.

"Come on, slow poke," he called out to me.

While we walked down the sidewalk, Miss Travick stood at the door watching us. I considered turning around and telling her about my mama's made-up death. She would wrap her arms around me, and the necklace would tickle my skin. Her butterscotch scent would rub off on my clothes, and everybody would know that she had hugged me. But fearing that a moment of affection might turn into a full-blown case of pity, I decided to follow Nana's advice and keep my mouth shut about grief.

Nana continued to pick us up from school long after Johnny was buried and the cleaned casserole dishes had been returned. Bonita not only didn't want to talk about Johnny; she didn't want to talk period. She lay in bed most days and kept the bottle of painkillers closer than a baby with a pacifier. While Nana cleaned the house and washed clothes, she always kept Bonita's bedroom door shut. Making up a question to ask Nana, I ran down the hall just before the door closed. Through the crack I saw twisted sheets on the bed and a matted mass of red hair on Bonita's head.

"Harvey made spoon bread today. Said he sure wanted to make sure you boys got some," Nana said as we pulled up to Nap's Corner. Tucked on the edge of a clump of oak trees and a bend in the river, the restaurant lived up to its name. It was a flat-top building with wooden pilings that formed a makeshift boat ramp designed to cater to hungry fishermen. Faded red paint matched the rust that covered the front-door awning. Spanish moss from low-hanging trees fanned across the ventilation pipes. As soon as we got out of the car, the smell of fried fish caused my mouth to convince me the place was a five-star restaurant.

"All right, now," Harvey called out from behind the counter. He was wearing yellow plastic gloves as he shucked oysters.

A woman with frosted hair and pink eye shadow smiled real big. "Hey, girl," she said and flipped the dishrag at Nana. Her voice went down a few levels when she looked at Beau and Josh and asked, "How y'all been getting along?"

"Fine," Beau said and shrugged his shoulders. "I hear y'all got some spoon bread today."

"Harvey made a batch just for you." She turned to look at me. "And honey, I know who you are. You're all this girl talks about."

Nana played with my shirt collar. "Yeah, Brandon, this is Karen."

"I work the lunch shift with your granny," Karen said. "And I tell you what, there haven't been any cuter men that walked through that door today than the three I'm standing here looking at."

"You better watch what you say," the man behind Karen said.

When she turned around, the badge was the first thing I saw. He looked seven feet tall and was holding a felt hat with the words "Florida Highway Patrol" etched on a gold pin. I felt Nana's grip grow tighter on my shoulder. Words from the script circled my mind, and I wondered if Nana would help guide me by the pressure of her fingers. The image of the man from TV flashed through my mind. A ventriloquist Poppy had called him, and the doll that sat on the man's lap and opened and closed his mouth was the dummy.

"Parker Townes, you better stop," Karen said. "Hey, have you met Pauline before?"

"I don't think so," the officer said. His smile revealed long pointy teeth, and the way Nana gripped my shoulder as he approached she must've thought for sure that he would bite.

"How do you do," the man said with a nod.

She cleared her throat. "Hello."

"Pauline works the lunch shift three days a week," Karen said. "This here is her grandson, Brandon."

Parker leaned down and looked right into my eyes. At first my eyes darted away from looking into the blue circles, but fearing that he'd think I had something to hide, I forced myself to stare back. His eyes pierced through me, and I hoped that he could not see all the way inside my heart. The same one that was running wide open.

I only breathed again when he turned to Beau and Josh. As Beau repeated the same old lies that everything was fine at his house and that his mama was doing better, I felt Nana ease her grip.

"Parker, order's up," Harvey called out from the kitchen. Opened oysters and a lemon wedge filled the plastic container on the snack bar.

"That Parker Townes is my weekly eye candy. Too bad you're not working when he comes in," Karen said in a stage whisper.

"Does he live around here?" Nana asked.

"Oh yeah. Just the other side of the post office. You know his wife up and quit him. Couldn't handle little-town life. Don't let the door hit you on the way out, I said. I'm just tickled that he's here, you know to keep crime outta town."

Sweat gathered around the edges of Harvey's gray hair. His skin glistened like well-oiled mahogany. "Here you go, boys," he said. Beau grabbed the bag that had started to stain from the grease inside. Josh had already reached inside and started eating before I could get to it.

Harvey cut his eyes towards Nana. "Me and my wife want to know, how's Bonita really?"

Nana stuck out her lips and shook her head.

"You tell her me and Sister Delores gonna be by real soon."

Before we could get out of the door, the patrolman called out to us. "Oh, and Pauline . . ."

Nana gripped the door handle, and the neon sign that advertised fresh seafood buzzed overhead.

The patrolman smiled and pointed with a tiny fork. "I'm sure we'll be seeing each other again."

Ten

———◆———

It was Beau's idea to make the bag swing for Josh. Filling an empty oyster sack with dirt, I never let on that I used to have a tire swing back in North Carolina and fought the image of Mary Madonna and Mac now swinging on it. Josh's bag swing would be even better. Like that guidance counselor with the pitiful smile had told me, sometimes the past is better left buried.

We heard the music from the red Impala before we saw the car. Holding the edges of the coarse bag, I looked up at the same time Beau did. Organ music and drums mixed with the loud voice of a woman singer. The music made the vehicle seem like a mini version of the juke joint that fed our campground songs late at night.

"Hey, babies," Sister Delores tried to shout. Her words garbled with the singer's moaning. When the car engine was turned off, the music disappeared, but she sat there a moment longer and smiled. "Umm, I'm crazy about that Mahalia Jackson."

Beau lodged the shovel deeper. "Who's she?"

Sister Delores struggled to get out of the car and paused just as her dress rolled up to reveal knee-high stockings. "Who's she? Only the best gospel singer in the entire United States of the whole America. Who's she? Who's she?" By the time she got of the car, she was laughing even harder. Tight black curls bounced around a face the color of peanut butter.

"Hey, I remember you," Beau said. "You're Harvey's wife."

"You mean Harvey's my husband." She handed us grocery bags and talked all at the same time. Talked about the weather, the new workers hired down at the marina, and how lost everybody was at Nap's Corner without Bonita.

Double-armed with groceries, Beau squinted at her. "I hope these ain't for us."

She tilted her head back until a long nose hair was visible. "Then what you want me to do? Leave 'em out here and let the seagulls tear into them?"

"We don't take handouts," Beau said.

"Boy, get yourself into that house before the cream melts and you make me go back to the store." It only took one look at her raised eyebrow before Beau started walking towards the porch. "You tickle me acting all grown like you're a little man or something."

Inside the house Sister Delores took on the actions of an oversized flea. She jumped from the kitchen sink to the mop and then started on the bathroom. Part of me was aggravated at her for driving in with her loud music and trying to take Nana's place as house manager.

When she began running water in the tub, the pipes let out a holler that vibrated the side of the house. Bonita's door creaked open, and she stuck half of her head out. Her eye was padded with puffy skin, but the front of her hair stood at attention. "What's all that racket?"

Beau pointed towards the bathroom. Sister Delores's wide behind stared back at us as she leaned over the tub pouring cleanser and singing "What a Friend We Have in Jesus."

Clutching the top of Johnny's work shirt, which had become her uniform, Bonita eased into the hallway. "Excuse me."

The sound of bristles stripping away grime provided a rhythm for Sister Delores's song. "Excuse me," Bonita said louder.

"Oh, hey baby. I didn't see you standing there. Excuse me for not getting up. This knee is giving me fits. Doctor said I need to loose weight, but when your husband is a cook, there ain't no way to put down that fork. You hear me now?"

Bonita massaged her eyes. "I'm sorry. Who are . . ."

"Baby, you know me. Sister Delores. Harvey's wife. I picked up that smoked turkey down at the restaurant right before Christmas . . . Well, anyway, I been planning to come by for some time, but with this old knee acting up and everything." She turned back to the tub and scrubbed faster. "You just get yourself back in that prison. We're managing just fine."

Bonita sighed in protest, but by then Sister Delores was back singing.

"Mama, you ought to see the kitchen," Beau said. "So clean we could eat supper off the floor if we wanted to."

"She brought groceries too," Josh added.

Bonita's eyes glassed over even more with the details. She took three steps and then rested her head against the wall, tilting a picture of two men standing on a boat. Leaning against the flowered wallpaper, she continued towards the kitchen and rubbed the place on the shirt where Johnny's name was stitched across the pocket. She looked down at the kitchen floor. Black-and-white tile glistened back at her. The gold-colored refrigerator tucked in the corner now seemed as good as new. She reached out like she might touch it, but stopped halfway there. We gathered around like a seawall ready to catch a crashing wave. I held my breath until my ears filled with a ringing noise. But then just as slow as she had walked out, Bonita turned and drifted back behind the bedroom door.

"Yes," Beau said, with his fist clinched in victory. "In the kitchen today. Out in the living room tomorrow."

Outside, we had finished filling the bag of sand by the time Sister Delores was leaving. She clutched a shiny black purse and watched as we struggled to lift the bag up to the rope that dangled from the tree.

"You boys stop that before you tear up your insides." She reached down and ran her stumpy fingers across the sack. "So you're fixing a bag swing, huh? I remember when my daddy fixed me a bag swing for my birthday one year. All us kids had the best time on that thing. My brother had a pit bull and that dog would clamp her teeth a hold of that swing and wouldn't let go for nothing. Yes sir, we had fun on that swing." She got into the car and leaned out the opened window. "Harvey and a man from my church will be out tomorrow to fix that swing for y'all. I'll see to it. A boy just needs to be a boy."

"What kinda church you go to?" Beau asked.

"God's Hospital. Right over yonder on Magnolia Street. And little man, I don't go to it. I'm the pastor."

"Pastor? You're a woman."

Sister Delores coiled back and opened her mouth. "And I didn't hear God checking in with you, little man, before he called me to preach. I sure did not. If I ain't the pastor, then why am I called Sister Delores?"

Fearing that she might really be mad, I searched my mind for a different topic. "What about that dog? The one that swung on the bag with its teeth?"

Cranking the car, Sister Delores looked straight ahead at the windshield dusted in sea salt. Organ music swelled while the singer's voice moaned in a way that dug up feelings in a hollowed-out place inside of me.

"Oh, her. Some man shot her one day. Shot her swinging right on that bag."

"Why'd he do that for?" Josh asked.

"Don't you never mind about why. Y'all don't be studying about that old dog. You hear me? Harvey's gonna fix that swing for you. Y'all just laugh and cut up and be sweet boys. That goes for you too, little man." With a point at Beau she drove away, leaving exhaust smoke and a distant crackle of music that stayed in my ears long after the car had disappeared.

Poppy worked longer and longer hours until it got to where the crickets had already started chirping by the time he opened the door. His shoulders would hunch over, and he'd remove the cap with the marina logo to reveal matted hair. Whenever Nana would complain about him overdoing it, he'd say "Time and a half beats tired bones any day." A restaurant-sized pickle jar served as their official bank. Locking the door, Nana would count the money every Friday right before we called Uncle Cecil.

One day while Poppy was working overtime, Nana and me called Uncle Cecil on our own. It was the first time I got to speak to him.

The February wind was brisk, and the man who owned the station stayed inside most of the time. The burnt orange sign that advertised an oil change swung back and forth to the beat of the wind.

"Hey, boy," Uncle Cecil said.

I gripped the phone receiver tighter against my ear. The whining sound of trapped wind from the nearby bathroom tried to distract me. Words to all the questions I had planned to ask stayed locked in my throat. My mind would not let me speak anything other than small chatter saved for bored old ladies. "No, sir, it's not real sunny today. The wind is all over the place."

Questions about my mama edged closer to my lips. I wanted to blurt it all out. Did you let her eat Christmas dinner with you? Was she still in town? But I just stood there with one hand buried in my pants pocket and the other growing numb holding a line to the past.

While Nana talked about the amount of money she was going to send him for the mortgage payment, I slid farther away towards the gas station door. Inside, the old man leaned against the counter and acknowledged me with a motion of his chin. Pressed against the concrete wall, I was free from the cutting wind but felt the burn of being Sophie Willard's son all over again. The ghost of yesterday slapped me around harder than the wind flapped the metal sign by the pumps.

The clanging sound of a cowbell tied to the gas-station door made me flinch. "Lord have mercy, it's cold out here," Harvey said as he zipped the jacket higher towards his chin. A black poncho draped Sister Delores, and a zebra-print hat was pulled down low over her ears. "Don't be crying to me. I tol' you to wear a heavy coat. Your blood pressure liable to fall slap out from this cold, and you without a decent coat."

I eased by the trash can and watched as Harvey raced to his truck. Sister Delores moved slower and kept flailing her arms under the black material. When her pocketbook dropped to the ground, she leaned down and saw me. "Hey, here. What you doing hanging out with trash?" She pointed to the orange trash barrel and laughed.

Her hand was light when she touched the top of my head. The musty smell of cornmeal clung to the poncho. "What you doing out here freezing?"

I pointed to the corner of the building. "Nana's talking to Uncle Cecil. He's all the way up in North Carolina." By the way the wrinkle above her nose deepened, I was afraid I'd said too much.

"North Carolina? Oh no, so far from home. I hope he can get down here close to family. A man needs his people."

I smiled and got onto myself for saying too much.

She pulled the hat down farther. "Listen, baby. Your friend's been coming to my church. Did he tell you?"

"You mean Beau?"

"That's the one. But I call him little man on account of how he tries to act so grown. Anyway, I was just standing here wondering if you'd like to come. We're having homecoming this Sunday, and I promise you you'll go home fed."

"Uhh . . . well, I need to ask Nana." The vision of Nana walking down the beach by herself every Sunday morning came to mind. The part of her that still hadn't found its way down to Florida.

"Where she at, round here on this side?" Sister Delores pointed towards the bathrooms.

Sliding along the cold block wall, I eased my head around the corner. The wind whipped until my eyes watered, but I still made out the shock on Nana's face.

"Hey, here. Sister Delores. Harvey's my husband. You remember me. Anyway, I just seen your grandson and he wants to come go to church with me. God's Hospital right down there off Magnolia. We got a carpool and everything. You won't have to fool with carrying him. I been picking up some of his friends, and I said to myself that boy of yours need to be in there with them. They fill up my whole car. One more sure won't matter."

"And uh . . . and uh . . ." Nana kept repeating into the phone. She nodded her head faster and faster until Sister Delores drifted with the wind back to Harvey's truck.

Poppy stared at me when I walked out with my hair all combed down. Our show *Navigating the Nation* was just coming on. While the host, Hoyt Franklin, talked about a house built like the U.S. Capitol, I sat down on the camper sofa.

"It's Sunday. Why you wearing your school clothes?"

"I'm going to church with Beau and Josh." Looking at the man on TV who claimed to be the richest man in Texas, I could feel the glare of Poppy's eyes.

"What's the name of this church?"

"God's Hospital."

"God's what? What kinda name for a church is that?"

Nana shook the plastic head bonnet out and tied it around her head. "It's that church that Harvey and his wife run. Over on Magnolia Street."

"That's the colored church."

"There's a few whites that go there too," Nana said and zipped on her jacket.

"Well I'd like to know what class of whites go there. How come you didn't say nothing about all this before now?"

"I did. Nana knew about it."

Nana paused at the front door. Her sigh could be heard over the TV. "Harvey's wife caught me talking on the phone to Cecil. She was talking so fast I hardly had time to make out a word she was saying."

Poppy rubbed his chin. "I don't like the sounds of this one bit."

Crisp air drifted inside when Nana opened the door. "Oh hush, A.B. They're good people. He'll go this one time and probably won't fool with it anymore. Besides, you think the Lord keeps it all separated up in heaven?"

After Nana left for her Sunday morning walk down the beach, we sat there letting Hoyt Franklin do the talking for us. The car horn was honking before Sister Delores made it to our camper. Poppy stood at the door behind me. Rows of children younger than me lined the front seat. A pink crocheted cross swung from the rearview mirror and, with each dip in the driveway, the black and white heads bobbed up and down. "I don't like this a'tall," Poppy whispered.

"Hey, baby," Sister Delores said with one foot out of the car and the other inside. "We're running late. I still gotta go by the McFarland place. Hey, sir. How you?"

Poppy halfway waved and closed the door. I found Beau and Josh sitting in the backseat. The same music that had greeted us in the front yard of their home was now blasting louder from the car speaker behind my ear.

"Y'all feel like singing back there?" Sister Delores cranked up the volume and started singing until Beau laughed out loud. "Ain't nothing funny about singing to the Lord, little man."

Biting my tongue, I sunk down in the seat and tried to hold it back. Just when I thought I might bust wide open, I looked out the window and saw the plastic rain bonnet. Nana was walking down the beach with her arms folded, never looking up from the sand that guided her. Two pelicans flew overhead while the choppy water seemed to be mad at the world. With Beau nudging me, tempting me to laugh, I kept watch and prayed with my eyes wide open.

Even more shocking than seeing blacks and whites in the same church was the smell of the building and how easy people laughed out loud. The white building with a gold cross painted on the wall over the doors was at one time a crab plant that Harvey and Sister Delores bought when the owners went broke. She told us all the details and praised the Lord from a pulpit covered in green indoor-outdoor carpeting. Marking the church's fifth birthday, she cried a little bit and laughed a whole lot more. I couldn't picture Brother Bailey showing out like that. Especially at one point when the whole entire church started laughing about how her stuck-up teacher told her she would never amount to anything. Maybe that's what I should have done whenever Mama's boyfriends told me the same thing. Just laugh right in their ugly old faces.

After the service we ended up outside underneath the magnolia trees. Sawhorses and plywood boards were transformed into a full-fledged buffet. While the paper tablecloth fluttered with the wind, we served our plates and ran back inside for warmer climate. A band with an electric guitar and drums was just getting started. The men all were dressed in green jackets and wore string ties. They were the first black cowboys I had ever seen.

When the lead singer pressed his lips on the mike like he might make it his lunch, Beau leaned over and poked me. "You know I'm just coming here so that she'll keep coming by to help my mama." His brown eyes were wide, and a piece of chicken clung to the side of his lip.

Shrugging, I turned back to face the music.

"'Cause I don't want nobody at school to think that I need this or nothing. You know with them being colored and everything. Some people might get the wrong idea."

After Mama Rose found out that Beau and Josh had been going to God's Hospital, I understood why Beau worried about people knowing that he shared a church pew with a black family. Mama Rose called two weeks later after the cold snap had moved through. The warmer weather was a signal for a markdown on the leftover goods from the fall line. This time she agreed to pay us a dollar each to help move merchandise.

A wig the color of strawberries draped down her neck. "I want all the shell lamps on that table right there marked forty percent off. Josh, precious, you take the orange-shaped pencil sharpeners and put them out on that full-price table. The one right over next to the T-shirt display. They'll go plumb nuts over the pencil sharpeners."

Moss hung from the oaks like chandeliers in the finest New York City store. An American flag discovered at a VFW was the latest find. It flapped in the soft breeze next to the pole that Alvin had set up. "I'm just so proud to live in the U. S. of A.," Mama Rose said each time the sound of flapping nylon caught her attention.

I ran my finger down the plastic girl dressed in a bikini. Her blonde hair and long eyelashes reminded me of Miss Travick. And as much as I didn't want it to be so, her wide smile was too much like Mama's. Beau pinched the pointy breasts and laughed until Mama Rose stopped staring at the flag. "Quit fornicating over that doll. Hand me that thing," she said. "I swear, Beau Riley. You come by it natural, don't you. Sorry as that mama of yours just as sure as the day is long."

Beau twisted his mouth until his chest bowed out. His soiled nails dug into the red construction paper that covered the display tables. He was still staring at the paper when the music caused us to look up. The Impala drove pass and then stopped at the next street and turned around. Sensing trouble had become second nature to me. "Mama Rose, you might need to check on Josh," I said. "He was looking inside some of those boxes you said for us not to get into it."

She continued wiping off the Florida-shaped key chains and never looked up. "Nobody likes a tattletale. You just finish unpacking that box."

The steady beat of the drums made Mama Rose look up before Sister Delores had parked the car. "What in tarnation?"

"Hey, babies," Sister Delores said as she struggled to walk up the hill towards the display tables. Beau looked at me, and the fear in his eyes matched the way I felt.

"Uh . . . hey," Beau said. "Mama Rose, I think the phone's ringing inside."

"I don't see how you can hear anything over that hoochie-koochie music roaring."

Sister Delores tilted her head and smiled. "How you doing? We met when your son passed. I'm Sister Delores. Harvey, down at Nap's Corner, is my husband."

Mama Rose squinted her eyes until specks of powdered makeup crumbled. "Yeah, well if you see anything you like, I don't give credit. Cash and cash only."

Sister Delores laughed. "Oh, baby, I just stopped by to speak is all. You know if you don't have plans this Sunday we're having . . ."

"Here," Beau said. He grabbed the doll by her breasts and lifted it towards Sister Delores. "You might want to buy a surprise for Harvey."

Rolling her eyes at Beau, Sister Delores laughed even louder. "Little man, you know I got no use for a baby doll. I just stopped by to tend to my flock. See if there was anything y'all needed or something."

"Tend your flock?" Mama Rose had her hands planted firmly on the sides of her bony hips.

"Sister Delores," Josh yelled. He came running out of the house with a red, white, and blue streamer flowing in the breeze.

"Hey, baby. How you doing?"

"You know her?" Mama Rose pointed at Sister Delores.

"She's our preacher."

Mama Rose bugged her eyes like she might curse for everything she was worth and then fell straight backwards. Orange-shaped pencil sharpeners and key chains the shape of Florida were scattered on top of her.

We stood frozen while Sister Delores ran around the other side of the table, the part Mama Rose said was off limits to customers.

"Y'all help me get her up to the house," Sister Delores said. When she leaned down to lift, I tried not to look at Sister Delores's ivory-colored bra.

Beau fanned Mama Rose with the fifty-percent-off sign. "No, Sister Delores, I don't think you ought to."

"Little man, you best start lifting. As big as you might want to be, you can't lift this woman all by yourself."

Josh ran ahead to open the door. Mama Rose sank down as we lifted. The thick material of her jacket could no longer hide the bony arms. Halfway there, the wig fell to the ground and rows of bobby pins shined all through the gray hair.

Inside, Mama Rose moaned when we plopped her on the sofa. Sister Delores rushed into the kitchen and came back with a wet dish towel. She pressed her finger against Mama Rose's throat and nodded. "Heartbeat is strong. Keep on fanning, little man."

"Sister Delores, we got it. Really we do. I'll call Uncle Alvin. He'll get her to the doctor. You go on now. Really."

The way that Beau said the word *really* made Sister Delores wrinkle her brow. "Well I just hate to leave you boys with this." She looked around the house and took a step backwards when she saw Mama Rose's cluttered desk. A Confederate flag and a cross with the gold medallion hung like diplomas overhead.

Mama Rose moaned and licked her lips, struggling to get up. When one eye landed on Sister Delores, she slid back down on the sofa. The crazed scream made us all jump. "Get that high-yella nigger outta my house!"

Sister Delores held up her hand and nodded. "Don't get yourself excited now."

"Out!"

Sister Delores never looked at us as she turned to leave. Even if she didn't want us to see her face, there was a slouch in her walk that couldn't be hidden. Standing at the door watching the Impala drive away, I pictured her in the car with the music cranked wide open. Music to wash away the pain of yesterday and to shine on the promise of brighter tomorrows.

By the time the dogwoods started blooming and the wild lilies appeared in the ditches, a renewal swept into Abbeville right along with the warmer Gulf breezes. Miss Travick certainly caught the fever. When we started studying about Florida wildlife, she talked the principal into letting us take a field trip all the way over to Wakulla Springs. She told us seeing a real-life alligator would make the pages of our books come to life.

Miss Travick must have thought it would help Bonita come back to life too. Beau came to school one morning reporting that Miss Travick herself had called to invite Bonita to come along. "Between her and Sister Delores, Mama is getting her head back on straight," he said.

The janitor hadn't yet raised the flag before we started boarding the bus. Miss Travick wore blue jeans and a T-shirt with a globe of the earth painted on it. Her thick yellow hair draped down over her shoulders, and blood rushed my face when I tried to imagine what it would feel like to touch it. I tried not to stare as she greeted us at the bus door.

"Mrs. Riley. I'm so happy that it worked out for you to come."

My face wasn't any redder than Bonita's. "Yeah, well, me too," she mumbled.

As the bus jerked to gain speed, Miss Travick yelled over the steady roar of the engine. "Wakulla Springs is a natural habitat for all kinds of animals. Some found only in Florida. We'll see fish and turtles and hopefully a gator or two. So listen up when we get there, because driving back I might ask some questions."

Beau nudged me with his elbow. "You ever seen a gator?"

"Not a real one. But back at my old school we went to the Capitol one time." Beau seemed unimpressed and turned to talk to the girl across the aisle. I wanted to knock his leg with my knee and tell him how I had stood on the floor of the Senate and got to sit face-to-face with the lady senator back in North Carolina. But the new script didn't have any scenes for Senator Strickland.

A fancy hotel the color of beach sand stood guard over the spring. As the bus circled to find a place to park, the rows of oak trees and grass the color of new money seemed just like a place Hoyt Franklin might show up at in his motor home. That's why I didn't ooh and aah like everybody else when Charlie the tour guide told us that movie stars had been to Wakulla Springs. Even Tarzan.

"Did you hear that?" Beau said and slurped back the spat of his excitement.

We stood on the dock and waited to board the glass-bottomed boat. Dense forest with cypress trees draped in moss greeted us on the other side of the water.

"Now everybody with Miss Travick's group, step to the side and let the other folks get in first," Charlie said.

While men and women Poppy and Nana's age filed pass, Miss Travick and Bonita shepherded us to the side of the boardwalk. Just when I turned to see how many people were in line behind us, I saw her.

She was standing with her head turned talking to an older man with a white captain's hat on. The teased black hair looked as fresh and kept as it had during the first reunion at Dairy Queen. Watching as she waved her hand in the air like she didn't have a care in the world, I felt my knees lock, and I grabbed a hold of the rope that separated me from the water.

From the side, the white sunglasses put the official stamp on my fear. I looked around to see if I could slip away and hide back in the hotel reserved only for movie stars. Legs lined with varicose veins barricaded a quick escape. Hearing a woman squeal, I turned my head only slightly and tried to brace myself for a headlock, slurpy kisses, and the familiar smell of whiskey and mouthwash. I pictured myself being drug away from Bonita and Beau and driven away in the fancy Cadillac that the rich boyfriend would have waiting for us in the parking lot. The braided rope vibrated against my hand as sweat trickled down my forehead.

The man with the captain's hat rubbed the small of her back and then looked right at me. Spinning around, I ran right into Miss Travick. The clear water below sloshed against the boat as the tour guide helped passengers board.

"Brandon," Miss Travick said.

"I might need to go sit down up at the motel."

Her hand was cool against the damp part of my neck. "You're pale as a sheet. Here, let's find you something to drink."

"Hey, where you going?" I heard Beau but never looked back as Miss Travick guided me directly into danger. I tried to bow my head until a ring of skin rolled up to my chin. Maybe they would think I was fat and let me slip away. But just when we walked by the man, he reached out and touched Miss Travick's arm.

"Miss, I couldn't help but notice. Is everything okay here?"

Blood drained to my feet, and I almost reached up to grab a hold of Miss Travick's hair for balance. Out of the corner of my eye, I could see her again. This time she was turning to face us. Turning to find her son who had run off after that judge ordered him to stay put and live with her.

Miss Travick's words sounded slow, like the movies at school that get tangled in a jammed projector. "I think he might have gotten a little seasick. You know, with the dock rocking and all."

I pulled away trying to run ahead, but her grasp was stronger than my determination.

"See to it that he sips a soda to help the nausea. The snack bar should have saltine crackers. That'll help."

When the woman looked down and pulled up the white sunglasses, I knew it was over. But the eyes. They were green, the color of the spring water below. "Poor thing. Getting sick and missing the boat ride. What a shame." The voice was light and polished. No matter how much grooming, my mama could've never talked so sweet. Fear let go of me, floated across the water, and got tangled in the Spanish moss of Tarzan's jungle.

We sat high above the boat dock under an umbrella of live oaks. I sipped a Seven-Up, ate crackers, and tried to ignore Beau's wave from the boat's stern. I slid along the wooden bench until my shoulder rubbed against the faded bumper sticker that read "Love, Not War." Watching the woman who had tricked me into panic move closer towards the boat, I tried to convince Miss Travick that all was better.

She reached over and stroked the back of my hair. "But I can't risk having you out on the boat. What if you get sick again?"

The woman's laugh rolled up to the hill where we sat. She clutched the tip of the tour guide's fingers. Then her black hair and white sunglasses were lifted onto the boat. Not even the cool touch of Miss Travick's hand could put out the anger that flamed under my skin.

We spent the week of spring break in the inlet obeying Sister Delores's command to "just cut up and be boys." Ignoring Beau whenever he told me about the boat ride that I had missed, I kept my eyes on the murky water at my feet and my net on guard to latch a hold of the granddaddy of all blue crabs. But no matter how disciplined I was, whenever the cold water slapped against my jeans, I couldn't help but wonder if that was how the light green water at Wakulla Springs would have felt. "This is cold now. You reckon God put a bunch of ice cubes in here last night?"

Beau slapped across the water and pulled his arms to help break free from the marshy mud. "Quit your whining. That's how come we left Josh back at the house. I don't need another baby."

With the cuffs of our jeans flapping against the air, we rode our bikes back down the bridge and towards the marina. From the highest point, the marina's white awning and blue sides reminded me of a birthday cake.

Arriving in the parking lot, I could see blue and yellow sparks flying off of a boat engine as the welder held the torch down below.

Poppy was standing by the Coke machine when we rode up. His gray overalls were patterned with engine grease. At the gate men with matching blue caps stuck cards into a time clock.

"How come all those men get to go home and you're still working?"

Poppy brushed the sweat from the bottle and never looked up. "They got no choice. We lost a contract today. They're laid off."

Waiting in line, the faces never raised to show any eyes. White and black, there were only eyelids that drifted pass the green box as the men fed time cards into the machine.

At Nap's Corner I felt almost ashamed to take Harvey's money for the five crabs that scaled the walls in our bucket. The empty faces of the men at the marina seemed suspended in my mind. Beau stuck out his hand while Harvey dropped a stream of fifty-cent pieces. A fiddle's whine from the jukebox and the rotating fan that hung from a corner beam struggled to be heard over the noontime chatter.

"Lord, I hope L.C. didn't lose his job," Karen said. She wiped her hands on the apron. "Did you see L.C. standing down there?"

Beau wrapped the money in a paper napkin. "I didn't see nobody. Except Mr. Hewitt. Now I did see him."

Karen reached over and grabbed Bonita's arm just as she was walking by with a tray of fried mullet platters. "Lord. Nate Hewitt got laid off. His wife's got lung cancer on top of all this."

Nana moved pass the jukebox with its neon lights pulsating to the beat of the music. "You girls stop worrying now. We got jobs and just need to keep our minds set on keeping them." Before Karen could open her mouth, Nana had given her three menus and was greeting tourists at the door.

When Sister Delores found out about the layoff, she never worried either. She just got to work assembling a small army to help take action. The following Saturday morning we lined up inside Nap's Corner and waited for our drill sergeant. Sister Delores kept a whittled-down pencil tucked in a curl on the side of her head. The paper listing laid-off families popped to attention when she snapped it open.

"Baby, you cover the Larson place out on 98, but be sure to stay close to the car. They got a dog that's bad to bite."

Bonita grabbed a grocery bag full of canned goods from the jukebox. Nana and Harvey stayed busy in the kitchen wrapping up fillets of mullet in yesterday's newspaper.

The smell of fish guts spread out into the dining room, and the stench caused me to think about all the morning cartoons I was missing because of Sister Delores's call for help.

Nana used the yellow rubber gloves to wipe away sweat while at the same time ensuring that the bloody fingertips didn't touch her hair. She placed the folded comics into a Styrofoam cooler and patted the side of the box. "And this one is ready to go."

"Look out, now," Sister Delores said. "I never thought I'd meet another woman who could outwork me."

Part of my job was arranging the Piggly Wiggly bags in the seats of Sister Delores's Impala. Tall bags took the place of the typical Sunday morning passengers. I helped mark off the list of deliveries and stapled cards to the bags. The plain white cards were all written in her third-grader block writing: "If you don't have a friend in the world you have one here: God's Hospital."

"Now you go on and run this up to the doorstep and knock as loud as you can. Don't lollygag and get caught. Don't nobody want people feeling sorry for 'em."

Cans of peaches sloshed as the bag crinkled in my arms. The house sat on cinder blocks and a green piece of material with tiny orange flowers covered the front door. As I stepped on the chipped porch step I heard the door hinges squeak, and turned back towards the car. The pink cross that dangled from the rearview mirror was my finishing line. Running so fast my lungs couldn't take in enough air, I jumped into the car feet first.

As we drove away, I turned to look across the tops of the bags in the backseat and saw a blanket of white dust sweep over the front porch. A woman with orange curlers put a hand on her forehead trying to catch a glimpse of our getaway car.

Sister Delores laughed in that deep-gutted way. "People running around chasing after dope ain't got a clue. Now right back there is the only kinda dope I'm studying. Getting high on giving to the needy. Thank you, Jesus."

"Boy I wish my mama could . . ."

"What, baby? What's that you say about your mama?"

The paper bag made a crumpling sound when I snatched it closer to me. "I just was fixing to say I wish my mama could've lived so she could help people like you do."

Her hand was soft when she reached over and patted my knee. As we pulled away, I stared out the window at the kudzu that snaked around a fence post. Even though my tongue would not let me confess it, I wondered how things might have been different if my mama would've gotten a hold of some of Sister Delores's dope.

As we clutched our fishing rods with one hand and steered our bicycles with the other, all we could do was nod to the policeman who sat in the parked car next to the phone booth. A woman with a floppy white hat didn't seem to notice. She pointed to the words "U.S.A.'s Smallest Police Station" as a man dressed in blue-checked shorts, dress socks, and white tennis shoes took her picture.

Rounding the corner to the dime store allowed a soft breeze from the river to break through the sting from the late May sun. Beau snaked his bike through the parked cars that lined the street, all the while keeping his eyes on the boardwalk across the way. "Good. No-body's out fishing today. We'll get first dibs."

It was his idea to check out the fish at the dime store. He was sure that minnows from the fish tank in the back of the store would be cheaper than buying them from the bait-and-tackle shop.

"Dog. This place ain't got the first minnow. You think these yellow-and-white stripes might work? Kinda looks like a shiner."

As I watched assorted colors of fish swim around tanks with blue rocks and plastic reefs, the smell of bagged fertilizer stacked on the cracked wooden floor kept me from making any big decisions.

The old man with a gut that draped over his belt sat in a lawn chair at the front register. The crinkle from his newspaper occasionally competed with the humming from the fish tanks.

"Only ten cents each. Let's try one of these yellow ones. If I catch something we'll come back." Just when Beau grabbed the plastic bag and fish net, we heard that piercing voice.

"Let me see the goods first and then I'll tell you if we have a deal."

Beau slowly turned around. Even if I'd not known the voice my-self, I could have told by the arch of Beau's eyebrows that the one thing that managed to scare him was in the building.

The man laughed until he went into a coughing fit. "All right, Miss Rose. See for yourself."

We hunched behind the shelf that was lined with matchbox-sized containers of fish food. Over the dusty containers we saw the black wig that curled around the top edge of her leopard-print coat. An electric fan behind the cash register kept the edges of Mama Rose's hair in a state of flutter. She held up a multicolored stick painted like a bird with a straw hat.

The man tried to pull his pants up higher. "Not a thing in the world wrong with them except the bottom broke off. I still got the cups. All you have to do is glue the bottom part and then she's good as new."

She ran her finger down the length of the bird and massaged the broken part. "What makes you so sure they'll dip for water?"

"Got this magnet thing in the bird so that it draws him to the water. All the big tourist places down the state are selling 'em like wildfire."

Beau inched down lower when Mama Rose turned her head. He stayed down as they bargained back and forth until the deal was sealed.

The man wiped his pasty forehead with a folded handkerchief and studied Mama Rose's coat from shoulders to ankle. "Rose, you been feeling okay? Haven't seen you in a while."

The black wig moved back and forth with her head. "My nerves are just tore all to pieces. I guess you know that ex-daughter-in-law of mine is now a certified nigger lover. Oh yeah, even going to one of their churches."

"Didn't know. You still taking the pills that doctor . . ."

"She always was nothing but common trash. Next thing you know she'll have a nigger man shacked up in Johnny's house."

Before I could stop him, Beau hit the shelf with his fist. Specks of fish food scattered as the sound of vibrating metal made its way to the front of the store.

"Hey, what's going on back there?"

We scooped up boxes of fish food as if it was a game of hot potato. The man's crinkled black loafers were planted inches from our fingers. "Y'all broke anything, you're paying for it."

Rising to face further judgment, I breathed deeper when I noticed the front of the store was empty. Outside the tall window Mama Rose pulled a red wagon with her latest find. In the noon sun her black wig glistened like crow feathers. A crow with a call so loud and shrill that others followed.

In the backseat of Sister Delores's car, sweat from the girl with underarm hair pressed against my shoulder. She was one of the new people picked up, thanks to us giving away bags of food.

"We sure gonna have church today, babies." Sister Delores's car was packed extra tight. The fruits of her labor spread across the ripped seat and onto laps.

I pictured the car rolling down the highway with the back end slumped down from all the weight, sparks flying behind us. It was a good thing that Beau and Josh had begun going to church in Bonita's car.

"That truck is about to run over us," said the girl next to me.

With her shoulder pinning part of me against the slick car seat, I could only turn my head part of the way. But the steel bars that imprisoned the truck hood gave Alvin away. Sliding down the seat, I could hear the roar of Alvin's sawed-off muffler.

Sister Delores kept both hands on the steering wheel and one eye in the rearview mirror. "Don't pay no mind to that truck." But the sweat that ran like a tear down the side of her neck convinced me otherwise.

When Alvin started honking the horn, the smaller children in the front seat craned towards the back window. Lined up against the headrest, their skinny necks stretched out like cowbirds ready to take flight.

Alvin's truck roared forward until we could see a stain of red clay on one of the front tires, tires fit more for a bulldozer than a vehicle. One of the little kids up front went to crying when he laid down on the horn again.

Sister Delores held the steering wheel and wiped away tears all at the same time. "No need crying over this silliness."

But when he jerked the truck into the passing lane and was lined up directly next to us, even I dug my fingers into the ripped place in the backseat.

Two men sat in the front seat as the CB antenna slapped wildly in the air. The one closest to the window stuck his head out. The back of his hair fanned out across his head, but the front remained slicked down. He held out a bat and waved it as if he might twirl it in the air. His words vibrated as if spoken into a rotating fan. "Nigger, you best watch out." He pumped the bat higher, and his scowl spoke louder than the words the wind tossed about.

"Roll up the windows," Sister Delores said. She jerked the knob on the door harder until the glass had cut out the breeze. The truck roared a final time and lurched forward until the antenna was nothing but a speck of silver far ahead of us.

"Bye, now." Sister Delores waved when the truck was a distance away. "If anybody ever needed Jesus, it was that poor thing. Oh now, babies, don't y'all go to studying about them men. You just seen something ugly is all. Just ugly and devil-filled right down to the core."

When we arrived at God's Hospital, Sister Delores parked right in front of the church with the gold cross painted above the front door. She led us in a prayer that asked for peace and for God's help to reach the man who held up the bat. Then she ran her fingernail down the pink cross that dangled from the rearview mirror. Smiling, she closed her eyes and seemed to draw strength from the touch, the same way my mama did whenever she held one of her nerve pills.

Soft drumbeats escaped from the doors, and Sister Delores led the little children by the hand. They formed a brightly colored chain of pastel dresses and sailor shirts. Inside, most of the new people had already found seats. I saw one man with a shirt just like the one Poppy wore, a blue pullover with a pocket painted the color of the Marina logo. Beau was too busy matting down the back of his hair to notice me slide into the pew.

"Boy, you're sweating like a hog. Get off me." He moved closer to Bonita, and she moved along the pew until Josh was pinned up against an old man with white socks and black dress shoes.

The organ started to whine, and I told Beau about the baseball bat. While the rest of God's Hospital sang "'Tis So Sweet to Trust in Jesus," I whispered the details to Beau.

Harvey stood at the podium in front of the church and nodded to the keyboard player, and voices in various keys soon filled the building once again. Beau looked down at the hymnal and ran his blistered finger across the stanzas. "Did you see Alvin?"

"No, but it sure was his truck. Those big bars on the front."

"How do you know it was him driving? Could've been somebody else. Maybe somebody borrowed it."

Bonita leaned down, and the gold cross she wore twirled playfully. For a second her hair spray wiped away the lingering smell of crab. "Hush. Now I mean it."

So I did hush. I never told Beau he was a fool. I just sat there and watched his finger guide across the hymnal. He wouldn't have known the truth if it had been written in the pages for him to sing. He couldn't hear it on account of the brain infection I diagnosed him with that day. Infection of fear and loneliness.

By the time Sister Delores got up from the tall wooden chair with a cross carved in the back, the amens had died down to a few coughs. She glided across the green carpet and took her rightful place at the podium. Her head shook until the curls rang back and forth like bells that had been silenced. "I'm just standing up her thinking about Jesus and how good He's been to us. The Lord told me back there five years ago that He wanted me to take His loving words to all His people. I said all His people. Black, white, yellow, half-breed, it don't make no difference to the King now."

"Amen, amen," a man with patches of gray hair said from the pew in front of us.

"Now God's Hospital is growing faster than most hospitals. And ain't that wonderful. A hospital should be pulling in the hurting. We got no use for people who don't think they need nothing. Bring me the hurting ones. That's what my Mother Hightower used to tell me when I was a little girl. She'd tuck me in at night and say, 'Baby, you gonna be used one day to help this hurting world, but even still this world is not your home.'"

"No, it's not. Sure not," a woman down in front said. A baby started crying, but it didn't break Sister Delores's stare on the Bible pages that fluttered in time with the corner fan.

"I was gonna preach on Abraham and his trip to Egypt, but coming here this morning something happened that tore at my heart. Tore it right down to the quick. Come on, somebody."

A woman with hair the color of sand waved a purple handkerchief at Sister Delores. "Preach it, Sister."

Right then I wanted to punch Beau in the ribs and stand up and shout that Alvin was the one who tore up her heart. But Beau was too caught up in drawing a picture of a spaceship on the church bulletin.

"Love is a precious gift, and some people don't want nothing to do with it. They act devil-filled to the heart, and it just breaks mine in two." Sister Delores grabbed the microphone from the lectern, and it squealed louder than the crying baby.

"Jesus told his disciples to bring the little children to Him, and that's what I was trying to do. Just like Mother Hightower brought me to Him. Now y'all know we got no secrets in God's Hospital. They tell me I wasn't no more than three days old when I was put up in a place for orphans. Nobody knowing any of my people until one day Mother Hightower walked in and picked me out. Said she seen sweetness in my eyes. Mother Hightower's hand was rough as day-old cowhide, but let me tell y'all something: it belonged to a heart softer than fine silk. We'd say our prayers, and then she'd pull that big ol' heavy Bible down from the kitchen cabinet and read the words from Psalms. Over and over until I had them stitched on my heart. 'The Lord is my light and my salvation. Whom shall I fear? When my father and mother forsake me, then the Lord will take me up.'"

The buzz from the lights filled the room and not even the baby cried out. Beau looked up and hit my knee with his. "She's fixing to cry."

I just sat there staring deeper into the soft brown lips that curled into a half smile. Sister Delores had found her daddy and her mama in one person, and by the way her nerves stayed so settled, I knew it was for keeps.

She moved down the stage steps and stood face-to-face with the congregation. "Do you know Jesus? Is He your daddy and your mama or just a crutch you pull out when the pain tears you a part? He wants you to lay it on down, and come home now. Come on home to Daddy Jesus."

Harvey had not taken his place at the podium before the words and music flew around us. Words as soft as the place I imagined Sister Delores's heart to be. *"Softly and tenderly Jesus is calling. Calling for you and for me . . ."*

The woman with the purple handkerchief was holding both hands high in the air while Sister Delores kept her head bowed in prayer. My heart slowed even more when I looked up and saw Him. Sitting in the tall preacher's chair behind Sister Delores, He was wearing a long beige shirtdress and His hair was the color of honey. His eyes never left me. They were magnets pulling out layers of poison from a wound that wouldn't heal.

When I moved from behind the pew, not even Beau's yank at my shirttail could keep me still. It was Jesus, looking just as sun-tanned as He had on the funeral fan. Only this time Jesus was smiling and threw His head back. When His hands reached out, I saw the holes and wanted to touch them. To put my hand in His and believe. To believe that He would fill the holes that my own mama and daddy had left in me.

With each step I made down the aisle, I saw Him waving me on to the finish line. His fingers were long, long enough to pull me up to where I belonged. *"Come home. Come home. He who is weary, come home."*

I reached up as high as the woman waving the purple handkerchief. Higher than any hurt I had ever been given. Just when I had made it to the first step of the altar, Sister Delores pulled me closer to her. The silky material that covered her round stomach brushed against my cheek. Floral perfume and the scent of grease from Nap's Corner were trapped in the dress. Smelling salts that brought me back to this world. A world that was not my home.

Eleven

———◆◇◆———

A mist of rain danced in the air the day I got baptized. The
cowboy singers stood under the concrete canopy at the
state park right next to a bucket of chicken. Their harmonized lyrics floated with the breeze and came in and out like an am-
plifier that was on the blink. Sister Delores stood knee deep in the
ocean water dressed in a white gown. When she first told me I'd have
to wear the dress, I resisted until I was convinced that others would
have one on as well. We lined the beach in various sizes, with our bare
feet digging deeper into the soggy sand. A man Poppy's age stood in
front of me wringing his hands until Sister Delores called out for him
to move forward. Church folks spread out across the concrete benches;
their various shades made me think of a bunch of brown M&Ms with
a cluster of white ones that somebody had forgotten to paint. I
searched the crowd until a woman dressed in a red dress moved away
to wipe her baby's nose. In the gap I saw Nana's face appear and disap-
pear with each swipe of the truck windshield wipers. Poppy leaned
next to the concrete piling as if he was holding the shelter up.

Between the clip of windshield wipers I watched Nana turn her
head away each time the crowd yelled a war chant of "Glory" to signal
another person had been dipped into the ocean. When it came my
turn, the cool water chilled my spine. Sister Delores reached out for

me and smiled as wide as I'd ever seen her smile. "Come on, baby, I got you. I got you."

The pull of the sea kept us in a steady rocking motion. She put her fingers over my nose and held up the other hand high towards the graying sky. "Brandon Davidson, by your profession of faith in Jesus Christ and your willingness to turn you heart over to Him, I baptize you in the name of the Father, the Son, and the Holy Ghost." With a slight shove, Sister Delores pushed me under the choppy water. Even though her fingers pinched my nose, it did not stop the saltwater from rushing down my throat. All the while I kept worrying whether the baptism would be for real because Davidson was not my real last name.

Rising up to the water's surface, I heard the crowd shout "Glory" once again. Brushing away the stinging salt from my eyes, I looked towards the truck just in time to see the windshield wipers take away a mist of rain. This time Nana did not look away. She stared straight at me and dabbed her eyes.

"I don't know why you wanted to get dunked for," Beau said at the school the following Monday. "You looked funny coming outta that water with your hair all stuck together and wearing that dress."

Opening my notebook, I ignored his comments. Ever since Parker Townes and his shiny black patrol car had started stopping by Beau's house, he seemed full of piss. Sister Delores told us the Bible says not to give pearls to a pig or something along those lines. Since Beau was acting like a pig that wanted to woller in slop, I decided to let him.

That afternoon for the first time Bonita and Parker Townes picked us up from school in the patrol car. Groups of kids from our grade and those younger gathered around the car, which was so shiny their faces gleamed back at us. I jumped inside the back of the car, where Josh was already pretending to be criminal clutching the bars that separated the backseat from the front. Bonita laughed, and waved for Parker to get out of the car to greet the students. His big silver gun stuck out as if it was an extra bone on his hip. While he answered questions about whether he had ever shot anybody, Beau moved away towards the door to the front office. Then it occurred to me that, given my circumstances, I too should be hiding from the patrolman with snaggled teeth instead of being piled up in his backseat. From the backseat, I watched Beau jerk away when Bonita tried to rub his shoulder. After a pull at his arm, he walked obediently back to the car and never looked up as the younger students squealed when the flashing lights of the patrol car came on.

At the camper Nana greeted me with the usual Pepsi. She waved at Bonita, but I was too busy trying to reach my snack to see if Beau waved back or not. The smell of fresh-baked cinnamon rolls hung in the humid air. Inside, Nana turned off her afternoon story on TV and motioned for me to wash up. My eyes never left the plate of rolls as she slid a knife through the bread and white gooey icing stretched towards her.

"I'm glad Bonita and Parker are seeing more of each other."

I decided not to tell Nana of Beau's recent bad attitude or to remind her of how scared she acted the first time she had met the patrolman at Nap's Corner.

As I ate the warm rolls, Nana would reach over and occasionally wipe icing from my chin. "Is it good to you?" she'd ask.

She was caught up in the flavor of it all as much as I was and that's probably why neither of us heard the knock at the door the first time.

"Hello. Anybody home?" Sister Delores's voice never did seem right outside of church. "I'm telling you, it's hot out there today." She filled the entrance of the camper, and Nana nervously reached for a paper napkin.

"Thank you. I just wanted to stop by to see how y'all doing. We sure did miss you at the baptismal."

"Oh, I was there," Nana said. "That sprinkle of rain kept me inside the truck, but don't you worry none, I was there."

Sister Delores wiped her brow. "I figured so all along."

Nana looked at the schoolbooks I had scattered over the so-called

sofa. "Brandon, pick up those books so Sister Delores can have a seat."
I cut my eyes back at Nana. It was the first time she had called the
preacher by name.

"Oh, I know how these boys need time to do their lessons. I don't
want to be in the way. Maybe we could just sit out here under this
shade tree."

Nana looked at Sister Delores the same way she did the new
people we met in town who tried to press too hard with questions
they had no business asking. "I've got just a few minutes before I have
to get supper started."

Watching them sit together next to the cook-out grill that was
guarded by concrete blocks, I felt as if I was watching a movie with
two actors I had known from different TV shows. Their lives seemed
like an H with me being the line that connected them. I cranked the
window handle just enough to hear their voices, and their words
floated in on waves of wind.

"I've been seeing your husband at church a time or two."

Nana brushed away invisible lint from her pants. "A.B. never was
one for religion. Back home, uhh, down the state where we're from,
he never did care for our preacher."

"Oh, I know what he means. I got no use for religion."

Nana slowed her nod. "Beg your pardon?"

"Oh, you know, a bunch of folks all the time talking about rules. I
got no use for such as that. Those kind made me quit church back
when I was just a Sunday morning Christian. Now relationship is
what I'm after, not a bunch of laws. I want to lead my church the
same way Jesus did it. He stirred up those religious people just like a
bunch of hornets. He sure did, now."

The afternoon train sounded in the distance. Sister Delores looked
towards the beach across the road. "You got yourself a good boy. You
raising him right."

"And just so you know, as long as he's lived with me he's been in
church. I just got to work some things out right now. You know, just
me and the Lord. Everybody goes through a desert now and again."

"You're right about that, now. We'll always have us a desert to pass through. Well, call if y'all need me." Sister Delores reached for the edge of the grill and pulled herself up from the picnic table.

Nana wiped away chips of concrete from the table, her eyes never following the steps of our guest.

Sister Delores's words competed with the creaking of her opening car door. "We all go through those dry spells from time to time. We sure do. But just be careful. If you stay around in the desert for too long, that camping tent you pitched just might end up becoming a fine brick home you don't want to give up."

Sister Delores drove away, and Nana's arms remained folded long after the Impala had disappeared down the driveway.

The day the Spring Fair opened, we stopped by the gas station to make our weekly call to Uncle Cecil. While Nana and Poppy huddled closer to the phone receiver, I stood at the corner watching the rows of trucks and cars that lined the entrance to the fair across the street. Tents and trailers transformed the empty lot into a place of high excitement. The owner of the gas station played with the change inside his pants as we stood watching the traffic. Jingles from the change accompanied the only words I had ever heard him speak.

"A fella from Waycross come down here to put that Ferris wheel together. Said it was the biggest one south of Albany. Said you could see all the way over to Tallahassee on a clear night." He raised up on the balls of his feet and stretched his head high. His words were almost as intoxicating as the multicolored lights that lined the side of the Ferris wheel. The commotion and noise from across the street got Nana and Poppy off of the phone faster than I could have.

Grass killed from the scorching sun crunched under our feet, and the smell of corn dogs blanketed the air. Passing people I knew from town and school made it feel more like a family reunion. Right then my old life back in Raleigh seemed like nothing more than yellowed photos in a dust-covered album.

We met Bonita and Parker at the shooting booth. Dressed in blue jeans and a western shirt, Parker looked smaller without the uniform and pistol. But his marksmanship gave him away as an expert shooter. Bonita held the three teddy bears to prove it.

"Here, Pauline, take one of these. I'm running out of hands." Bonita handed Nana the teddy bear dressed in overalls.

Poppy laughed and snuggled the bear closer to Nana's chin before she swatted at his hand.

Not looking up from the gun, Parker said, "Brandon, your teacher came and got Beau. She needed him at the snow-cone booth. You might want to check it out." Bullets clipped as I turned to go.

Nana grabbed my shoulder. "Now where exactly are you going to be? That white tent right over there?"

Poppy gave her a look, and then she let me go. All the while I felt her eyes watching each step I made.

After we had poured blue liquid on the last snow cone of our shift at the school booth, Beau and me took Josh for a ride on the Ferris wheel. We waited in a long line while the man who operated the machine told us all the details that the gas station owner had already spilled. I watched the way he smiled at the girls and whispered close to their ears until they laughed. Right down to the belt buckle engraved with the words "Groove Thing," he seemed like somebody Mama would bring home. Maybe that's why I didn't laugh at his one-liners the way Beau and Josh did. He locked us in the yellow-seated cart and kicked us off in such a way that the cart began to spin. Josh clamped harder on to the handle and tried to make us think he liked it by yelling real loud. The night sky filled our senses as we moved higher and higher towards the stars.

"I bet this is what the astronauts see right when they're taking off," I said and threw my head back until the rocking of the cart made me feel dizzy.

"Look at them down there. They look like little bitsy ants." Beau pointed at our classmates selling the snow cones. Miss Travick's blonde hair might as well have been straw pasted on a stick figure.

"They say you can see clean over to Tallahassee," I added.

When the Ferris wheel suddenly stopped, Josh never looked down. "What's that over there?" Josh let go of the safety bar long enough to point in the direction south of town.

Red streaks rose up from a clearing of trees. The flames danced higher out of the darkness and clawed at the stars.

"It's Dead Man's Curve. See it? There's a fire right over there." Beau's finger held the position, and he turned to look at me.

Due south of Dead Man's Curve could have been either of our places. I pictured our camper boiling in flames and ashes of money from the pickle jar drifting all the way up to the Ferris wheel.

We must have had the visions at the same time, because all at once we started yelling, "Fire. Fire. Let us down!"

Josh was flailing around, making the cart swing faster than it did when we first took off. The man down below was laughing with a girl who had her hair pulled back in a braid. She pointed up, and only then did he snatch the lever that made us come back to earth.

Beau was the first to reach Parker at the booth with basketball hoops.

"Fire! Something's on fire just pass Dead Man's Curve."

We followed Parker across the street to the gas station. On the same phone that we used to communicate with our past I watched Parker dial the sheriff and then the volunteer fire department. All the while my stomach twisted in a knot that I had thought it had forgotten how to tie. A knot that was supposed to be left back in North Carolina.

The big cross planted in the middle of the churchyard seemed to be filled with electric currents. Angry flames shot out in all directions. The symbol that was stamped on the Bible that Sister Delores had given me suddenly seemed like something ugly. Behind it the roof of God's Hospital caved in and flames busted upward towards the trees. Even the whine from the fire-truck sirens couldn't break my stare.

When the church steeple broke off and tumbled to the ground, I pictured the same soot that rose up in the sky dirtying my insides.

Men still dressed in clothes they wore at the fair began spraying water on the sanctuary. Magnolia trees that had blanketed us for dinners on the ground now popped and twisted against the flames.

Beau looked at me and then ran towards the trees. He pulled the garden hose from the house next door and began spraying. "Are you just gonna stand there?" he yelled. But as much as I wanted to move, all I could do was watch as God's Hospital, Sister Delores's church, my church, sank down right along with my spirit.

Twelve

S ister Delores sat in the back of the sheriff's car with the door wide open. Sounds from the radio crackled and then fell silent. I figured Sister Delores, like the radio, was all cried out. Tears had left a map down her face. She just sat staring at the smoke that drifted away from what remained of the charred building. The lone cross that had been electric with flames in the churchyard had long since fallen and lay broken in two pieces, charred and blackened.

While men in orange shirts walked around kicking the edges of the building and placing pieces of the church into plastic bags, Bonita and Nana stood with Harvey behind the sheriff's car. With the rhythm of an old hymn, Bonita kept a steady pat on Harvey's shoulder.

Parker and two deputies took a piece of the cross and placed it in a bag. When one of the gloved men peeled away the gold medallion, I stretched against the barrier of yellow tape. The deputy held it up as if it might be some treasure unearthed in the scorched grass. Part of the gold circle was twisted towards the grooves. My heart raced as the strange necklace and medallion that Josh found the day we cleaned out Mama Rose's attic swept through my mind.

Regular church members crowded behind the sheriff's car. They stared at Sister Delores like she was one of the women the fair had left behind. A woman with snakes growing from her hair. The crowd began to mumble when Sister Delores stepped out of the car. Harvey ran to her and whispered something unknown but to God and the two of them. She pushed his hands and slid underneath the tape.

She moved as if the cross might revive and produce a new spray of flames. When she kicked it, a trail of smoke escaped. Not even the crunching sound of burned wood could mask her scream. A scream so piercing that I turned to look for a protective nod from Nana, a nod indicating only a minor setback. But Nana was like all the rest, her brow wrinkled and jaw clinched as she took it all in.

Sister Delores fell to her knees, and Harvey stood behind her trying to pull her up. She lifted her head high towards the trees; pine straw filled her clinched fists. "Lord, I did everything you told me. But I can't do this no more. You promised strength to the weary and power to the weak. Well, Father, bring it on, because I just can't do this no more."

By the time Parker and Harvey had lifted Sister Delores from the ground, she was moaning a deep growl that I had first heard playing on the eight-track tape in her car. But this time my heart managed to translate each octave of pain.

Within a week, traffic was able to pass by the church without so much as slowing down. The charred foundation soon seemed nothing more than an unfilled cavity.

It began slowly at first, with the clearing of black crumbled wood, and then two weeks later new pilings began to rise up along with our spirits.

"What in the world . . .," said Nana as we drove pass the church. Cars, trucks, and church buses filled the lot next to the place where the cross had once burned. Nana, Poppy, and me got out of the truck to find makeshift tables covered with plastic coffee cups and boxes of doughnuts. Men with construction aprons began unloading boards from a flatbed truck.

"Let's rock and roll," Miss Travick said. Her smile was as wide as the truck that held the lumber.

"Where did all these folks come from?" Poppy asked.

"Well, after the story ran, I got my friend at the *Tallahassee Democrat* to cover it too. Then she got her friend at the TV station to mention it. Before you knew it, my phone was ringing off the hook."

"Look, there's Frank McCloud, preacher down at the Church of Christ." Nana pointed at the man carrying a saw.

"And Darrell Harvey," Poppy said. "He works down at the marina."

"Praise Jesus," Sister Delores said as she walked towards us dressed in blue jeans. "I sure do appreciate y'all coming by."

"Listen, gal. We just appreciate how much you've done to help those men at the marina feed their families." Poppy looked away at the group unloading the wood. "I'd better give them a hand."

While Sister Delores went around hugging everybody, Miss Travick paired us up. Beau and me were given a bucket and scrub brushes. We scrubbed the concrete steps leading up to what used to be the door until our knuckles were raw.

Every so often Beau would pause long enough to look at me and whisper, "I don't care what you say. Alvin wasn't in that truck." By the third time, I dropped the brush into the pail and slipped away behind the vehicles.

As much as I wanted to ignore the events that led up to the burning of God's Hospital, Poppy couldn't stop talking about them. We stood outside of the filling station making the regular call to Uncle Cecil as if nothing had changed. A thick wind of early summer cut through the cracks of the bathroom door and stirred with a howl of anger.

Nana reached for the phone, but Poppy turned his back.

"Don't worry, we slipped away when all the newspeople showed up."

By the time Nana got to talk, the look of disgust had swept down from her wrinkled brow to every crease around her lips. She snatched the phone from Poppy and only spoke a few sentences before the operator announced time had run out.

Inside the café downtown, she held the menu decorated with sketches of shrimp with top hats and never said another word. But Poppy was making up for anything she might have wanted to say.

He was smearing butter onto a cracker and talking all at the same time. "They tell me the Klan meets down at the swamp. Old Joe down at work said his cousin used to belong. Said if anybody got to talking out of turn about their plans they'd just cut the man's tongue . . ."

The table jarred, and pieces of cracker wrappers drifted to the floor. "Will you please hush about burning churches and cutting out tongues. As it was, you wasted the entire call with Cecil worrying about business he doesn't care a thing about. Never once thinking to check about the note on the farm."

Nana turned back to the menu, and a young girl with braces flipped a new page in her pad. "Can I get you something to drink?"

"Yes, ma'am. I think I'll take me the biggest glass of tea you got in the place. How 'bout you, Brandon?"

"Pepsi."

Before Poppy could turn to look at Nana, the bell on the door chimed and she had walked out. Acid grew in my throat as I watched a pair of seagulls fly away from the railing of the boardwalk. The waitress's thighbone brushed against my shoulder when I slipped by.

Nana's pant legs slapped together as she walked faster towards a bench by the river. By the time she sat down, I was standing behind her.

"Where are you going?"

She reached up and patted my hand. Her fingers felt as tattered as the shrimp nets that lined the boardwalk railing. "Don't you worry about all that. He just never did care about the farm the same way I do. To him it's just land. Land that's got my family's sweat and tears in every square inch of it."

A soft breeze made the collar of her blouse flutter. The beat of her heart pulsated against my thumb as a small mullet boat drifted by with a pack of seagulls hovering behind it.

Poppy's footsteps were heavy on the boards of the dock. He stopped right when a seagull cried out one last time before flying away from the boat. "Brandon, I grabbed a mess of hush puppies. Why don't you go see if they're interested in feeding."

Grabbing the clumps of meal inside the napkin, I watched Nana smile that way she had. The smile that said worry was a nuisance that we did not have space for in our new lives. Poppy slid down on the bench and patted her leg.

While seagulls circled in mid-flight around me, I watched the two of them more than the birds. She never responded when he reached over to hold her hand. She simply gazed at the boat as if it could carry her back to dry land that was reserved for the past.

Bonita and Parker had set the trip up right after the church burned. Little did I know when I accepted their invitation to spend the day at the amusement park in Panama City that Beau and me would communicate only through Josh.

"Hey, let's ride the Spider," Josh said.

I shrugged my shoulders and looked down at Josh. Blue food dye from the cotton candy outlined his lips. "I'll do it. But I don't know about him. He's too chicken."

"You tell him that I can ride that dadgum roller coaster with my hands straight up in the air. I'll ride that thing, but I won't sit by him."

By now Josh had gotten used to being a translator and was tired of repeating the words that he had first said through broken laughter. The joke died down before we entered the park gates.

As we rode the Spider, black metal arms stretched out low over the park. Bonita and Parker looked like action figures standing in front of the shooting gallery. The cart would spin out of control before they had a chance to hear us call out their names. It was the first time that day that we had all laughed at the same time.

Beau's words were clipped as rock music blasted out of the cart's speaker, but I did not need a translator to understand them. "I don't know why you think Alvin burned that place down."

Josh was pushed into Beau as the cart made another dip towards the ground. His face was twisted even more than the arms of the ride. "Burned what place?"

"Brandon thinks Alvin burned down God's Hospital. Said that gold thing they found on the cross was the same one Alvin had at his house the day we went out there."

"That's stupid." Josh cut his eyes to Beau for confirmation.

When we turned again, Josh slid over to me but grabbed the metal bar and pulled himself away.

"I said it looks like the same one that was on that cross Alvin had. And hey, you're the one who held the one at Mama Rose's house."

"Alvin carves stuff for people all the time." Beau leaned up trying to make me look at him. "That's how he makes a living. Doing woodwork and stuff." Rotating to the side for one final time, the cart suddenly became still. "I tell you what, I'm gonna prove once and for all that Alvin don't know nothing about that fire."

"What you gonna do, walk up to him uptown and say, 'Alvin, do you burn crosses with gold things on them?'"

"No, we're going back out to his place. Next Saturday when he takes Mama Rose to the grocery store."

"You crazy? I'm not going out there again."

"What's wrong, you know you'll be proved wrong? Or maybe you're just too yellow-bellied to do it."

Josh leaned forward and the words whistled from his missing tooth. "Yeah, chicken."

"Let's put it this way." Beau touched his fingers together better than the mobsters he had seen on TV. "You don't go out there with us, and I'm telling Alvin what you said about him."

Poppy's words from the restaurant filled my ears louder than the electric guitar down below. I pictured Alvin hog-tying me and then sharpening his knife until the tip reflected the sunlight of his private hell in the swamp. A chill iced the image of my tongue hanging on a pine tree right between the others decorated with snakeskins and hubcaps.

The following Friday we stood outside of the gas station while rain dropped from the edge of the rusted roof. Rainwater filled the holes in the asphalt the same way that the fear of Alvin had begun to fill my body.

"Hello, is Cecil Willard there today?" Nana propped her blue umbrella against the bathroom door outside of the gas station. Beads of water ran down the phone booth and settled at her feet. "Uhh . . ."

Nana slammed the phone receiver down, but her fingers kept moving as if she was tapping Morse code back to North Carolina.

"What's the matter?"

"That woman wanted to know who I was again when I asked for Cecil."

I kicked a bottle cap into a puddle, but she didn't even try to stop me. "That's what secretaries do. They take messages."

Nana grabbed the umbrella and nudged me towards the car with her elbow. "Something's not right. This is the second week in a row. It's just not right, I tell you."

By the time we drove to the marina to give Poppy supper for the night shift, Nana was tapping the steering wheel to a beat all of her own. Poppy stood at the opened window with rain dripping from the brim of his cap. "Probably just got sick or something. Maybe Loraine took ill. You know how she likes to be petted. Oh, it ain't nothing." But the words of comfort never seemed to soak into Nana's mind, and I can't say that I cared. With the threat of having my tongue cut out, a missed Friday afternoon call with Uncle Cecil was nothing more than child's play.

The multicolored Christmas lights were still burning even though it was five till nine in the morning. Looking up at the faded glow of lights that hung above the door of the Lazy Lounge, I suddenly wanted more than anything to be one of those lights.

The clicking sound of a loose bike chain made the muscles in my neck tighten. Beau wore a camouflage hat and began laughing when he saw me. "I bet you done pissed all over yourself wondering if we had already gone on to Alvin's place and told him about you blaming him."

Josh trailed behind in a zigzag motion and tried to make his laugh sound just as genuine.

Dust and specks from broken beer bottles flew up when they braked. Beau directed us towards the highway with a tilt of his chin. "You're fixing to be proved wrong, and I want to be there to see you eat crow."

"I'm about to kill and dress that crow. Then we'll see who's gonna eat it," I yelled back.

Other than an armadillo that skirted across the road, it began to seem like we were the only signs of life in the county. Squinting up at the sun that pounded our sweat into the asphalt, I began to wonder if everything else had more sense to stay tucked inside the thick forest that lined the edges of the road. Josh reached for the fake-leather canteen that clamped on to the handlebar. He used one hand to steer while finding relief from the container with Davy Crockett's picture on the side. Looking down, I stared at the washed out places that swept by and pedaled harder. Invisible cotton hung in the back of my throat. As much as it might hurt, I vowed never to ask anything of the Riley boys for the rest of my life. No matter how short a life it might be. It was then that I wondered if me dying would cause Mama to be welcomed back into the family, out of pity if nothing else.

We rode until the grooves of the bike seat seemed like a natural extension of my backside. Beau pulled off onto a driveway covered with pine straw and thick vines. Oil-colored water touched the tip of the cypress branches that hung like claws over the edge of the swamp. Mosquitoes the size of half-dollars danced around our bare necks. Slapping sounds echoed from the moss-draped landscape.

The roughness of the overgrown path seemed to rattle nervousness deeper into my body. Breathing started sounding whistlelike. Beau turned his head and then reached under his bicycle seat. He slowed enough for me to reach him and stuck out a thermos. "Here. You look like crap."

Beau stopped when we saw a portion of Alvin's shed. Part of the rusted tin was missing to reveal a post that held up the structure. We followed Beau's lead and tucked our bikes under the fold of a pine tree.

The cry of a bird rolled down from a cypress tree, and soon its flapping wings broke the stillness. Josh jogged up closer to Beau and cautiously looked back at me as if I was about to ambush them. The same sensation that had caused me to wet the bed overpowered my insides. Dryness seemed to cover the back of my throat the same way weeds covered the hems of our jeans.

A stack of wood speckled with mold greeted us at the edge of the shed. An upside-down horseshoe and a raccoon's tail dangled from the tattered door. Now the whole injustice of the church burning seemed nothing worse than burning leaves on a windy day. Maybe that gold medallion fell off somebody's car trunk just the way Beau had explained. Then we moved pass the woodpile, and my legs buckled when I saw the truck in front of Alvin's house.

The rusted-out tailgate held Alvin's latest work. Round cypress tables lined what was once the truck's brand-new body.

Beau turned and sighed. "Come on. That truck ain't nothing but his work truck. He's half way to town by now."

A rooster pranced around the side of the shed and stopped to glance at us before pecking dirt. Lumber in all sorts of colors and sizes lay scattered under the house.

Dust and dead bugs clung to the window of the front door. When Beau wiped the glass with his palm, an outline of his fingers offered us a look inside. "See there's nothing in there that nobody don't have in their own house."

Pressing my nose against the hot glass, the red of the Confederate flag that hung on the wall looked darker behind the dirt. Stacks of boxes covered the sofa, and a corner TV with aluminum wrapped around its antenna completed the tiny living room. The closet door that had housed the cross and the gold medallion was leaning sideways. A rusted hinge held the top of it to the door frame. The rooster crowed, and I jumped backward at the sound.

Beau nudged Josh, and both were laughing.

"So what? The cross I saw was probably the one he set on fire at God's Hospital."

The door squeaked open when Beau pushed it. "If you're so smart, then go on in and find another one."

Musty smells rolled out onto the porch, and my heart beat faster. "You crazy? He'd have grounds to kill me for sure."

They were still laughing when I looked behind them and saw the small window of the shed. A droopy spider web clung to its edges. "What about checking that window?"

With hound-dog precision Beau followed my point, bounded down the stairs, and started pulling at the shed door. Strips of white paint peeled away from the frame, and the top part of the door seemed bolted on the other side.

Beau glanced at the perfectly stacked firewood that was the most organized thing on the property. The bottom log caved in when Beau put his weight on it. The faster he moved up the stack, the smaller his arms looked as he balanced himself by clinging to the side of the shed. He wiped the window with his elbow and mumbled something just as the rooster crowed again.

"I told you so," I said climbing up the pile. The back of Beau's sneaker was in direct view when I heard Josh pulling himself up behind me.

The shed window was filmed with neglect, but the evidence was crystal clear. Inside, crosses lined the room like tombstones for giants. The gold medallion was smack dab in the middle of every one of them, just as it had been on the one burned at Sister Delores's church. A rope the color of saw grass dangled from the corner. Attached in the noose was the head of a black doll, its eyes bugged and a tongue painted red hanging from its mouth. A tongue ready to be cut and hung on a tree. Then the black rag doll turned into my face, and the limp body was mine. Tongue dangling out like a dead cat's, I watched myself twist in circles. Holding my crotch, I fought the urge to pee right in front of them. A curtain began to fall on the scene, and blood drained to an empty pit somewhere outside of my being.

The grinding truck gears caused us to look back towards the house. Steel bars on the truck grill glistened while the miniature Confederate flag hung limp on the antenna. Alvin's body looked bigger than ever riding towards us in the raised vehicle. As I scrambled to get down, a piece of splintered wood lodged into my palm. Just as I heard Beau yell, "Look out," the log slipped out from under his feet, and the vision of my mama came into full view. She was standing down below, right next to the water pump with her arms extended wide. The ends of her jeans were painted with flowers and flapped like an angel ready to carry me away. The soft red lips formed a smile so peaceful that I tried to reach out for her. But the earthly scream I heard was one of torment as logs rained down in a clap of thunder. All the while, the arms of my mama kept stretching but never managed to reach far enough.

I heard the moaning before I saw the soles of Josh's shoes turned sideways. Logs slanted in all sorts of directions covered the bottom part of his body. Beau jumped up right after I did. A stream of blood ran down the side of his head. Our arms moved so fast that they blurred with the logs we yanked and tossed away. A force slammed me down to the ground again, and I watched Alvin shove Beau away. As if they had been made of toothpicks, Alvin flung the pieces of wood to the side.

The sound of Josh's teeth chattering was the only noise I heard. Alvin jerked him up in his arms and moved towards the truck that weeks earlier had only been able to terrorize. Josh's legs were knotted to the right, and blood was beginning to soak through the jeans.

"Open the damn door," Alvin yelled. "Open it!"

Beau's eyes danced with panic as he struggled to pull it open. A scream as piercing as the one Josh had let out was heard as the door hinge scratched against metal.

• • •

People from the church and the regulars from Nap's Corner trickled into the hospital. Bonita kept folding a tissue and paced the lobby filled with low-seated chairs while a fluorescent lightbulb cast ghost faces on those who sat below it.

"Y'all had no business out at Alvin's place. No business at all," Bonita balled her fist up and said. I stared at the specks on the tile floor and wished more than ever that I would've stayed home that morning. Nana only shook her head and frowned. The heaviness of her eyes landed on me as hard as the logs that had pinned Josh.

"I ain't told mama nothing about any of this," Alvin whispered to Bonita.

"Oh, Lord, please don't. The last thing my nerves can take is Mama Rose up here." Bonita unfurled the tissue and covered her eyes. Parker massaged the inside of his patrolman hat and looked into it as if the brown felt might give him the right words to say.

Alvin's eyes burned my skin as he leaned against the case that held the fire extinguisher. His eyes kept a steady dance between me and the silver clock on the wall. It had been two hours since Josh entered surgery. The doctor told Bonita that one of his legs was shattered, and metal plates would have to be put in. I pictured Josh rolling around in a wheelchair with braces and brown lace-up shoes like the people on the Jerry Lewis Telethon.

Beau hit my arm and got up from the two-seated chair we shared. He glanced back over his shoulder, and I followed him pass the nurse's station. We paused inside a doorway filled with drink and snack machines. "You're not gonna say nothing, are you?"

"About what?"

Beau rolled his eyes. "About what. About why we were out at Alvin's place." He glanced around the room as if it might be bugged. "Now we can stick to the story about fishing. We'll say my line broke and we were seeing if Alvin had any."

"What if they ask how come we went all the way out to there to go fishing? What if they want to know how come we didn't go out to the cove like normal?"

"That's the question I got on my mind." I turned to see Alvin filling the doorway with both arms on the side of the frame. Edging backwards, I felt the drink-selection buttons pressing against me.

"Uh, hey, Uncle Alvin. Doctor come out yet?" Beau shook his head better than any actor on TV. "I sure hope he'll be able to walk again."

Alvin used his tongue to floss a front tooth. He looked down the hallway and never turned when he asked, "How come you boys been out at my place?"

Beau shifted his weight and stammered just for a second. "We went fishing. That's all."

"My fishing hole's filled with nothing but gators. Fact of the matter, I'm surprised they didn't track y'all down for stepping foot on my property." Alvin leaned down so that he was eye to eye with us. A flake of dead skin clung to his eyebrow and it raised upward with his words. "You boys snooping for trouble?"

"Uhh, no sir. We just wanted to fish someplace different. That's all."

"I take a man on his word, Beau. But I got no use for liars. You best remember that." Alvin turned to me, and the lines in his eyes were as red as the drink machine. He tried to smile, but his lips would only pull sideways. "Boy, Beau took you in like a brother. Family sticks together and fights for one another. They say you ain't got no mama and daddy. We look at you just like you was one of us. You're just the same as us."

Pressing harder into the machine, I nodded until Alvin had stood back up.

"Good, I'm glad we understand one another. With Josh in there on the operating table, now's the time we gotta stick together."

His hand reached closer until I could see dirt on the side of a bloody scab. Just when I braced for him to slap me, he pushed me to the side and slipped coins into the machine. "Now go on and pick out a drink to take back to the waiting room."

• • •

By the time Josh was able to be pushed in a wheelchair, Beau never left his side for a minute. Not even when Mama Rose came to visit with a plastic Snoopy that was missing one ear.

Josh pointed towards the concrete patio outside, off of the hospital lobby.

"That nurse said for you to stay inside," Beau said.

Josh whipped his finger in the direction of the sliding glass door. "Outside!"

We sat on the concrete table with a yellow umbrella big enough to cover Texas.

I used the black marker to sign my name at the top of Josh's knee, right below a patch of freckles. At the bottom of the cast I saw the scratchy name that looked like it might have belonged to one of Josh's first-grade friends. Alvin. My stomach deadened as I moved my attention back to the clean place on the cast. "When you think he'll go home?"

"If you want to say anything, you say it to me," Josh said.

"Well, when then?"

"Next Saturday. Sister Delores is letting me pull that string that's covering up the new steeple."

I looked at Alvin's name once again and then up at Beau. His eyes darted faster than a moth on a porch light. "Hey, we gotta go back inside before that nurse finds out we're out here," Beau said. He never looked back as they turned the corner and disappeared down the hallway.

The church dedication had become a hot topic in Abbeville. Not only did the paper have a front-page article, but the townspeople got into a buzz again when the Tallahassee TV station came back for a follow-up story. We stood pressed together on the steps of the restored God's Hospital. The tin roof reflected the morning sun like a premier spotlight. Against the freshly painted walls Sister Delores's bright pink dress resembled an oversized azalea bloom.

Her voice boomed at us in a way that reminded me of how policemen use bullhorns to talk down potential suicides. "He who is in
me is greater than he who is in the world. Come on, somebody. They
tried to scandalize us, then burn us out, but let me tell you something.
God showed up and then He showed out. He said it's time to rebuild,
and y'all got busy answering that call."

As if on cue, the singing cowboys got up on the porch steps and
started harmonizing about a new day. Growing bored with the oldest
one who kept his ear cupped and kept leaning down towards the
green welcome mat by the door, I turned to watch the crowd.

Bonita, Parker, and Beau stood up front next to Mr. Livingston,
who owned the marina. Two reporters from Tallahassee scribbled into
their palm-sized pads and ignored Josh's glances. He sat in the
wheelchair with his graffiti-covered cast standing out at attention towards the cord that snaked up to the steeple. The soft sounds of the
sheet flapping against the steeple tempted me to look up, but I kept a
gaze on those scattered across the churchyard.

I saw the top of the motor home's TV antenna before I heard the
screeching brakes. It was right when the singing cowboys were finishing their highest note, so nobody turned to see the new load of guests
being transported to God's Hospital. Nana was still clapping when I
slipped away.

The motor home made the van from the Tallahassee TV station
seem toylike. The end of the motor home had a steel ladder, and
soon a man with long sideburns got out and climbed to the top.
Jagged antennas popped up all over until the motor home looked
more like a flying saucer. When I saw the red stripe down the side
and the shape of the United States on the front door, I froze. Songs
from the church steps faded as another man wearing a red checkered shirt and signature safari hat stepped out of the door. He looked
right at me and smiled. As he moved forward, others followed behind, and my jaw flinched.

"Hello, there. Seems like quite a party you all have going on."
The man lifted his chin and rubbed his stomach all at the same time.
In person he didn't seem as tall as he did on TV.

"It's . . . they . . . I mean we're having a church dedication."

"So I hear. Did you help rebuild the church like the others?"

Scrubbing those steps had to count for something, so I nodded my head and looked down at the freshly shined boots. His hand reached down and broke the stare.

"I'm Hoyt Franklin. Hoyt Franklin with *Navigating the Nation.*"

"Brandon. Brandon . . . um, Brandon Davidson."

"Well, Brandon, do you mind if we move up front and meet some of the other people at your church?"

Leading them towards the group, I felt an inch taller with each step we made. I could sense Hoyt's eyes burning the back of my head as strong as the summer sun had burned the grass we were crunching. At first, no one seemed to notice the man who traveled the country seeking stories that were shared on his TV program. But when the man who owned the bait shop turned and spat tobacco inches away from Hoyt Franklin's boots, the nudges began and continued rippling until finally even Sister Delores was peering over the heads.

"Please, please. Don't mind us. We didn't come to interrupt anything," Hoyt said.

"That's the man off TV," I heard Harvey say to Sister Delores.

She shadowed her eyes with a pink handkerchief. "Well, praise Jesus. Don't stand back there and be bashful. Come on up here so we can get a good look at you."

The crowd divided faster than the sea that Moses crossed. Mumbling grew in a beehive fashion. I followed behind the camera crew until a jerk of my shirt collar pulled me into the thick of the others.

"Stand over here and behave yourself," Nana whispered. She and Poppy kept slipping farther from the porch steps where the only TV star I had ever seen was standing. The cameraman leaned down on one knee and focused his attention on Sister Delores.

"Through the affiliate we heard of all of the great things you people have done."

"Things that God did," Sister Delores said with a point to the sky.

"Well, in any case this town used adversity to form a partnership. I, for one, think America wants to hear about it."

A thunder of mumbles rolled through the crowd, and now even those who had been stone-faced were smiling.

"If you wouldn't mind, Reverend, I would like to stand back and let your crusade continue. And folks, don't be shy of Bart, our cameraman. Just act as if that little black machine on his shoulder wasn't even here."

While the cameraman squatted down in all sorts of positions and pointed the small black lens up at the porch, Sister Delores stiffened and pronounced each word in a way that made me think of Nairobi. The edge of her notes twitched as her words grew louder and more exact with each syllable.

"The Lord did not always promise sunshine and cloudless days. But in Him we have a comfort that not even Mr. Daniel Webster himself could define. Peace that surpasses all understanding. Yes, I am talking about peace."

A hush fell over the crowd, and the humming of the camera began to blend in like a chirping bird that would not fly away. No matter what Sister Delores said about peace, the words were lost on Nana and Poppy. They kept moving farther outside of the crowd until only the top of Hoyt Franklin's safari hat was visible from where we stood. Nana kept a steady grasp of my shoulder, pressing me away from the man with the black camera as if he had a water moccasin strapped to his shoulder.

Weaving in and out of the cars and trucks that filled the churchyard, I kept looking back at my last chance for fame. The chance to look into the little eye of the black machine and tell the whole world the real story behind the church burning. I pictured the sheriff circling around Alvin's house and talking him out with a bullhorn. He'd cry and beg them not to take him to jail, and the handcuffs would keep him from reaching for my tongue. I'd stand with Hoyt Franklin while his crew recorded every detail. They would pat my back and offer me a guest spot on his show. We'd move to New York and live in a big apartment, the kind that Jody and Buffy lived in on *A Family Affair*. Except instead of Mr. French, Nana would see after the place. She'd have thick sheets on the bed and a hot batch of cornbread to welcome me home from my many travels. I'd even talk Hoyt Franklin into giving Mama a job doing hair for everybody on the show, and she'd travel with us from each end of America.

Climbing into the truck, I heard the applause just before the door closed. Through the rear window, I watched Josh pull twice on the rope. The sheet glided away with the grace of a dove. A walnut-colored cross rose up above the top of the magnolia tree and closer to the sky. The sheet landed on the edge of the roof, and its ends dangled in the breeze. As we drove away, the crowd grew smaller, but the tip of the cross reached over the treetops. Even from the highway, the marker that stood guard over God's Hospital could be seen. Pressing my head against the back window, I watched it grow smaller until finally the limb of a live oak tree had clipped the celebration away for good.

When we pulled into the campground, the man and woman with Missouri license plates waved. Poppy lifted his finger in a half salute, but Nana turned her head towards the trailer office.

Heat from the long afternoon had not yet escaped through the front door before Nana started closing the blinds. Poppy fanned himself with his cap and managed to turn on the air conditioner with the free hand. Rays of sunlight illuminated the plastic blinds the way a flashlight exposes fragile bones on a hand.

"That woman from Missouri looked at me twice. Twice." Nana opened the cabinet and ran her hand down the pickle jar stuffed with wads of cash.

"Nobody's looking at nothing. You need to sit down and rest your nerves."

Instead, Nana peeped outside of the back window. "I knew this would happen. I knew it. Only a matter of time."

"Woman, please. The only thing that will get people curious is the way you're carrying on." There was an edge to Poppy's voice. The same shrillness that I had heard the night Nana grabbed the butcher knife and cut her hair. A panicked warning that she was heading down a dangerous path and didn't know the way home.

She played with the buttons on the shirt Bonita had given her for Christmas, the one reserved for special occasions. Her green eyes held Poppy's gaze and then softened as they drifted down towards me.

Poppy switched on the TV just like always. The glow from the screen filled the room and comforted the same as a campfire.

"All this mess today has worn me slam out," Nana said stumbling to the back bed.

A diving contest in Acapulco played on the TV screen, and I wondered if Hoyt Franklin had ever made it that far south. Poppy's chin pointed straight up to the air conditioner, and each time he snored his Adam's apple disappeared under the skin.

Looking at the screen, I pictured the next episode of *Navigating the Nation*. Josh's smile would be so wide the gap from his missing tooth would be a black pit. He'd nod to the camera and then pull the sheet from the new steeple that his uncle had sought to destroy. Beau would stand behind him with one hand propped on the handle of the wheelchair, while Sister Delores led the group in praise songs. They would be stars and life in New York City would be theirs for the asking. All because Nana had acted in a way fit for the Mama Roses of this world we missed it. Turning away from the TV, I flipped through a book that I decided was too young for me. The walls began to feel like iron bars, and the air conditioner overhead seemed more like a surveillance camera.

Keeping the door from squeaking was not as hard as preventing the natural sunlight from waking Poppy. Sun spread across his pasty face as the Adam's apple sunk deeper inside his throat. To be safe, I stood outside of the camper and heard the heat pop against the tin walls. The manager's cat paused to look at me before trotting away.

At the entrance of the campground, I fought the desire to turn left and join Hoyt in a cup of homemade ice cream as I outlined the details of our search of Alvin's cabin. As mad as I might be, I understood the fear that Nana had felt. The only difference was I had swatted it away as easy as a pestering gnat. So I turned right and tried to convince myself that Poppy would explain to Nana that a man needed time by himself.

Stacks of new crates were propped against the oak at Mama Rose's place. Pedaling faster, I looked straight down at the white line that separated the paved road from the ditch. "Beau Riley, is that you?" But by the time the words had found their way to the edge of the road, I was already too far ahead to turn back.

I rode along the path of the river. It snaked the corners of yards lined with plastic swimming pools and fishing boats. Pink flamingos, the type that Mama Rose sold in the spring collection, dotted the edge of the principal's house. Streamers of moss dangled from the branches of the oak trees as if even nature itself was celebrating Hoyt Franklin's arrival.

When I first approached town, it looked empty except for a hound. Her tits dangled inches above the sidewalk, and she wagged her tail as I drove by. The dime-store window was draped red, white, and blue.

It was not because of the motor home that I braked. I did not see it until the crowd moved to the side. It was Beau that caused me to break. He was laughing and throwing his head back like he really thought he was the king of the town. For a second I thought of pedaling faster and faster until my bicycle flag fluttered in a caution-light red. I pictured Beau hitting my handlebars and landing flat on the ground. As I edged closer, Beau saw me and waved before he could help it.

The top of Hoyt Franklin's safari hat was set high above the group. His deep voice and smooth tones were even more defined than they were through the TV speaker. "And that's when I knew that it was time to stay put in New York for a while. The streets of Manhattan were nothing compared to Marge Wheeler of Ridgeport, Michigan, and her twelve gauge."

Without laugh tracks, the crowd roared to life again. "I don't see how you keep all those names straight," the man who owned the dime store said.

"Good work if you can get it. And so, that leads me to the end of the road, ladies and gentlemen." Hoyt held up his hand even before the crowd moaned in disappointment. "All good things must end. So with that, I would like to get one last shot of this famous police station. The smallest in America, you say?"

"You won't find any tinier," the mayor called out.

Hoyt nodded, and the man with long sideburns inched backwards with the camera still strapped on his shoulder.

The camera made a clicking sound. The sound of a snake that is tired of being tricked. Edging away to the side of the phone booth, Hoyt Franklin looked right at me. "Hello again. Say, why don't you and the other boys get behind me with your bikes."

Beau almost tipped his bike over trying to line himself up with the camera. Hoyt propped his arm against the telephone booth, right next to the words "Police Station."

Clicking rang in my ear. It was as if a bomb had been tucked inside the lens and at any moment would explode without warning.

Beau licked his hand and ran it down the front of his hair. Through the corner of my eye, I saw Hoyt Franklin looking down at me. The piercing stare was more polished than his words.

Watching the moves of the small black lens, I edged to the far side of the group. Two boys pressed against Beau as if they were his girlfriends. But the clicking sound of the camera . . . tick, tick, tick . . . kept me playing hard to get.

"What is a community? Flesh and blood who come together to share experiences for a lifetime. Blacks and whites who share hard times as well as the good. Towns tucked away in the hidden parts of this country. These boys know community. And what they witnessed in Abbeville, Florida, today will be that of stories passed down for generations. Of flesh and blood. One white and the other black coming together to make a community that refused to give in to hate."

When Hoyt stepped aside, the cameraman got down on one knee as if he might propose to the phone booth. He slowly slid the camera towards the group. My heart beat as fast as the tick of his machine. Leaning away, I tried to lift my bike and make a run for it.

I heard the elastic rip in my shirt collar and then felt the material sag. A force was yanking me into the darkness of the lens. Beau was giggling as he looked into the camera and pulled my shirt all at the same time.

I kicked at his bike, but the only thing I hit was a cracked Coke bottle. Tick, tick, tick. The man's shoulder swung towards me and suddenly the darkness was peering right at me. My reflection in the glass was nothing but wide-eyed wonder. It did not show the dryness of my throat or the thumping in my chest. Tick, tick, tick. Little did I know how far that black hole would reach.

Thirteen

—◆—

The day of the Fourth of July celebration I awoke to the sound of aluminum wrap being folded into submission. Nana was pinned in the camper kitchen carefully wrapping the cupcakes she had made to sell at the booth for God's Hospital. A dim light the size of a pencil flashlight shone down on her, and even in the darkness I could make out her arm twitching.

She never even saw me slide down from the bunk bed and step towards her. Her robe with tiny purple flowers moved around the cramped space as if a hurricane had swept up a batch of wildflowers from a distant field. Her brow was deep with wrinkles once again. Soon she'd tear open a packet of BC powder and reach for a cup of water. It was a ritual I had seen played out every day of the past month. Worry left scars of white powdery medicine clinging to her lips like milk rings.

Before she could reach over and open the refrigerator door, I wrapped my arms around her waist. Her stomach molded into my touch as if it were stuffed with feathers.

Her flinch did not tear me away from trying to settle the storm that boiled inside of her. "I didn't hear you get up," she whispered.

For a second we just stood there against the music of Poppy's steady snore from the back of the camper. Her familiar smell of fresh soap and summer rain filled my head until I no longer cared if I was too old to be holding on to her this way. She squeezed my hands in a type of coded language that only I could understand. It's going to be fine. I'm just going to have to work through this concern about Cecil. There's no use worrying over it anymore. And with a pat she let go.

Later at the town celebration, the "Street Closed" sign stood directly in front of Main Street. A dunking booth built by 4-H members and card tables representing every good cause in town lined the sidewalks. The singing cowboys harmonized about Beulah Land down by the river, as citizens armed with candied apples meandered through the street like misguided ants. At the other end of the street grills were hitched to the backs of two trucks and chicken-flavored smoke cut into the air. A deputy stood guard over the police station. The afternoon sun cut flecks of gold through his hair as he took one last drag on a cigarette before pressing it out against the phone-booth door.

Poppy stood nearby with his hands tucked inside pockets and watched as Harvey lifted the gigantic grill cover. Harvey twirled the skewer stick as if he were a majorette, and soon flames shot up until the chicken pieces sizzled. With his new crutches, Josh barreled up right next to Harvey.

"Josh, is your mama and them coming?" Poppy asked.

Josh simply pointed a crutch at the truck behind us. Beau and Bonita had gathered lawn chairs out of the back and were trying to maneuver through the automobiles that lined the side streets.

"Hey, lady. Let us help you out," Poppy said.

Bonita tried to laugh and grab an ice cooler that was slipping away from her. "Lord, please!"

Beau nervously looked at me and then back towards the crowd. I reached for one of the chairs, only to see him jerk it away.

"Is Parker coming?" Poppy asked.

"No. He had to work." Bonita's red hair shook with the complicated details. "Lord, I can't keep his schedule straight."

Bonita stopped in front of the drugstore and talked to two ladies selling leather bracelets with stamped names. But Beau trudged ahead with the chairs, making his way to the worst cause in town. Even though I couldn't make out the words from the distance, I could see Mama Rose's beaklike mouth moving as fast as a bird warning a hawk to keep away. She chose a red wig for the celebration and even had a sparkly American flag pinned to her rabbit coat. Just looking at the clump of brown fur that was wilted flat by the hammering sun caused a trickle of sweat to tickle my ear. I was just about to turn in the other direction when I was jolted by the touch of ice against my neck.

Alvin was holding three bottles with slivers of ice melting down the sides. "You want a cold one? I got a mess in the back of my truck."

The baggy sockets his eyes rested in were as ugly as pure sin. Instead, I looked down at the threads of torn jeans that tried to hide his military boots.

A woman with legs mapped with blue veins blocked me from being able to warn Sister Delores to move her stand down the street. She had enough problems without having to sell baked goods that Alvin might slip over and pepper with poison.

"Hey, baby. You looking for your grandma? She went down there for a drink."

I followed Sister Delores's point, and saw Nana standing at the soft-drink trailer. The concern that had trapped me when I first saw Alvin faded into relief. She was smiling and shaking her head to something Mrs. Rockingham, the head clerk at the Piggly Wiggly, was saying. Nana laughed right out loud and patted the back of her hair. Through the smoke that was drifting from the cooker I could not recall how long the virtuous braid had been. The nestlike clump of hair that had rested on the dining-room floor from days past was now nothing more than a skin she had shed in North Carolina.

A piece of paper broke my stare. "Here, Sister Delores." Josh was waving a piece of Mama Rose's construction paper in the air.

"What's this here?" Sister Delores held the paper as if it was laced with poison ink, and I tried to confirm the suspicion with a wink.

"It's my autograph. Mama Rose is selling them for a dime apiece, but you can have one free. Seeing as how you got me on the news and everything."

Sister Delores rolled her eyes and laughed that deep-gutted howl. "Now, here you go acting all grown like that brother of yours."

While Sister Delores clutched the paper to her chest and smiled as if Josh had delivered a million dollars, Alvin glared from across the street. Mama Rose was holding up a flag paperweight and shaking it right in front of his face, but he never looked away. The longer he watched us, the smaller his eyes seemed to become. He hadn't made it pass the stage before Beau caught up with him and together they headed towards the parking lot.

By the time the high school band began to play "America the Beautiful," I had already made it down the street twice. Standing on the edge of the gazebo down by the river, I surveyed the people below. A sea of heads connected the river and the town. It was only when I looked out over the parking lot that I began to sense something was not right within the family.

Parker's brown hat stood high above the others. The gold letters FHP reflected in the sun, and two other policemen walked alongside of him. They glided through the crowd and stood in front of Sister Delores's stand. The policeman who had been leaning against the telephone booth was now talking into a walkie-talkie. A patrol car and a white sedan pulled up at the edge of the street closest to me. Two men dressed in uniform and a white-haired woman got out. They forked their way through into the crowd just as a policeman got up on stage.

Alvin. They finally figured out it was him who burned the church. I leaped from the railing and didn't even feel the shock of hitting the ground. Running through the crowd, I only slowed down when my arm was caught by a wayward purse strap. By the time I got to the edge of Sister Delores's table, her mouth was gaped open.

"I wanted to tell you, Sister Delores, but he'd cut my tongue out. See, we saw the crosses in his shed that day."

She leaned against the table and never even noticed when a stack of wrapped brownies fell to the sidewalk. "Baby, you just stay here with me till this mess gets through with." Folds of her sticky underarm were like quicksand, keeping me from pulling away.

Parker's gun never was drawn. It was still locked on his hip as always. The crowd began to stare as Parker walked towards Mama Rose's stand. She saluted and said, "God bless America and the road patrol that keeps this place decent." But Parker and the two men had a mission greater than a town simpleton. Drifting through the groups and pass the parking lot where Alvin had slipped away, Parker kept his head held high. I pulled away wanting to tell Parker that Alvin had probably made it back to his home in the place called hell.

"Shh, now. Just stay right here with me," Sister Delores whispered.

Bonita jogged up to Parker, but his face never broke from the stone mask. As the crowd moved to follow Parker, Bonita ran back across the street to us.

"What in the world is going on around here?"

By the time Parker and the men reached the trailer that sold drinks, Nana was already chewing the ice from her cup. The two men that followed him stopped a distance away. When he touched her shoulder, pieces of ice scattered across the sidewalk.

Parker led her by the elbow as if she might be twenty years older and in need help crossing the street. By the time they had made it to the stand for God's Hospital, she was biting her lip. "See after my boy."

It wasn't supposed to happen this way. Not yet. Don't cry, I screamed inside my head. You cry, and they'll all see you. The tiny lens of the camera that Hoyt Franklin had brought to town could not have captured the details any better than my mind.

The woman with white streaks in her hair touched my arm and squatted down in front of me. "Hey, buddy. We're going to take you back to North Carolina now. This is all over, and your mom is waiting for you." Her words were slow and loud, the way a person might talk to the deaf.

The taste of waste filled my throat. Resisting the urge to punch the woman right on her crooked nose, I yelled as loud as I could. "I want to see them."

"I don't think we can do that, big guy."

"You better let me see them!" Even Sister Delores could not hold me at that point, and a fleck of spat hit the woman's arm.

"I'll walk with him over there if you need for me to." Sister Delores was nodding her head.

"We can't allow . . ."

"Listen, I know the head man down at Florida Highway Patrol. Honey, I think you just might want to make an exception." Bonita's hip was flung out to the side, and a red streak ran down her neck.

She walked in front of us directing the crowd, who stared like it was me, not Josh, who had an autograph to give away. "Go on, move over," Bonita yelled.

The smell of the cooker made me want to throw up all over the shoes of the people who lined the street. A salty taste tickled my tongue, and I knew that it was not the air but the taste of blood. Moving to clamp down on the other side of my lip, I once again ordered myself not to cry and prayed all the way to the car that Nana and Poppy would be dry-eyed as well.

Poppy was the first one we came to. The patrolman opened the car door, and he was sitting in the backseat with his hands tucked behind his back. The marina hat was twisted to the side, and his pointy chin trembled. "Son, don't you worry none. This will get cleared up when we get back home."

This is my home, I wanted to scream. But fearing any more attention, I looked down at the gravel parking lot and kicked a half-eaten chicken drumstick.

Sister Delores guided me like a blind person to the police car Nana sat in. The light inside the car made her seem even paler. She smiled as if I had just gotten home from a bike ride. "Hey, there. Now Sister Delores and Bonita are going to see after you while I'm away."

Sister Delores and Bonita harmonized behind me. "We sure are. Oh, yeah."

Nana sat with her hands tucked between her knees. The top of the handcuffs would have seemed less obvious if she had been a woman who wore bracelets. "Now you be a good boy. I don't want you studying about all this. No need to worry. You got a pile of people who love you and don't forget I'm at that the top of that list." When her voice broke, she turned to look out the window.

A white sedan pulled around in front of the cooker, and Harvey rested his wide hand on my shoulder. "You come from good people. Don't let nobody tell you no different."

Josh hobbled up as the woman with white hair was telling me how wonderful it would be to be back home again. "Mama, what's that lady doing with Brandon?" Bonita's words mingled together with the hushed whispers of the others who lined the car.

A crease on Sister Delores's forehead marked the spot where the Uncle Sam hat had been earlier during the celebration. "Baby, I found out where they taking you. Back up to Raleigh. Don't you worry none. Sister Delores sees after her flock, and you one of mine."

Her words were empty. I looked through the crowd to see if Jesus was among them. He could take me out of all this and unlock those chains on Nana and Poppy all at the same time. But the only faces I saw were those of tired, fakey smiles that had pretended to connect with me. Me, a poor boy stolen from a good and decent mama.

It was a movie, I told myself. A rehearsal for the role I would play on Hoyt Franklin's TV show. Everybody in town had jumped at the chance to be an extra. Repeating the assurance helped my hands not to shake as bad.

"Brandon, you be good, hear." Bonita's scrunched-up eyes filled with tears, and she backed away with the others.

A man with hair the color of tomatoes got in the driver's seat. Said his name was Tony and called me "buddy" just like the woman did. "Hey, buddy, we'll stop off and get us supper. Anywhere you like."

·Tony had just pulled the gearshift when a hand with dirty fingernails and a fresh blister snaked through the small space in the window. Beau tried to smile real big, but it ended up lopsided like all the others. I shook his hand and glanced over at the woman who sat next to me. She patted my arm. A pull between the old way of living and what was yet to come. Finally, Beau's fingers slipped through my hand

and disappeared for good. The woman reached over and rolled up the window just as Mama Rose moved closer. "I knew that boy was trouble the first time I laid . . ." The window sealed off her last comment, but she still pointed the clawlike finger as the car moved forward.

Tony drove slowly as the faces I had come to know through God's Hospital and Main Street drifted together as easy as the changing tide. Beau ran along the side of the car waving and waving. But I did not wave back. It was a matter of survival more than shame. I kept my hands tightly latched between the slick seat and the flesh of my bare legs. They twitched with fever force, and I knew if the woman next to me saw how scared I really was, she would baby me the whole way back to my past.

Climbing to the top of the bridge, the car shifted into overdrive. The special kingdom filled with my own subjects of crabs, saw grass, and pine trees was far below us. Trying to gather it into a postcard memory, my eyes scanned it all. Before I could make out the roof of Nap's Corner, we had glided down the bridge and were on our way back to the place the woman called home.

Fourteen

By the time we got back to North Carolina, the lights from the homes just beyond the interstate flickered like a dying fire. Pressing my head against the car window, the glass was cool to my skin, but it didn't bother me. As soon as we had crossed over the Georgia line, my body felt like it had already shut down. I saw my blood being pumped by the heart, a memory branded in my mind from all of the old black-and-white science films that Miss Travick had shown us. But now I saw my blood as cold slush, like the Icees I used to buy at the gas station back in Abbeville.

I watched the soft lights of Raleigh pass by us with one eye closed. The eye closest to the woman with white hair had remained shut as soon as we crossed over into Georgia. When we passed through Jacksonville, she came clean and told me she was a mind doctor sent to help me deal with everything that was happening. But before we had made it to Tallahassee, I had already figured that out. They all had that smile and carried a bag full of questions: "How do you feel about leaving Abbeville? How do you feel about your mother finding you?" By the time we had passed the fifth Stuckey's restaurant, I stretched out my arms wide, yawned right in her face, and leaned against the car window.

The car blinker ticked, and I measured it against the beat of my heart. We turned off onto a side street in Raleigh. The houses were still and dark as a ghost town. A yellow porch light cast an eerie glow over the driveway we turned into. The car headlights hit the windows of the brick house, and a motion inside made the sheer drapes dance against the glass.

A woman with a black hair net and legs shaped like oversized marshmallows stood at the door. She clutched the top of her robe, and I closed both eyes when the mind doctor leaned towards me. They tried to shake me, gentle at first and then harder. When the inside car light came on, I kept my eyes sealed tight and tried to hold my breath. Maybe they would think I was dead. Tony, the driver, lifted me out of the car and carried me right into the house.

Cracking an eye, I made out a plastic-covered sofa with printed roses. Torn places on a lampshade fanned with the movement in the room. The sofa made a crinkling sound when Tony put me on it. Soon a pillow was tucked under my head, and a blanket fell over my legs. Mumbled words intertwined with the squeaking hinges of the front door.

"I'll come back to check on him tomorrow," the mind doctor said. "Here's the information we discussed."

Papers rattled, and a coo-coo clock chimed.

"Let's see, his name is Bobby?" the woman with the hair net asked.

"Brandon," Tony and the woman doctor said at the same time.

"Brandon," the other woman repeated. "Well, he'll be happy here. The children will make him feel right at home."

The door closed and locks clicked. I kept my eyes closed until I heard the woman's feet shuffle against a plastic runner down the hall. Light seeped in from the streetlight, illuminating a painting of a beach. The waves broke at the shore, and two seagulls hung in mid-flight. I stared at the painting, fighting hard against the temptation to blink. Never leaving the sofa, I finally tasted the salt of the air and heard the waves crashing. I wiggled my toes hoping to feel the grit of the sand between them. Soon the waves began moving, and the seagulls were dipping and soaring against the wind. The painting became a TV screen of wishful thinking. Suddenly Nana was at the end of the beach with the plastic bonnet on her head. She held the strings to the bonnet with one hand and waved with the other. Poppy walked up behind her and held up a piece of driftwood that had found its way back to shore. As I clutched the picture in my mind, the waves pulled away the emptiness that weighed down my chest. The sound of the tide rose and sank until sleep took me away from it all.

The sound of pots rattling from the kitchen woke me, but I kept my eyes closed hoping to avoid the people in my new home. Sweat from the night's sleep made the plastic-covered sofa cold to the touch. Relieved that it was only sweat and not one of the old accidents, I knew then why the big-legged woman kept it covered.

In the car the mind doctor told me that the woman who ran the place was a Foster mother. But I was determined that the woman with big legs and the hair net could be Foster's mother all she wanted, but she would never be mine.

She was in the kitchen humming a song. The sounds of butter sizzling in a frying pan and a refrigerator door opening drifted into the foyer. Try as I might to fight it, the smell of melting butter managed to make my mouth water. I was just about to give in when the sensation of eyes looking down at me ate up any hunger I had. I could feel the heat of their bodies as much as I felt their stares. Their eyes sizzled on me the same way I pictured the butter melting in the frying pan.

Trying to peek at them, I heard the one closest to me speak first. "We see your eyes a-fluttering. You're awake." At first only one giggled, and then two others joined in.

A girl with stringy brown hair and freckles on her nose pulled down at her shirt and laughed harder.

"If you knew I was awake, then how come you were leaning over me?"

Two boys with crew cuts and matching T-shirts looked under the sofa and around the side of the corner table. "Why don't you have a suitcase? They always bring some clothes."

"Because he's jailbait."

A bigger boy with a stomach so low that it made me think of men who walked the streets of Abbeville came into the room. His fiery red hair matched the heat of his words. "The police brought him in here last night. They carried him in like some retard all bundled up in that baby blanket."

"What you been in jail for?" one of the twin boys asked.

They all moved forward and widened their eyes, scanning the length of my body as though I was a mannequin on display at Mama Rose's stand.

"Nothing much."

The big one rubbed the tip of his elbow. Flakes of dead skin fell to the sofa while he tried to flex a muscle. "Son, you better tell us or I'm fixing to nail you but good."

"I said nothing much. Just this thing about cutting a boy's tongue out."

"What?" the girl asked.

"Un-huh. You're lying," the bigger one said.

"That's why they had me all wrapped up last night. I get these spells that make me jerk all over. If I don't get to my medicine, they get real bad. Like that time this boy in school got to picking at me. I started jerking all over and reached for my pocketknife. It was like watching a movie, you know, but I was the one playing in it. I just walked right over while he was laughing and cut his tongue clean off." I held up my index finger and showed the scar left by a wayward hook from a fishing trip with Poppy.

"This scar is from him near biting my finger off. When he did that I went real crazy then. My legs went to flopping around like a puppet or something. And before the teacher could get a hold of me, I put my knife right in the middle of his rib cage. Blood went flying all over the place. They had to call in extra janitors from other schools just to clean it up." I stared straight ahead at the painting meant to bring peace and twisted my jaw. "Those pills usually keep me calmed down. That's why they put me in here last night, in case I went crazy and killed one of y'all."

The girls slid to the edge of the wall, but the redhead stood his ground. "You're making that up."

"You'll see. All kinds of mind doctors are coming to see me. Ask one of them if you don't believe me."

"I'm gonna ask Miss Madelyn," he said.

"Go on, but you think she knows? Last night I heard the doctors say they weren't gonna tell her and get her all nervous. But right before they closed the door, they did tell her to keep that butcher knife locked up." I sat staring at the scene of the ocean and jerked my shoulder up to my neck.

The twins darted out of the room first, followed by the girl. Just before he left, the older one lifted up his leg and farted. "That right there is what I think of you and your story." But as he left, he walked out backwards. His eyes remained on me until he bumped into a shelf stacked with angel figurines.

"Quit your roughhousing, Pete," the woman called out from the kitchen.

"Yes, Miss Madelyn."

For good measure I jerked again before he skipped into the kitchen. My eyes never left the painted beach or the tiny seagulls that hung over the water.

The woman with the black hair net came and got me for breakfast. She tried to smile and told me her name was Miss Madelyn. I didn't tell her that the others had already given it away.

We sat on dinette chairs covered with daisy-printed plastic. Miss Madelyn made the others say their names with mouths full of scrambled eggs and bacon. Charlie and Caleb were the twins, and Trudy was the little girl's name. The fat boy mumbled his name in such a way that I would have never guessed it if I hadn't already heard Miss Madelyn call him Pete. I glanced up as they chatted about a new cartoon that was coming on TV. Their eyes circled me like pestering houseflies that never land. I tried to ignore them right down to their names. The least I knew about them the better off I'd be. Besides, I had more to worry about than some new cartoon character. My grandparents sat in jail for a crime that I had caused them to commit. It was up to me to get them out.

• • •

A week after the mind doctor stopped by again to assure me everything would be fine and that I would be back with my mama in no
time flat, the real help came. She stood at the door that was outlined
with wrought iron.

"Can I help you?" Miss Madelyn was wiping her hands on the
dishrag. Even while watching from the kitchen, I could make out the
tall turban through the screen door. The purple stack of material rose
up over Miss Madelyn like the point of a new crayon.

"Yes, my name is Nairobi Touchton, with the Child Advocacy
Network. Brandon Willard is my client. Social Services said they were
going to notify you . . ."

"Oh, yeah. Well . . . come on in, I guess."

Even though I knew she was my only chance, my last chance, my
legs froze. The shame of what we had done settled on me.

"Bran-don," Miss Madelyn yelled.

The steady sound from the coo-coo clock was all I heard.

"Bran-don. Let me see where he is." Miss Madelyn hadn't made it
ten steps when she found me standing by the refrigerator. "Didn't you
hear me calling you? There's some woman in there to see you. Now
go on and talk with her."

With a slight shove by Miss Madelyn, I was in Nairobi's presence
again. She stayed seated on the edge of the sofa. Her back was as rigid
as her smile was warm.

"Long time, no see," she said.

I turned to Miss Madelyn for guidance, but she had already
made it back to the kitchen and was pulling canned goods from the
shelves. All I could do was nod and look down at her buckled
shoes.

"You've been missed."

Her words were soft and hurt worse than if she would have
screamed them at me. I put my hands in my pants pockets and pressed
the edge of my shoe into the carpet.

"Everyone has been asking about you."

"Who?"

"Everyone at the Advocacy center for starters. And Senator Strickland. She asked about you just the other day. You remember her?"

"The woman with the bright yellow hair."

She laughed right out loud. "Yes, hair the color of daisies."

The coo-coo clock chimed three times. As soon as the bird had disappeared again, she spoke. "Brandon, we need to have a talk."

When I looked up, her eyes were as inviting as blackberries warmed by the sun. For a second I wanted to run and hug her neck. To break free and cry real hard. Then the sound from the TV made me come to my senses. Pete and the others would be in the room in no time flat if they heard me break down. And long after Nairobi was back behind her desk, the moment would forever seal my fate at Miss Madelyn's house.

"I'm sorry, okay. We should've stayed but . . ."

"You don't have to explain anything. I'm your friend."

The sound of dishes being stacked rang out from the kitchen. Moving closer, I could smell the sweetness of her skin. "What did they do with Nana and Poppy?"

"You know, I have a philosophy. Children are simply growing adults. So I won't lie to you. They're being held, and they'll face a trial."

"What about somebody buying them out like they do on TV?"

"That's called a bond."

"My Uncle Cecil can get them out. He can go down to the bank and . . ."

Nairobi put her finger to my lips. "I tried to contact your uncle." She looked down at the tiny ceramic dogs that lined the coffee table. "Brandon . . . I don't want you to worry when I tell you this, but your uncle was injured at work and now . . ."

"What happened?" I moved to the edge of the sofa, and the vision of us standing at the pay phone in Abbeville trying to reach Uncle Cecil swept over me.

"A bulldozer he was driving flipped and pinned . . . Look, it's not good for you to dwell on this. The point is that I called and spoke with his wife."

"I want to call him." I jumped up from the sofa. "He can sell something. Write a check or something."

"Brandon, please. Let's just first talk about . . ."

"I want to call him. I'll do it whether you let me or not. She's got a phone right in that kitchen, and I can use it anytime I want to."

Nairobi gazed down at the alphabetized blocks that one of the twins had left scattered on the floor. "Brandon, I truly want to help you."

Her words were empty, and I pointed right at her chest. "Then make him help us. I know he can!"

Nairobi grabbed my arm. "Your uncle is paralyzed."

The plastic was still warm when I leaned against it. The picture on the wall in Nana's house was the only thing my mind would let me see. The one of Uncle Cecil dressed in a uniform, hunched above the ground with his fingertips touching the field and his football helmet at his feet. Ready to leap forward to protect and defend.

"Look, I did not intend to go into all of this. He is at home with your aunt. He's resting. Simply resting in a deep sleep. Now, promise you will not take your uncle on as another worry."

Worry. Nairobi's words were just like all the others. A tag line that brushed against my skin, but never entered the pores of my soul. I stared once again at the beach painting, but all I saw were dabs of paint. "Did you tell Aunt Loraine about me being over here?"

Nairobi exhaled real loud and said the word "yes" at the same time.

"Can I go stay over there? Just until . . ."

"Well, you know she has a big commitment taking care of your uncle. A lawsuit has been filed. She said she doesn't even have enough time for her own children right now."

We sat in silence. I wondered if she was waiting for me to deliver the next line. But there was none to offer. While she kept her hands clutched on the lap of her purple dress, I used the tip of my shoe to knock over one of the alphabet blocks. The letter W stared back at me.

The next day the woman from Social Services came by. It was the same woman who had first tried to get me reacquainted with Mama before we took off to Abbeville. She reviewed the questions for me with one hand on the edge of her cat-eye glasses and the other positioned on the clipboard. Miss Madelyn sat on the chair shaped like a queen's throne, the one piece of furniture not covered in plastic and forbidden to be touched.

"Your mother is so very pleased to have you back in town," the government woman said and then grinned the way she did after completing all of her sentences.

"We're sure gonna miss him, but we know how much he is looking forward to having his own mama back," Miss Madelyn said and crossed her ankles. Wads of skin bunched up over the tops of her shoes.

"Now, young man, do you have any questions for me before I send in this report?"

Turning to the woman, I looked at the tiny pearl chain that clamped on to her glasses. "When I can see Nana and Poppy?"

The smile slowly sank into pursed lips, and she flipped through the pages on the clipboard. "Now, that is not healthy. Just not healthy in the least."

Miss Madelyn shook her head. "No, not a bit."

The woman cut her eyes at the throne-shaped chair, and Miss Madelyn stopped moving her head. "Now do you even know how many young people I deal with on a daily basis? Well, it would just boggle the mind. But you're a smart one. I can tell. And a smart boy would look at this as a second chance. You and your mother have had some rough spots along the way, but that's in the past. The only thing missing in her life is you. And I know you feel the same way whether you know it right now or not."

Miss Madelyn cleared her throat. "You're blessed, Brandon. Not all of the boys and girls who come through my door get to go back with their mamas."

Later that afternoon while Pete, Trudy, and the twins ran through the water sprinkler in the backyard, I sat on the iron chair on the flat piece of concrete that Miss Madelyn called a front porch. Clips from Miss Madelyn's afternoon TV stories drifted from the open window.

The dog at the end of the street started barking just as the announcer on the TV inside declared that *Guiding Light* was coming on. He was a stumpy mix breed that the man kept chained to a tree, a sight that caused Miss Madelyn to shake her head and mumble "white trash" each time we drove by.

With his front paws raised in the air, the dog kept barking towards the end of the street. Barking and circling the water pipe that secured his chain. The wide cedar at the corner of Miss Madelyn's yard kept me from seeing what was causing him to act up worse than usual.

Walking pass the cedar, I turned back to see Pete running wide open through a spray of water. Trudy and the twins lined up to follow him. I could see the back of Miss Madelyn's head from the window. Against the glow of the TV, the orange curlers on her head seemed to come to life in a spray of fire. When I passed the cedar tree that separated Miss Madelyn's house from her neighbor's, I began to feel that I was breaking out of prison and that any minute a man with a rifle would come hunt me down.

The dog reared up as I passed by the car that his owner kept on blocks. His focus was fixed on the green taxi just the other side of an open lot. When I moved closer, the taxi driver turned to look towards the backseat, and then the passenger door opened. Standing dead center in the middle of the street, I stared at the person waving her hand. It wasn't until she pulled her hat off that my heart skipped a beat.

A grease-stained grocery bag was clutched to Sister Delores's chest. She waved bigger as I pinched myself just to make sure it was real.

"Come over here, baby, and give me a hug. How you doing?"

The fried smell of Nap's Corner clung to her blouse, and I only pulled away when she grabbed my shoulders.

"Now, I told you, I'm gonna see after my flock. Didn't I say so? It took me a few weeks to get the money together, but I'm here now. Sister Delores keeps her word, baby."

My own words clung to the back of my throat, and I thought if I forced them to come out tears would follow.

"Baby, you look good. They been feeding you all right?"

I managed to only nod.

"We all been praying for you. Had a special prayer meeting the night y'all got hauled off. You feeling our prayers, baby?"

I choked on words and tasted the tears that slipped down to my lips.

She pulled me closer and rubbed my back. "Oh, I know it. Now don't you forget that the Good Lord knows about all this here. He sure does. He knows right where you are. He ain't forgot you, baby. That's how come He sent me here. Sure did. Sent me right on that Greyhound."

A utility truck drove pass, and we both turned as if a crime was being committed.

"That lawyer told me where you been staying. Said she wasn't supposed to, but you know I got it outta her. The night they hauled y'all off we didn't just pray, but we collected too. Even that man that owns the marina put in some money. I done took it up to that lawyer to help cover some of the bill."

"You saw Nana and Poppy?"

"Seen them this morning. Brought them both a pound cake that Bonita made. They're doing good, now don't you worry. 'Cause if you start worrying, then they gonna start worrying." She shook the wrinkled grocery bag. "Brought some of your things. They been giving you clean underwear?"

Each time I nodded, she would stare off towards Miss Madelyn's house. "You believe you can get this bag inside without them knowing who brought it? We don't need them all in our business."

"So what? I don't care if they know."

"Now don't start acting like that friend of yours, that little man. This ain't no time for that kinda attitude."

As we walked towards the cedar tree, the dog barked and his chain rattled. The chain stretched and jerked the same way I pictured my nerves behaving. Words that had been locked in a clamp of fear suddenly broke free. "Sister Delores, I know who burned the church."

She stopped and looked as if I had just scratched a scab off a wound that hadn't yet healed.

"When you said little man, that made me think of the whole thing again. It was Beau's uncle, Alvin. The one that lives over in Hagan's Hell. We saw a cross in his shed. The same kinda cross that was burned. I wanted to tell, but Beau . . . I just should've that's all. I'm sorry. I feel real bad and now with all this happening to Nana and Poppy."

Her eyes narrowed and the sight made me want to pull away. Just then she brushed the hair from my eyes. "Baby, don't you think about that no more. And don't start thinking God's punishing you for not telling me. Besides, it don't make no difference. The law wouldn't do nothing about it anyway. It's always the same ones. We just gotta pray for them is all."

The dog stopped barking when its owner came out of the house wearing a sleeveless T-shirt and camouflage pants. He stared at us for a second and then began dragging the water hose to the dog's bowl.

She leaned down and looked so deep into my eyes that I thought for a minute my soul might be pulled out of me. "You're hurting. I know it because I love you. And that grandmama and granddaddy loves you too. You got a whole bunch of people loving on you. Listen to me, now. Through all that love, that's how you know God's still here. Baby, no matter what the lawyer or the judge or anybody might do to you, God's not gonna leave you and He sure won't forsake you. He knows you by name, don't you forget it." As her face pulled away, I leaned up to kiss her cheek. Turning away, she stared at the man and his dog across the street. "We love each other. But, baby, you can't kiss me. Some people just don't see the world the way a child do."

When we got to the edge of the cedar, she handed me the grocery bag. "Now, I don't fool with good-bye. I'll see you again. If not in this world, then in the kingdom."

And she never did turn back. She just kept walking until her broad backside had reached the taxi. When I heard the engine crank, I took off like something gone wild. I had only made it to the corner of the neighbor's house before I saw her drive away in a blur of green paint. Without warning, the car turned down a side street and then slipped away for good.

Clutching the crinkled bag full of my possessions, I held on to it as if a piece of Nana and Poppy were tucked inside. The sun beat down upon me as hard as the heaviness of the moment. I moved to the side of the street seeking relief in the shade of the tree limbs. It was just for a little while, I tried to reassure myself. But my heart didn't pay any attention to my mind, and teardrops added new stains to the worn-out bag.

"Who was that, your mammy?"

Pete stood guard at the edge of the cedar tree. His belly button hung down over his swim trunks and jiggled when he laughed.

"Shut up, Pete." I fought the urge to wipe away the tearstains that were left on my cheek and hoped that if I lifted my head high enough, pieces of sun that seeped through the treetops would dry them.

The twins hid behind the cedar tree, peeping through the gapping limbs. Their giggles rolled down the street.

"Oh, look at the little girly baby crying over her mammy," Pete said.

"I ain't telling you again, fatso. Shut up!"

"We saw you hugging on her. Crying like a little baby. I was betting that you would go to nursing on her any minute." He poked out his lips and made a sucking sound that made the twins break into laughter.

The twins leaned lower on the cedar branches until the limbs sagged closer to the ground. Pete began rubbing his eyes and sucking air all at the same time. "Bran-don's a nig-ger lover," he began singing.

As if a dam of boiling water had broken, I began to feel my chest rise with each word he sang. I gripped the folded creases in the bag until the paper ripped. "Shut up!"

When Pete began circling around in some sort of dance, I saw his real face. The face of the man from Hagan's Hell. Alvin, the boy-man who had burned down the church. The one I had let slip by without saying so much as a word until it was too late. Just as he was turning back around to egg the twins on to more laugher, I felt my feet lift from the ground. My yell made him turn, and for a split second I saw a speck of fear in the brown eyes. He hadn't yet made it completely around when I slammed into his rib cage. The sucking sound of a nursing baby was changed into the sound of gasping for air. His belly was as soft as a trampoline, and for good measure I slammed my elbow into it twice before he hit the sidewalk. Another gasp let lose from his mouth as his head landed on the cement. My fist hit his nose until blood oozed like the ketchup he poured on corn dogs.

The twins screamed. "He's bleeding pure blood! Pure blood."

The grip on the back of my arm bit through the shirtsleeve as though a stinger had gotten me, but the black hair net covering orange curlers above me was madder than any hornet I knew of. Miss Madelyn arched her drawn-on eyebrows and screamed.

She tossed me aside and ordered the twins to help lift Pete. Streams of blood ran down his neck and his nose. He moaned as Miss Madelyn spread his red hair away to find the source of the flow. "I hope you're satisfied. You busted his head wide open. Liable to need stitches. You and your meanness."

One of the twins ran out of the house with a plastic garbage bag, and Miss Madelyn wrapped it around Pete's head like a mummy. Trudy was holding an ice pack and pretending to cry. They piled into Miss Madelyn's car the same way Poppy's pigs would line up for the trailer that took them to market. The car only stopped long enough for me to jump inside.

Trudy pinched me when I landed on the backseat, and the twins turned around to stare. Pete moaned for good measure, and Miss Madelyn kept a steady glare from the rearview mirror. Her eyebrows arched higher than usual. They all looked at me like eternal hell was just around the corner.

"It's a good thing your mama is coming to get you tomorrow or you'd be shipped off to the state home. It's a good thing for sure."

Fifteen

———◆———

A mist was in the air the day my mama arrived. She stood at Miss Madelyn's door with tiny drops of water clinging to her black hair. As much as I wanted to hate her at that moment, I felt a sense of pride. She wanted me, and that was more than I could say for the mothers of Pete, Trudy, and the twins.

When Miss Madelyn pulled the door open wider, Mama's eyes grew big and she pulled at the rain jacket.

"Bran-don," Miss Madelyn shouted.

Miss Madelyn grabbed at her dress collar when I stepped from behind the coat rack. "Oh, he's a regular little clown. We sure are gonna miss him."

The government woman with the pearl chain tied to cat-eye glasses stepped forward. "Today is a very special day for you. Your mother is tickled to have you back where you belong."

Mama looked over the woman's shoulder and winked.

The woman with the clipboard pulled my shoulder until I was standing face-to-face with Mama. Clutching the same torn bag that Sister Delores had given me, I smelled what was left of the scent from Nap's Corner and looked right into the eyes of my future.

Blue eye shadow made her lashes look like feathers on a blue jay. Tears puddled as she tried to laugh. "Well, can you give me a kiss?"

Feeling the stares from Miss Madelyn and the government

woman, I stepped into her arms and heard the women sigh. The perfume tempted me into believing she was as fresh as the scent.

She kissed me three times before I pulled away and pointed to the nearest distraction. A red sports car sat underneath the streetlight. "Is that yours?"

My mama laughed again and used her pinkie to dab the corners of her eyes. "Can't pull nothing on you, can I? Yeah, we bought it last month. Kane says that it will go sixty in two minutes." She looked up at the women. "Not that I've ever tried it or nothing. He just said it will is all. Kane, I mean. Oh, Kane is great. Brandon, you're gonna love Kane. He is so excited to meet you. He's got his own business fixing . . ."

His name floated around me, and I pushed it away. I ran to the car and looked inside at the white fur seats. The smell of cigarettes filled the car, and I jumped right in it like I was addicted to nicotine.

The government woman smiled at Miss Madelyn and then scribbled something on her clipboard. Miss Madelyn lined Pete, Trudy, and the twins on the concrete slab in front of her door. As we drove away, they all waved like they were riding on a float in the Thanksgiving Day parade. All except Pete, who wore a white patch on the back of his head to hide the souvenir I had left. When Miss Madelyn turned to say something to the government lady, Pete lifted his hand and gave me the finger.

Mama pointed to three eight-track tapes lined up on the dashboard and told me to pick the one I liked best. I picked the one with the picture of a woman sitting barefoot on a windowsill.

"Oooh, I love Carole King. She's so deep."

Watching her drive with one hand and slide the tape into the player with the other, I kept reminding myself what Sister Delores had said. I had more people who loved me than anybody else at Miss Madelyn's house. At the end of the street, I looked towards the vacant lot where the taxicab had sat. Mama tapped her finger to the music and leaned down to light a cigarette. She talked of new beginnings and a new apartment. A new job as a cashier down at Winn-Dixie. A good job with insurance and sick leave. All the while, I listened and never looked back as we turned left at the stop sign, the opposite direction from the one that the taxicab had taken.

Knotted rope the color of orange Kool-Aid held a small fern. It dangled from a hook by the front door of our new home. The duplex sat across the street from a gas station.

"Drinks and crackers anytime you want them. Just right across the street," Mama said. She stood at the door and clutched her hands the same way I'd seen Mary Madonna do in beauty pageants. When she reached for the paper bag, I pulled away.

"Well, come on in. This is our home. It's real nice. You're gonna be so surprised. I cleaned for three days fixing it up for you." Her words came out as a song as she ran ahead of me.

Gold shag carpet lined the living room, and big speakers sat in the corners. "That's Kane's stuff. He's all into electronics. Got his own business fixing TVs and stereos. Plays in a band too." She turned around to look at me, but I just kept walking towards the kitchen. "You want a snack? Some milk? Or a drink maybe? I can run right over across the street and get you one."

I shook my head and turned to walk down the tiny hallway. The smell of cigarettes and air freshener clung to the concrete walls. She skipped ahead and flipped on a light in the first bedroom. "Now, this is your room." She said it the way a game show host might announce a new refrigerator. A small bed, a red dresser, and a lamp decorated with Charlie Brown characters filled the space.

Dropping the bag on the bed, I began unpacking my things. Each one of them covered with the fingerprints of Nana. Sadness kept fluttering around as I fought hard to keep the smile on my face.

"You like it? I found this lamp down at the flea market last Saturday. They had a matching bedspread that I thought we could go back and get if you wanted to."

I nodded and pulled out a pair of underwear and hid them under a T-shirt.

She pushed the neatly piled clothes to the side and sat down on the bed. When she closed her eyes, some of the blue eye shadow flaked onto the bed. "Honey, I know things are hard right now. I know all this is . . . kinda weird I guess. But I really did want you back. I fought hard to get you, and I don't want to lose you ever again. I'm your mama. I need you." She used her pinkie to dab her eyes, and this time a tear broke free and rolled down her cheek. "Mama loves you."

"I love you too."

She grabbed me and squeezed real hard. "It's gonna work. It will, I mean it. All we got is each other and we'll show them. We'll show them all."

My arms wrapped tighter around her back until I could feel her spine. It was pointy and as fragile as the angel figurines that Miss Madelyn protected in her china cabinet. Objects too tiny to amount to much and too fragile to handle. I was like medicine to her soul, she had told me a long time ago. And with Mama addictions died hard.

The following weeks we fell into a routine, and it felt good. Mama enrolled me in the fourth grade down at the school. My new teacher, Mrs. Joplin, had so many wrinkles that her face looked like a crow's claw had gotten a hold of her. I sat in the last seat in the second row. Distant faces turned to look back at me that first day of school. I cared as much about knowing them as I had the kids at Miss Madelyn's house.

Each morning we'd pull into the school parking lot, and then I'd watch Mama drive away in her Winn-Dixie uniform. Whenever the kids congregated on the sidewalk would point at the red car and ask if she was my mama, I'd nod my head and enjoy the feeling that settled deep inside me. The sense of pride would sink so deep that sometimes it would push away the worry over Nana and Poppy.

Kane was better than I thought he'd be. He had reddish-colored hair and long sideburns like Elvis. The gray van he drove was stenciled with the words K. T. Electronics. K was for the part of the business that Kane owned. It didn't seem too bad having him live with us because most of the time he was out working. Mama claimed he worked harder than anybody she had ever known. I knew deep in my gut that nobody could work harder than Poppy.

The week of the October state fair Kane took off an entire day to take us to the fairgrounds. He competed with me to see who could knock the most milk bottles over, and I know he missed one of them on purpose so I could be the one to give Mama the stuffed bear. Walking by the rows of cows and pigs showcased by 4-H members, I felt the past hit me again. I breathed in deep while Kane pinched his nose and Mama laughed. A boy with a cowboy hat looked up at them and then back down at the speckled hog.

From a distance the landscape that framed the barn looked pretty. Tree limbs caught the sunlight in a way that made me wonder if they had been dipped in gold. Across the highway leaves twirled to entice me closer, but it was the bob-wire fence that made my legs go dead. At the end of the barn I could see the sign perfectly. A prison with miles of fence and wire to keep in the guilty and tall trees to keep the free satisfied.

"Hey, get a move on. We still got the monster Tilt-a-Wheel to ride." Kane glanced across the highway. "What's wrong?"

"Nothing. Hey, last one there's a rotten egg."

Mama squealed like one of the pigs as I flew pass her. My feet pounded the concrete slab harder and harder while the thud of Kane's boots trailed behind me. The boy with the cowboy hat stopped brushing the hog long enough to look up. Just another family enjoying the crisp October air and living free.

The usual crowd was just beginning to drive up for the Friday afternoon get-together at the duplex. Lynyrd Skynyrd blasted from the new speakers that Kane had bought. His business partner, Tony, set them up out back with the ice chests filled with beer Mama had bought with her employee discount. Tony had long black hair and girllike features. Maybe that's why he wore the skull tattoo on his right bicep.

Cheyenne, the girl from the end duplex, was the first one to see the uninvited guests. "Cool, it's Granny-D with pearl cat-eyes." She was pointing right at the government lady with the clipboard. Nairobi stood next to her and pulled at the pink wrap around her shoulders just as Cheyenne's cat drifted out of the front door.

Mama's eyes turned wild when she saw them. "Well, hey. We were just, uhh . . . It's Kane's birthday, so . . ."

"I left a message for you to call," the government lady said while adjusting her glasses.

"Well . . . uhh, now . . . I don't think I got it."

The group in the house kept moving outside through the kitchen door, and the music finally softened.

"It was left with the manager at Winn-Dixie. You are still working, Miss Willard?"

Mama flapped her hands like she wanted to take off in flight. "Oh, yes ma'am. Got a raise two weeks ago. I'm doing real good."

"She's doing great," Tony yelled from the back door. The girl with beads hanging down the side of her head leaned against the door frame and laughed until the government woman glared.

"Miss Willard, may we speak in private?"

When they slipped out of the front door, Kane tried to pull me back, but I brushed his hands from my shirt. Peeking through the crack in the door, I watched Cheyenne's cat circle around the porch railing.

"Miss Willard, we need to discuss your parents. As you know they've been sentenced and, well, before they go away they're asking to see the boy."

"No way," Mama said.

"I can understand how you must feel. But please, Miss Willard, this is not about whether you three agree or not. This is about Brandon," Nairobi said.

"Right here is where he belongs." Mama put her hands in blue-jean pockets and bowed out her hip. "Do you even know how much they put me through by running away with my boy?"

"I know it was difficult," Nairobi said.

"No, shug, you don't know. You ever had your natural-born intestines pulled out? Huh?"

The government woman played with the pearls on the chain. "Miss Willard, really."

"Well, I'm so sorry. I've towed the line on ever single thing y'all told me to. Hadn't I? I said, hadn't I?"

"Yes, you've progressed satisfactorily. Now, no need to get so excited."

Nairobi cleared her throat. "With all due respect, Miss Willard, this is not about you. Have you asked Brandon if he wants to see them?"

"Give me a break. All that brainwashing they did to him. He don't know what to think."

"My question was have you asked?"

The government lady clicked her tongue and looked at Nairobi. She then touched Mama's arm. "You have done well with him so far. We don't want to push you now. You just think about this."

Nairobi stepped closer. "This is just a chance for him to see . . ."

"This is just a chance to see if you think he's up to it," the government woman said without looking away from Mama.

"I just don't. Not right now. Maybe later. Hey, listen I know we have check-up time and everything, but one wasn't booked today. I got people over for Kane's birthday, so . . ."

Before the government woman could turn around, Nairobi had already opened the front door. I hoped she had not noticed the way I jumped backwards when the door swung open. The pink lipstick matched the material she wore around her head. "Brandon. How are you?"

Before I could speak, Mama and the government woman were standing behind her like two guard dogs ready to leap at the first syllable of the wrong question.

"You're looking good. How's school?"

"Fine."

She glanced behind her. Smiling, Nairobi winked at me. "Time for us to go, I see. But I'd like to talk with you again."

Mama trailed behind them as they walked towards the official blue sedan. Words describing the fun we had had at the fair were offered even after the car doors had slammed. I met her back at the porch, and she brushed the hair from my eyes. "Nobody's ever gonna hurt us again."

When she pranced back inside and cranked the music up, I smiled. She bit her lip, closed her eyes, and acted like she was playing an electric guitar. She liked it when I laughed, so I did that too. Soon the crowd circled us again. Their cups bent, and beer fell like waterfalls. Don't worry, I told myself. It's the same color as the carpet. We won't get in trouble with the landlord.

Later that night after I had fallen asleep on the couch, Kane carried me to bed. The smell from the bonfire Tony had built clung to his shirt.

A bottle being broken jarred me out of sleep. Characters from the Peanuts lamp looked blue in the darkness. They lined the lamp like dummies in a store window.

Stillness had swept over the duplex, and only the sound of crickets and a barking dog let me know anybody else was up. I lay still and listened to them chirp and bark in some sort of song. My heart pushed against my chest until finally I gave in and breathed. Staring up at the glow-in-the-dark stars that Mama had taped to my ceiling, I thought of Uncle Cecil. I dug my nails into the sheet and fought hard not to move one inch of my being. I pictured him laid out on the couch of their trailer, listening to whatever the others had playing on TV. The next time I thought I heard a glass break, I jumped.

The smell of the bonfire had found its way down the hallway. Mama's door was partly open, and I pushed it with my toe. The comforter we found at the flea market dangled at the end of the bed. Her teased hair looked like the end of a mop that had been painted black and propped on top of a pillow. Kane snored with one leg thrown over Mama.

Empty beer cans and paper cups were scattered across the living room. Hamburger buns and clumps of coleslaw remained on the kitchen counter as if more guests were expected. When I sat down in front of the TV, the carpet was damp, but the glow from the screen was warm. With an adjustment of the antenna Lucy came into view. I laughed right along with the audience until my mouth felt dry from the effort.

Turning to go into the kitchen, I jumped when I saw Him as plain as daylight. Leaning against the stove, He had his arms folded like a wayward guest who had roamed in after the bonfire died. Just standing right there smiling at me as easy as He had in front of God's Hospital. Laughter from the TV grew weaker as I looked into the eyes. The same deep-set eyes that had been painted on the funeral fan back in Abbeville now radiated right into my nerves. Standing there looking up at Him, I felt the embrace of Nana wrap around me. Soft edges of her underarms and scratchy patches of dry flesh were light against my bare shoulders.

"What the hell are you doing? It's four-thirty in the morning." Mama played with the collar of her T-shirt. The side of her hair was matted to the scalp and the other side stood straight out at attention.

All I could do was point at the stove. "Jesus."

"Watch your mouth," Mama said and reached for a pack of cigarettes. "You had a bad dream or something?"

The words swirled in my mind but never did come out of my mouth. I stared at the black scratch mark on the side of the stove next to where He had stood.

"You still like Lucy, huh?" With her cigarette Mama pointed at the TV and giggled. When she stretched out on the couch, she patted the space in front of her. The charred smell of the bonfire lingered in her hair. The ends tickled my neck when she kissed the top of my head. All the while my eyes never left the kitchen, and the warmth never left me.

"You remember how we used to watch TV on Saturday mornings? You'd eat Pop-Tarts and lean up against me with your head on my chest. You always did have the thickest hair. The one good thing you got from . . . anyway, you remember?"

I stared at the kitchen and nodded.

"It was just me and you then. You know, I miss it sometimes." She pulled up and looked me square in the eyes. "Quit looking off in the kitchen. You just had a bad dream is all. Listen, now. You know I love you. You know that, don't you?"

Nodding, I prayed that Jesus would come stand right in front of her too.

Leaning back against the sofa, she sighed. "You like Kane, don't you?"

"Yeah. You gonna marry him?"

Her laugh was deep, and she ended up coughing. "Well, I guess I ought to if you like him. About time you liked one I picked."

The TV glowed while Lucy held up the edge of her dress and stomped grapes in the wooden barrel. Mama laughed, and I decided that if she laughed one more time before the commercial I would ask her.

"Mama, if you marry Kane and we become a family, will we go spend Christmas and stuff at Uncle Cecil and Aunt Loraine's? And then go see Nana and Poppy . . ."

"Now don't start getting on my ass about all that." She leaned back up and ran her fingers through the side of hair that was still teased. "What, you don't want to be with me?"

"No. I just want to . . ."

"Brandon, cut me some slack. Why can't you just be happy with you and me like it used to be? Huh? Remember how we used to watch cartoons?"

She lay back down and pulled me closer. I could feel her pulse under the bony part of her chest. She rubbed my arm until the beat was steady again, all the while Lucy ran circles inside a barrel of grapes. Running, but not going anywhere.

The paper turkey wobbled in time with the circulating fan. The display that until yesterday had sat at the end of Mama's checkout line at

Winn-Dixie now stood guard over our kitchen. A real turkey snug in a tin plate rested next to the display. Band music from the Thanksgiving Day parade on TV competed with the electric guitars that flowed out of Kane's speakers. He ran around taking pictures of Mama preparing our meal. She had that wild look in her eyes that made one of them look bigger than the other.

"Smile," Kane said.

Mama sighed real hard and closed her eyes before a tense smile formed.

"Kane, is your mama and daddy coming over to eat with us?" I asked.

"Looks like we need more film."

When he turned to fish through a stack of paper sacks on the kitchen table, Mama stared right through me. She slowly shook her head as if to warn that a danger zone was ahead.

But none of Kane's blood family or ours, either one, showed up that Thanksgiving Day. Just the people that Mama called our new family. Cheyenne and her baby were the first to arrive. The baby, whose name I couldn't pronounce, wore Indian moccasins on her feet and tiny gold balls on her ears. She wobbled over to the TV and pitched face first into the beanbag. Cheyenne's voice roared louder than the music. Her laughter drifted around the room in currents that seemed to ease Mama's tense face.

Next, Tony came carrying a case of beer in one arm and a bag of ice in the other. The girl with him was somebody new. She used her knee to help balance a bag from the liquor store and closed the door all at the same time. Pieces of her frizzy hair stood out, and I wondered if it might be on account of Cheyenne's electricity. She had told Mama that electric fields were around her all the time. All I could imagine was the electric fence that Poppy put up at the farm to keep the hogs locked inside. As I watched our guests twined together in the kitchen, the thought made me wonder what had happened to the hogs back at the farm. Did Uncle Cecil take them to market before he got hurt and couldn't move his body?

A picture of us all gathered at Nana's table for the usual Sunday dinners flashed across my mind like the slide shows my teacher gave on life in Mexico. The vision put the usual pain inside my stomach, and I looked away at Cheyenne's baby. She was staring at me just like she could read my mind. A stream of drool slowly ran from her opened mouth, and she pointed over my shoulder. Turning to look, I saw nothing but the artificial tree that covered a hole in the wall. But she just kept staring. Her dark eyes were wide, and she twisted her mouth like she was about to say something. That she would speak right out loud and make them all know what I was really thinking. Before she could blink, I ran to the stereo and turned up the music. As I turned, my arm slammed into Tony. He jerked his arm up in the air, and the drink tumbled to the floor.

"Damn it," he yelled. "You blind or something?" His mouth twisted, and the skin around his eyes tightened. Laughter died, and music from the TV and stereo began to sound like sirens.

Mama was on her knees wiping up the drink with paper towels. The sweetness of liquor soon replaced the smell of the floral air freshener she had sprayed. "Brandon, watch where you're going, okay," she said. The words sounded weak and tiny rising from the floor.

The next day Kane was awake before I was. He sat in the kitchen smoking a cigarette and sipping coffee. As he riffled through the advertising section of the paper, there was an old-man way about him that made me think he could be one of Poppy's friends. "What you think about us going up to the mall and doing some Christmas shopping?" His words sounded like the Spanish my teacher would speak each time she showed the Mexico slides.

"Well yeah, but . . ."

"But what? You got other plans?" He flicked his cigarette in an empty beer can and laughed.

I didn't want to admit that Mama couldn't afford it. But it didn't matter. Mama's money was no good that day. Kane paid for everything including a walkie-talkie set for me. We walked around the mall laughing and eating from the box of popcorn that Mama had wanted.

She tried on clothes and even walked away with a pair of new shoes that Kane put in for her to have. Conversations bounced off of the mall ceiling to the beat of the water fountain. Anybody else might have thought it sounded like a crazy house, but to me the organized chaos was a release. That day we were just like the other groups who walked around checking off lists written on the backs of envelopes or in little notebooks. We were a family.

After lunch at a cafeteria with chandeliers, Kane and me sat on the bench next to the fountain dotted with good luck pennies. We could see Mama inside the store filing through the clothes on the rack. Kane kept making faces at her until she finally stuck her tongue out, and we laughed.

He leaned back and rubbed my head until the last bit of laughter was released. "You know, we're a family so I need to come clean about something. Yesterday you asked about my parents. Well, the truth is I hadn't talk to them in a while."

"They're dead?"

"Just in my mind. They've got money and everything. You know, always thought I should act and do things they wanted me to. I was never much for school. Not smart like you." Kane turned to look at me directly in the eyes. "Yeah, school's important. You keep on making good grades. But it just wasn't my thing. For a while I kept up with my mom. But then she didn't like . . . she didn't like some of the people I was messing with."

Striding out of Sears, she swung her blonde hair as if to tell the world she was on the premises. They gripped bags in both hands and laughed real loud. With each step they came closer to the fountain. The pug nose and frosted hair gave her away. It really was Aunt Loraine. Mary Madonna was looking up at her, talking and flapping her wrist around all at the same time. The once soothing fountain roared like a waterfall, and Kane's words of a lost home clapped in thunder. If they walked by and heard him, they would forever write Kane off as the same trash that his mama and daddy thought he was. Leaning down like Kane, I tucked my head and even tapped the tips of my fingers together. Maybe they would think that I was some little man. A midget talking to another old man about the weather and how women spent too much money on shopping.

The bags they carried ruffled against the legs of the people they passed. Aunt Loraine's perfume of wildflowers drifted ahead of them as a warning scent. I tucked my head lower until it must have seemed that I had dropped something under the bench. The taps of their shoes were as loud as the marching of a thousand troops. A giggle, light and airy like the way Mary Madonna used to laugh whenever we ran through the woods, tempted me to look up.

"What you finding under there? Somebody drop some money or something?"

I ignored Kane and kept staring at a lipstick-scarred cigarette butt resting at the foot of the bench.

"Hey, what is it man?"

When I slowly looked up, a woman with white pants so tight you could see the outline of her underwear was standing in front of us. She was staring at the mannequin in the store window across from us. Staring as if nothing at all had happened. Then the water from the small fountain behind us began to soften and the voices of the crowd grew lighter. "I just thought I saw something . . . something I lost."

In the distance, Mary Madonna's hair swung to the rhythm of the shopping bag that Aunt Loraine carried. I watched them grow farther away until they opened the big glass door and disappeared into the parking lot.

Sixteen

"All your ass does is sit around talking about work. Work, work, work. I get so sick and tired of hearing about that shit," Mama said. She reached for a pack of cigarettes just as Kane tried to squeeze her shoulder.

Tony straddled the kitchen chair and used his index fingers to play a drumbeat on the table. "Quit your bitching, Sophie. Today we grow from two trucks to three. Hey, we're a monopoly."

Kane tried to laugh and looked at Tony and then at Mama. She rolled her eyes and stormed off towards the front door.

I tried to block it and pointed to the TV. "Remember tonight's when Miss Kitty gets kidnapped on *Gunsmoke*."

"Brandon, not now, okay. I just gotta breathe."

The red tip of her cigarette led her like a tiny torch down to the duplex six doors away. Every time Mama went over to Cheyenne's, she would come back laughing all night. Wacky weed is what Kane called it. One time I saw them sucking up smoke inside a long tube that looked like a gun barrel the pilgrims used to carry. The first time I asked her about it, she said it was genuine medicine that people used to help them calm down. That was when I got nervous. Anything that helped settle nerves always ended up making Mama worse.

Sitting in front of the TV, I first tried to ignore the conversation Kane and Tony were having. But when the screen kept showing the jail with the keys to the cells hanging on an iron ring, I soon lost interest. No matter how many times I turned to look away, the vision of Poppy and Nana standing behind those black bars confronted me. Soon even loudmouth Tony was more appealing than the show.

"Man, we can do this, I'm telling you," Tony said. He took a long drag off of his cigarette and blew smoke over Kane's head. "We got the business. See, we get this truck and we'll be playing with the big boys. No more bullshit stuff."

Kane nodded and kept flipping through the bank papers. "If we get the loan."

"Man, please. You said your brother told you he'd help. We're set. Now's the time to hit him up."

"I don't know," Kane said.

"What's to know? He told you he'd help. Go ask him to co-sign." Tony took another drag and stared at Kane without even blinking.

Two commercials ran before either one of them spoke. Kane kept flipping through the papers like he might find the answer buried deep inside the loan application.

The day school let out for Christmas break, Mama came to pick me up with a Christmas tree tied to the top of the car. When she jumped out in her green uniform skirt, silver hair bow, and go-go boots, I felt proud. That moment, she looked just as good as the other mothers who circled the driveway to the school. Even the principal turned and looked.

As we drove away, I watched everyone stare as if we were secret agents. "How'd you get this tree on top of the car all by yourself?"

"Shug, when you got legs like mine, you can manage to get a man to do most anything. Besides, that little slow boy, you know the one who bags groceries, he's always wanting to help."

Her burst of energy did not end in the car. She ran around the duplex tossing silver strings like confetti. Icicles draped every piece of furniture we had, even the lamp and TV. There was a childlike innocence in the way she slung the strings in the air, and soon even I was tossing them at the tree. "Rock Around the Christmas Tree" blared from the speakers, and we both laughed when Mama hung icicles on the end of her silver hair bow.

She ripped open a new box of balls and handed me one to hang on the tree. "Hey, what about the lights?" I asked.

"You're always worrying about details," Mama said. "Let's just be free."

She reached inside a grocery bag and pulled out carvings for a nativity scene. "I got these down at the flea market. The man gave me these manger ornaments for only ten cents each." She held the tip of Mary and tried to wipe away a black stain from the figurine's face. The past that I was trying hard to forget appeared as easy as the smudge on the Virgin Mary's face. Various colored wise men lined up on the coffee table and could have just as well been at home on the roadside stand in front of Mama Rose's house back in Abbeville.

Pulling ornaments out of the shopping bag, I saw a box of cards tucked in the very bottom. Mama was still dancing with icicles clinging to her miniskirt. Her smile was warm and inviting, just like the smiles of all the other mothers at school. I held up the box and approached her. "You got cards too."

She never looked away from the tree and laughed. "We're gonna do it up right this year."

"Can I send some out?"

"Okay, go on over there and start working on your little cards. I'm gonna have this tree so covered in icicles that you're gonna think you're in the North Pole."

Stacks of mail and icicles covered the dinette table. In my best penmanship I carefully wrote a happy note to Nana and Poppy. The beginning of the last line, "I want you to be home real fast," was scratched out and rewritten. "We want you to be home real fast." Whether she knew it or not, I decided that Mama needed them too, but just hadn't figured it out yet.

Addressing the envelope was the hard part, and in all the excitement of tree decorating I let my guard down. "What prison is Poppy and Nana in?"

The happy music continued to fill the room, but the holiday spirit was sucked away. Mama stood with her back to me, holding an ornament. "Why?"

Trying to ignore her, I started working on the second card, a safe card, one to my teacher, Mrs. Joplin.

"Why, Brandon?"

Slipping down lower in the seat, I felt my heart begin to rev up. "I just thought I . . . uhh . . . we . . . could, you know, send them a card."

The sound of the ornament slamming into the wall caused me to sink lower. Pieces of red glass rested on the floor like a shattered eggshell. "Nothing's ever good enough for you. I bust my ass trying to get to the store and make this a special Christmas and you don't appreciate it."

"Mama, I do."

"No, you don't neither. All you want to do is sit there and think how much better life would be without me. Stuck off God knows where in some dumpy camper. They probably wouldn't even had room for a Christmas tree." She paced circles around the tree, snatching off icicles and ornaments. "Just forget the whole damn thing."

I pulled at her sleeve, but she jerked away.

"No matter how hard I try, nothing is ever good enough for you. Working my ass off to please you, but all you want is to be with them. You hate my guts. No matter what I do that'll never change. I'm just not gonna put up with this shit."

Trying to wrap my arms around her back, I yelled the words as loud as I could. "Mama, I love you. I do. Really."

"No, you don't. Don't nobody love me. You're just like the rest. I'm better off to just leave this place and never come back."

Her words stung worse than the needles on the tree, and the reflex caused me to kneel and beg. The slick vinyl of her boot slipped through my hands, and the bedroom door slammed.

The shag carpet brushed against my face. Lying on the floor, I looked down the hall and saw the gap between my Mama's bedroom door and heard her cries. There were pieces of her behind that door that I wanted to fix, but could never reach. Instead, I tried to clean up what was right in front of me.

Carefully, I put the pieces of the broken Christmas ball into the dustpan. The icicles were returned to their proper places on the tree. When I couldn't reach any higher, I pulled the dinette chair over and stood on it. Eye to eye with the golden-winged angel, I wished that God would make me one too. An angel who could fly off with Jesus. Maybe that was why He had come to see me to start with.

When Mama came out of the bedroom, her head was tucked and her makeup smeared in circles making her look like a spotted puppy. The words were slow, as if she were learning a new language. "Do you love me?"

It was my cue, and before I knew it my arms were back wrapped around her waist. "Mama, please don't go. I love you. Really now."

She halfway laughed and squeezed me extra hard. Then with the back of her hands, she smeared the makeup even worse. Sifting through the stack of eight-tracks, she stuck one into the stereo. Al Green's voice drifted across the room and she smiled again. Words from "Let's Stay Together" rose out from the speakers, and she waved her arms as if to welcome them in. With eyes closed, my mama mouthed the words like ointment was being applied to the scorches on her soul. Then right in the middle of the icicles that still littered the floor she reached for my hand. "It's about time your mama teaches you how to dance."

Even through the black smudges, her eyes were the color of blue snow cones. They glistened in a way that drew me closer until her breath was warm against the top of my head. Her hand was sticky as she placed her fingers in mine. I stood on the tip of her boots, and she led me in circles until I laughed again. She spun us around until the Christmas tree became a blur of silvery green. We just laughed and laughed until the past had spun away for good.

Seventeen

———◦◆◦———

The day after Christmas, Kane showed me the gift that would change everything. We stood outside the duplex next to the hot-water heater. Cold breezes clawed across our faces as Kane pulled the gold box from his coat pocket. Against the sun, the tiny diamond sparkled like a sliver of a star.

"You think she'll like it?" Kane asked.

All I could do was stare. The only other time a man had given Mama a diamond ring, it turned out to be a fake. It was from Roger, the husband who worked construction and raced stock cars. After their first fight, Mama had tried to scrape it down his car window to see if it was real and ended up with buckle scrapes down her back.

"It looks like we're going to have a double celebration New Year's Eve," Kane said. "Christening the new truck Tony and me got and giving Sophie this ring. I can tell this is going to be a good one."

The day the new van appeared all white and shiny with black lettering that read K. T. Electronics was the same day Tony handed Kane a new work schedule. Jobs piled up and so did Kane's hours. He would come home late and often leave before Mama had gotten up in the morning. Whenever Mama would complain, Kane would only mumble about having more bills to pay.

New Year's Eve was the big day, and just as Kane was moving the furniture out of the living room to make room for a dance floor, the phone rang. A man down in the rich section of town said his TV was on the blink. The man told Kane that Guy Lombardo was a tradition with his wife and that if Kane would come fix it on a holiday, there would be more work down the road.

"But the man manages Sears," Kane repeated to Mama. "He can give our names to everybody that buys a TV in that place." As Kane zipped up the navy jumper with his name stitched on the pocket, Mama stomped her foot.

"One damn night, Kane. Just one night we need you. You know, just forget it. Go. Go on and leave us. I don't even want to see your face." Before Kane could take a step towards her, she ran into the bathroom and locked the door. He sighed and thumped the ring of keys on his belt, the ring holding the key to the new van. The jingle of keys faded as he made his way out the door.

Even without Kane the usual crowd flowed into the duplex, and music began to jar the walls. Tony showed up with a bottle wrapped in a paper bag and kissed Cheyenne right on the lips. He ran his hand through his long black hair, and from the back anyone would have guessed that it belong to a witch.

Mama weaved through the guests sipping a beer. Her hair was teased up extra high, and she wore a purple choker necklace that kept sliding down. When she found me sitting on the edge of the sofa staring at the beer bottle, she rolled her eyes. "Damn, it's just beer. There's hardly any alcohol in this thing." Spinning around, she landed right up against Tony.

"Look at you, Miss Thing." She never pulled his hand away when he grabbed her thigh.

Everybody laughed when Tony stuck his finger in the cake that Kane had made for the party. I watched Tony take his slice and wipe it on the face of a guy with a peace symbol hanging from his neck. In the corner, I took a plate of cake and spat on it. Smearing the spat on the cake, I walked it over to Tony. "Here, Tony. Hurry up and eat it before he gets you back."

"Thanks, man." Tony took his finger and ran it through the icing. He never noticed that my shoulders rose a little higher.

When Cheyenne brought out the long pipe that looked like a pilgrim gun, a group of people headed back to my bedroom. Cheyenne pulled her baby from the room and sat her in front of me. "Keep an eye on her, kiddo."

The TV showed us the ballroom of a fancy hotel in New York. Guy Lombardo kept his band in line with the small white stick. Turning to look for Mama, I remembered that she was not with the group that followed Cheyenne into my bedroom. Nor was she standing in the kitchen passing a funnel of beer. I took Cheyenne's daughter by the hand, and we followed a trail of ashes down the hall to Mama's bedroom. There in the darkness, I saw their silhouette framed in the glow of the hall night-light. Tony was facing us with his arms wrapped around Mama. They were kissing as big as Dallas right in front of us. Before I could cover the eyes of the baby I was supposed to protect, Tony used his foot to slam the bedroom door.

Running to the living room, I threw a bowl of potato chips back into the bag.

"Hey, I'm munching on these things," a guy with kinky blond hair said.

"Time to go," I yelled.

They kept laughing as I yanked bowls from the table. A stack of napkins fell to the floor as paper plates were tossed into the pantry.

"Get out! Get out or I'll call the cops!"

I began shoving stomachs and arms in all sizes until their owners' laughter rang in my ears. When I felt myself being lifted from the floor, I kicked over the lamp. The guy with kinky hair kept looking back at the group in the kitchen. His arms gripped my elbows and ankles as he held me up over his head as if I was a sacrificial joke. I spat and jerked, but that only made him spin me faster. The people standing in my kitchen began to swim around, and a burning sensation crept up my chest.

"Put him down, asshole!" Kane's voice clipped the laughter of our guests. The guy tossed me on the sofa and brushed hair from his eyes.

"It's cool. Just having a little fun."

Kane only glanced at me before he knocked the kink right out of the guy's hair. The guy lay on the floor with a trickle of blood coming from his nose. The group in the kitchen moved closer to the back door when Kane slammed the ring of keys on the table. "Where the hell is Sophie?"

"She got one of those bad headaches and had to go lay down," I said.

Kane's jaw tightened, and I tried to hold his leg as he walked down the hall. "She's sleeping. Just sleeping."

Before I could pull his hand away from the bedroom door, he jerked it open. Screams pierced through the walls and in an instant slit a hole right into our future.

When it was all over, Tony ran out of the duplex with nothing more than his underwear on and blood running down his mouth. Mama sat in the bathroom crying like a kitten that was being weaned from its mother. The others had long scattered, and the stereo had already been knocked over. A crack ran down the cover that was supposed to protect the record player.

Kane had stopped on his way out the door long enough to shake his head at me and mumble, "Sorry." Pieces of his clothes littered the hallway like bread crumbs on a one-way journey.

Outside, the cold air stung my bare arms enough to remind me that life was still going on. I found the gold box sat right next to one of Kane's shirts. The diamond ring looked less bright underneath the sparkle of the stars. Picking up the clothes, I tried to think of a plan to get him back. I'd get Mama to go over to his parents' house and tell him she had really messed up by drinking beer. She could call him and tell him that we had his clothes. He would come back for his things. But then I remembered what he had told me about his family being rich, and no matter whether he had been talking to them or not, I knew they would welcome him back to where he belonged. Kane didn't need his clothes, or us either for that matter. He could buy more clothes, and he already had a family.

A smell that was stronger than the scent of spilled beer overtook me. When I looked up, Jesus stood right where Kane's van had left tire tracks. He held up His tanned arms and the edges of His sleeves flapped until I wanted to run and hold on to Him for good. As if she had been standing on the roof, Sister Delores's words fell down on me. *"The Lord will be your mama and your daddy. He won't leave you and He sure won't forsake you."* A tin can rolled with the wind down the street, and when I looked back, it was over. But this time the fresh smell that comes after a hard rain lingered, and the peace that had first found me at God's Hospital poured over me once again.

After Kane left, Mama stayed in bed for eleven days. She'd sip the chicken soup I made straight from my thermos. Cheyenne brought over a bag of groceries, and I kept up with my schoolwork as if life was the same as usual. But it was not the same. The big boss down at Winn-Dixie got tired of Mama's flu bug and laid her off on the eighth day. That's the day I heard Cheyenne tell Mama that Tony said he wanted to come over.

Backfires from a motorcycle let me know when Tony had arrived. From my bedroom I heard Mama speak broken words in that little-girl way that I thought she had forgotten. Tony kept coming over until soon Mama had learned the language all over again.

Life in the duplex with Tony made my nerves coil up like a spring ready to pop, but seven steps across the street, life at our new neighbors', the Pickerings, made it all smooth again. Mr. Pickering was only slightly larger than Mrs. Pickering, and both made crinkling sounds when they walked. Mr. Pickering talked about playing baseball in high school while Mrs. Pickering kept pound cake as moist as Nana's protected underneath tinfoil. The best part of being big for their daughters, Bethany and Destiny, was softball. They could knock a softball farther than any boy I had ever known. When Mr. Pickering took us down to the recreational park to sign up for the season, the coach first protested about having girls on a team designated for boys. But then Mr. Pickering pitched Bethany a ball and the crack of her bat made it soar pass the sign advertising cigarettes. "What'd you say your name was again?" the coach asked Bethany.

After softball practice, Mrs. Pickering would pick us up and then stop by McDonald's for french fries. When we pulled up to our duplex, a woman dressed in white boots was walking away. "You have the most company," Mrs. Pickering said. There was an edge to her voice that caused me to pull at the loose stitch in my glove.

"My mama sells Avon." Mrs. Pickering smiled and nodded like it made all the sense in the world.

The sweet smell of the merchandise engulfed me when I walked through the door. Mama was standing with her leg propped up on the barstool painting her toenails. "How was practice," she asked without looking up. I slammed my glove on the coffee table. A box of sandwich bags slid to the edge.

"What's the matter with you?"

"Nothing."

She motioned towards the table. "Go on and get you a drink. The money's on the table."

"Maybe I don't want a drink."

"Okay, then. Hey, I need you to stay in the back tonight. Tony said they're bringing a shipment in and I don't want you in . . ."

"I'm sick and tired of this! Sick of lying about you selling that stuff."

"Well, I guess you hate this roof over your head and the clothes on your back too. How's about that nice glove and that jersey I just had to pay for? You hate them too?"

I stared at the floor until her painted toes blurred into the color of the fiery hell I thought I'd face for lying.

"Look, I'm doing the best that I damn sure know how to do. And if you get to acting too uppity, I'll stop you from hanging out with those fat asses. They're probably making you think you're some do-gooder or something."

"They're nice people."

"Oh yeah, and I'm just a piece of trash. I forgot." Her blue eyes were lit brighter than the Christmas lights that still hung on the front porch.

"I didn't even say nothing," I said.

"You don't have to. Look, if you want to live with them so bad, then go for it. End up weighing three hundred pounds like them too. See if I care."

Tony began talking the minute he stepped through the front door. He pulled out the wacky weed from the grocery bag. "Okay, we gotta get moving here. Maurice is stopping by at eight to get everything moving. We need to call . . . Hey, get moving. You hearing me or not?"

Mama waved her hands in the air in such a way that I didn't know if she was still drying her nails or wanted Tony to hush.

Tony kicked the edge of my cleat. "What the hell's wrong with her? You talking back?"

I kept staring at his black cowboy boots. They were pointy at the ends and could corner a roach if he wanted to.

"I need her helping me tonight. Why don't you go spend the night with your girlfriends, Rotunda and Bigass."

Gripping the edge of the bat, I raised it over my shoulder. The steel was cold against the fire of my flesh. I aimed it right between his eyes and pictured the bat slamming into his slanted nose.

"Punk, you want some of me?" Tony pointed into his chest. "You want some of this?"

Mama stared from the kitchen and called my name three times before I breathed again. "Just go on over to the Pickerings, okay. Tell them I'm having one of my Avon parties."

Easing my grip, I drug the bat to my bedroom. Tony was still laughing when I tucked it underneath the edge of my mattress, the same place where Poppy used to hide his pistol.

Eighteen

———— ·•◆•· ————

The Child Advocacy Network letterhead was stamped with December 9 across the top. Written on stationery with charcoal drawings of children running down the side were Nairobi's words.

The letter was found by accident, folded in squares and tucked in the corner of Mama's dresser. Nairobi's precise voice rang in my ears as I read the last line: "Miss Willard, I urge you to think of the best thing for the sake of the child. Brandon needs to see his grandparents as much as they need to see him."

The picture of Nana and Poppy alone and cold in a prison cell flashed through my mind as did the guilt in knowing that they probably thought I did not want to see them.

Mama came home smiling and showing off all the new clothes she had bought for me. "Tony did real good on that run down to Myrtle Beach. He even said we could go next time and stay at one of those big motels right on the beach. You don't like this new shirt? Too bright?"

"I just had a bad day at practice. I don't feel good."

When she put her palm on my head, I fought the urge to bite a chunk of skin out of her hand. "You seem a little warm. Why don't you go lay down for a little while? You want a chili dog from Dairy Queen? I'll get us a milkshake too."

I tried to fake-yawn. "That'd be good."

Watching her drive away through the cracks in my bedroom blinds, I realized how Nana must have felt the day my mama drove away from the farm.

Weeks went by and the letter or my grandparents were never mentioned. Life at the duplex was just as we had rehearsed. Mama helped to fix bags of wacky weed, Tony made the deals, and I went to school and to softball practice.

"You sure it's okay to leave you here all by yourself?" the coach asked.

"Yes, sir. My mama knows about it. She's on her way to pick me up."

The coach pushed up the brim of his cap and then pulled away from the softball field with a load of my teammates in the back of his truck. The man from the recreational department nodded as he mowed the grass surrounding the bleachers. Nodding back like all of this was supposed to be happening, I climbed the steps to the highest point. Looking out over the tree limbs, I thought I could see the top of the big bank building. As high as I was, Mama was still nowhere in sight.

The letter kept pushing up to the front of my mind until I had scripted out every hateful thing I could say to her. She was unfit, just as a teacher had once whispered to my guidance counselor. The shrillness of her voice played out in my mind like it was coming from the loudspeaker overhead. Crickets began to sing, and soon the sun dipped away. Just when I had made it back down the bleachers and the vision of walking home seemed more like a reality, I heard the roar of her car. A cloud of gravel swept over it as she jumped out, pulling at her miniskirt. Biting my lip, I forced the anger to stay locked behind my eyes.

"Sorry. I got all tied up with an order, then had to run over to the beauty shop for some . . ."

"Shut up!"

She flinched as my voice echoed from the other side of the field.

"All you do is lie. Lie about selling Avon. Lie about being late. You lie about everything."

Her eyes widened, and she played with the ruffle on her blouse. "Damn, I mean I was late, but come on. I'm sorry, okay." She tried to bend down towards me, but I jumped up.

"Just like you're sorry you kept me from seeing Nana and Poppy!" The aluminum bleacher vibrated when I stomped my foot. "I told you I wanted to see them. I told you."

"What the hell?"

"You know what. I found that letter from Nairobi. They wanted to see me but you stopped it. I hate you!"

Tears were on my cheeks, and tears were natural enemies to Mama just like water was for the witch in *The Wizard of Oz*. She began to sink and bend forward to the point of breaking.

Her words were as soft as mine had been loud. "Hate me. I deserve it."

I ran up and down the bleachers, shouting and screaming. Nothing broke her faraway stare. She just sat there with her hands folded in her lap staring at the gap between the bleacher seats.

Crickets were singing, and lights from the nursing home across the field lit up. But Mama never came back on. She just sat there staring into the darkness. Coldness settled in the aluminum before either of us spoke.

"Let's just go home," I finally said. Like an obedient child, she followed me down each step. Her platform shoes clanked until we had made it to the last seat. Feeling guilty for telling her that I hated her, I turned to say something reassuring. But she had already slipped out of my reach. With a fling of her shoes, she raced up to the top bleacher.

"Come on, let's go. I'm hungry," I yelled up to her.

She reached for the railing and climbed on top of the last bleacher. With outstretched arms, she stood on the edge of the rail and looked straight out over the gravel parking lot.

Running around to the back of the bleachers where I could face her, I felt a chill snake down my neck. I looked up, trying to mask my fear with a plea. "Mama, quit playing. You're gonna get hurt."

A mascara-stained tear slid down her cheek, and edges of hair fluttered with the evening breeze. "You're just better off without me."

In the distance a siren sounded, and I prayed that the policeman would take a wrong turn and end up with us. "Mama, don't now. Come on down."

Her left arm wobbled when she stretched it out. "All I ever wanted is for you to love me. That's all I ever wanted in my entire life. But you don't."

"Mama, I do love you. Get down."

"No," she said. When she shook her head, the aluminum popped and her legs shook.

"Please, now. I promise. I really love you."

She began to cry harder and reached over for the edge of the beam. When her fingers slipped, she bowed forward. Her face was void of expression as she reached up to the stars and moaned.

A trail of urine snaked down my leg. "Mama!"

Aluminum rang out when she fell towards the seats. A flock of sparrows flew from beneath the bleacher in a fury that was as chaotic as my actions. Running up the steps two at a time, I wondered what I would do if she was really dead. Who would I call? Where would I end up?

Her leg was bent and a line of blood wove a path to her foot. Smeared makeup made her look like a car-wreck victim, and she screamed as I approached.

Kneeling, I pulled her head against my shoulder. "Mama, you're gonna be okay."

"I'm not okay. I'm awful!"

"No, you're not." No matter how many times I said the words, she never seemed to hear them.

"They were right. All of 'em." She gazed off in the distance just like she had done while standing on the back of the bleacher. "They were all right. They told me I shouldn't have had you." She traced her finger through the blood on her leg as if it was war paint and she was preparing for battle.

"At first Mama and Daddy wanted to send me away. Said it was for the best, but I wouldn't listen. I wanted my baby. And it wasn't my fault. I kept telling them that. It was not my fault." She leaned her head backwards as if trying to reach for the past.

"I told them it was that preacher's son. But he said I had this spirit thing and tricked his boy. He even made me go down to the front of the church and tell everybody how I'd acted. I decided if they wanted to hear the nasty details, then I'd tell every single bit of it. I still remember that man, that Brother Bailey, pinching my elbow and leading me out the door of his church. I kept waiting for somebody to stand up and do something. But Mama and Daddy just kept looking down at the floor. Just kept looking down. All I did was stand up there and tell the truth."

The blade of her words stripped away layers of make-believe that had filled the empty place in my being. Her breathing was deeper, and when she let out a scream, I wanted to run away for good.

"The next day my suitcase got packed. Daddy told me no whore was welcome in his house. Said it was for my own good and would make me straighten out. I still remember them standing there on that porch. They looked at me just like the people had in their church. My mama and daddy hated me that day. And me with nothing but a suit-case and a baby in my stomach. They stood right there on that porch not doing nothing."

She gripped my shirt harder and cried so deep that I thought some-thing inside of her had torn loose. Searching the lights of the nursing home across the field, I wondered if I should run and ask for help.

"When you were born, I was over in Charlotte working at Grady's place. After they cleaned you up, you kept the tightest grip on my fin-ger. Wouldn't let go of it even when that nurse tried to put you back in the nursery. Right then I knew you were all mine. Man, you held on to me. You held on to me for everything you were worth. But none of that seemed to matter to them. Mama kept telling me that it took more to raise a baby. So I tried to get fit. I married that bartender, a son of a bitch if I ever laid eyes on one. But you know none of that even really mattered because I had my baby boy. My baby kept holding on to me. You gripped my finger. I mean, you gripped real tight."

She turned and reached for my hand. Our fingers pressed together until the blood from her wound felt like paste. For the first time it all seemed real. She was not my sister or my friend or my child. At that moment Sophie Willard really was my mother.

During the following days my mind tried to shuffle the details as if they were trick cards stuck together. No matter how many times I tried to picture Nana and Poppy sending Mama away, I could not bring it into focus. Dissecting the details even cost me extra time at school. It happened when Mrs. Joplin called on me to answer a question during social studies. But I had more pressing things on my mind than the capital of Minnesota so I just kept staring off in the distance.

While I wrote "I will pay attention in class" one hundred times in detention hall, my mind kept coming back to that night at the softball field. To make order of it all, I gave passes to Nana and Poppy. It was Brother Bailey's fault. He probably had told them to kick her out. He made them do it just like he had made Nana write down how many times a day she prayed. Soon, the glue on the other cards began to sling free with a violent force. No matter how hard I tried to change the players on the cards, the reality was that my daddy was not a long lost businessman with a yacht and a fancy motorcycle. He owned a candy-red Firebird with black stripes down the side that stayed parked outside of Rock Creek Holiness Church. It was him. Murphy was my daddy. That meant Brother Bailey was my granddaddy. My fingers went numb, and the pencil tumbled to the floor. Picking it up, I erased a misspelling and at the same time tried to erase my past.

That night Tony left to make a delivery in Asheville. Usually I liked it when he was gone, but tonight I watched my mama like she was an unknown woman sent to take care of me. She stood at the stove poking a pork chop until the popping grease made her step away. When she caught me looking at her, she started laughing. "What? I got flour on my face or something?"

"No. I just was thinking."

"You know, you do too much of that. You gotta learn to be free." She raised the long metal fork in the air and laughed again.

Laughter was always a good time to slip in something important. "Hey, you said that Poppy was at church . . . you know, the night you know . . ."

Her laughter weakened down to a gargled cough.

"But Poppy never goes to church."

The grease popped, and she turned the pork chop over. "He used to go. Went all the time."

"When did he stop going?"

"After I left. Mama claimed he blamed everything on that Brother Bailey. Funny, he never said nothing to me about it. Listen, let's stop talking about all that." She stared into the bubbling grease as if it would tell her what to say next. "Now, I don't want you freaking out over all that stuff. You just gotta learn in life some things are better left dead."

"But I just want to know. Did Murphy ever know he was my dad . . ."

The fork slammed down on the skillet, and grease sloshed over the edge. "Damn it. Don't ever mention his name again. You understand me? Now look what you made me do. Grease all over the floor."

When she leaned down to clean up the mess, I slipped away to my bedroom. Trying to do homework, all I saw were miniature red cars in place of fractions. The car Murphy drove was my strongest memory of him. The only other thing that came to mind was the night I saw the girl from church sitting in the car. She was stripped down to her underwear. I guess like my mama had been. I slammed the book and turned on the radio. Turning the volume louder and louder until it was nothing more than garbled static.

The Beach Boys screamed through the transistor radio while I tried to hold on to my version of the past. Part of me wished I could have gone back to the night Mama climbed up to the top of the bleachers. Watching her fall to the ground might've been easier than having the truth land on top of me. With one hard slam, the radio hit the side of the wall, and batteries scattered across the floor.

Nineteen

———◆◆———

The night of the softball banquet, I stood in the Pickerings'
living room admiring the queenlike woman on my trophy.
Mr. Pickering passed by me and patted my shoulder again.
While Bethany and Destiny chomped on the jawbreakers the coach
had given us, I kept staring at the trophy.

Mrs. Pickering had to repeat her question twice before I took my
eyes away from the torch-bearing woman. "Why are so many cars
parading up and down the street tonight?"

"Avon party," I said. "That's how come Mama couldn't go to the
banquet."

My words were as stale as the nachos that Mrs. Pickering was
serving. Words not laced in disappointment, because I liked sitting
with the Pickerings at the banquet and making people think I was a
smaller version of them. Maybe people thought I was premature and
never got to be their size or maybe they had decided that I was a boy
rescued from some orphanage.

After the lights were all turned out and sleep had covered my
neighbors' duplex, I thought the steady chime was from a clock that
had gone haywire. When I turned over, the sharp edge of the trophy
scraped across my arm. I bolted upright and for a second forgot that I
was spending the night with the Pickerings. Lights came on, and in

the haze of sleep I could make out Mr. Pickering stumbling to the door dressed in boxers and toting a sawed-off shotgun.

Before he could crack the door, the squeal gave her away. Mama stood outside rubbing her shoulders and darting her eyes in a million directions. "Brandon here?"

Mr. Pickering massaged his ear. "You know, it's after three."

"It's an emergency, okay. We gotta go to Asheville."

"Asheville?" Mr. Pickering repeated the word as if she would have said we were going to the moon.

My heartbeat began to speed up, and I reached for my pants. I heard Mr. Pickering trying to convince her to let me stay, but I had come to know the desperation in her voice all too well. When she got like this, it was best to just give her whatever it was she needed. And in some spot deep inside me, I liked being the one to rescue her.

"Look, you want to call the cops or something? He's mine and he's coming with me."

Before she could point her finger at Mr. Pickering, I had slipped through the crack in the door still clutching my trophy.

"Brandon, call if you need us," Mr. Pickering yelled as we got into the car.

The keys chattered in her hands and she dropped them on the floorboard before leaning back against the seat. Her cry was soft, and her breathing heavy. When she hugged me, her skin felt as if it had been dipped in ice. "Oh, honey, this is bad. Tony got arrested. He just called and told me to get over there right now. I'm just so . . . I don't know what to do."

"Mama, we'll make it."

Tony came back into the apartment smelling like wool that had been left out in the rain. When he left again the next day, with him went a piece of our dignity and the stash of money Mama kept hidden in an empty cereal box.

While Mama continued to scream and cry about not having

any money, I watched as Bethany and Destiny played hopscotch out in the street. Their pigtails bounced at the same time, and they began to look as if they had been hosed down with bleach. Holding my arm up against the window, I tried to compare my skin with theirs. Skin so white and pure that it sparkled against the afternoon sun.

Mama stayed in bed most of the time and eventually even Bethany and Destiny quit inviting me outside. We were wrapped in a cocoon of overdue bills, nerve pills, and darkened windows.

Only splinters of light managed to come in through the cracks in the blinds. Staring at the gaps of light, I tried to will myself back to Abbeville. A man on TV had once willed himself back in time by staring at a dot on the wall. I stared at the rays of light until my eyes blurred, but the memories did not. They drifted me back to Sister Delores, Bonita, and Beau, back to everything that made my insides still and quiet, back to Nana and Poppy.

"What the hell are you doing?"

Her voice made me jump, but it was the sight of her that surprised me. It was the first time she had gotten out of bed since Tony had left. The outsides of Mama's eyes were lined with eyeliner and the eyes themselves with red streaks. The front of her hair was teased high, and when she turned I saw a gap that looked as if a small bird had buried eggs deep inside the black nest.

"Get up from there and stop staring like you're retarded. Brandon, it came to me. Every day we got a choice to be pitiful or powerful. That's what they teach in those rehabs. Up in Canada they told me that I needed to make my own destiny. And I got to thinking this morning." She glanced at the clock on the stove. "It's eleven twenty-seven in the morning on whatever day and Sophie Willard is fixing to make her own destiny."

That afternoon we drove to the grocery store, and while I stood guard at the end of the aisle, Mama made her destiny by stuffing a package of chicken under her coat. Next came the jars of peanut butter and jelly.

The smell of sugared cereal made me light-headed, and my hands began to sweat. Nana would have had a fit if she'd caught me stealing and would probably have blistered Mama and me both. For once, I was glad that she was locked up and not able to see everything that was taking place at the Piggly Wiggly. Then the image of Jesus standing right in front of our duplex flashed through my mind. Nana may be locked up, but Jesus sure wasn't. What if He walked up right as Mama was trying to sneak through the checkout line?

When an older woman with bright red lipstick and a wide nose came walking up, I moved backwards until the cardboard display for a new oatmeal pressed against my back.

"Excuse me, young man. I need a box of this oatmeal."

I moved to the side, and she walked away with her purchase. Her wide hips swayed, and a shiny pocketbook dangled on her arm. Most likely she was a woman like Nana. A church-going woman who wouldn't put up with sorry excuses or lazy behavior. Even though I still felt like a foreigner in this new land that Mama called her destiny, the woman's words lingered in my mind. She had called me a young man. Not "darling," "sugar," or "sweetheart"—names handed out to babies. But she had called me a young man, and for the first time since Abbeville, I felt that I had an identity again. I was a man in this new land. The only man my mama could count on.

Sister Delores had once told us that every child of God's has a gift. I was beginning to think that Mama's gift was a fast hand and quick feet. When Mama mastered the art of walking away with merchandise from Woolworth's, we soon had a stream of visitors at the duplex once again. "It's a business, okay. They make so much money they never will miss any of this stuff no way. Besides, it's better than being on welfare." She repeated the lines to me every time she came through the door with a new supply.

The day she and our neighbor Cheyenne left to take some stock to the pawn shop, I waited five rings before answering the phone. The voice was deep and serious.

"Hello, Brandon."

I could hear the rattle of my breath against the phone mouthpiece.

"This is Nairobi. How are you?"

The sound of typing echoed in the background. I was silent until she called out my name for a second time.

"Hey," I finally said.

"Can you talk?" The way Nairobi asked it made me think that maybe she knew about our new destiny.

"Umm–hmm."

"It's been a while. Your grandparents wanted to know how you're doing."

Her words began to swarm around me like mosquitoes wanting to suck me back to the past.

"I'm doing good. *Real* good."

"That's nice to hear. And how's your mom?"

"She's doing good too. She started her own store and everything. So . . ." My words trailed off at the idea of Mama walking in the door and hearing me tell all of our business.

"Oh?"

My eyes were locked on the doorknob of the front door. "She's trading stuff. You know, like a flea market."

The clicking sound of typing returned.

"I'm just checking in more or less. Letting you know I'm still your friend. Your grandparents keep asking me if you . . ."

"You still see them?"

"I do. Not as much as I'd like but . . ."

"They ask about me?"

"Oh, yes. Every time I see them they ask."

"Are they behind glass when you see them?"

Nairobi cleared her voice the same way Mama did whenever she was fixing to get onto me. "No, they sit right across from me at a table the same way they would if we were in my office. Don't worry because they are . . ."

"I hear somebody knocking. Gotta go."

I slammed the phone down faster than she could say good-bye. But try as I might, I could not stop her words from slamming up against my heart.

• • •

The week before Memorial Day, we made the pilgrimage over to Wool-worth's. Red, white, and blue flags, the kind that decorated rodeos, hung from every entrance. A man with a wrinkled face and strands of hair plas-tered to his forehead glanced at us. He stood right next to the gigantic trampoline that had a "Do Not Sit" sign propped up on it. A miniature American flag hung down from his shirt pocket. The name tag with the Woolworth's logo read "Mr. Mackingham." When I ran my hand down the bright red trampoline rails, he looked over and smiled. But the greeting did not last long. When he looked up at Mama, his jaw clinched. Ignoring him, she just slung her big straw purse into the buggy and marched forward. First she browsed a row of new bathing suits and then, before I could make it to the toys, she pulled me closer.

Her words fought with the "Yankee Doodle" tune that played throughout the store. "That man was watching me. Is he still looking? Don't make it obvious. Just turn your head a little bit like you're look-ing for somebody."

A flock of people with short sleeves and sweaty faces were enter-ing. The man was leaning sideways, trying to look pass a woman wearing a dress with orange flowers.

"He's fixing to look."

Mama bit her lip and darted her eyes faster than the people streaming into the air-conditioned store. With a tilt of her chin, she motioned for me to follow. We walked through the crowd of people and pass a display for new lounge chairs. Pass the rows of TVs that played a soap opera and underneath the air-conditioning vent that blew silver streamers back and forth. Finally we were at the back of the store near the entrance to the snack bar. Mama craned her neck high above the others behind us. "Go on in there and get us a cherry Pepsi while I look everything over."

As I sat at the counter sipping my drink, I noticed for the first time a group of older men holding court in the booth behind me. One wore a black hat and chewed the end of a straw. His high-pitched laugh reminded me of Poppy's. Soon the shame I kept trying to chase away was buzzing around me again.

"Sweetie, you need something else?"

Before I could answer the waitress, Mama was standing beside me. She smiled and shooed away the woman away with one glance. "Come over here, Brandon, and let's sit at one of these booths."

Mama leaned over the table and whispered like the best secret agent. "You remember how you and those big girls next door used to play James Bond? You know, y'all would act out the scenes. Well, I thought you and me could play it too. I just want you to go in that store and fall down on the floor. Act like your stomach is hurting so bad it's about to kill you. Then . . ."

"No."

Mama batted her eyes until I thought the false eyelashes would fall to the table. "What did you say to me?"

"I'm not doing it."

"I'm fixing to tear your ass up. Now listen to me, Mr. High and Mighty, there are bills to pay."

I glanced over her shoulder at the old men in the booth behind her. The one chewing the straw looked over and casually nodded.

"Fine," Mama said. "Just go on and mess everything up. You don't even know what I had them put on layaway. If you knew, you'd feel real bad about how you're acting. I mean, real bad."

"What?"

"No, never mind."

"Come on, tell me. What?"

Mama patted her hair and then brushed scattered salt from the table. "Nobody can give you surprises. You won't let them."

"Come on, what? I promise I'll still act surprised."

"If you won't help me out this one little bit, I won't even be able to finish paying it off so it don't matter no way."

The feeling of having to urinate started to make me flinch around inside the booth. "Please . . ."

"Just that trampoline is all. That's what I've been paying on. Already talked with Cheyenne about going in on it with me."

The vision of the red railings sparkled as bright as diamonds in my mind. I ran over to Mama's side of the booth and tried to hug her.

Her bony shoulders were as limp as the crumpled napkins piled at the end of the table.

"Yeah, so what. If you'd help out, then maybe I could make another payment. I was figuring on having it paid for by August." She stared down at the table so long I thought she might start crying. "All I wanted was for you to do this one teeny-weeny thing for me. Just this one little thing."

After three more soft drinks, my stomach really did ache. Mama had gone over the details until she made it sound as simple as make-believe. We strolled right up to the jewelry counter, where a woman with soft brown eyes began opening the trays and displaying the goods. Gold necklaces sparkled against the black felt cloth. Mama put one on and glanced at the small mirror on the counter. "This might be too flashy. What do you think, Brandon?" She looked down and smiled as innocent as a Sunday school teacher.

"You look beautiful."

The clerk chuckled and then began pulling out more display cases. Just when she bent down to unlock the bottom counter, Mama nodded. Like a trained dog, I fell to the floor and began screaming so loud that I thought the ceiling might cave in on top of us. All the while, the red trampoline railings glittered even more as I pictured myself jumping on it.

"Lord have mercy." The clerk was the first one to come to my aid. A spray of spat hit my face, and I rolled to the side clamping my stomach. "Is it his appendicitis?"

Mama was kneeling beside me. "Baby, what's the matter? What, baby?"

I held my side just as we had rehearsed. When she touched my hand, I screamed as loud as I could.

A crowd gathered and someone mentioned calling an ambulance. "Oh, my baby," Mama kept yelling. Her eyes jumped from me to the jewelry counter. When she turned ever so slightly, I noticed one of the gold necklaces dangling over the top of her purse. I tried to get her attention by casting my eyes in that direction, but she was too busy playing her role of upset mother. Mama might have missed the hint, but the employee with the American flag flapping out of his shirt pocket did not. He barreled around the jewelry counter so fast that the flag on his pocket was flopped sideways. The lines on his forehead became deeper as he looked down at me. I kicked my leg up, hoping to direct Mama to the back of the crowd. But she just squatted over me and shouted, "Somebody get the ambulance."

Between the legs of the crowd Mama turned to look for help. Her purse swung with each movement of her shoulders. When the man with the American flag looked down at us, I began to scream louder. He never did look at me. He just kept staring at the big purse on Mama's shoulder.

"Darlin', I promise the ambulance is coming," the jewelry clerk kept repeating. But it was useless. No amount of screaming or reassurance stopped the man with the flag from reaching down. The sleeve of his checkered sport coat seemed as powerful as a crane when he reached for the big purse. At first the crowd looked at him the way they might look at a cat killer.

Mama fell sideways and used the tips of her fingers to steady herself against the speckled tile floor. Panic gripped her eyes as she tried to hold on to the purse and steady herself at the same time. It was as if we were watching a movie in slow motion. Necklaces scattered to the floor like a nest of gold-encrusted snakes looking for their home.

"I knew it. I knew it," the man kept repeating. Before he could scoop up the necklaces, Mama was crawling through the crowd on her knees. By the time the man reached down and grabbed her shirt like she was a misbehaving toddler, it was too late. The policeman had her by one hand, while the man with the flag kept saying "repeat offender." As the handcuffs clamped her wrists, Mama turned sideways. Pieces of hair formed a web over her eyes. The words might have been broken but the scream was strong.

"Don't worry. Don't worry about nothing. I'm gonna sue these bastards for everything they're worth." Her words stomped me deeper into the floor. As she was led pass the shiny trampoline and out of the store, the eyes of the crowd drifted back to me. All I could do was lay there and let them stare.

Turning my head, I saw a cigarette butt that had been squashed. Seeing the tips of the polished police shoes inches from my face, I began to shake.

"Son, are you all right?"

All I could do was shake to the beat of Mama's voice. "We gotta make our own destiny . . ."

Twenty

The clicking of the typewriters filled the small room of the Raleigh police station. A policeman with hair that stood up like porcupine quills kept asking the same questions over and over. My lips were as tight as the springs to the trampoline back at Woolworth's. I stared at the keys of the typewriter while the man next to me made them sing in a noise of controlled chaos.

When the woman with curly brown hair sat down in front of me, my mind began to change channels and a beach fog drifted over them.

"Today has not been such a good day, huh? Now, we all want to help you here. Why don't you just tell us how old are you."

The man sitting at the desk next to me glanced over and then rolled the typewriter platen to the next line on the form. The words "No Response" ran across the paper. A trickle of sweat snaked down my armpit and landed at the top of my underwear. The chill of it all caused me to tuck my hands underneath the chair. Then I saw the final word scroll across the typed page. "Abandoned."

Burned coffee and cigarettes clung to their breath. Black vinyl chairs, stacks of files, and a steel desk surrounded us.

I had no one. The words on the paper told me as much. While I rocked back and forth, various faces drifted through my mind as easy as a changing tide. Sister Delores would come. I could get her to take the bus and come up here and get me.

When the policeman with the porcupine hair coughed, it sounded like a distant foghorn calling me back to shore. "Son, do you have some kin we could call?"

The vision of Uncle Cecil stretched out on a hospital bed with bandages wrapped around his body like a mummy made me shake my head. The policeman took it as a no and moved on to the next question. His words tangled with the clicking of the typewriters, and I wondered if this was what Sister Delores had meant when she preached about speaking in tongues.

Sister Delores's words filled my mind as fast as the coffee that the policeman poured filled his mug. I could see her standing at the altar at God's Hospital. Her hair hung in ringlets, but it was the smile that made me want to tell them I had family in Abbeville. Besides, she had told me that she was my sister in the Lord. Her voice wailed in my mind as loud as a ship horn. *"God will never leave you or forsake you."* I turned to see if a miracle had taken place and if she had walked into the room. But my heart fell a little lower when all I saw were two policemen in the corner laughing. One had his leg propped up on a chair and was pulling at his trousers as if all he had to do was stand there and laugh. But laughter was not about to drown out Sister Delores's voice. *"I'm telling you straight, Brandon. God will never leave you. No sir, He sure won't do it now."*

By the time the second policeman sat in front of me, I had drifted so far back to Abbeville that his words were nonexistent. I could see his mouth moving, but all around him were the people and scenes from another way of life. Just pass his shoulder where a gray file cabinet sat I saw Beau and me crabbing in the marsh. Above the policeman's head the round light fixture became the night-light that Nana kept plugged in at the camper. A light that led me to the bathroom and reminded me that darkness was only temporary. On the black-streaked floor were the grease stains from the kitchen counter at Nap's Corner, and I watched as Nana scrubbed the counter until it began to sparkle. My mind played out a home movie of Nana setting out a plate of hush puppies on the counter. They were golden brown and steam began to rise where the butt of a cigarette rested on the floor. I reached down to pick it up and smelled it long and hard. The smell of used nicotine was replaced by the sweetness of the hush puppies, and just when I started to stick it in my mouth, the policeman snatched it away. The jerk jolted me away from Nap's Corner, away from the marsh and the safety of our camper. Darkness was back again, and with it came the crashing wave of fear.

The twitching at my feet erupted up to my head. It was a soft moan at first, much like the sound of a sow before she gives birth, but then I began to get louder and louder. Soon they were all in front of me, the woman with the curly hair, the policeman with the crew cut, and the man who typed the report. They just stood there looking down at me while the tears ran and my mouth opened but no words came out. Nothing except the sound that caused the reaction I hated more than anything else—pity.

When we pulled up to the building with the white sign out front, I leaned up from the backseat of the police car. White buildings with iron bars on the windows were scattered across the landscape.

Like a robot, I followed in between the man with porcupine hair and the woman towards the building with white columns. I guess because they thought I was mute, neither of them said a word. When the man pulled the door open for us, I saw the word "Administration" engraved on the inside wall. The smell of bleach and aged dust greeted us. Lining the wall was a bulletin board with different-colored letters spelling out "Summer Fun." Photos of different children and two retarded people were scattered across the board. Some held up baskets in the photos while others were standing by a swimming pool. While I sat out in the hall in a wooden chair, the woman walked over to examine the photos and turned to offer a reassuring smile. Words from the office echoed out into the hallway. I heard the policeman with porcupine hair use that word again.

"He must be abandoned. His mama was using him to shoplift for her. And she won't tell us anything. Keeps screaming about suing."

The sound of a woman clucking with her tongue followed his words.

"We had him downtown trying to figure out his name and so forth. And just like I told you about his mama, he won't say a word. He just sits there rocking back and forth. And, oh yeah, he had that fit that they called you about."

The woman clucked with her tongue again. "We've got him scheduled for an examination."

While I was looking at the photo of a retarded man holding up a straw basket, dread swept over me. I had heard Nana and Poppy talk about this place. The home for feeble-minded they called it. A place shared as a joke whenever Poppy would forget where he put his glasses.

That policeman was right. Everybody had abandoned me. Any person who cared a thing in the world for me was either in jail or in a state too far away. Sister Delores's words were like a song you want to forget but just won't go away. *"God will never leave you or forsake you, Brandon."*

Only then did the image of Jesus settle on my mind. The last time I had seen Him was outside of the duplex. When I looked over at the bulletin board, the bright words and sad pictures seemed to fade. Instead I saw a photo of Brother Bailey's snake eyes looking down at me. The sun on the bulletin board was now a ball of fire just like the hell I knew I was facing. I had sinned right there at Woolworth's. I had helped my mama steal in front of everybody.

Abandoned. The word from the police report clung to me like mildew on the walls. "Jesus," I moaned.

The woman turned away from the bulletin board. "What did you say?"

Sister Delores's reassuring words kept clinging to me as if I had walked through a spider web. What if she was right? Maybe Jesus was out there somewhere waiting for me. The long hallway lined with big tall doors and topped with high ceilings seemed mazelike. A maze that hid the prize. Every sense of my being told me that the time at hand held my last hope.

When I got up from the chair, the woman turned to me. "Dave, he's talking. He's talking and getting up." Her fingers brushed the back of my shirt, and I moved faster towards the first door. The knob was sprinkled with rust and seemed weightless when I pulled it open. The smell of musky papers filled my senses, and I yelled louder than I had at Woolworth's. "Jesus, I'm here. Help me."

I fought the policeman's pull and then felt the arms of another on my back. Kicking, I bent backwards and slammed my head into the chin of the person behind me. Sounds of metal chairs screeched across the floor behind me. The man with porcupine hair had me pinned down on a table that was cold to my face. A prick on my arm made me think his hair had struck me. Soon the room began to spin, and my legs fell limp.

There was nothing but white. White walls, white floors, and a single white toilet. Heaven, I first thought. Sitting up, I felt like I had been spinning around and around until I had gotten so light-headed I fell down. A door with a square piece of glass at the top was across from me. White nurse hats in different heights drifted pass.

Only the specks of dead bugs on the ceiling broke up the starkness of the place. Then the reality of where I was and what had happened at Woolworth's slapped me back down. Fighting hard not to let the emptiness overtake me again, I turned my head towards the toilet.

At first, the darkness of His feet made me jump. Scanning up, I saw the robe and then the outstretched arms. The familiarity of His face allowed me to breathe again. Jesus was standing right next to the toilet just as casually as He had the night outside of our duplex. When He smiled, I felt a vial of peace being poured into every part of my being. Sister Delores's words once again sang in my mind. *"God will never leave you or forsake you. The Lord will be your mama and daddy."* Sitting on that bed in front of Jesus, I felt a sense of place that I thought had been lost the day I left Abbeville. The urge to beg for help was far away, and all I wanted to do was to touch the hand that reached out. To see for once and for all if I was deserving of the feeble-minded hospital.

Easing off of the bed, I stepped closer while the voices from God's Hospital sang louder. *"Come home. Come home. All who are weary come home."* The floor was cold to the touch, and the paper gown ballooned from my body. But it was His eyes that drew me closer, closer home. Eyes not colored the way they had been on the funeral fan back in Abbeville. They were colorless and filled with a love that drew me closer than my mama had ever been able to do. He was the one I wanted to grip and hold on to until He had taken me up in flight. We'd soar above the hospital, pass the duplex, and above the marshes of Abbeville the same way the eagle soared to its nest. Each step became steadier, and just when I had reached the edge of the toilet, a popping sound from the door caused me to look away.

"Oh, were you about to use the bathroom?" The woman began writing on a pad attached to a steel clipboard.

I turned to look at the corner, but He had slipped away again.

"Okay, Mr. Brandon Willard," she said and rolled her eyes down at me. "Your mama broke down and told them your name." She pulled a thermometer from her dress pocket and began fanning it back and forth. Her hair was pulled up in a bun, and a yellow pencil kept most of it in place.

As I got my temperature taken, "regulation" she called it, I heard all about my schedule for that day and the nice doctor who would be checking me out. "He's just as sweet as he can be. Just a little thing not much bigger than you. He's from Taiwan. Just a regular genius. Except everybody thinks he's from Vietnam, so that's why he can't get on at the bigger hospitals."

When I sat before the balding doctor with red-frame glasses, all he did was point at different cards. "What this?" he kept asking. All I saw were splats of black ink on cards that looked like they should have been used as flash cards for a spelling bee. My mind was still on Jesus. As we sat in the room with steel tables and humming lightbulbs, I kept my focus by looking around the room for another divine sign that help was on the way.

• • •

It was not until the third day that my prayers were answered. It happened right after lunch and just before my afternoon dose of medicine. Through the glass I saw the white nurse's cap and the gold turban. Standing before me were Nairobi, a pretty woman with long black hair, and a nurse holding a plastic bag. I couldn't help myself, and before I knew it, I had my arms wrapped around the stiff material of Nairobi's waist.

"Well, now aren't you a sight for sore eyes," she said.

"I need you to get me outta . . ."

"The judge placed you into Foster Care, and that's why we're here. This is Millicent, your new social worker." The young woman reached out to shake my hand, but all I could do was stand there frozen, wondering if they were only temporary visitors.

"I expect you want to take off that dress you're wearing." Nairobi handed over the plastic bag with my clothes in it.

While she waited outside, I changed clothes so fast that I almost tripped over my pants leg. Before I escaped, I made sure to look around the room one last time. Words that Sister Delores planted in my mind blasted louder than Mama's stereo. *"God will never leave you or forsake you."*

Walking out to the car, I fought from asking about Mama, especially with the social worker standing right there. No telling what she had already heard about Mama. Besides, I knew Nairobi didn't like Mama and was probably glad she was locked up. But she did like Nana and Poppy.

"When will Nana and Poppy get outta jail?"

"Two lawyers who do nothing but take on cases such as theirs are looking into the situation. We're working on an appeal and . . . regardless, let's just . . ."

"Let's just try to think about new beginnings," Millicent added. She looked down and smiled in a way that made me think of my teacher back in Abbeville.

"Where are y'all taking me?"

Nairobi stopped just shy of her car. Moisture glistened on her broad nose, and I shaded my eyes to get a better read of her expression.

"You recall Senator Strickland. The woman we all met back when . . ." Nairobi glanced away and I saved her from having to dig up the details of our past right in front of Millicent.

"The lady with hairlike daisies," I said.

They laughed at the same time, and I felt even freer.

Millicent tapped my shoulder. "She's one of your biggest fans. Senator Strickland just jumped at the chance to have you stay with her."

Nairobi cut her eyes towards Millicent. "Brandon, as soon as we learned what had happened, I wanted to take you in myself . . ."

"But it was determined . . ." Millicent raised her eyebrows.

"But it was determined," Nairobi continued, "that it would be best if you stayed with another party. I contacted Senator Strickland and, well, that's when she stepped forward." Nairobi bent down towards me. Her long necklace of beads twirled around in circles. "I'm sharing these things so that you will know just how many people want you."

All the way to the new place, I held on to Nairobi's words as tight as I'd hold a fistful of lightning bugs.

Senator Strickland lived in a part of Raleigh that I thought only existed on TV. The cream-colored blocks of her tall house matched the suit she was wearing. She stood by a hedge cut into the shape of a golf ball. The brass lion's head on the door looked down at her like he would scalp her yellow hair any minute.

A woman with a black uniform that was filled out at every angle stood in the background wiping her hands on a dishrag.

Nairobi and Millicent got out of the car at the same time, but all I could do was sit there and look at the fountain in the middle of the driveway. It was only when Nairobi opened the car door that I slinked out.

"Hello, hello," Senator Strickland said. "You remember me now, don't you?" She batted her long eyelashes and bent down so low I could see a mole on her chest. When she hugged me, I felt a roll of fat clinging to the side of her skirt.

Senator Strickland motioned towards the door and the woman

wiping her hands stepped forward. "This is Esther. She's been with me for, oh Lord, how long now, Esther?"

"Since time began, I suppose." Esther's nasal words made me think she must've been swimming in the water fountain. Her chin pointed forward, and she sniffed when she spoke.

Senator Strickland smiled big enough for both of them. "We're just a little family. And we're just pleased as punch to have you with us."

When we went inside, I remembered the day my school visited the governor's mansion. Her house looked even bigger and caused my insides to tense up. I cautioned myself not to touch anything for fear of breaking it and being sent back to the torture of reading ink splashes. Crystal chandeliers sparkled as if they were Senator Strickland's own private star collection. The front room was filled with white furniture, flowers, and paintings of Chinese people.

"Welcome to my sanctuary. My sunroom," she said. The sofa we sat on was covered with some kind of flower print. The material made her hair look so yellow that I figured she was supposed to be the sun part of the room.

She scooted close and the sweet-smelling perfume helped to melt away the tension. "Now sweetheart, you just make yourself right at home. Now, I thought one thing that might make you feel better about all this is having you call me some pet name. You know a name of endearment. I got to thinking about it this morning and came up with one." She opened her eyes so big I could see the red lines that zigzagged around blue circles. "Now before I tell you, I just want you to know that I don't have any use for that Miss business. That's a name fitting for old ladies, and I'm hardly old. Anyway, the name I came up with is Aunty Gina. Do you like it?"

By the way she smiled and nodded her head all at the same time, I figured there were no other options. Besides, I was still trying to figure out why she thought she was young. Her hair was bright and the skin on her face was tight, but the brown spots and raised veins on her hands could have fit on Nana easy.

She hugged me again and this time patted my head. "Oh, you and Aunty Gina are going to have the best time."

Walking through the stores with Aunty Gina was like walking in a parade. Every step we made there were people who knew her by name. And she never paid for a single thing. "Just put it on my account will be fine," was her standard response.

At Belk's department store two salesladies tried to help me and Aunty Gina both at the same time. They fluttered around us like birds protecting their young. By the time we had stopped for lunch at the cafeteria, the boxes and bags we carried seemed fitting for a real-life Santa Claus. In the back of my mind, I kept wondering how this would all work. I decided I'd treat the shoes, shirts, and pants with the same extra care I was giving every other item in her house. If Nana and Poppy had to pay her back for my new clothes, we could just return everything to the stores in good condition.

Between bites of chicken salad, Aunty Gina kept one eye on the people who walked by and one eye on me. Every chance she got, she pulled someone over and introduced me as her new son. After the third time, reading the facial expressions became a game. The eyes of the ladies would widen, and then they'd flash a glance towards me. Aunty Gina would wink at them, and then they'd nod. One lady with bright red hair that flipped up like permanent wings was particularly curious.

"Brandon, this is one of my oldest friends, Mrs. Raymond McMasters." Aunty Gina held on to the edge of the woman's sleeve like she was a misbehaving child.

"Nice to meet you, young man. Are you a nephew? Oh, is this one of Kenton's boys? How are they?"

"No, no, but Kenton's fine. Brandon is my new son. He arrived yesterday."

Mrs. McMasters raised her drawn-on eyebrows to the edge of the red bangs. Her saggy eyes lifted for a second. "Oh, I see. Well, young man, you're in fine company." With a smile and a bat of the eye, she turned to Aunty Gina. "Now Gina, with motherhood and all, are you still able to meet for bridge next week."

"I'm still planning on it. That governor keeps talking about a special session, but I just hope to goodness he'll come to his senses."

Mrs. McMasters returned to her table. Soon the other three ladies were turning around. They all smiled in that upside-down way that I hated.

"My gracious, you're already on your dessert. You've got to learn to slow down. Be kinder to your digestive system. By the looks of it, you like banana pudding as much as I do," Aunty Gina said.

"It's pretty good, but I think my Nana makes . . ." Looking up at her, I tried to gauge whether mentioning the names of my real family was allowed.

Aunty Gina patted my hand. "It's hard to be separated from loved ones. My late husband, Preston, was my life for so long. But we have memories now don't we?"

I refused to let her think I was counting Nana and Poppy and even Mama for that matter as dead. "I've never had nobody in my family die."

"It leaves a hole in your heart, but somehow time really is the best medicine. And staying busy helps, of course. Right before Preston passed on, he talked to me about running for his seat in the state Senate." She kept squeezing the napkin until it became a round circle.

"He was a senator too?"

"Oh, was he ever. The best you could know. The party had talked to him about running for governor and then came the cancer. That's when I knew that if he wanted me to run, I had to do it. I didn't have any use for politics, and between you and me I still don't. But if Preston asked me to do anything, I did it."

The server appeared out of nowhere. When the ice and tea began to pour into Aunty Gina's glass, she flinched.

"Anyway, enough about such dreary subjects. Now, Mr. Brandon, I expect we need to find you a suit fitting for church."

. . .

Before we went to church the first time, I stood in front of the long mirror in my bedroom and wondered who I was. The bow tie had been tied by Esther, and my new black shoes shined to the point of sparkling. It's just like being a guest star on a TV show, I tried to convince myself. Even so, insecurity was my closest companion on that ride to church. Esther drove the big car while Aunty Gina sat in the passenger seat putting on lipstick. She kept chirping about how handsome I looked while fancy homes and big trees drifted by us.

Looking up, I saw the eyes of judgment. Esther's gray eyebrows and almond-shaped eyes were framed in the rearview mirror. For a second I thought she was about to ask me a question, but then her eyes darted away.

When we arrived at the Episcopal church, I played the role and stayed right next to Aunty Gina. It gave her the opportunity to mother me with her introductions, and it gave me an excuse not to sit by Esther. During the service I looked around at the rows of balding heads and wide hats all the while wondering what Sister Delores would say about such a fancy place. I think she might have liked how everybody knelt down on the padded footrest and prayed. We got up and down so many times saying all kind of prayers that I wondered how women as old as Aunty Gina and Esther held out. I could just hear Nana, "All that bending is tearing my knees to pieces." With my hands clasped and knees bent on the soft pad, I almost laughed right out loud. Then wondering what God would think about me laughing while I was supposed to be talking to Him, I bit my tongue.

Opening one eye, I looked up at the minister who stood on a special little stage surrounded by winding stairs. A ray of purple light from the stained-glassed window streaked across his bald spot. An air conditioner caused his robe to sway in a way that made me think he could soar above us. He was a powerful giant, and all of the sudden I wanted to stand right up there with him. I'd wave to Aunty Gina and stick my tongue out at Esther. Probably tell her she might go to hell for staring at me all the time. Remembering how Sister Delores talked about Jesus telling people they should visit the prisons, I'd stand up there and ask everybody to help me set Nana and Poppy free. I might even tell them about Mama and ask for a special prayer. But before I could move, it was time to kneel back down and pray again.

When the minister began to talk about waiting on God, my attention drifted to the stained-glass windows and high ceilings. Organ pipes stretched above the altar and at the very top hung a gold crucifix. From where I sat, Jesus looked pitiful hanging on that cross with thorns on his head. He was much skinnier than the Jesus I had seen. Looking up at Him, all I could think about were the words Mama had shared before she set out for her destiny. "Every day we got a choice to be pitiful or powerful."

After the service Aunty Gina stood under a magnolia tree and fanned herself with the church bulletin while Esther pulled the car around. All different sizes of women came by to kiss her cheek and pat my head. Just as we were getting into the car, a man with square glasses with gold frames came towards us. He stepped high like a horse and waved a paper in the air. Seeing him wear the same pokka-dotted bow tie I had on made me want to jump in the car.

"Hold on, Gina."

Aunty Gina laughed the same way I'd seen my cousin Mary Madonna do in beauty pageants. "Jackson. You're going to have a heatstroke carrying on so."

"Have you seen the paper this morning?"

"Do you ever stop with all your foolishness? Right here at church, mind you."

The man popped the paper open and pointed at one of the stories. "He is doing his best to stop that session. I went over this with him just yesterday, and he told me he would not interfere. Now look here."

"Jackson, he is the Senate president. There are a few decisions the man can make without consulting you. Besides, as I told you before, whatever he wants to do is fine with me. I'm not bucking him."

The man shook his head. "Gina, I'm telling you right now, we're in a fix. If we lined them up, we'd have cases stretching from here to Charlotte. We're bogged down. That courthouse annex best get funded—now this is our best shot."

Aunty Gina fanned and pulled me closer all at the same time. "Enough of such talk on Sunday. Brandon, I want you to meet one of my oldest friends, Judge Jackson Avery. Judge Jackson is one of the finest superior court judges in the state of North Carolina."

"You can only flatter for just so long." The judge smiled at Aunty Gina before looking at me. "Pleased to know you. Put it there, young man." His wide hand stretched down, and all I could think of was the Santa Claus–looking judge that caused Nana and Poppy to go to jail.

"Well go on, honey. Don't be bashful. Go on and shake his hand."

As I stuck my palm in his, I looked down. An edge of cement had cracked away from the street drain. I could hear Aunty Gina and Judge Jackson chuckle. Their voices were in time with the organ music that spilled from the church doors. Kicking a chipped piece of concrete, I wanted to slide down the drain with it. No matter what Aunty Gina said, in my book judges were the same as government women with clipboards who show up your house to cause problems but never solve anything.

After Sunday lunch the house grew still. Chimes from the clocks and creaks from settling floors were the only sounds I heard. Aunty Gina and Esther had settled in for their afternoon naps. They walked up to their bedrooms at the same time, but went to opposite ends of the house. Aunty Gina took the main staircase with its marbled steps, while Esther walked up the pine stairs tucked in the kitchen corner.

The main staircase swept down into the foyer. One of those big chandeliers hung right in the middle. Rubbing the slick marble railing, I walked up the stairs twice before getting up my courage. A whistling snore came from the end of the house where Esther slept. Straddling the marble railing, I was just about to slide down when a small door down below caught my eye. It was as tall as me and tucked in the space between the end of the stairs and the downstairs bathroom.

When I pulled the handle, the creaking door made me stop and count to twenty. Visions of a disfigured monster came to mind. Probably a tortured child that Esther kept chained to the steps. A long rope dangled, and when I pulled it a lightbulb swung back and forth.

Concrete steps led down to a slab floor. The smell of preserves and dampened dust filled the room. Jars with tomatoes and pickles were scattered across a table that looked like it might have once been in a dining room. The room was small, with a ceiling so low that it blanketed me. Instead of torturing children, I pictured Esther canning just like Nana. In that room their way of living didn't seem as strange. Crates and a cabinet filled with wine bottles were the only things that were different than in the farmhouse. After I ran my finger over the jars of tomatoes, peaches, and pickled cucumbers, I felt as if I had brushed against my past. Running up the steps, I decided it was time to find my own destiny.

The library was right next to the sunroom. Photos in color and black and white lined the dark shelves. Books as big as family Bibles filled the built-in cases. I used the fancy ladder that leaned against the wall to get a better look at the photographs. Stepping up to the highest point, I saw photos of Aunty Gina as a younger woman with a fur wrapper around her bare shoulders. There were pictures of her husband posed at a desk with the state flag draped behind him. Climbing down the steps, I missed one and regained control by gripping the railing tighter. The ladder tilted to the left and I held my breath, praying that it wouldn't topple over. I'd be back at the feeble-minded home for sure.

Steadying myself, I reached out and lightly touched a silver frame. A color picture of Aunty Gina in a ball gown with her husband. On either side were President and Mrs. Nixon. I looked closer, wondering if the faces had been glued on the same way Mary Madonna had done with a picture of Miss America. But there were no cut lines or glue marks. Just the smiles of people who looked like they were as close as family.

Twenty-one

I t was the word "pecan" that made me serve time in Miss Helda's White Gloves and Party Manners School. I was in the TV room minding my own business when Aunty Gina called out from the library, "Sugarfoot, why don't you come in here and try one of these chocolate squares."

"Now, Gina, they're swirl bars. My girl Corinth finally managed to copy the ones they have down at the bakery. I told her I might just keep her on my payroll after all." Mrs. McMasters fanned her red winged hair with the cards and kept a steady gaze on me.

Through a fog of cigarette smoke, the glistening desserts were scattered on silver trays. Aunty Gina got up to fix me a plate of the swirl bars. "How many do you want?"

At the end of the table my eyes landed on the pecan pie, its edges dusted in brown sugar. A twin to the pie that had sat on Nana's kitchen counter before the Thanksgiving meal was served. The sound of cackling women could have been the laughter of Aunt Loraine and Mary Madonna. The words flowing around the table changed from those of fashion shows or men who ran around, and became the words of Poppy and Uncle Cecil talking about a tractor that was for sale.

"Brandon, how many, honey?"

"I'd rather have some of that peecan pie."

Their laughter chased the memory away. Mrs. McMasters kept fanning herself with the cards while the big-chinned woman next to her held her chest and leaned forward. The heat of embarrassment ran up to my forehead.

"It doesn't matter how you pronounce it, it still tastes good." Aunty Gina put an extra big piece of pie on my plate and sent me back to the TV and the world I knew best. I had just made it pass the bookshelves and the painting of the man in an army uniform when Mrs. McMasters led the assault.

"Sweetheart, a *peecan* is something our mammies placed underneath their beds. A pecan is something we eat." I heard them laugh again, and I moved so fast that the pie slid sideways on the plate.

In the hallway, I pressed my head against the door, both wanting to hear what was being said and trying to pull myself away all at the same time. "Bless his sweet little heart," Mrs. McMasters said. "No telling what sort of rearing the poor thing has had. Proper training, I tell you, that's what he needs."

"Oh, my little grandbaby, you know Nell's daughter, anyway she just started party school. Old lady Helda Kipshaw's training them how to be proper little ladies and gentleman. Just as cute as can be."

"Lucille, you might just be onto something with that school," Mrs. McMasters said. "Gina, I'd register that boy before he ends up embarrassing you to death out in public somewhere."

"Honey, if you kept your mind on this game as much as you do on everybody else's business, maybe we wouldn't lose all the time."

But Mrs. McMasters did win that night. By the end of the week, I was dressed in my church suit and sitting at a long dining-room table learning how to be one of Raleigh's finest.

Miss Helda was more ancient than I had imagined. Watching her shuffle across the dining room, I figured that she had probably trained all of the women in Aunty Gina's bridge club. A gold bumblebee guarded the back of the white hair as if it was the bee's very own hive. Skin hung from her neck the same way pearls dangled from the socialites she trained.

I kept my distance from the four girls and three boys who joined me at Miss Helda's table the same way she said we should keep our distance from complaining about a bad dinner party. At the beginning my fellow travelers on this pristine journey looked at me with the curiosity reserved for a new kid at school. But by the time we were learning how to stir our tea without making the spoon clank against the cup, they were more interested in the boy at the end of the table. He wore glasses and had hair the color of cornstalks. But it was his hands that made them all stare. Even I found myself watching him clutch a spoon in his webbed hand. Four fingers moved together in such a perfect unison that only God could have glued them together.

"Now boys and girls, it's time for us to practice our formal introductions," Miss Helda said. A trickle of sweat ran down my neck and was captured by the starched collar. When it came my turn, the chandelier dangling above us might as well have been a spotlight. Questions that would follow blared in my mind: Why are you staying with Gina Strickland? Where is your own mama? The past had been washed away the day Mama was taken away in handcuffs at Woolworth's. Now I was going to have to come up with a whole new story. Maybe this was what movie stars meant when they talked about having to wing it.

"Thank you, Master Brandon Willard. Master Willard is a summer guest of Mrs. Preston Strickland. She reports that his visit has been a ray of sunshine. Welcome, welcome." The way Miss Helda dressed up my mumbling, even I was beginning to believe that I was a rich nephew who had arrived by train with a cartful of bags, ready to entertain the lonely aunt.

By the time we had made it to the boy with webbed hands, Miss Helda had moved to the opposite end of the table. From certain parts of the room her hearing was as faded as the gold drapes that hung in the window.

The boy pushed up his glasses and looked at Miss Helda, who was nodding even though he had not spoken. "Hello, I'm Winston Rickards. I was born in Trenton, New Jersey. My family moved to

Raleigh three years ago. I'm very pleased to be here . . . and oh yeah, pleased to meet you."

Miss Helda continued to nod as the boy across from me leaned over and smirked at us. "He means, he moved here from the ocean. Didn't you Lobster Boy?"

Giggles from the others became a piercing alarm to Miss Helda, a type of high-pitched noise that not even dogs can tolerate. "Silence. This is a dinner party, not a circus."

"Oh, yeah? Just look at the freak show at the end of the table," the boy whispered.

Although Miss Helda had already moved on to the importance of writing thank-you notes, I could tell that Winston stayed behind. His eyes cast across the table but never landed on any dish. When he caught my eye, I held his gaze, but only for a second. Pity was as ugly as the way Miss Helda described eating with your fingers.

With the legislature moving forward with a special session, I saw less of Aunty Gina and more of Esther. She would pick me up after Miss Helda's school and drop me off at the park once a week, where I'd meet some of the other kids Nairobi was helping for what Aunty Gina called "recreation." But the recreation was limited to our tongues. When the pretty girl who usually answered the phone had us sit in a circle and talk about our feelings, my inclination was to go jump on a swing. I'd swing higher and higher until I landed right in the middle of the farmhouse porch marked with the year my family had built it.

When the session was over and everyone was brushing grass from their pants, the pretty girl walked towards me with a paper sack. She bent down and tousled my hair the same way she did with the little kids. "Nairobi wanted me to give you these. They found them when they cleaned out your mom's apartment."

While my mind wanted to dig right in and pull out the past, my heart wanted to toss it in the trash barrel. The girl's smile faded a notch when I didn't open the bag.

"Don't you want to open it?" She reached in and pulled out a stack of envelopes tied together with a ratty string. "Letters from your grandparents." She laughed and ran her finger over the edges the way you might expect someone to shuffle cards. "All of these are letters just for you."

Riding in the backseat of the car staring at Esther's short gray hair, I tried to convince myself that, like Nana, Poppy, and Mama, I too was in prison. Esther was my warden and the state was giving me three meals a day. I stuck my hand in the bag and secretly ran my fingers across the sharp edges of the envelopes. I pictured Nana and Poppy riding in the backseat with me. Poppy would be asking all kinds of questions about the car engine, and Nana would be ordering him to keep quiet with a shake of her head. Watching the big two-story homes pass by, I tucked the bag behind my back. The letters, like my past, were secrets that Esther had no business knowing.

It wasn't until we were a block away that the anger managed to find my new address. Mama had hidden the letters just like she had the letter from Nairobi. She had kept them away on purpose just so she could keep on hating Nana and Poppy.

Back home Esther sent me outside and then proceeded to lock all of the doors. She peered through the sheer curtain of the patio entrance. "I don't need you tracking up my waxed floor. Keep outside until I call you."

A familiar sound of water rolling over the rocks by the creek back at the farm caused me to turn. A statue of a little boy peeing into a big pit filled a side of the backyard. Trees as tall as the ones at the farm towered over me and shadowed patches of the grass. A backyard so neatly trimmed and decorated that it didn't even seem like real life. A tall hedge of shrubbery made a fence that divided the property. Over the top of the shrub I could make out the roofline of one home. At the end of the shrub, I squeezed through the prickly branches. Behind the hedge, communities of trees surrounded a swimming pool and tennis court. A tall brick house with a glassed patio stood guard.

Leaning against the back of a tree, I opened the first letter as if it might disintegrate right in my hands. Each syllable and pitch of their voices sank deeper into my being. Poppy was taking classes and liked science the best. He wanted to take a bet on who could make the best score, him or me. His tiny words told me that he was working with the dairy cows and for me not to worry about him. "Worry" was the word both of them used over and over, as if their sentences would protect against it. Nana's swirled words updated me on all the news from Abbeville. Sister Delores kept in regular contact and had even sent a fruitcake for Christmas. Bonita had married Parker, the highway patrolman, and Beau seemed to be liking him better. Nana was even leading Bible study at the "place," as she called prison. While I was reading the last letter, a tear fell on top of the blue ink, and I carefully tilted the paper so that it would roll away from the rest of her words. *"You've got a whole lot of people who love you and don't forget I'm at the top of that list."*

Packing the letters back into the bag, I felt emptiness circling around me, but I wouldn't let it in. Peace was the gift their words had given me. Hope was found inside those stained envelopes, just as it had been the day I first walked the aisle at God's Hospital.

The voices of Nana and Poppy were back in my mind to encourage me not to worry, to keep me plugging along, to remind me that tomorrow is a better day. While dragging a stick down the hedge the way I had seen prisoners rattle cups on cell bars, in old movies, I discovered the oasis of my former life.

Nestled at the far end of the hedge was a small garden. Splinters of wood framed the tilled dirt, and a line of string secured vines of the tomato plants. The dirt was warm to the touch, and the damp scent of the earth transported me. Some of the leaves of the tomato plants were cut with perfect circles. "Dad-gum bugs," Poppy would surely say. All of the plants had the signs of unwelcome guests. Rows of cucumbers and squash looked just as bad, but I kept telling myself that they weren't down for the count just yet.

A squirrel jumped from a tree branch. The shaking leaves caused me to turn, and when I did, a tennis court was in full view. The boy from Miss Helda's class clutched a racket in his webbed hand. He swung the racket so hard that I figured he was picturing the ball as the face of his tormentors. It was that same determination that drew me closer. Dead leaves and sticks crackled until I was just feet away from his afflicted hands.

"Brandon. Brandon Willard." Esther's voice rang out. I raced back through the hedge, hoping that the boy would not hear the warden calling my name.

"What are you doing back there?" Esther's hands were planted on the wide hips, and for good measure she curled her lip.

"Nothing . . . I was just . . ."

"You're smoking cigarettes back there, aren't you?"

I shook my head extra fast.

"Well, then, what's in the bag?"

"Nothing." I tucked the bag deeper inside the front of my pants.

"There's something in there all right. If you don't want me to know, then it can't be any good." She reached for the waistband of my pants, and I shoved her arm so hard she almost fell.

"They're letters, okay. Just letters from my grandparents."

Wrinkles around her mouth twitched. Esther said nothing as she turned to walk back inside. I obediently followed, thinking that if she told Aunty Gina it would be all over.

While Esther washed a sinkful of dishes, I tried to figure out my next step in our dance. Maybe I should turn up *The Brady Bunch* real loud so that Esther could hear how a real housekeeper was supposed to act. You don't see Alice acting this mean to the Bradys, I thought. But Esther took a step before I could. A click echoed from the kitchen, and voices from a TV soap opera filled the front of the house.

When I eased the cellar door open, moist air cooled my legs. Voices from the soap opera rolled through the air-conditioning vent. They were so clear that I turned to see if Esther had broken into my sanctuary. But the big oak door was still sealed as tight as my emotions. Moving closer to the end of the room, I noticed one of the crates slightly ajar. With eyes glued to the door handle, I carefully lifted the lid. Yellowed, curled photographs were scattered among old tissue paper. One photo showed a young girl standing beside a magnolia tree, its blooms busting out towards her. On the back, written in unsteady penmanship, were the words "Ginny Mae age 11." Other photographs were of the girl and a dog standing on a front porch sprinkled in snow. An old couple sat in chairs next to them. By the time I examined the fifth photo, I had painted a grim history for the girl. Probably some long lost stepdaughter of Esther's, whose pictures had been hidden after the girl was killed by her. The air-conditioning system clicked on, and the door popped. I clutched the box of evidence and only breathed again when I heard Esther's footsteps and then the sound of running water.

Laying the photographs and my letters across the table with the canned fruit, I stood with all the respect I'd give a church altar. Behind the table a daddy-longlegs spider crept up the block wall towards a crack. Watching him escape, I continued to study the past and began to map out a new destiny.

Twenty-two

———◆◆◆———

A t breakfast I watched Esther's question mark–shaped body
move around the kitchen. When she served hash browns, I
picked around the food searching for some sign of poison.
The way I figured it, she had already killed one girl and I didn't want
to die before Nana and Poppy got out of jail.

"Good morning, my precious," Aunty Gina said and kissed me on
the forehead like she did every morning.

"What time did you get in last night?" Esther asked the question
in such a way that made me think Aunty Gina worked for her.

"Ten o'clock. Can you believe it? All this special session nonsense
is just about to wear me to a thread."

The doorbell chimed, and Aunty Gina rubbed her temples.
"Who on earth? It's not even eight-thirty yet."

Nairobi and the pretty social worker walked in with clipboards
and smiles. After they declined Aunty Gina's invitation to join us for
breakfast, it was time to get down to business. The questions were
routine, about an insurance policy to make sure I was living an adjusted life with Aunty Gina. I knew all the answers by heart, but when
Nairobi tricked me by asking a new one, I froze.

"Friends, Brandon. Are you making any friends?"

Aunty Gina tried to pat Nairobi's arm, but Nairobi's eyes never left me. "Oh goodness, yes. He's making all sorts of new friends at Miss Helda's school," Aunty Gina said.

"Do you ever have friends over to play?"

"Umm, no, but there's this boy behind the house."

Esther stopped wiping off a pot long enough to give her two cents. "Behind the house?"

"Winston," I said while watching the social worker make notes.

"Oh, why yes. That family from up north. You know, Esther. The man who runs that copier company. His little son."

"What do you all like to do?" the pretty social worker asked.

"Umm . . . well, he plays tennis, but I don't . . ."

The china cup sounded like a chime as Aunty Gina put it back on the saucer. "Oh, what a fun idea. You boys can take lessons down at the club. Why, Esther can set up the lessons and drive y'all each morning. Why don't I call his mother and set it up?"

"Uhh . . ." Before I could think of anything to say, Aunty Gina was already on the phone explaining about my need for friends.

Satisfied that I would have a recreational outlet two days a week, Nairobi and the social worker got up to leave. Aunty Gina walked them to the door, reassuring them of happiness each step of the way.

"How much longer do you think you'll be in session?" Nairobi asked.

"Lord only knows," Aunty Gina said. "Judge Jackson is walking those halls night and day fighting for that courthouse annex."

"That budget is so heavy-handed," Nairobi said. "Social Services needs some of those funds. Not to mention . . ."

"Now, Nairobi, as I told you before, I am just one woman on a committee full of grown men. Well, at least most of the time they act grown." Aunty Gina attempted to chuckle.

"Just one woman who sits on the Ways and Means Committee." Nairobi turned to the social worker. "Senator Strickland serves on one of the most powerful committees in the legislature—the one with the purse strings."

"Now really, Nairobi . . ."

"Shall I stop by this afternoon? We could go over the line items offered by Senator Dayton."

Before Aunty Gina could say a word, Nairobi and the government woman had walked through the door and begun their journey.

Winston didn't ask about Mama until the third tennis lesson. It was right after his maid had removed our lunch plates from the patio table. He asked as easy as he would ask about my backhand. "So, where is your mom anyway?"

The glass of iced tea was cupped in his webbed hand, and I resisted knocking it out to create a distraction. "Huh?"

"Clean the wax out of your ears. Your mom. Where is she?"

The steady clipping of the sprinkler system matched the way his question clipped me. "She's dead. Killed down in Africa." The lines I had used to curse my mother back in Abbeville came out as a reflex. A forbidden spot, much the same way I saw his hands. A part that was untouchable.

"Man. What was she doing in Africa?"

"Look, I don't want to talk about it, okay." Tossing the napkin onto the table, I gave in. Running pass the vegetable garden and through the hedge, I tried to hate him for making me lie again. Safe in the compound of my new life, I struggled to dump the mental image of Mama screaming at Woolworth's. No matter how hard I tried, her claw gripped me tighter than I had clung to her as a baby.

While Esther took her after-lunch nap, I scooped up ash from the fireplace and sprinkled it around the infested plants in the vegetable garden. But no matter how hard I tried, the words I shared with Winston followed me like a prophecy I couldn't escape. As the ashes hit the edges of the vegetable leaves and floated down to the ground, I wondered if this was what a cremated body looked like. The woman on Esther's soap opera had cremated her husband and then scattered his ashes at the beach. The stench of burned material filled my senses, and before I could stop them, tears began to seem as natural as Winston's webbed hands. Through the tears I stared while ashes fell in a rain of dust, all the while knowing that I was sprinkling away Mama for good. Deep in my being I knew her second chances were used up. Reforming her was a dream that had been spilled just like the necklaces that spewed from her purse at Woolworth's. There were only so many people I could save, and Mama was beyond my grip. She always had been.

That night long after Esther had gone to bed, I sat in my bed and thought about Mama. Aunt Loraine had been right about Mama. She wasn't dependable and never would be. Deep inside I knew that she was gone for good, and the thought that I was better off without her scared me to the core. I was sure the road to eternal hell had been paved by such bad thoughts. Besides, the Bible said to honor your mother and father. My mother was in jail, and my father didn't own up to me even after my mama gave him the chance. Straining to hear the voice of Sister Delores remind me that God would be both my mother and father, all I heard was the steady chime of the grandfather clock.

The steps were so soft that at first I thought Jesus had come back for me. Jumping out of bed, I flung the door wide open. She was standing slump-shouldered with her earrings in hand. The embarrassment of being caught in my underwear swept over me, and I ran back to bed. Even slamming the door and burying my tearstained face in the pillow could not stop her.

"Brandon, honey. Are you all right?"

Aunty Gina's sweet perfume tempted me to look up. Her face was twisted in a half smile of pity. The night-light formed a halo around her yellow hair, and at first I thought she might be a real-life angel. She wiped the tears from my eyes. "What, honey?"

I shook my head, hating my tears as much as I hated being alone.

"Do you miss your grandparents?" Her words were so sweet that you could almost drink them up, and I did just that.

Words flew out of my mouth like a bad cough. "I want them out. I want them out right now."

"Oh, honey, I know." Aunty Gina pulled me closer. The material of her suit padded my chin. "It's all right to cry. Just go ahead and let it out."

Pulling away from her, I finally did let it out. "Please get them out. Get them outta that jail."

"Why, honey, I wish I could, but there are . . ."

"Call President Nixon. I saw you with him. Saw him in that picture down in the library."

Aunty Gina halfway chuckled, and I fought the urge to pull away from her completely. "That picture is probably five years old. Just a silly fund-raiser with so many people you couldn't stir them with a stick. I was just one of hundreds, many hundreds, who paid money for that picture."

The begging surprised Aunty Gina as much as it did me. Words long lost from the play now poured. "But you know lots of people. You can do stuff. Please, Aunty Gina."

The hallway light flowed over her and streamed across the bed. Clinching her fist, she patted it against the skirt. "I just don't . . . we'll see."

"What have you put all over my garden? Poison?"

Esther was standing in front of the TV screen holding a tomato plant, its vine still carrying the light dusting I'd given it.

Sliding backwards until the arm of the sofa pressed against my leg, I tried to put out the fear that was sparking in the same old place. "It's ashes."

"Ashes? I knew it. I knew you were smoking behind that hedge. Smoking, weren't you?"

Shaking my head, all I could do was stare at the plant she held up like a hunted duck. "Answer me," she yelled.

"No . . . no, ma'am. It's from the fireplace."

"What are you doing with ashes from the fireplace?"

"It helps fight bugs. I saw . . . I saw bug bites all over the leaves and . . ."

"And you decided you'd throw ashes on them? I'll be lucky if they don't die for sure now. Where did you learn such a crazy idea? In that juvenile delinquent home, I'm guessing."

"Poppy told me."

"Who?"

"My granddaddy. He used to put ashes on his garden."

Esther looked at me for a long time before she marched back into the kitchen. That evening while she ate her meal downstairs, I stayed upstairs waiting for Aunty Gina. As soon as I heard the downstairs door open, I let out a howl and flopped down on my bed. Pity had been my biggest enemy. Now it would be my best friend.

I counted to twenty-seven before Aunty Gina had made it to my door. "Honey, what's wrong?"

This time I did not let her see my dry face. I would just holler and stiffen every time she tried to roll me over. It was a routine I decided would be played out every day until Nana and Poppy were released. Either she would break down and call the White House or she'd send me back to the feeble-minded house.

One night after a particularly loud tirade, I eased down to the cellar and pulled the stepladder underneath the air vent.

"I just don't know what in the world to do with him," Aunty Gina said. "You said he won't eat."

"He didn't eat a thing all day," Esther lied. As much as she may have wanted me out of her house, I wanted to get out even more.

"Oh, there's only so much I can handle."

The sound of iced tea being poured trickled down the vent. "Now, Mrs. Strickland, like I told you before. He's not your son. The boy's got a family."

"Esther, I am his family for the time being. That sorry excuse for a mama is not going to be out of jail anytime soon. He's better off here with us."

"Well what about the grandparents he's screaming so about?"

"Lord, there's just so much red tape with these types of things."

Esther cleared her throat. "Well what about that colored lawyer? Can't she help do some . . ."

"Enough of such talk. My head is about to split wide open. Anyway, all I'm saying is that I want you to take extra measures with Brandon. Think of him as a little fragile bird or something. Why, you're crazy about birds. Just think of him as a little sparrow with a broken wing."

When the vegetable garden took a turn for the better, so did Esther. It all happened the day Winston and me were playing tennis at his house. Winston saw her first. His eyes grew wider when Esther came tearing through the hedge that separated her way of life from his own.

By the time she reached us, beggar weeds covered the bottom part of her stockings. Her eyes swept across the sparkle of the swimming pool. Anywhere to keep from looking at me. "You like strawberries, I suppose."

Thinking she might have gone crazy, I looked at Winston for guidance. He just stood there gripping his racket, a line of sweat rolling down his neck.

"Umm . . . yes ma'am."

"I bought an extra pint this morning and was thinking about making a strawberry pie for dinner." She pulled at the top of her uniform and tilted her chin towards the pool.

"That would be good."

"You want ice cream to go along with it?"

"Uh . . . yes ma'am."

"Vanilla?"

"Vanilla's good."

With a nod she stormed back through the hedge. It wasn't until the branches had stopped shaking that either of us said a word. "What was all that about?" Winston asked.

"I think she might've just said she was sorry."

That night Aunty Gina called to say that she had to go out to dinner with a group from the legislature. The dining-room table had already been set for two. Esther wiped her hands on a dish towel and picked up the glass of wine she had poured for Aunty Gina. "No use in letting this go to waste."

For the first time Esther and me ate together in the same room. Her words were stiff and spoken with the unsteadiness of a bad actor. "What type of vegetables did your grandpop grow on his farm?"

But as the wine got lower in the bottle, her words became looser. She even laughed when I told her the story about Mary Madonna flying into the hog pen.

Licking a strawberry from my wrist, I asked, "Did you grow up on a farm?"

"Not a farm really. Well, my dad had a small vegetable garden. He was the manager of this estate up in Newport. That's in Rhode Island." She twirled the wine until it looked like it might cascade over onto the arm of the chair.

"How'd you get all the way to North Carolina?"

"That's a long story. And besides, it's my story."

The pictures of the girl down in the cellar came to mind. Maybe that was the reason she didn't want me to know. She didn't want me to find out she had killed her stepdaughter. "That girl in those pictures down in the cellar. Is she kin to you?"

The wrinkle between her eyes grew deeper. "Been snooping around down there, have you?"

"Umm . . . no, I mean I just found . . ."

"Those are Mrs. Strickland's things. I don't think she'd want you sneaking around down there."

"No, I just . . . saw this picture and everything."

Esther poured the last of the wine into her glass and chuckled. "Poor little Ginny Mae. Mrs. Strickland's birth name. Nobody knows that except me. When she met Mr. Strickland, she changed all of it. Oh yeah, she went right down to the courthouse and erased her whole past, as far as I'm concerned."

As I sat up at attention, the carved chair pressed against my back. If Aunty Gina erased her past, maybe she could do the same for me.

"That's why she's soft on you, I suppose. Her being taken in by her grandparents and so forth. I still can't believe she let that colored woman talk her into . . . Well, I guess she aims to do good." Esther tilted the glass towards me, and a spray of wine landed on her plate. "And don't think I don't know what's behind all that crying you're doing. I've been around the block enough times to know and . . ."

"How long you worked here?"

She nodded and took another sip. "I worked for her husband's family first. Years ago they had a summer place in Newport. Then when he sent the family into a tailspin by marrying little Ginny Mae, I was sent to show her the ropes. At first I was going to be the nanny, but that just wasn't meant to be. Let's see how long has it been?" Esther clutched the glass with two fingers and used the others to count against the rim. "Well, her birthday is coming up, so it's been around thirty-four years. And by the way, we'll all be prancing around here celebrating her fifty-fifth birthday next week. But mark my word . . . she's really fifty-six." Esther winked and almost slipped as she got up from the chair.

That night while she washed dishes Esther even sang. The words to "Happy Days Are Here Again" rained down to the cellar. Holding the faded picture of the long lost Ginny Mae, I stood directly under the vent and let her words about better times drench me.

The night of the birthday party Esther was in high excitement. As she barked orders, waiters moved in all different directions. Trays of crab cakes and salmon-draped biscuits drifted above the heads of the guests as hired help weaved in and out of the crowd. Following the tray with boiled shrimp, I passed Mrs. McMasters and the other ladies from the bridge club. Men in ties and ladies with sparkling pocketbooks flooded across the hall and into the library. Strains from the jazz band called me out to the patio. Aunty Gina was leaned against the piano playing with a long strand of pearls, while Judge Jackson and two other old men held court around her.

One man lit a pipe and blew the smoke straight up at the stars. "Now, Gina, I know you're sick to death of this special session, but if Ways and Means would go ahead and get that budget out of committee, we could all go home."

"We're working on it," the other man said. "I figure by the end of August we'll be free."

"The end of August," Aunty Gina moaned. "Lord, that's just about the craziest thing I've ever heard. I've got to be out before then. Brandon will be ready to start school. I'll have missed the whole summer."

"She's right," Judge Jackson said. "The end of August seems extreme. Besides, all the papers will hang you boys for spending taxpayer money on such a long session."

The man with a pipe nudged Judge Jackson. "Oh, I know the solution. Just go ahead and fund that annex of yours and then we can all go home."

Judge Jackson smiled and held up his glass just as Aunty Gina spotted me.

"Well hey, honey. Come over here and speak to these old friends of mine." As she adjusted my tie, the men winked at each other. Nairobi entered the patio carrying a glass of champagne and wearing a turban that matched Aunty Gina's hair.

"Look, Nairobi's here."

"Well, if it's not Harriet Tubman herself."

"Now, Conner," Aunty Gina said.

"Excuse me," the man said, "but there's just so much social good I can stand in one night."

Esther was directing everybody outside when Judge Jackson found Winston and me in the library counting out the drink umbrellas we had collected. "Young man, Gina's asking for you."

When I finally made it through the crowd, she was standing on the band stage. As she bent down to whisper in my ear, the dampness of her breath tickled. "Honey, there are going to be so many candles on this cake I need your help blowing them out. Are you up for the job?"

When the biggest three-tiered birthday cake I had ever seen came rolling out on a cart, the band took the cue. Soon the entire group fanned over the grass and down to the hedge was singing "Happy Birthday." With her hands draped around my shoulders, all I could do was glance up and see her smile. Faces from Raleigh's finest shone back at us, and in the crowd Nairobi's yellow turban was the brightest of them all. Winston and his parents stood in the middle. He waved, and I lifted my hand, but then resisted doing anything that might cause embarrassment. The people who looked back at me on that stage seemed like those I'd find in *National Geographic*, foreigners from distant lands. And, like the photographer who took those magazine pictures, I was just a visitor passing through.

"Are you ready now? Make a wish and we'll share it together," Aunty Gina whispered. Leaning over the cake, she clutched her chest and the bottom part of the pearls swayed. Against the candles she looked younger and batted her eyes the same way I imagined Ginny Mae doing whenever her grandparents gave her a cake. At the same time we closed our eyes and strained to blow away the past.

After the last guest had left and the band was packing up, Aunty Gina and me sat on the patio steps. She had pulled off her shoes and rubbed the ball of one foot. Esther stripped away the cloths from the scattered tables. "Esther, come over here and rest before you work yourself into a stroke."

"I'd rather keep going. Once I stop, then I'm afraid I won't be able to get back up." She was carrying an armload of white linens up the steps when Aunty Gina reached up to touch her hand.

"Thank you for a wonderful birthday. I declare, it was the best yet. Well, the best since Preston left us."

"Oh, don't butter me up. I'll still plan the next one too." Esther patted the armful of linens. Before walking inside, she reached down to touch Aunty Gina the way I thought she might do if she was in a fancy store and tempted by fragile china.

"Isn't the sky just gorgeous tonight?" Aunty Gina sighed. The spray of her breath warmed my arm.

Stars dotted the sky like the diamonds she wore on her fingers.

"This is the type of sky that makes me think of western North Carolina, up in the mountains where I grew up. My grandfather used to say if you could grab a handful of stars on a clear night, your dreams would come true. I'd try for that cluster right over there to the right."

"What did you wish tonight?"

She giggled but never looked away from the stars. "Now, honey, you're not supposed to tell or it won't come to pass. Look at that Big Dipper. Mercy, that is gorgeous."

When the last piece of band equipment was packed, chirping crickets were the only music we had, and it settled on me like the wine Esther enjoyed.

"Why did you ask about my wish, honey?"

"After we blew out the candles, I thought maybe we should've wished for the same thing. You know, maybe it would make it come true if we both wished for it."

"I know what you wished for, honey. I know." Her eyes sparkled as easy as the stars. Before I could think, I reached over and held her hand. The rings were cool to the touch, but the skin was as delicate as her dress. There was nothing to gain or any games to be played that night. Aunty Gina was just one more person I could add to Nana's list of people who loved me.

Twenty-three

E sther was the one who told me that company was coming for dinner. It happened on a hot Saturday morning while we pulled weeds from the garden. Tufts of hair tangled with sweat and were pasted against her forehead. "Mrs. Strickland's planning for company tonight. Cut off some squash on your end. She told Judge Jackson my squash casserole is even better than the one in that Junior League cookbook."

The comment was offered in her usual no-nonsense tone, but the very name caused me to stop digging.

That night I greeted Judge Jackson with a firm handshake and solid eye contact that would've made Miss Helda proud. While a Lawrence Welk album played on the library stereo, Esther served drinks. The dining-room table was set with roses and the big candleholders that Esther had polished special for his visit sparkled even brighter than usual. Nervous energy and Aunty Gina's perfume tangled the air.

After I gulped down supper in the kitchen, I stopped by the library.

"Good night, Aunty Gina." I kissed her the way I had the night of her birthday, but my eyes were on the judge.

"Good night, honey. Sleep tight."

She didn't even have to remind me to stop by his chair and stretch out my hand. "Good night, sir."

As I walked up the stairs, I stomped extra loud. Halfway to the top I turned and ran down to the cellar. The swinging lightbulb cast shadows across the letters lined up on the table, and strains from Lawrence Welk's orchestra hummed like a nest of wasps. Under the air-conditioning vent, their words sounded as if I was hearing them on an out-of-range AM radio station.

"May I freshen your drink before we go into the dining room?"

The judge coughed extra loud and then cleared his throat. "One more please."

When they moved into the dining room, I drug the stepladder over to the opposite side of the room. A spider's web and clumps of dust dangled from the corner of the ceiling. When Aunty Gina reported that Bobby and Sissy on *The Lawrence Welk Show* were really married, I almost gave up straining to hear. Besides, Esther was the one who had told her that anyway.

"I don't get the opportunity to look at much television. With this session I don't see how you make the time."

"Oh, gracious, I don't. I just have two TV bugs in my house. Brandon keeps it going round the clock."

"You're coaching him to be a charming young man."

A fork dropped on the table, and the sound drowned the judge's words.

"Well, speaking of Brandon, have you had a chance to look at his grandparents' case?" Aunty Gina asked.

"You know we've talked . . ."

"Blah, blah, blah. That's all we've done. Now, did you read those case notes?"

A silence followed that made me curl my toes and desire a bathroom.

"Gina, let's skip shoptalk tonight."

"Did you, Jackson?"

"Now, Gina. What you're asking me to do breaches on unethical. I mean, reducing a sentence for people who crossed state lines with a child . . ."

"Honey, that child you're talking about was their grandson. They saw fleeing as their only way to protect him."

"I just don't know . . . You know usually I'd help anyway I can."

"So I've been told."

"But this is a murky situation. Murky at best. A custody battle be-tween grandparents and a mother. At the time there was no just cause why she shouldn't have had him."

"Well let's see . . . The girl is sitting over in jail for shoplifting. Not a soul in the world to even bail her out."

"Gina, I'm sorry. It's just not ethical for me to reduce sentences . . . Now for the sake of justice . . ."

"If you'd just look at the case instead of having your law clerk flip through it, then maybe you'd see what's best for the sake of this child."

"Now, Gina, you simply don't understand all of the procedures involved, but I always . . ."

"I understand enough to know you've done it before, Jackson. How about Doug Sippling's boy? The one caught embezzling . . ."

"Now that was a . . . who told you about . . ."

"And Jackson, you mentioned ethics. Well, it just seems to me that if an authority figure were to hear about this case and that au-thority figure didn't step up to the plate . . . well, I'd question what sort of ethics he had to start with."

"These are rather harsh statements, Gina."

"I've made up my mind about this thing. If you don't step up and do something, that precious little courthouse annex of yours won't see the light of day."

Judge Jackson laughed in a gurgled tone. "Gina, I'm impressed with how fond you've become of the boy. Really I am, but this little game of cat and mouse . . ."

"Honey, there's no playing to it. I've got the votes and that col-ored woman you saw at my party is working it too."

The music floated out again, and I pictured Aunty Gina dressed in a wrestling cape with the judge pinned beneath her.

"Now hold on, Gina . . ."

"Jackson, by the time we're through slicing up your precious bud-get, the only thing anybody will be holding will be your testicles. The

Senate president will hold them out for all North Carolina to see. Every day he's adding up the dollars this special session is costing tax-payers. He'll be more than glad to blame you for every bit of it. And do you really think that your buddy the governor will stand up for your little courthouse then?"

The sound of a fork tapping a plate cut the air like a radio weather advisory.

"I seem to have found an ice queen this evening."

"No, Jackson. I just found my voice is all."

Stillness settled over the house in those early days of August; anticipation brewed with the heat. Each evening I waited up for Aunty Gina, and each night she'd come in with her pocketbook and briefcase in tow. I kept expecting her to come in with a big smile and maybe a cake decorated with the words "Welcome Home, Nana and Poppy." But each night her smile seemed weary and her eyes a little sadder. For the first time I recognized the eyes as those of the little girl in the yel-lowed photographs. As she hugged me and kissed my head, I realized that I knew more about her than she did about me. I wanted to hug her tighter or pat her back. Wondering if this was how people felt when they found out about my past, I fought the urge to squeeze back and instead carried her briefcase into the library.

At night she would continue to work at the desk with legs shaped like eagles. Her words of steel and sugar floated up to the staircase where I waited. Perfume-laced battle strategies that sounded like secret codes in a World War II movie.

While the news anchors talked about the long special session moving forward, I moved forward with a make-believe life. Esther en-rolled me at the private school downtown where Winston had signed up. Two weeks before school was scheduled to start, we completed our tennis lessons and for once I was able to beat Winston. The ac-complishment was hard to accept. The entire time we swam in his pool that afternoon, all I could think was that he let me win out of sympathy over my dead mother. I was just beginning to make a dive when Esther's voice roared out from over the tall hedge. "Brandon. Brandon Willard."

Winston's webbed fingers brushed water from his eyes. He treaded water and stared as if my name had been called out from the intercom at school. Such a call could only mean trouble. I ran barefoot towards the hedge and nicked my leg jumping a fallen limb. Branches raked across my side the way that bad memories tried to yank me back to the past. I fought the image of Aunty Gina killed in some car wreck or worse yet, dead from a heartache caused by work on my behalf.

Esther was standing on the patio steps shielding her eyes from the sun. "You're scratched to pieces."

My breath was as tangled as the dishrag she held. "What's the matter?"

"Mrs. Strickland just called. She had to go in for a vote. But anyway, they're coming home. Your grandpop and grandma are coming home." Esther smiled as best she could and reached for my shoulder. Her pat was swift but her words were as sweet as Aunty Gina's. "They're coming home."

I rose with the sun the day Nana and Poppy walked out of my memories and back into my life. The morning paper lay on the brick driveway. Clutching it, I wondered if delivering the paper would be the last thing I would ever do for Aunty Gina. When I saw her picture on the bottom of the paper, I took off running towards the kitchen table.

"What in the world . . ." she asked.

"You're in the paper." I waved the paper like a flag of victory.

When I flipped the paper open, her picture looked even bigger. She was shown with her head turned smiling at Judge Jackson. The headline read "Special Session Over: Budget Passes." It was set right below the fat banner that declared the end of the Nixon administration.

After breakfast I changed into the shirt and pants I had hidden in the bottom part of the dresser. They were the clothes I had shown up wearing, and they would be the clothes I would leave with. Sitting on the bed, I studied the room and tried to sketch the objects in my memory, the same way someone might do in an art museum.

"Honey, you better start packing up your things." Aunty Gina stood at the door fastening her watch.

"Uh . . . I already have."

She searched the room with her eyes. "What about your tennis outfit and your church suit?"

I hated to tell her that Nana and Poppy couldn't pay for any of those things, so I just sat there. Aunty Gina began pulling everything out in the drawers in a frenzy suitable for spring cleaning. She saw shirts and shoes that morning, but all I saw were mounting dollar signs. "We don't have the money to pay for all this stuff, okay."

She stood there holding my underwear and looking as if I had slapped her. "Honey, these are your things now. I gave them to you." Sitting down on the bed, she outlined what else she was giving me. The tuition to school was paid in full for the year; so were next summer's tennis lessons that she convinced me would offer companionship for Winston. Nana and Poppy didn't take to charity, I could've told her that much. "Oh, it's just a loan here and there," Aunty Gina said with a toss of the hand. "An agreement between the three of us."

Before I left, Esther handed me a bag full of vegetables. "Until your grandpop can set out a garden." She used the back of her hand to iron a wrinkle out of her uniform. "Now you keep working on your tennis. You're a real natural."

Riding pass the fountain, I looked over at the driver's seat. It was the first time Aunty Gina had driven me anywhere. She smiled and nodded as if to acknowledge the milestone.

As I watched the mansion grow smaller in the side mirror, it began to look like something out of make-believe. A miniature castle made out of blocks. And a piece of me had been left in that castle.

Down in the cellar tucked deep inside the crate of photographs of Ginny Mae were the letters Nana and Poppy had written me. Sacred memories tossed together in strips of faded tissue.

We drove through downtown Raleigh and then headed south. "The farm's back the other way."

Aunty Gina pulled tighter on the steering wheel. "You've got a new place now. It's just as cute as it can be. You'll have all sorts of neighbor children around."

"Why aren't we going back to the farm?"

"Honey, now I don't know all the details. Your aunt has her mother or somebody living there now. I'm talking behind Nairobi, so I think it's best you ask your grandparents about all that." She turned and looked at me with all the seriousness that I pictured her giving Judge Jackson. "But just remember a home is wherever your people are. Boards rot and concrete cracks, but it's the people inside that really matter."

When I saw Nairobi and the pretty government lady standing on the concrete porch, a familiar feeling swept over me. It was not the farmhouse. The tiny brick house had just one tree in the yard, and the neighbor was so close I could see the glow of the TV. But the corner fern that dangled from the wrought-iron post was what I focused on.

I pinned my hands under the seat so I wouldn't jump out before the car had stopped. When they saw us, Nairobi turned, and Poppy stepped from behind her. He was a little heavier, but the John Deere cap was the same. Nana came out of the house patting the sides of her hair. It gathered like white yarn at her shoulders. The way she balled her fist and covered her mouth, I knew she was fixing to cry. Before Aunty Gina could turn off the engine, I opened the door. They were all looking at me—Aunty Gina, Nairobi, and the government lady. As much as I knew they expected me to cry, I fought to keep any tears pushed down.

Poppy lost his fight. "Hey there." The words had hardly gotten out of his mouth before he chewed them back with emotion.

Nana's soft green eyes searched me in a way that only Jesus had managed to do. A breeze swept across the yard and when her hair blew up, she began to look even more like an angel. I buried my head against the doughy part her stomach and held tight trying to keep her from being lifted away. Poppy's arm helped anchor us as he snaked it around us. Her words were stable and rolled out in the whisper of an ordinary afternoon. "I got you a Pepsi. And you might even find a piece of pound cake on the kitchen counter. Come on, let's go on inside. Let's go inside."

That evening we sat in the cramped kitchen with the refrigerator that jerked each time it defrosted, and I baked in their warmth. The food opened a door to the familiar: a plate of fried chicken that bubbled up at the bone, a skillet of cornbread baked until the edges crackled with sweetness. Even the card table and used folding chairs had a comfort to them.

As easy as the wind shifted outside the cracked window, our words floated back and forth from a censored past to a promising future.

"It was all Aunty Gina's idea for me to take tennis lessons." The word Aunty had not yet left the air before Nana looked at Poppy.

"She's a good woman," Poppy said. He clutched his fork like a baton and told how Aunty Gina had secured a job for him at the vet school taking care of the livestock. While he went on about a new breed of cattle they were studying, Nana cleared the supper dishes like she had all the times before.

Livestock was the perfect lead to ask when we would be moving back to the farm. Clutching plates, Nana moved back to the table. She and Poppy glanced at each other in a way that always made me think they could read minds. Reaching for my glass, Nana spoke as if she was learning a new language.

"Maybe one day we'll go back, but right now Aunt Loraine has her mama there. She's been having those ministrokes and with Uncle Cecil being in the shape he's in . . . Well, it might just be for the best right now."

"How come she gets to let her mama live there?"

"Son, she owns the place now." Poppy leaned forward and pointed his fork. "We just gotta remember if it wasn't for Loraine stepping in the way she did when Cecil got mangled up on the job, the place might not even be in the family a'tall."

"After her mama gets to feeling stronger, Loraine said we could talk about buying it back," Nana said.

"She did keep up with the mortgage note and all the taxes," Poppy said. "I keep trying to tell myself that it's only fair that . . ."

"It's not fair," I yelled. Before Poppy could reach my arm, I jumped from the chair. Screeching metal cried as loud as my voice. "I hate her. I hate her!" When I snatched the plate of sliced tomatoes, Nana touched my shoulder.

"Watch yourself," she whispered. "Now, we don't hate nobody in this house. We might not like their ways, but we don't hate. You're mad and you have ever right to be. Poppy and me felt the same way. But the thing that I know from living this long . . . Well, I know that it all comes clean come wash day." She grabbed the other end of the plate and I let it slip through my fingers. "It all comes clean come wash day."

Mama only filtered through the conversation one time. It was that first night when Nana stopped by my room to check on me.

When the door creaked open, I jumped up and reached for my shoes. Nana clutched the top of her robe, the one with Aunty Gina's initials stitched on the pocket. "Son, why're you dressed?"

She stared at the jeans and shirt I had on. The worn-out box springs whined when she sat next to me. "What's behind this?"

"I thought somebody might . . . I thought we might have to leave."

She pulled me against the fleshy part of her arm. "There won't be any more leaving at this place." Slamming car doors and laughter rolled in from the street. A car cranked and then drove away. "Is this about your mama?"

Never answering, I chose instead to concentrate on the tiny hole and wood shavings in the corner. But there was no escaping. Words spewed out of Nana like a handful of nails too hot to handle. "Sophie's good-hearted. Real good-hearted. She just got into some messes along the way."

I wanted to pull away and become one of the spiders from Aunty Gina's cellar. Racing across the floor, I'd jump right in the hole head first.

"Just some people can't see Sophie's heart. I guess neither could I. Now just yesterday I was thinking about the time she found a baby squirrel and had Poppy fix a . . ."

"I don't want to talk anymore."

Nana looked down and then offered a kiss. "All right, then. Goodnight. I love you."

Their words jumbled together, my mama's and Nana's. They crossed a dividing line I had placed in my mind to keep them separate. I didn't need to hear how much she regretted making my mama leave the house. It was already etched in the lines around her eyes and the wrinkles on her forehead. A road map that led to regret.

Nana never did mention Mama again. Not until the day we learned that she had slipped away for good. It wasn't a rhino that ended up getting her or the collapse of an oil rig in Canada; it was her own demon. A demon too strong for a boy to exorcise.

The end was in Roanoke Rapids, Virginia. She was found frozen to death at a rest stop after trying to walk away from a bar. The day I learned the news we sat on the concrete steps. Poppy's mouth sprayed a ghostly mist in the January air as the facts flew around as fast as migrating blue jays.

Cold from the concrete seeped through my jeans as I listened to Nana sob and Poppy comfort. The tip of a rock was sticking up out of the red clay that edged the steps. I could only think of one thing—the day I scattered ashes across the garden at Aunty Gina's mansion. The type of home that was supposed to be reserved for heaven.

Nana kept her arm tight around me. Folds of her stomach vibrated as she cried. But I never cried that day. The tears would come later in life and at unplanned moments. Some would be shed simply when riding down the road and listening to the words of a Carole King song on the radio. More were shed the day we took my oldest daughter home from the hospital. The piercing blue eyes were as radiant as the mother I had wanted but never knew. In the structured cubicles of my mind, Sophie Willard would end up being a favorite sister who had left for college and never looked back. Her memory would remain as pure as the patches of snow that clung to the ground that day.

Aunty Gina, Esther, Nairobi, and Winston all came to the funeral. They sat scattered in the funeral home chapel while the Baptist minister from our new church stood over the silver casket and tried to piece Mama's life together. When I turned to look for my friends, Aunt Loraine blocked the view. She sat behind us dressed in black from head to toe. A pearl necklace with a diamond chip wrapped around her neck like a dog collar. A possession paid for with the same funds that secured the farm—settlement money from Uncle Cecil's accident. She tilted her head, smiled sweet, and slowly shook her head. Mac and Mary Madonna sat next to her and nervously looked away. They sat in the pew draped with the red velvet cloth stitched with the word "Family," and just when I started to reach over and snatch it off, Mama's words called out. *"Every day we got a choice to be pitiful or powerful."*

After the service, we went back to our brick home. The church family had prepared lunch. Ladies with bubble-shaped hair buzzed around the kitchen while Esther directed their moves. A peace lily plant filled the corner of the living room. Like a blind person, I stood in the corner rubbing the words on the card: "Blessed are those who mourn, for they shall be comforted. Remember, we sure do love you, Sister Delores and God's Hospital."

When no one was looking, I pulled the card and placed it in the pocket of the suit Aunty Gina had bought me. She was sitting on the love seat that had a rip down the side talking with Nana as if she had found a new bridge-club recruit. Their shared words of what was best for me floated as free as the scent of Aunty Gina's perfume. Through the window, I saw Poppy sitting on the porch step. With his pocketknife he carved a piece of oak that was beginning to take the shape of Uncle Sam. Winston stood next to him as shavings gathered around the concrete step.

Nairobi's silky material tickled my hand. She sat on the folding chair next to me and watched Esther line up the food. "You do realize Senator Strickland predicts we'll see you playing the U.S. Open one day. But I said no, not Brandon."

Looking up, I saw a sly smile drape across her mouth.

"No, I told her. I predict we'll see him playing in a different game. Congress, maybe. And do you know what that woman said to me? She said, 'Nairobi, Brandon Willard can do whatever he makes his mind up to do. And he'll do it well.'"

"I believe we're about ready to eat." The minister looked over at Esther. She nodded and sucked in her cheeks. "May we say grace," he said.

As the requests for comfort and protection went up to the One who Sister Delores promised would be both my mother and father, I kept a steady gaze on those hedged around me. Esther's chin pointed to the ground, but her eyes were wide open. Aunty Gina smiled softly as her eyelids twitched in time with the minister's words. "Yes, Lord," Nana whispered and kept a fist balled at her lips. The bloom from Sister Delores's peace lily brushed against Poppy's pants as the ceiling light formed a halo around his bald spot. Nairobi stood next to me, pressing her palms together the way I'd seen little children pray.

With each word the minister prayed, I breathed in deep and pictured a mist going deeper inside me, protecting frayed nerves once and for all. Jesus didn't have to appear for me to feel God's love that day. It was found in each of the people who formed a wall around me. While studying their various shapes, colors, and imperfections, I realized I was a part of them. A family joined together by ties stronger than blood and land. Joint heirs of past and future combined.

Epilogue
2003

The rusty "No Trespassing" sign is slanted sideways, its words missing sections of black print. From the car I watch it keep time with the February wind, an almost forced dance with the front door. Patches of white paint still cling to the porch railing like snow trapped past its time in the shadows of the sun.

Staring at the weathered farmhouse and its shattered living-room windows, I stuff my hand deep inside the jacket and massage the rough edges of the deed. After all the struggle and cost that dollars can't compensate for, I think it strange how thin and fragile it feels. As fragile as the end of the porch that once firmly upheld generations of my family, but now bows in submission towards the ground.

Once I thought the house of rotted wood was a palace. A place of safe passage that was as fine as any home I had been introduced to from the television nestled inside the once-cramped living room. Now, thirty years later, the building looks as tiny as the house of matches I had seen the summer Nana and Poppy took me to Ripley's Believe It or Not Museum, and just as delicate.

Cold dirt cracks under my weight, and I pull the top of the jacket closer to my neck. Even the dirt that once produced food and income for my family now seems dead to the touch. When a gust burns my face, I suddenly remember Poppy's favorite thing about our trip to Ripley's Museum—the warm Florida weather.

A steady screeching noise echoes from the swinging "No Trespassing" sign, but I ignore its order. With the force of my shoulder the scarred door opens, and suddenly I am back in the sanctuary, if only in my mind. The foyer wallpaper that once jumped out to welcome guests in patterns of cheerful daisies is now torn and worn down to mere smudges.

Inside the living room I use my foot to sweep beer cans that have been deposited. "The very idea of drinking in my house . . ." Nana would surely say. But it's the broken kitchen window, the window that once poured sunlight onto our breakfast table, that shows me how life has really changed.

The crack across the window distorts my view. A bulldozer sits silent and still where the tire swing used to hang. Clumps of trees are left scattered as if the machine had been polite enough to leave a calling card. Flawless homes line the surrounding property like fortress walls protecting a new way of living.

An empty nest, either the home of squirrels or rats, is piled where the supper dishes once rested in the kitchen sink. Although not visible, at least some living force still exists in the house, and for that I am thankful. A section of the linoleum floor sags where tired wood has given way. The cabinets, though covered in years of dust, still retain the same sturdiness they had the day Poppy made them. Wiping away the dirt, I smell the surface, hoping the scent of Nana's fried chicken and okra remains entombed in the wood. Only the howling wind through the cracked wall reminds me that there are modern-day problems lurking outside.

Walking around the small shell of a home, I force my mind to picture what used to be and try to convince myself that it can still be exhumed like a chest of treasures.

• • •

Driving towards town, I pass the entrance to Hathaway Plantation. A towering home with a tall American flag rests beyond the stone gates. A sign next to the entrance says it all. Aunt Loraine and her new husband, Coach Johnson, are standing back-to-back holding matching cell phones. "Plantation Living Starting at the $290s. Jingle the Johnsons and Move in Next Month."

After Uncle Cecil died, she waited seven months to marry Coach Johnson. When the first wave of transplants arrived in the area, the operation gradually boomed. At first real estate was Aunt Loraine's side business, a hobby discovered when she developed tennis elbow. Now, as reported in her last Christmas newsletter, she has a floor of office space and twenty-three employees. She was always spoken of in polite terms at Nana and Poppy's house. An apparition that would appear with Mac and Mary Madonna each Christmas with courtesy gifts. As Mac and Mary Madonna became older, the relationship became more awkward. They are now more like pen pals from a distant world rather than family from red-colored soil.

It wasn't until I graduated from the Naval Academy that I began receiving yearly Christmas newsletters from Aunt Loraine. That year her broad letters scrolled above a picture from a Tahiti cruise: "We're just all so proud of you back home. I knew you could make something of yourself. Keep going!"

Keep going—the one piece of advice I did take from Aunt Loraine. After Aunty Gina helped secure a congressional nomination to the academy, I became a member of the tennis team. I even used the party manners Miss Helda taught me to marry an Annapolis debutante, a woman whose childhood was filled with tea parties and sailing lessons.

The latest strip mall and brick fast-food restaurant now sit where my friend Poco and his grandfather, Mr. Calato, farmed. Rows of cloned homes jumble together like stacks of dominos ready for the fall. At the intersection where Nairobi's Child Advocacy Network once was, a dead deer rests in the median, its legs broken and twisted along with the landscape. A tire store has taken over Nairobi's center. She now lives in Washington, D.C., and teaches law to the next generation at Georgetown. E-mail and phone calls allow our paths to cross, but there are many others I wish I could pick up the phone and call. Age and disease have claimed them as fast as the developers have leveled the farms and shops that I once knew.

Sister Delores comes to mind, as she often does. No matter how many times Nana told her she had joined the Baptist church, Sister Delores refused to take our names off of the membership at God's Hospital. The last time I saw Sister Delores I was about to graduate from high school and had driven to Panama City with Winston for spring break. As I started to pull away from her house in Abbeville, she ran up to the car and used the back of her hand to clean the side mirrors. "Baby, keep your eyes on the road and don't keep looking back," she said. Looking back now, I understand why she never told anyone about the bone cancer. It was not her way, her husband, Harvey, reminded us, when he called with the news of her death. Sister Delores and I were alike in that respect. Pity was worse than terminal illness.

Aunty Gina and Poppy both slipped away within the past two years. The stings remain fresh to the spirit. Memories tempt me to drive by Aunty Gina's home too, but I recall my wife's advice and keep the car straight. "You have to release the past," my wife tells me. But she only knows a polite fraction of my story. There is so much to be said. The price for saying it, a stripping of the soul that, at age thirty-nine, I am still not yet willing to pay.

Winston would be a good excuse to pass by Aunty Gina's neighborhood. I see him most regularly of all. When I can convince him to take time away from his law practice, our families summer together at his home on the Outer Banks. Gripping the steering wheel, I force myself to stay away from the exit that leads to Winston's old-money world of inside the beltline. Instead, I follow the road towards the ghost of betrayal that Winston has helped to uncover.

Two large portraits hang above the reception desk. A young woman plays with the headset mouthpiece and asks if she can help me in a way that lets me know she has more urgent matters at hand.

"Brandon Willard. I stopped by to see Loraine. My aunt."

When she walks towards the French doors in the back, the portraits leap out at me. Mac and his children are sitting on the beach all dressed in matching khakis. The lines on his face favor Uncle Cecil, and I wonder if he still feels the loss of his father. His wife is exactly what someone like Aunt Loraine would prescribe for a doctor's spouse. In the portrait peeling skin on her tipped nose is held down with makeup, and her teeth are as white as the sand she is standing on. The other portrait is of Mary Madonna and her three boys. Her blonde hair is curled at the ends and drapes over her shoulder. Divorced, she now owns the largest bridal and formal outlet in the Carolinas. At least some things remain the same.

The receptionist's voice is a welcome distraction. "She asked if you could have a seat. She's finishing up a closing."

The seat of the leather sofa is hot by the time Aunt Loraine bursts through the French doors with opened arms. Her face is tight, and only the lines on her neck give her age away.

"Brandon, how are you? Oh, I see a little gray at the temples. You and Mac are both lightening up on top and I want you to cut it out. It's making me feel old." The cell phone in her suit pocket begins playing "Rhapsody in Blue," and she holds up a finger. "This is Loraine . . ."

While she discusses an escrow account, I move to the wall lined with photographs of her with every elected official in North Carolina. I wonder if she would believe me if I told her that Gina Strickland had willed a portion of her estate to me. The knowledge would only be a slight intrusion on the perfect world she's carved for herself.

"Come, come, come," she says and snakes her hand under my arm.

A white sofa and floral pillows make the spacious office seem like summer. "Now, I'm just going to redirect this phone to voice mail and sit and visit." She punches numbers on the desk phone and tosses her hair back. "What did we do before voice mail?"

This woman who had frightened me as a child suddenly seems a mere child herself, and I unzip my jacket.

"So tell me. How are Nicole and the girls?"

"Everyone is fine."

"And you're still in Atlanta? Still working with computers or some sort . . ."

"Still in Atlanta. Still have the software business."

She fans the polished nails across the suit jacket. "I know Nana is so proud of you. Why, we all are."

"Thanks. Yeah, speaking of Nana . . ."

The cell phone begins to play the song again. "Hold that thought. This is Loraine . . ."

As I leaf through the stack of magazines on the coffee table, a brochure for Hathaway Plantation slides out. An illustration shows homes with Williamsburg-style shingles and children riding bikes down the street. I wonder if the artist would have ever guessed the setting was once the strip of land where we rode our bikes around hog pens.

"I'm so sorry. I don't think some of these people could breathe if I didn't tell them how." She laughs in that nasal way I remember. The part of her that money couldn't change. "Now what was I saying?"

"Uhh, I think we were about to talk about Nana."

Her smile lowers, and she shakes her head. "You know I need to go by there and see her. Now tell me, how's her hip? How long has it been since she broke it, five months at least . . ."

"About a year now. She's adjusting to the new place, but it's hard. I can tell she's lonely."

"Now, Brandon, you have nothing to feel guilty about. I know all of the owners of the nursing homes. You put her in the best, I'm here to tell you."

Another verse of the song plays on the cell phone, and she laughs right out loud. "Can you believe this? It just never stops. This is Loraine . . ."

Scanning the photos on the wall, I notice one with Lars Hathaway, the developer of Hathaway Plantation. Aunt Loraine and her husband are guarding him on either side.

Playing with the sapphire pendant, she shakes her head. "Mac was asking me just last week if I had gotten over there to see Nana. I keep intending to . . . well, you know how it is."

"Yeah, I guess it's true what they say. You know, about the road to hell being paved with good intentions."

Releasing the pendant, she straightens her suit and tries to laugh. "Yeah, well. Now is this just a social call or . . ."

Picking up the brochure for Hathaway Plantation, I lean forward. "I was just wondering, were you ever going to mention this to me?"

"What? Well, it's just a new venture we're trying." When the cell phone comes to life again, I snatch it from the coffee table and press the off button.

"Brandon, I am expecting an important call. What's gotten into you?"

"I guess I've had a splinter for the past thirty years and it's finally festered is all."

When I stand, she slides to the edge of the chair, seemingly nervous that the past may start boiling over into her orderly life.

"I don't know what bothers me more. The fact that you're trying to turn our farm into an amusement park of two-story homes or that you don't even bother to consider that I might care."

"Brandon, with all due respect. That farm was mine to sell to Lars without your permission. Let's remember that I'm the one who had to pay the mortgage when Nana and Poppy chose to run off with you."

"You never gave them the chance. Not one damn chance to buy it back!"

"Would you hush that yelling. Now, I will talk to you, but only if you act like you've got some sense."

"Don't worry about everybody knowing. People already know. You know how the game works."

She continues to shake her head. "You've absolutely gone and lost your mind. Speak in English please. I can't understand riddles."

"Lars Hathaway. A friend of mine plays on his tennis team. He told me months ago about all this. So you know what I did? I just turned around and bought the land back from Lars."

"What?" The squeal is back to the Aunt Loraine I remember. "You can't do that. They're already building."

"I hired the lawyers. The section of land I'm buying was grandfathered out of the city years ago. So it's not zoned."

"I just talked to Lars this morning. Besides, where did you get the money to . . ."

"I've got the deed. It's done."

While she searches me with her eyes, I feel the discomfort of standing on the iron steps of her trailer all over again.

"Oh, well. We'll just keep selling those lots and stacking them up behind your run-down shack. It's just one section anyway. It won't hurt us one bit."

"You're right, it's just one little section. But I tell you what. Next week I'm getting the biggest trailer I can find. Then I'm loading that thing up with as many hogs that will fit in it. Then we'll put up a fence and start unloading. By the time it's over, the stench will be worse than you ever remembered."

"Okay, I see where this is heading. How much do you want for it?"

"You just don't get it."

"Look, I don't have time for your sanctimonious attitude. I did the best I knew how to do. I took care of Cecil until the day he died. I tried . . ."

"You never tried as far as we were concerned."

"What's all this about? That I didn't let them buy the farm back? Look, I needed the investment. I had a vegetable for a husband. No income. It was all I could do to make ends . . ."

"Here we go. I guess you're forgetting about the money from the lawsuit. Or about how you tucked Uncle Cecil away?"

"You know, that's it. Brandon, you need to leave now."

When I get to the French doors, her voice whines for the last time. "Is all this really about your mama? Some sort of little exorcism you're performing at my expense?"

"No, Loraine. It's all about wash day."

• • •

She's sitting in the cafeteria listening to a gospel quartet sing from a miniature stereo. Cardboard Valentines blare from the white wall as if they are blots of wet red paint. Her face is gaunt, but the green eyes remain the same. A black woman glides past me in a wheelchair, and when I move, those eyes fall on me.

Clenching both fists, Nana giggles right out loud. By the time I reach her, the smell of rubbing alcohol and steamed cabbage reminds me this is not her home. "Get over here and give me a hug," she says. "I thought you were coming Thursday."

"Yes, ma'am. Today is Thursday."

"Lordy me. In this place I'm doing good to keep my name straight."

"Are you about ready to go get a milkshake?"

With the walker stashed in the backseat of the car, I listen to her talk about the kindergarten class that distributed Valentine candy and the latest quilting-club member who died. "You remember Amanda, the one from Morgantown? Her funeral was yesterday. They tell me she wanted to be cremated. I can hardly stand such a notion. When it comes my time, don't be doing me like that."

"Well, you better not leave anytime soon."

"I got to studying about it last night. You know, I'm proving there is such a thing as living too long."

By the time we pass the turnoff for Dairy Queen, she knows. "Where are we off to?"

Pretending not to hear, I continue straight down the highway that runs north of town.

"Son, I'd just as soon not go out there. There's not a thing in the world I can do to change it, so I just choose not to study it." She looks across the land at freshly stripped pines and hardwoods stacked on red clay.

When we stop the car, she's still staring straight ahead as I pull the paper from my coat. Her bony fingers hold the document inches from her glasses.

"Nana, it's the deed. I couldn't get it all, but I managed to save the old place. I was inside earlier this morning. It needs a ton of work. I think the kitchen floor's rotten and the porch is caved . . ."

Before I can finish preparing her for reality, the car door opens and she steps ahead. Sprinting up behind her, I hold out the walker, but she ignores the offer. Her arms halfway stretch out as if to provide balance to her toddler-sized steps, but the eyes remain determined. Does she understand? Has the place with screaming patients and Valentine decorations made for children stomped out the solid places of her mind for good? Her steps are uneasy, as if walking through a minefield. The wind lifts the edge of her plastic bonnet, but she never seems to notice.

She grips the edge of the porch railing to steady herself. Next to a gap in the wood are the crude numbers, 1918. Her crooked finger reaches up and traces each number as if it was in Braille. When she speaks, her voice cracks as easily as the steps that lead into the house. "My daddy was a sharecropper. Mama always claimed working so hard for the down payment on this place drove him to a early grave. Daddy used to tell us kids we had Carolina clay running through our veins."

She cups her hands and offers the story up like a prayer. Words of sacrifice and survival pour into the scorched places that the world and weather have left maimed. Even though I know each sentence as well as a child can recite a favorite bedtime story, I listen as if hearing it for first time. Picking at splintered wood on the porch rail, I lift a piece and tuck it inside my shirt pocket. Nana searches the roof and porch as if a piece of the structure will lift her back to the past, and all at once I miss the boy who once could make himself shrink away in time. We are quiet as a roar from a nearby dump truck tempts us to look away and acknowledge the modern-day changes.

In the car she just pats my arm. "Son, you're my world."

At the edge of the highway, minivans and European cars thicken the road. In the rearview mirror the homes of Hathaway Plantation sparkle in the sun. Pieces of the roofline glisten like diamonds yet to be mined, and a flag on the model home flaps in the wind at full staff.

It is then that the need to protect overtakes me. "You've got so many people who love you," I say.

Her hands are as beaten as the porch floor and stay obediently folded in her lap. She stares straight ahead, almost resigned to the future, never seeming to notice that I am heading in the opposite direction of the nursing home. We just keep driving down a highway that now seems like a trail of untamed wilderness.

As I grip the steering wheel, my shirt stretches across the chest. The splintered wood from the porch rail presses against me until it's almost an extension of my being, much like a birthmark or a scar. A discolored piece of jagged wood that is a souvenir of the boy I was as much as it is a compass for the man I want to become.

Acknowledgments

As always, I am grateful for the never-ending encouragement and support that I receive from Melanie. She's not only an outstanding "first" editor for my work but also a wonderful wife and best friend.

The idea for *Slow Way Home* came before I wrote my first novel. During a business trip to Fort Lauderdale I passed an RV park packed so tight with campers that they were nearly on top of one another. My first thought was that someone could get lost in such an environment and then the image of an older couple and a young boy came to mind. If it had not been for the guidance of Judge Shelley Desvousges this story would still be floating around in my head. She led me through a legal maze of custody hearings and federal versus state law in such a way that even I could make sense of it. With that said, any and all mistakes are mine. I'm also grateful for the legislative clarification I received from my friend Jack Graham.

Others offered early comments on the manuscript or promotional help that led me to this point. I appreciate the support that I've received from each one of them: Tina Baker, Sonny Brewer, Megan Brier, Stacey Howell, Marsha Marks, Robert Segedy, Karin and Keifer Wilson, and Betty Joe Wolff. Special thanks to my in-laws, Tom and Dixie Sanderson, who shuttled me to many book signings and yet still remain just as enthusiastic.

Thank you, Laurie Liss, for your advice and advocacy as my agent. Your talent and persistence are motivating.

I also appreciate the talent and kindness of my editor, Renée Sedliar. Renée, everyone should be so fortunate to have an editor as qualified and nice as you.

To my parents, Larry and Elanie Stroud, I am grateful for your love and ongoing support. It doesn't seem that long ago when all of this was simply talk fit for air castles.

To my grandfather, Curtis Whitfield, thank you for your love and stories. No one makes oral history come to life the way you do. And finally I acknowledge the impact my grandmother had on my life. Audrey Whitfield gave me an unconditional love that only God Himself can surpass. She graced this world for seventy-two years but her love and wisdom live on in the lives she touched.

It is estimated that 2.5 million grandparents are raising grandchildren in the United States. Most are doing so with little or no financial support. I thank them for taking responsibility for the future and offer my humble gratitude.

4/